The Guilty

by Jason Pinter

Jason Pinter

Copyright © 2008 by Jason Pinter

eISBN 978-1-947993-19-8

First published March 2008 by MIRA Books
Reissued November 2017 by Armina Press

The Guilty

Jason Pinter

Also by Jason Pinter

The Henry Parker Series
THE MARK
THE GUILTY
THE STOLEN
THE FURY
THE HUNTERS (novella)
THE DARKNESS

THE CASTLE (standalone)

Prologue

They say it's better to have loved and lost than to never have loved at all.

I disagree.

I've lost before. I lost the affection of my parents before I was old enough to know that the world looked upon an estranged child with sad eyes. I lost my first love because I was too cowardly to protect her. I nearly lost my life due to circumstances beyond my control. All of those losses created holes in my life. Holes I've attempted to patch up, to cover, but they'll always be there, even if they don't leave a mark.

Doesn't mean I can't try to forget them. Through life. Through work.

Through Amanda.

If she wasn't here, lying next to me in our bed, her head inches from mine, I wouldn't be here at all. It's not that I'd be back in Oregon, paying my dues at the news desk of the Bend Bulletin, skiing at Mount Bachelor, thirsting through thirteen inches of annual rainfall, and paying two hundred bucks a month in rent.

If she wasn't here, I would either be rotting in the ground somewhere or in a jail trying to stay alive while cursing a simple twist of fate.

Her soft brown hair cascading down her back, eyes so bright and big I get lost in them.

One year ago I was running for my life. A total stranger saved my life. Without her, everything would have been lost.

And God help me I can't lose her, because I don't have the strength to patch that kind of hole.

So as I lie here, watching Amanda's chest rise and fall, all I can do is hope I'm here to witness every last breath of her life. And hope that, finally, the stories I report won't be my own.

Chapter 1

The limousine pulled up to the curb outside the Kitten Club, and like a cult waiting for its leader, dozens of heads turned at once. Hundreds of eyes widened. Pulses sped up, hearts raced.

A black-clad bouncer stepped to the limo and opened the door. A slender leg stepped onto the curb. Then it stopped, its owner making sure the cameras had time to swallow up every inch of perfect skin. Then another leg slipped out. The crowd moaned, her body glitter giving the girl's normally pale skin a translucent glow. The crowd gasped as her full form emerged. Those who weren't too stunned to move pressed against the velvet ropes, the bouncers going into full push-em-back mode.

Flashbulbs popped by the dozen. She flashed that million-watt seductive smile, the one that had seduced and captivated people all over the world. They shouted at her. Nothing she hadn't heard before. Yet as she stepped onto the red carpet, rolled out just for her, listening to the throng of fans chanting her name, Athena Paradis couldn't help but feel that the world had given itself to her.

She waved to the dazed crowd, stopped to sign a few autographs and blow air kisses through ruby lips, laughed at the mismatched chunky schlubs who would be fantasizing about her that night as they lay alone in the dark.

One-thirty in the morning, but the flashes and screams made it seem like broad daylight. Just late enough for the party to be in full swing, just late enough to make sure she'd be the last memory of a night her fans would never forget.

Despite her seeming nonchalance, Athena spent many nights in breathless anticipation of these delicious moments when all eyes would be on her. Hearing digital cameras beeping, fingers tapping on cell phones as flabbergasted fans sent grainy images to their friends. Young men trying to give her the same lame sultry looks she'd seen and laughed at a million times. Yet she would always smile just enough to make them think they had a chance.

This was Athena's world, her oyster, and it was delicious. Everyone else watched from outside the snow globe, hoping that one special night they too might be touched by her magic.

In three days, Athena Paradis would release her very first album, The Goddess Athena. Her promotional tour was in full swing, and tonight at the Kitten Club was a prime stop. She was scheduled to guest DJ, spin and sing tracks that had never been heard outside the recording studio (created with the gentle touch of some very talented—and patient—sound producers, vocal coaches and technicians). Athena's autobiography, HOW YOU CAN BE LIKE ME, was ghostwritten by a pleasant sixty-year-old Jew named Herman Goldstein. It spent eight weeks on the New York Gazette bestseller list. Her signings all required extra security. Herman wasn't allowed to attend.

Three bouncers the size of minivans controlled the crowd. The mayor's office had sent several off-duty cops just in case. Athena's manager and publicist had called Mayor Perez's office nonstop requesting massive police protection for their twenty-two-year-old gold mine, but the second-termer refused. Not that he wouldn't have wanted to help. The mayor was well known for his reliance on sizzle over steak, providing a good show to distract people from their woes. He'd written three self-help books and was constantly photographed alongside celebrities, including Athena Paradis. But the union was busy organizing a new contract, and they were squeezing him hard. Adding additional unnecessary force tonight would only make people angry.

Every nightclub Athena graced with her presence would fatten her bank account by fifty thousand dollars. The hotter—or more desperate—the club, the more they paid. Most promoters, like the Kitten Club's Shawn Kensbrook, tripped over themselves to pay Athena ungodly sums of money for a simple appearance. She would show up, pose for the camera, down a few kamikaze shots, dance on the bar, and within a week the patronage tripled. Best advertising in the world, and a hell of a lot more entertaining than an ad in a movie theater or those worthless postcards.

Tonight, though, wasn't about appearances fees. If she seduced the crowd, it would be worth its weight in platinum for her album.

Athena sauntered past the throng of gawking men and starry-eyed women, slipping into the pulsating darkness. Her entourage was immediately met by Shawn Kensbrook, club promoter extraordinaire and co-owner of the Kitten Club. Just three years ago, what was now the Kitten Club had been an abandoned warehouse in Manhattan's meatpacking district. It was destined to be torn down by developers or vermin, whichever got there first. Kensbrook was able to mount an army of backers to buy what was widely considered a sinkhole. Through his A-list Rolodex, Kensbrook turned a pile of rubble into Gotham's hottest nightspot since the heyday of Limelight. Its clout had grown to the point where New York Magazine had referred to it as "The Oprah Winfrey of music promotion." If you had to jump on one couch to get maximum exposure, the Kitten Club was the place to jump.

Shawn was decked out in a wool Versace suit that ran $2,200 and burned off a thousand calories a night. Shawn had purposefully bought it a size too small, the fabric stretching over his taut frame. Athena knew the only thing he worked harder at than promoting his club was promoting his body. Unlike most in the entertainment field, Kensbrook accomplished it solely through weightlifting, protein bars and the best personal trainers money could buy. Bastard didn't even drink.

Shawn pecked Athena on the cheek and ushered her through the crowd to the DJ booth in the back. She shook hands with a guy Shawn introduced as DJ Stix, a light skinned black man wearing sunglasses rimmed with diamonds. No doubt they were real. Kensbrook would want his employees to dazzle in every way, no matter the price.

Athena's manager, a twitchy man named Eddie, would be standing by in case she got the crazy urge to sing without proper electronic vocal support. Athena had an army of producers who made sure she sounded perfect in the studio. Live, anything could happen.

After the current song ended, Stix turned down the music and Kensbrook picked up the house microphone.

"Ladies and gentlemen, kittens, cats and lions of all ages," he said. "It is my pleasure to introduce you to the Queen of all Media, her royal highness herself, the woman whose debut album drops this Tuesday, give it up, show your love, for the beautiful Athena Paradis!"

The crowd roared as Athena waved, blowing imaginary kisses, flaunting her body and striking glamorous pose after pose. She was a god amongst mortals. She knew it, they knew it, and they all loved it.

The Guilty

Suddenly a deep, throbbing bass began to reverberate through the club. Squeals of joy leapt from the lips of heavy-breathing men and women. Then, after a dozen bass thumps, the synthesizer kicked in, and the club came alive.

The sweaty bodies congealed into a solid mass as the expertly arranged rhythm sent ripples through them, electricity making every person sway, every person bounce, every one of them belonging to her.

Sweat coated her upper lip. She licked it, shuddered at the sensation, and knew the night would be a memorable one. The blue Missoni dress clung to her body, the fabric clinging to her curves like tissue paper. The dress had been air-mailed by Ottavio Missoni himself, specifically for Athena to wear tonight.

She could feel DJ Stix's eyes drinking her in. He didn't even pretend to look away. Even Shawn Kensbrook couldn't help but steal an eyeful as she danced and spun to the beat. Athena looked at them with a seductive grin, then raised the volume a few notches, the bass thumping harder.

The music consumed the night. And then Athena jumped on top of the turntables.

The crowd stopped dancing, stared at her, cheered her on. She ran her hands over her body, made every one of them feel like they could be her lover.

Athena owned them. Every single one.

Somebody handed Athena a clear glass. She drank it in two gulps. Vodka tonic. With a hint of lime. She could feel the ecstasy tab kicking in. The whole world became a velvet dream, soft, wet and inviting. She kissed the air, watched as her lips sent waves of passion through hundreds.

When the song ended, Stix took Athena's hand and escorted her back to her nine hundred pounds of bodyguard. The lips pleaded with her to stay, reaching and pawing as she was led through the crowd.

Shawn Kensbrook ducked through the prying arms. Athena's lead guard recognized him, parted the way. Shawn was dripping with sweat. She envied that he could experience such ecstasy while sober. He threw his arms around her. Whispered into her ear.

"Athena, hon, that was off the charts."

"No," she said. "Come Tuesday, that's number one on the

charts." Shawn smiled, nodded.

"Look at this, I mean, will you look at it? All these people here for you…what's that feel like?"

She smiled at him, flicked her tongue into his ear. She felt him shiver. Felt him grow hard in an instant.

"You'll never know."

Shawn watched as the bodyguards whisked her away. The bouncers parted the curtains, flung open the doors. Eyes waiting on line widened. Her limo waited just beyond the red carpet. It would take her to Nikos's SoHo loft, where he'd have champagne, strawberries and other goodies waiting. They'd do it all night before passing out naked on his satin sheets. Tomorrow she would see her photo in newspapers across the city.

Athena stepped onto the red carpet and waved to her fans. Her new fans. Her old fans. Fans who would give anything for her. She took one step onto the carpet. Smiled. And then a crack of thunder filled the air, and a bullet smashed through her skull.

And just like that, her blood staining the carpet an even darker red, the Goddess Athena died.

Chapter 2

I woke up thinking that Amanda must have hijacked my cell phone. That's the only way my ring tone could have been changed from the standard and satisfying triple beep to an electronic version of that awful new Athena Paradis song, "I Want UR Love."

And the only thing worse than hearing that song come from a tinny cell phone speaker was being woken by it at three in the morning.

Amanda grumbled. Her arm was thrown over my chest, but her sleep hadn't been interrupted. Figures I'd be the only one disturbed by her diabolical creation.

I reached across to the nightstand where I kept the phone, careful not to dislocate my shoulder since my other arm was pinned under Amanda. There are worse things in the world than having your arm stuck underneath a beautiful woman who loves you.

I covered the speaker with my thumb and checked the incoming number. Christ, not again; this was becoming a routine. It was Mya, my ex-girlfriend. Two-thirty in the morning. The third time this week Mya had called in the wee hours. I was having a hard time putting an end to it. I knew since last year Mya had been on a slippery slope. Calling from a bar, no doubt. I could practically smell the Stoli through the mouthpiece.

Mya and I dated for several years in college, a time I could hardly remember. When we met, I was smitten. She was tall, beautiful, with confidence like no girl I'd ever met. And for some reason she'd picked me. I don't know if I ever loved her, or simply loved being with her. Loved being with a girl I knew would be somebody.

We'd broken up a year ago. Right before my life had changed forever. Our relationship was probably doomed whether or not I'd been accused of murder, but after I nearly died and became a minor New York celebrity, she'd had a change of heart. Suddenly she wanted to give our buried love life another go.

She didn't love Henry Parker anymore. At least not the Henry she'd met years ago. Not the Henry Parker she used to kiss behind the stacks in the Cornell library. She loved the Henry Parker that had

11

been invented by the newspapers and magazines. The indestructible one who'd survived a three-day manhunt, only to live and regain his job at the city's most prestigious newspaper. Not the Henry Parker who could barely run without feeling the pain in his side from where the bone shards punctured his lung. Or the Henry whose heart beat fast every time he heard a police siren or a car backfire. That was the Henry that only Amanda knew. And I was happy she knew it. It felt real. Like it could last forever.

Mya loved the other Henry Parker. But that wasn't me. That Henry was a creation, a monster created by ink. I wanted nothing to do with him.

At the same time, the year Amanda and I had been together had seen incredible changes. When I'd first met Amanda—when I'd lied to her to save my skin—she'd been as lost as I was. Her entire life existed in a trunk full of notebooks she'd kept since she was a little girl. Notebooks she used to catalog every single person she met, writing down superficial details, mirroring the abandonment in her real life.

When she picked me up in her car, thinking I was a student named Carl Bernstein, Amanda wrote down her thoughts about that nonexistent man. I wanted her to know life wasn't something to be catalogued. With me, she could actually experience it. Soon after she moved in, the notebooks disappeared. One night, after making love, I'd asked about them. She said she didn't need a stupid pen and paper anymore. She said real memories were good enough. And that's what I promised to give her. Even if it meant her playing practical jokes with my ring tone.

I clicked the Answer button and waited. I could hear breathing on the other end. It was the fifth time this month Mya had called after midnight, in addition to the myriad calls to my office, always from unlisted numbers or pay phones. At night, I could chalk it up to her being drunk. During the day, I didn't know what to make of it. A week ago Mya had called at 3:30 a.m. She asked if I'd meet her for a drink. To talk about stuff. We'd never really had a chance to say goodbye, she'd said. I told her we did. And still she kept calling.

"Hehlo? Izzis Henry?"

"Yes, Mya," I whispered, watching to see if Amanda would wake up.

"Where are you?"

The Guilty

"At home."

"Why are you at home?"

"I was sleeping."

"Why are you sleeping?"

"Because I have work tomorrow." I waited. She said nothing. "Listen, Mya, you need to stop calling me."

"Oh stop it," she said, and I could picture her waving her hand dismissively. "You're not sleeping now. It's early, silly. Come out for a drink."

"Mya, there's no way…"

"Who is that?" I felt Amanda stir, her eyes fluttering open. "Is someone on the phone?"

"It's me," I said softly. "Go back to sleep. It's Mya again."

"Again? Does she think you deliver pizza or something?" Amanda said through a yawn. "Tell her to call Domino's and get out of our life."

I waited a moment until Amanda's breathing evened.

"Listen Mya, I'm going back to sleep. Please. Stop calling."

"I miss you Henry." Her voice had changed, choked up. I closed my eyes. Tried not to think about the last time I'd hung up on Mya late at night. I couldn't do it again. She had to choose to let it go.

"Come on Mya, I'm with someone else now. You know that. Please. Hang up the phone. Go back to your friends."

"I have no friends. Please, Hen. I really want to see you."

"Good night, Mya. I have to go. You should go."

"Fine," she said, and then I heard a dial tone.

I swallowed. Felt Amanda stir. Wished Mya hadn't gotten so screwed up after the whole mess last year. Wished she could be happy.

And then the phone rang again. Amanda bolted upright.

"Don't bars in this city have a closing time? I swear you need to get a restraining order. If you answer it you're sleeping on the couch."

"I don't fit on the couch."

"Then you get the refrigerator. I have an eight thirty tomorrow. It's hard to convince a child that their future is in good hands if their counsel shows up looking like Morticia Addams."

I pressed Answer. "Mya, I told you I'm with someone—"

"That's none of my business or concern, Henry, but if it makes you feel better Jack asked me to blow you a kiss."

Crap. It was Wallace Langston, the editor-in-chief of the New York Gazette. My boss. And he definitely wasn't calling because he missed me. Wallace was a good man, had hired me out of college, but I learned quickly that New York had a way of chewing up and spitting out its good men. Few newsmen were more respected, but readers didn't care much about professional courtesy. They wanted juice, gossip, and sadly often the lowest form of both. And that was one thing Wallace refused to give.

I'd gotten used to late-night calls from the office. Jack O'Donnell—my colleague and professional idol—was prone to doing it just for kicks. Like Mya, sometimes late at night I could smell the Seagrams on his breath through the phone. Jack worked late. He was unmarried, had no children. He just needed to hear a friendly voice, I supposed, because there weren't many in his life. So I didn't mind. And thankfully Amanda slept like wood.

"Wallace, what's up?"

"I need you at Thirteenth and Eleventh. Right away."

"I'm guessing this isn't so we can spend nine bucks on a beer at one of those clubs in the meatpacking district."

He ignored me. "Just get in a cab. There's been a homicide at some swanky shindig called the Pussy Club, I need you to cover it. I'd send Jack but he hasn't set foot in anything but an Irish pub since the seventies."

"Pussy Club...you mean the Kitten Club?"

"I mean it's 2:33 a.m. and if you're not here in ten minutes, we're going to get scooped by the Dispatch, the Observer and those crummy papers they give away for free on the subway platforms."

"Why me? Who's on night shift?"

"You're the only guy who's even remotely young enough to even understand this stuff. Now get dressed."

"What stuff? I don't follow."

"Athena Paradis was shot to death this morning. Looks like it might have been some sort of execution. Single shot, from a distance. I'm going out on a limb and saying you're more familiar with her, er, résumé than Jack is."

I was stunned. Athena Paradis. The world's most famous socialite. Famous for, well, something. She averaged three covers a month at the Dispatch. Wallace refused to give her that kind of coverage unless she cured AIDS or something. But murder changed all that, I guess.

"On my way," I said.

"I was never a fan of hers," Wallace said, offering more information than he needed to. "But the way it looks down there...she didn't deserve what this monster did."

Chapter 3

The New York night was muggy. Even at two-thirty in the morning, when the sun, like most of the city, is hibernating and waiting for the start of a new day, something kept the air thick. It was early May, and humidity already choked the streets. Late night revelers all wore shirts soaked through with sweat, foreheads shiny, content for the sun to never show its face again.

My cab slowed down and then stopped as we approached a tangled mess. I could see flashing lights nearly three blocks away. Kids my age lining the streets with worried looks. It took a lot to ruin a good night. I could only imagine what had happened here.

I walked the last few blocks to Thirteen, wading through honking cars and loaded partiers screaming on cell phones. I couldn't help but hear the panicked voices.

"Man, there was blood everywhere. I was right near her, man!"

"She...they think she's dead. Oh God, does that mean her album won't come out on time?"

I saw Wallace Langston talking to a cop and jotting down some notes on a spiral pad. Wallace didn't get out of bed for many stories. He left that to his city desk. But this wasn't just New York front-page news, this was a national headline. The kind of tawdry story that Paulina Cole and the Dispatch would be sopping up with a biscuit and squeezing dry.

I hadn't seen Paulina Cole in months, and I prayed she wasn't here tonight. I didn't need any distractions. Paulina Cole had once been a top reporter at the Gazette, left after penning a series of controversial yet shockingly popular articles where she insinuated that my murder accusation was merely the next story in a line of young journalists whose names always ended up in brighter lights than their stories. Didn't matter that my murder rap was bogus. The articles enabled Paulina to jump to the New York Dispatch, the Gazette's biggest rival. She got more money, more perks, and of course the chance to hoist her name among brighter lights.

Covering Athena Paradis's murder would be tricky. If we played catch-up to Paulina and the Dispatch's muckraking, they would dig a grave and bury us in a pile of our own moral righteousness.

Above the Kitten Club was perched a gigantic neon sign in the shape of a kitten. And not just any run-of-the-mill kitten, the kind of kitten that apparently wore a halter top and stockings and every few seconds tipped back some sort of pink cocktail that probably cost more than my pants and contained less alcohol than a glass of seltzer. Appearances. Atmosphere. That's what Kitten Club patrons came for. And last night they got it. In the form of Athena Paradis, world-famous socialite, erstwhile fashion model, nubile actress, soon-to-be recording artist, and, depending on who you asked, either your personal hero or the bane of your existence.

I had nothing against Athena personally, but a few weeks ago a colleague forwarded me a leaked demo of her first single. Not even three straight hours of Bruce and Dylan could rinse that stain off.

You'd think my generation would have more to offer. I'd like to say they do, but lying to yourself is pretty pathetic.

Within hours all those people soundly sleeping in their beds would wake up to find out that one of the most famous women on the planet had been murdered. That the suspect was still at large. That there would be a city-wide manhunt that would put all other investigations—including my own—to shame. Not to mention the resources that Athena's father—Costas Paradis—would likely contribute. Bottom line, if your finger pulled the trigger, you were a marked man. But as soon as the killer fired that round, the reverberations created a news story. It was my job to see all the ripples.

Problem is, New York is a city eight million strong. If you want to disappear and don't have a pile of mush instead of brains, you could disappear. Hundreds of crimes and dozens of murders went unsolved every year. All this guy did was raise the stakes. Raised them to a level that would scare off pretty much anyone without a death wish, but raised nonetheless.

I saw Wallace, approached him. The editor-in-chief of the New York Gazette was a tall, slender man. He wore a neatly trimmed brown beard flecked with gray, and though his stature was hardly imposing his intelligence shone through. He wore a light jacket, hands tucked into the pockets. Wallace and I acknowledged each other with a brief nod, then turned back to the scene.

A line of police tape had cordoned off a thirty foot radius around the spot where Athena's body had fallen. Even against the dark red of the carpet, I could make out a darker, more gruesome shade. The body had been removed from the scene, but forensics had taped off the angle at which her body had fallen. Several areas were marked with flags, presumably for ballistics and blood spatter experts. Some of the spatter appeared to be as far as ten feet from where Athena had fallen. Only a high-caliber slug could cause that much damage. I saw a flag on the carpet, in front of a piece of chipped pavement. Quite possibly where the bullet had lodged after exiting Athena's skull.

The other bars in the district had been emptied out by the cops. The music had been turned off. The only sounds were the sirens and the cops, but the fear was louder than all of it.

"Warm out tonight," I said. Wallace nodded, wiped his forehead with a handkerchief as though reminded to.

"Gunman shot Athena from a distance. Goddamn sick coward."

"Just what I was thinking," I said. I looked around. "Guy would have been noticed on the street," I said. Wallace lifted his head, looked at the rooftops, didn't need to say more.

"How do you shoot a woman like that?" Wallace said, to nobody. "Disgusting, that's what it is."

"Athena wasn't just a woman," I said. "You get that famous, you become bigger than yourself. Become an ideologue or something." Wallace looked at me, knew we were both thinking about what happened to me last year. When people thought I'd murdered a cop, I was no longer Henry Parker. I stood for something evil. And even when I was vindicated, the stench lingered. Athena lived in that spotlight every day of her life.

Police were questioning several young men and women who were sitting on the sidewalk, leaning against an ambulance. They looked visibly shaken. Eyes red, heads down. Confidence sucked out of them. Several were crying. I wondered whether they were crying due to the horror they'd just witnessed, or because the world had been robbed of Athena Paradis.

"Cops aren't going to get anything from witnesses who were

The Guilty

inside the club," I said. "Figure at least fifty paparazzi outside, all those strobe lights, every single eye was focused on her."

"How can you be so sure?" Wallace asked.

"Cause mine would be. You tell yourself you could care less about celebrities like Athena Paradis, but it's damn hard to turn away. And this was her scene."

I thought of Mya. Wondered if she was near here when she called. I hoped she'd made it home safe. I debated calling her just to be sure.

"This is page one," I said to Wallace.

"We're too late for the print edition," he said. "I want your copy on the Gazette website in an hour. And I want updates by the time Al Roker is smiling his way through the weather report."

"Awful generous deadline of you."

Wallace looked at me. "We mishandle this story in any way, the Dispatch will cannibalize our circulation rate and spend all winter bragging about its superior reporting."

"They couldn't report their way out of the 6 train," I said, expecting a laugh, but receiving none.

"Doesn't matter," Wallace said softly. "Story like this, it's all about how sensational you can make it. Who runs the cover photo of Athena in the most revealing dress. Gets the best quotes from her exes. Finds the most salacious angle to play up, even if it turns out to be bogus later on. You know Paulina will be all over this."

"So what do you want me to do?"

"You know the sign I keep by the elevators to all our news divisions, right?" I nodded. The sign Wallace was referring to was simply titled The Three Types of Reporters. It was a piece of paper, containing four short, handwritten sentences.

Some reporters are always one step behind.
Some reporters always keep pace.
Some reporters are always one step ahead.
What kind of reporter are you?

"Good. Then Evelyn will be expecting your copy in sixty minutes."

"I'm a lucky man."

19

Jason Pinter

Evelyn Waterstone was the Gazette's battle-ax of a Metro desk editor. All stories that focused within the five boroughs were doled out by her, met with her approval, and she had final edit. She was notorious for fighting for front page space, claiming that New York was the country's central nervous system, and that most relevant stories stemmed from there. So far she had treated me with kid gloves. Which left me uneasy. She always seemed to be much tougher on the other young journalists, the interns, the people who hadn't paid their dues. The fact that she liked me was fairly disconcerting. Like someone who smiled to your face while they held a Ginsu behind their back.

"Leave out the stuff about slug caliber and shooter vantage points," Wallace said.. "Too much conjecture. Let the Dispatch be forced to make retractions. We need to play this clean."

"I'll get it done," I said, trying to convince not only Wallace but myself.

"Don't worry, I spoke to Evelyn before you got here. She's aware of the time-sensitive nature, and is waiting for your e-mail. I'm asking you to play in the same scuzzy ballpark the Dispatch does, only you bat clean. You have an hour. Find an angle the Dispatch will miss. The entire country is going to be talking about Athena's murder, and we need to give them something nobody else will. I don't want any baseless conjecture. I don't want any name-calling. I don't want to stoop to their level. I want you to report this story the way a Gazette reporter would."

I nodded. Had no intention of doing it any other way. Since I returned to the Gazette full time, I'd worked my ass off in an effort to prove I could hack it at that level. My first go round had been sidetracked by a slight case of murder. I'd spent the better part of a year trying to live down my own story, and now it was time to return to what I did best. To what I was born to do. Find the stories nobody else could.

I looked back at the crime scene. Saw where the body had fallen. A ballistics expert used a pencil to trace an invisible line from the top of a brownstone several blocks away to the spot where the bullets had struck Athena. This club had security cameras outside, meaning Athena's death had undoubtedly likely been captured live and in color.

All those cameras. All those witnesses. No doubt a dozen people or more had taken cell phone photos and videos of her murder.

20

The Guilty

Who knew how many ghouls would post them publicly. Whoever had killed Athena couldn't have picked a more public place. It was as if the killer wanted people to see it, to record it, to spread his mayhem. It didn't make my job any easier, that's for sure. There would be a cacophony of noise tomorrow, and I needed to find a pitch that could rise above it.

I looked at the brownstone being eyed by the tech. Checked my watch. Under an hour to find a story. Didn't have to be the whole ball of yarn, just a strong thread. Sometimes a thread was all you needed.

Chapter 4

I pushed my way through the throng of eager reporters. Felt more than one elbow jab my ribs. I wasn't naïve enough to think they were accidental. Much of the NYC press corps still burned because of the publicity I'd received from my murder rap. Grizzled vets who resented the book and film deals I'd turned down. It was a Catch-22. They would have hated me just as much if I'd taken the money. The spotlight of fame exposed every jealous and spiteful emotion from those who wished they had it, and from those who wanted nothing to do with it.

I saw Curtis Sheffield on the cop side of the tape, holding back photographers and issuing no comments like they were going out of style. Curt Sheffield was a young black officer, two years out of the academy and the kind of cop who'd be one of New York's finest for years to come. Fit, tall, with a smile that got female witnesses offering more than their side of the story. I'd interviewed Curt a few months ago for a story on the NYPD's developing new body armor, how the upgrade was long overdue, and how based on gunshot wound studies the new vests, when implemented across the country, would likely save up to thirty lives a year.

Curt was glad the department finally kicked in the dough to save lives, but offered sincere remorse for the lives that had already been lost. He'd been honest and eloquent, and it was clear the public good was his passion. The department had recognized this—and recognized that his face would look good on a poster—and within weeks Curt was the centerpiece of a new NYPD recruitment campaign.

Despite our naturally combative professions, I considered Curt a friend. He was a great source because he knew any information he passed along would be treated with respect. A few weeks after the recruitment drive started, Curt admitted that most cops weren't big fans of do I know you looks. They don't like getting recognized in movie theaters or getting asked for autographs. So we had something in common.

Curt saw me as I battled the wave of gawkers barricaded behind police tape. He walked over fast, a stern look in his eye.

"Hey, back off," he said, approaching a grizzled paparazzo trying to sneak his camera beneath the tape. He eyed me, popped his head to the left. Come over here.

I followed him off to the side. Another cop held back the masses so we could talk in private.

"You believe this shit?" Curt said. "Don't know what's worse, cleaning up this mess or having Athena Paradis's stupid song stuck in my head while her blood is drying on the sidewalk."

"I'd say they're both pretty bad."

"Yeah. Pretty bad," he said, distracted. He was chewing gum. His jaw was working overtime, anything to keep his mind occupied.

"So you assigned to this mess?" I asked.

"You aren't assigned to shitstorms, they just happen to rain when you're walking by." Curt smacked his gum.

"Big story," he continued. "Not just any girl got killed here tonight."

"Don't I know it." I leaned in. "Listen, man, if I had to guess, Athena was killed by a high-powered rifle. High caliber slug." I pointed at the outcropping of rooftops surrounding the Kitten Club. "Your killer shot from the roof of one of these buildings. Guess it's up to your forensics and splatter people to figure out the angle and trajectory."

"Like Deadwood out here. Everybody saw everything, but nobody saw nothing. Know what I mean?"

"Yeah. Figure some sick asshole with a video cell phone will upload this to YouTube any minute now." I looked around, saw half a dozen half-drunk and half-asleep club goers fiddling on cell phones and BlackBerries. "Maybe sooner than later."

Curt kept chewing, nodded. "You see that building over there?" He flicked his head north.

"Which one?"

"Don't know," he said, eyes locked on to mine. "Maybe red brick or something."

I looked again. There was a red brick building two blocks north and one block west of us. I could make it out through the early morning haze.

"Seen a lot of my boys in blue checking it out. Trying not to cause a stir."

"That right?"

Curt nodded. "Hate to see those cockroaches at the Dispatch get the brass ring. You know they had a reporter over here from their gossip section, offered to write me up as one of NYC's hottest bachelors if I planted a bug in our briefing room? Fucking parasites."

"Hell, you'd be lucky to break the top hundred."

"Yeah, tell that to my girlfriend. I'd be on patrol with a GPS monitor up my ass the second she thinks my eyes start wandering." Curt looked around, coughed into his hand. "Can't say I was a fan of Athena's, you know, work, but Christ, the girl was only twenty-two."

"No kidding," I said. We stayed silent for a moment, then I remembered my deadline. "Hey, drinks on me this week. If I don't hit my deadline which is in, oh about six minutes, I'll be out of work and you'll have to pick up the tab."

"Then get the hell out of here." He clapped me on the shoulder. "Take it easy, Parker."

After saying goodbye I hung back for a minute. I didn't want to let anyone else know I had a possible scoop. Then I waded back into the soup of reporters, stuffed my hands in my pockets and headed north.

Two patrolmen jogged by me. I slowed down. There were several cops huddling outside of the building. As I got closer I heard radio activity. I stopped at the corner and peeked around.

A plainclothes cop stood by the awning, a walkie-talkie in his hand. A plainclothes cop, probably from the Forensic Investigation, strode up and spoke to him for a minute, then ducked inside. I took a breath, waited until the guard was alone, then rounded the corner and approached him.

"Help you?" he said. Nothing to see here, move along.

"Henry Parker, New York Gazette." I showed him my press credentials. Might as well have been a slab of lemon, the way his face scrunched up.

"Go on, get out of here."

"Something going on inside this building?" The cop locked eyes with me, then spoke deliberately.

"You know you don't have a whole lot of fans in the law enforcement community."

I nodded. Despite clashing often over jurisdictional authority, the NYPD and FBI still considered themselves part of the same noble profession. When push came to shove, they stuck up for one another. And even though I had never been brought for the murder of Officer John Fredrickson, if not for me he'd still be alive. And even though he was dirty as sin, that was something no cop or Fed would ever forget.

"Crime scene is over on Thirteenth." He jerked his thumb back where I'd come from. "You want a better view of the crime scene, might I suggest walking to the middle of the Brooklyn Bridge and then jumping off."

I laughed, pretended it didn't affect me. "I saw several officers entering and exiting this site."

"You saw wrong."

"Officer..." I said, looking at his badge. "Officer Lemansky. I know this is the building the killer shot Athena Paradis from. You and I both know this murder is going to make both of our lives a living hell until the killer is caught. All differences aside, the story is huge, and it won't go away just because you tell me to. Whether it's the Gazette, the Dispatch or the National Enquirer, you're going to have reporters up your ass until this psycho is caught. Do you read the newspaper?"

He nodded. "So what?

"So you must have read that story the Dispatch ran last week. Detective Pedro Alvarez, killed in the line of duty. Did you know him?"

Lemansky's silence was an affirmative.

"So you know the Dispatch ran a front-page story two days after his death. About his mistress. Lena something, right? "

Officer Lemansky sniffed. He shuffled his feet.

"Fucking parasites," he said. "Madeleine deserved better than seeing her family's name dragged through the mud." He looked at me. "Alvarez was a good cop and a good husband. If it wasn't for people like you he'd still be remembered that way."

I had my opening.

"I don't work for the Dispatch. I'm not interested in smear campaigns and ruining families to sell papers. If you don't talk to me, another reporter will get the story. You've read the Gazette. So you can talk to me right here, right now, or I can't promise what tomorrow's headline will be in the Dispatch. But I can promise you what the headline will be in the Gazette."

Lemansky was searching my eyes for the truth. Whether he

could trust me. I knew he could.

He nodded. "I give you something, it came from an anonymous source. I get quoted, or you do anything to go back on what you just said, I don't care if the papers start claiming we're fucking aliens from Mars, you'll get a mouthful of broken teeth before you ever get another story."

I said, "You have my word."

He looked around. I thought about Curt. Knew the cops just wanted to make sure the right thing was done.

"Forensics is saying they found a note scrawled up on the roof, below the ledge they think the shooter rested the gun on. They're analyzing it, but they say he wrote in block using a Sharpie so it's pretty much useless. They're sifting through about a ton of loose gravel up there, could take days to find anything else."

"The note," I said, speaking softly, half to calm the cop and half to slow down my heart. "What did it say?"

The cop looked around again. He reached into his pocket and pulled out a folded piece of paper.

"Some lab rat passed copies around, asked if anyone had ever heard of someone talking like this before. I didn't know, but..." He licked his lips. His eyes danced around, like somebody was about to leap from the morning shadows.

He handed it to me.

"Get out of here," he said. "And remember what you said." I nodded, took the paper and walked off.

I waited until I'd gone about three blocks and was out of the line of sight from the building. Then I opened my hand.

It was a simple piece of paper on which was written a single sentence. And if Lemansky was correct, besides a murdered girl, this was all the killer left behind.

I read the sentence. Felt my breath catch in my throat. Right then I knew why Officer Lemansky was scared. I knew what my angle was. A chill of fear ran up my spine, similar to the one I felt last year when I was accused of murder.

And I knew that Athena Paradis wouldn't be the last victim.

Chapter 5

I was sitting in Wallace Langston's office as he read a printout of the article. My palms were coated with sweat and my eyelids felt like they were being dragged down with two-ton weights. Evelyn had posted the text of my article at 4:22 a.m., holding it up just to confirm my source. When I told her the quote the killer had left at the scene, she paused.

"Why do I recognize that line?" she asked.

I took a breath before answering, "Because I wrote it."

The slip of paper Officer Lemansky gave me had one simple sentence on it. It read:

The only difference between the innocent and the guilty is that the guilty are the only ones who believe in their cause.

I had written that line several weeks after being cleared of the murder of John Fredrickson. When I was on the run, when the whole world saw me as a murderer, other than Amanda I was the only one who knew and believed in the truth. The article was in response to those who'd been so quick to pass judgment, including the Gazette's own Paulina Cole. I was happy to hear when she left for the Dispatch. I couldn't imagine going to work every day, sitting next to someone who printed such vileness without knowing the truth.

When the world assumed I was guilty, they looked at me as a degenerate, someone to whom committing murder was justified.

And now a killer had taken my words, used them to support whatever twisted reasoning goes through the mind of someone willing to steal an innocent life.

If my assumption was correct, the killer knew he was guilty. Only he didn't care. He had a cause. Causes don't simply end. Murderers don't simply lose interest. There were more victims out there.

"This came out well," Wallace said, mainly to fill the silence. We both knew the copy wasn't great, but contained all confirmed and pertinent facts and was as good as could be expected from a reporter running on Red Bull and a deadline.

He put the papers down on top of a copy of the morning edition of the Dispatch. Wallace had it delivered every day, though I couldn't remember him ever reading it.

The headline read, HEIRESS WHACKED: Police Search for Sex Symbol Shooter. It was actually one of their more subtle headlines.

"I give them ten points for alliteration," I said. "Search for sex symbol shooter. Almost poetic."

"Take off several thousand for subtlety," another voiced chimed in. I turned around.

Jack O'Donnell walked into the room, half a dozen newspapers under his arm. He looked well rested, energized.

"Least someone around here caught forty winks," I said.

"I think I caught forty winks total my first five years on the job, don't complain to me about sleep." He took the papers from under his arm, and I recognized the running heads of what looked like the morning edition of every major paper in the metropolitan area, as well as a few nationals. He tossed them on Wallace's desk one at a time, giving us a chance to read each headline.

I wasn't aware newspaper fonts could run that big.

"You have no idea how much it cost us to dump our page one and get the Paradis story in there," Wallace said. "None of them report anything substantial. That'll come tomorrow. With any luck we'll sell enough papers today to make up for the printing and shipping delays."

"Even in death Athena breaks the bank," Jack said. "You know some asshole found a highball glass from last night that still has Athena Paradis's lipstick on it? Bidding on eBay is up to ten grand. I'm thinking of joining the fray, resell the glass during the trial and retire."

"This case will never go to trial," I said, a sick feeling in my stomach.

"And why not?" asked Wallace.

"Fools with a cause don't go quietly. They don't put their hands behind their back, and they don't care about their Miranda rights. This guy's in it until the end."

"Let's hope you're wrong," Wallace replied. "Right now all we can do is our job. So let's talk."

Jack flicked my ear as he walked by. "What, no iPod today?"

I sighed, played along.

The Guilty

"I usually take it off when I get to the office."

"Hard to concentrate when listening to Bee-yonk, right?"

I didn't correct him, frankly would have felt like an idiot telling him the correct pronunciation was Beyoncé. A few months ago, I made the careless mistake of going to the bathroom and leaving my iPod on my desk. The mistake wasn't leaving it out in the open, but trusting someone like Jack to act like an adult. By the time I got back to my desk, Jack had scrolled through my entire playlist and taken votes from the entire newsroom as to which artists I should delete from the hard drive permanently. The results were tabulated, and for a week after that he would ask for the player to see if I'd complied. Finally I removed the offending songs, just to shut him up. According to Jack, any music created after 1986 should never be heard through my (or any other) speakers again. He said if not for the Dylan and Springsteen, he would have thrown the entire thing in the garbage.

"Henry," Jack said, his voice now without any condescension. "If you don't think this case will go to trial you're an idiot. Someone's getting prosecuted, even if it takes a few cases to get the right suspect. Costas Paradis's private jet is on its way to the city as we speak, and I can promise that he's bringing hellfire and brimstone and a savings account large enough to be a continent unto itself. Whether it's Shawn Kensbrook, the security staff at the Kitten Club, the killer himself, or Lord Zeus up on high, somebody's getting locked away while the key is thrown in the ocean. Half a dozen tabloid hacks are writing first drafts of quickie books that will be on sale in your local grocery store within the week."

"Cynical much?" I said.

Jack dismissed the question. "If you want to last in this business as long as I have, you'll have the cynical alarm on high 24/7. Question everything. You wouldn't be here right now if you hadn't done that last year."

"So why did a line I wrote end up at a crime scene?" I asked. "That's my question."

"Let's hope it's an eerie coincidence," Wallace said. "That it doesn't have some sort of meaning that plays into why Athena was killed."

"If this goes to trial," Jack added with a smile, "we can always claim libel, say the killer used Henry's quote out of context."

I absently scratched my ribs.

"Now the question for you both is," Wallace said, "where do we go from here? We've got the killer's message. Jack, you check with the NYPD, see if Carruthers has any suspects or leads."

"I want to talk to the ballistics department," I said. "Jack, do you know anyone there you can hook me up with?"

"Why ballistics?" Wallace asked.

"Athena was killed by a high-powered rifle shot from a rooftop three blocks away, and the killer left a message he wanted to be found. This is as premeditated as it gets, and was executed with careful consideration. No doubt the murder weapon will fit into that. Then we can run a check on the gun, find the store he bought it at, go from there."

"Jack?" Wallace said. Jack scratched his beard. It looked a little darker than it had the last few days, the brown a little more, er, not gray. With our coverage of the Paradis murder, we were going to sell a lot of papers. Jack wanted to look his best in case there were any photo ops or interviews. And who was I to question the omnipotence of Just For Men?

There was a beep alerting Wallace to an incoming e-mail. He clicked the mouse, eyes narrowing as he read.

"Mayor Perez called a news conference for noon today. Costas Paradis will be in attendance."

I looked at Jack, who was staring at the screen, thinking. The fire was just starting to burn, and I felt it too.

"I want you both there," Wallace said. "And I don't care what you do or how you do it, get something different to run with tomorrow. I need angles here that won't be covered by the other papers."

"Angle is my middle name," Jack said.

"Yesterday you told me it was Glenfiddich," replied Wallace.

"Mine is Shane," I said proudly. They both looked at me. I wasn't proud anymore. "I mean it's Angle too."

Jack shook his head. "Wine cooler. That's your middle name. Get a good story and I'll promote you to Zima."

"And Henry," Wallace said, "If anyone asks about the quote the killer used, you have your 'no comments' at the ready. Am I correct in assuming you're not hiding anything? That you have no reason to think this is anything but an awful coincidence?"

"I swear I have no idea," I said, honestly. "Trust me, after last year I'd just as soon stay out of the spotlight as much as possible."

"Then let's keep it that way. We have to assume the suspect used it simply because the quote was relevant, or that he has some serious bats flying around in his belfry."

"That might work better than a 'no comment," Jack said.

"Now get a move on," Wallace continued. "I have no doubt there'll be some fireworks at this conference. You won't want to watch from the back row."

Chapter 6

Paulina Cole sat at her desk, holding a warm cup in her hands. She took a sip. Coffee and Xanax. Better than toast and a runny omelet. She'd squeezed Dr. Shepberg's name into an article naming the best psychiatrists in NYC and ever since then the prescriptions arrived in her mailbox once a month.

Behind Paulina's desk were half a dozen picture frames containing front pages pulled from the New York Dispatch. Stories she'd broken, papers so hot they'd sold out their print runs and been dissected on blogs around the world. Since she'd joined the Dispatch, the paper's circulation had grown 1.5 percent, a number many tried to attribute to a new marketing campaign, but those in the know knew it was solely because of her. Ted Allen, the Dispatch's publisher, had said as much during the last shareholders meeting, and promptly given her a ten percent raise. He said Paulina Cole represented the bold new direction the Dispatch would be taking into the twenty-first century, that despite all the perils facing the print industry, technology simply couldn't compete with an old-fashioned nose for news. According to Allen, the Dispatch was tired of being the number two newspaper in New York. And come hell or high water (possibly both) they would eventually best their number one competitor. Even if it meant simply hiring away their top reporters.

That's how he phrased it. Their enemy. This wasn't business, this was war. The longer you stayed satisfied being number two the more likely you'd fall out of the race completely. Nobody remembered the guy who lost the election, the ex before meeting your soul mate. The second-best were forgotten, pulped. If you weren't willing to kill to grab the lead, you deserved to get trampled.

That was Paulina's job; to do the trampling, to sell newspapers.

And for all the battles waged between the two newspapers, the coverage of Athena Paradis's murder could be the Dispatch's Gettysburg. Athena was the most recognizable woman in the world, more than the president's wife, more than Princess Diana (hell, most of Athena's fans were too young to have even heard of Lady Di), even more than that lucky gal who scribbled the words Harry Potter on a notepad.

The battles lines had been drawn. More newspapers were going to be moved during the Paradis investigation than any event save a terrorist attack. Of course Paulina could argue that more people had seen Athena's reality show than had voted in the last election, so by sheer volume alone this was the biggest news story of the decade. Besides, the Lindbergh baby had never posed on the cover of her self-titled album wearing stockings and wrapped in a fire hose.

Until three o'clock this morning, Paulina had been digging into the personal life of David Loverne, congressional candidate, philanthropist, father of Henry Parker's ex-girlfriend Mya, and alleged keeper of somewhere in the vicinity of four mistresses. It was a cover story in the making. David was beloved. Tall, handsome, the kind of man other men looked up to and women wanted to look down upon. She was going to blow the whole thing wide open, expose the creep for who he really was. His fans and supporters would be demoralized. His detractors (yes, there were some) would eat it for breakfast. And every one of them would fork over their fifty cents to read it.

Over the past week, Paulina had interviewed two women who claimed to have slept with Loverne, both within the past year. One dalliance occurred in a limousine after a stump speech, the other in an airplane flying to Dubai. Taking Loverne down would sell papers. Getting in another dig at someone close to Henry Parker was just icing on the cake.

There was a knock on her door.

"Come in," she said. In walked Terrence Bynes, the Dispatch's Metro editor. Paulina's direct boss. The fact that he would lick between the subway railings if Paulina asked him to was implicit in their relationship.

Bynes was wearing suit pants with cuffs an inch too long, and a blue work shirt that looked like it had been fermented with starch. His eyeglasses were too big, not to mention unnecessary, considering Paulina knew his last eye exam produced 20/19 vision. And she'd be willing to bet there was a rolled sock (or two) down his trousers as well.

"I assume you read the Gazette this morning," Bynes said.

"Fucking online edition," Paulina said, taking another sip, feeling that delicious warm tingle. "Read only by cheapos and kids without the attention span to click the 'Next Page' button. Their print edition didn't have anything we didn't, that's all we should be concerned about."

"Tell that to Ted Allen," Bynes continued. "The man is pissed. He thinks we got scooped, and he's looking to point the finger."

"We did get scooped," Paulina said. "But that's like saying we got stabbed by a toothpick at the start of a knife fight. What Henry Parker wrote this morning won't be a blip on the radar tomorrow after Perez's press conference. So tell him if that finger goes anywhere near me I'm cutting it off."

Bynes smirked. "Why don't you tell him that?"

"Well, it's your job, but I'd be happy to. I'll e-mail him right now." She pulled out her keyboard and began typing. Bynes placed his hand over the keys.

"That was a hypothetical question," he said.

She stopped typing. "Don't ever ask me a hypothetical question again, or I'll hypothetically strangle you with your shoelace. I call every bluff I see. Remember that."

Bynes swallowed, flicked his eyes down to his wingtips. "So what do I tell Ted Allen? He's pissed this Parker kid got to the cops before we could."

Paulina leaned back in her chair. She closed her eyes. This Parker kid. This Parker kid.

Her eyelids flew open.

"This Parker kid is a good reporter. Give me pages four through seven tomorrow for coverage of the murder."

"That's a lot of copy. Are you sure you'll have enough to fill that space?"

"Don't ask me that again. I could give a rat's ass what you do with pages eight, nine and sixty-nine. Oh, and get Tamara Finnerman to do a write-up of David Loverne's speech at the Alzheimer's event last night. When my story runs, I don't want people thinking we've had it in for him. Tell her to use prose so syrupy and purple I'll be able to see the Crayola logo. Tell Allen that between these two stories, the Gazette will be limping within weeks."

Bynes laughed, then wiped a loose dribble of saliva from his mouth.

"I'm not going to tell him that. What, you think covering a story we've already been scooped on will suddenly have Wallace Langston quaking in his Doc Martens?"

Paulina smiled at him, crossed her legs.

"Every war begins with an opening volley. Parker's scoop this morning was the Gazette's opening volley. I'm not simply returning fire, I'm coming back with a Howitzer up their ass. You know my ex-husband was a state prosecutor. One thing I learned from him, other than that men are as useful as dirty bathwater, is that nobody remembers how you won, they remember if you won. We simply take what Parker has, know what he's going to know, and make it our own. Henry's a great reporter, but after last year he's nervous, twitchy, and doesn't want to rattle the cage any more than he already has. I have someone who'll shadow him closer than his beard stubble, and I'll be waiting to lay down the copy."

Bynes smiled. "I thought you said Finnerman was the one who wrote purple prose."

"Trust me," Paulina said. "It'll look better on paper."

Chapter 7

I was walking towards city hall alongside Jack O'Donnell, nearly having to sprint to keep up. And his legs had an extra thirty years of mileage. I dialed Amanda, figured I'd say hi before radio silence. She picked up on the second ring. "Hey hon, can't talk for long, just wanted to say hi. I'm heading to the press conference with Jack. Think I can smell the mayor's cologne a mile away," I said into the cell phone

"Hey babe. No problem," she said. "I'm about to go into the library and I think they've starting arming the cell phone police with automatic weapons."

"Good thing you finally learned how to use the vibrate button." Jack elbowed me. Amanda, I mouthed. He raised his eyebrows. Girlfriend. He opened his mouth to say ah. Then he ran his thumb across his throat. Cut it off. "Anyway, I'd better turn this off. Jack is giving me dirty looks. I'll call you as soon as this circus is over."

"Is it a three-ring circus, or does Athena Paradis warrant four?"

"You know, I think they might green-light the ever-elusive five-star circus. Just for Athena."

"The news ran video of Costas Paradis getting off his private jet this morning. I've never much sympathized with billionaires, but you have to feel for the guy."

I said nothing. Didn't have to.

"Give Jack my best. Knock the story out of the park, Henry."

"Will do," I said. "Stay quiet." I hung up. Jack was holding back a thin smile. "What?"

He allowed a small chuckle. "Like two sweet jaybirds, you two," he said. "Hope you don't mind my taking amusement in the love rituals of the young and naïve."

I eyed Jack's hand, barren of any rings or jewelry other than a swank Omega wristwatch. I knew he'd worn a ring, years ago. He never showed any desire to discuss it.

The Guilty

I took my press pass out of my pocket and looped the lanyard over my head. Jack did the same. We rounded the corner and immediately became two small fish in the biggest school I'd ever seen. There must have been five hundred members of the press corps standing outside of city hall. Dozens of cameras, many of them live, along with Brylcreemed reporters and onlookers peeking out of open office windows for blocks in every direction. Millions of people would be watching this conference, whether live or on the evening news. Which made our jobs near impossible. How do you find a shadowy corner when there are hundreds and thousands of eyes scanning every inch?

We ducked under a rope and tried to push our way to the front.

"Easier to dig to China," Jack said. "Screw this. I don't need to be close to hear Perez."

"He'll have the text up on his MySpace page within an hour anyway."

"Perez has a MySpace page?"

"Facebook too. Wants to hit the young voters."

"Do young voters like him?" Jack asked.

"I didn't vote for him," I replied. "A little too much self-promotion for my tastes."

Jack pulled a pair of folding binoculars out of his pocket. He stared through them, peered along the dais and around the surrounding area. When he was done he passed them to me.

I took in the scene. The marble steps leading to city hall were polished a gleaming white. The podium was empty, waiting for Mayor Perez and, I assumed, Costas Paradis. Three uniformed police officers stood on either side of the podium. They stood straight, arms at their sides, guns visible. I swung the binoculars from right to left. When I saw who was standing directly to the left of the podium, I nearly dropped the binoculars.

"I saw him too," Jack said. "He's not here for you. Be a professional."

"Professional," I said, my mouth dry. "Right."

Standing to the left of the podium was Detective Lieutenant Joseph Mauser. One year ago, Detective Joe Mauser had chased me halfway across the country, shot me in the leg, and barely escaped with his life after taking three bullets in the chest from his partner, Leonard

Denton, the man most directly responsible for the events that changed my life.

I had followed Mauser's recovery over the months. Visited his guarded hospital room and was turned away by the very cops who'd wanted me dead before they found out the truth. After two months in the hospital—fully recovered, minus one spleen, two ribs and twenty pounds—Joe Mauser transferred from the FBI to the NYPD. He attributed the transfer as a tribute to his fallen brother in law and in arms, John Fredrickson. The man whose death I was responsible for, indirectly or not. Mauser wanted to be closer to his sister Linda, John's widow. In various interviews, Mauser insinuated that he held no ill will towards me. That given the circumstances he would have defended his life and honor as well. But a wound is a wound, no matter how it's caused, and the simple fact was his brother-in-law would still be alive if not for me.

Mauser had sold the book and film rights to his story for a reputed seven figures. He said the money wasn't for him, but would feed his sister's family, educate her fatherless children. If not for Mauser, my life wouldn't have been saved by a beautiful stranger. The same woman who now shares my bed. I guess we could call it ever.

Mauser looked good, healthy and even a little tan. He looked like the kind of man who was proud to serve his city. And I was glad to finally be on his side.

I could barely hear over the noise as reporters chirped into cell phones, cameras ran their feeds. Suddenly a hush came over the crowd and I saw Mayor Dennis Perez stride to the podium through the massive columns bracketing city hall. Walking alongside Mayor Perez was Costas Paradis. The normally confident man looked pale, tired. But looking through the binoculars, I could see the anger that burned for his murdered daughter.

The mayor wore a striped gray suit and walked with a purpose. His mustache was neatly trimmed as always, but his eyes were bloodshot. He probably hadn't slept since Athena died. And Costas wasn't the kind of man to mourn. He was the kind of man whose grief turned to anger, whose anger turned to rage, and whose rage could scorch the earth. I just stood and hoped they found the killer before more families experienced that grief.

The crowd grew quiet. Though the majority in attendance were paid to speak, discuss and bloviate as loud as humanly possible, they also knew that if they missed a single word they could miss a scoop, fall behind, give people a reason to pick up a paper or watch a newscast other than theirs.

I thought about Wallace's sign by the elevators. Then I looked at the sea of microphones and suits. Just like a marathon, a giant mass beginning as one. But that wouldn't last. The good ones would break away.

Mayor Perez stepped to the podium. Costas Paradis stood next to Perez, and I could sense the mayor's discomfort, like a child forced to admit wrongdoing in front of an angry parent.

"Ladies and gentlemen," he began. His eyes traveled from right to left. Making sure he made eye contact with every camera he could. Give each station their half second of exclusive content. "At approximately one-thirty-seven this morning, Athena Paradis was shot and killed as she was leaving a nightclub. This is a shocking and heinous crime, perpetrated by an individual whose depravity knows no bounds. At this very moment we have unleashed the very best men and women upon the crime scene to establish just who is responsible for Ms. Paradis's death, as well as their motives in doing so. No stone will remain unturned, not a second will go by where Ms. Paradis's murderer will have a chance to breathe."

Jack was scribbling in a notepad. I was watching their eyes. Mayor Perez. Costas Paradis. Joe Mauser. There was worry in them. Right then I knew they had nothing.

The mayor continued.

"The true test of a city is challenge. The test of a family is grief. In this investigation, we will grieve for the memory of Athena Paradis, but rise to the challenge of bringing her killer to justice."

"Second book," Jack said, pen hanging from his mouth.

"What?"

"That line. From Perez's second book. Just made himself another ten K in royalties right there."

I shook my head as Perez continued. "What we do know at this time is that the shooter is most likely a lone assailant, the murder weapon a high-powered rifle which was discharged from the roof of a building several blocks away from the club where Ms. Paradis was performing that evening. We have taken casts of footprints discovered at that rooftop, and are matching them with known offenders as we speak."

Bullshit, I thought. Officer Lemansky told me the rooftop was covered in gravel. Unless they developed some way to detect footprints in rocks, they're throwing us a hollow bone.

He continued. "We have many unfortunate witnesses to the crime itself, but as of yet nobody has come forward who has been able to positively identify the assailant."

At this point Costas Paradis moved a half inch closer. His eyes seemed to be burning a hole through Mayor Perez's neck. The mayor swallowed. He held his hand up, index finger extended.

"Let me assure you that the NYPD is using every available resource to find this heartless and soulless coward, and the NYPD will not rest until the assailant has been brought to justice."

Perez's eyes became sorrowful and he lowered his head.

"At this time I would like to express my sincerest condolences to the Paradis family. I have known Athena's devoted father, Costas, for many years, and suffice it to say his daughter's death is not only felt by the Paradis family, but is felt by his family and friends both in this city and around the world. Justice will be served."

Hotel Paradis, Paradis Park, Paradis Skating Rink, I thought. Not only was there a murderer loose, but there were millions, perhaps billions of dollars at stake. Maybe Perez should quote a few more lines from his book. Catching Athena's killer was not only a moral and legal priority, but one the mayor needed to help pay for those campaign reelection ads with spiffy production values.

Perez went on for another few minutes. He spoke a great deal but said very little.

"I've seen mimes more eloquent," Jack said. He leaned in closer. "Listen, I've got a contact in the medical examiner's office. As soon as this little soiree breaks up I'll have him on the phone. I want you to talk to him before we file any copy."

"What do you want me to do?"

"He owes me a solid. After you talk to him, I want you to go back and canvas the area around the Kitten Club. People don't like talking to cops. Answering questions makes them feel like they're being accused of something. Too many freaking Law & Order spin-offs. Anyway, tell them who you are. A newsman, their voice, the voice of the people. You make 'em believe it, they'll let you hold their newborn."

"Got it."

At that moment, Mayor Perez said, "And now I'd like to turn the podium over to Police Commissioner Alan Bradley, who will answer further questions."

"Might be worth leaving now," I said. "Get a head start."

"Not yet," Jack said. "Leaving early is how you miss the big stuff."

Commissioner Bradley, a stocky bald man in his early fifties, shook hands with the mayor and Costas Paradis. He stepped to the podium with a look of gravity and sincerity. Then I noticed something strange.

Joe Mauser was flinching. He brought his hand up to his eyes, as if shielding the sun. I took the binoculars, followed his line of sight. He was looking at a building across the way. Then I saw what he saw—a faint glimmer of light off of…something—and then all hell broke loose.

Mauser dove to his left a millisecond before the air was shattered by a deafening crack. I saw a fountain of red explode by the podium, and suddenly hundreds of people were screaming and running and cursing and fleeing.

I heard someone yell, "He's been shot!" EMS workers sprinted up the stairs. I watched in slow motion detachment, arms and legs pummeling me as they flew past. A man and a woman in white knelt down beside a fallen person atop the stairs. Police had their guns drawn and were yelling into walkie-talkies. Their eyes were all looking up, guns drawn. At the rooftops. Where the gunshot had come from.

I looked through the binoculars to get a better view of the carnage.

I could see a group of cops ushering the mayor and Costas Paradis inside city hall. An ambulance was trying to get through the pandemonium but was having no luck. The cops were shaking, ready to fire at an instant's notice.

I saw the EMS crews working as fast as they could on the downed officer, but through the binoculars I could see one of them shake her head. Watching fingers of blood drip down the steps, I knew what she was thinking. This one can't be saved.

As they placed the cop on the stretcher, I increased the magnification. I could just make out the face.

My breath left me. I dropped to my knees. Panting. Felt Jack's hand on my shoulder. Felt the world swimming away. Saw the face again. Saw his brother in-law's face. Both men lying in a pool of their own blood.

The downed cop was Detective Lieutenant Joe Mauser.

Chapter 8

She was lying on her back. Propped up against three pillows. One more across her chest. One more by her right arm. She felt warm, safe, comfortable. Henry made fun of her for this. Said she was building a fort every night. Yet when the lights went out, after Amanda had burrowed into her pillow castle, she would push the pillows aside and gently by her head on his chest.

She would listen to Henry breathe. Listen to his heart beat. She knew when he was thinking about a story—his heart beat a little faster. She knew if the day had been long and challenging, or fast and invigorating. All this from his heartbeat.

She would glide her finger down his chest, tickling his side. She knew he was sensitive, but he never told her to stop. Sometimes she would run her finger along the scar where the bullet had come so close to ending his life. She knew that in some way she was responsible for that scar. For some reason, despite the pain it had caused Henry, she was glad it was there.

She knew he was awake. His breathing was shallow. Henry's eyes had sunk. His body looked as though it had been sapped of all energy, like one of those video game characters after some evil shaman sucks their soul right out of their body then yells something cheesy like "Fatality!"

Another death. Reporters weren't supposed to see lives end in front of them. Henry wasn't off in a tank in Iraq. How much more could he take?

Henry's breathing had grown steadier. Maybe he had fallen asleep. She hoped so.

And then the shrill noise of Henry's cell phone broke the silence, and Amanda kicked herself for forgetting to change the ring tone.

Henry didn't stir, so Amanda reached over to the nightstand and picked it up. She expected to see Wallace Langston or Jack O'Donnell calling about some urgent scoop.

But no, it was Mya Loverne. Undoubtedly calling again in the desperate and pathetic hope that her old boyfriend would return her affection. That some previously severed synapses would again begin firing.

Amanda stared at the phone and felt a terrible pressure beginning to settle behind her eyes. She pressed and held the power button until the phone went dark. Then she gathered all the pillows, held them close to her chest, and hoped sleep would arrive soon.

For both of them.

Chapter 9

The Boy sat on the bed. Elbows on his knees. Feet planted on the floor. He read the newspaper again. Third time he'd done so. Then he put it on the chipped wooden nightstand and turned off the light.

He lay in the dark. He could feel his heart beating fast. It wasn't just the thrill of the kill that did it, it was the beautiful anticipation. Then the memory of the blood.

His hands still tingled, gravel still stuck in the treads of his shoes. Amazing how he could read about himself in the newspaper mere hours after the killing, the ink drying quicker than the blood.

He thought about last week. He thought about the grave, that headstone he'd visited so many times, wanting to wrap his strong hands around the necks of all those idiots who'd stolen God knew how many marble replacements. It had gotten so bad that the graveyard proprietors had to construct a metal fence around the headstone. Didn't matter much. They couldn't afford good metal, and twice a year some kid would use a pair of eleven-ninety-nine wire cutters and steal it just the same.

After visiting the grave for twenty years the Boy didn't care about the headstone itself. All he cared about was the bones that lay underneath. The body that lay buried in that hard earth for over a century. People thought they knew the truth. They saw movies, read books, figured they knew everything. He was here to change that. Through blood and lead, they would know the truth, and they would know exactly why he died. The Boy's legacy, and now he was being baptized in the blood of the damned.

Every now and then he would bring a fresh bullet to the grave, dig a small hole with his hands and place the ammunition inside. It's what he would have wanted—to be close to the bullets. Up until now, those bullets were the only link between them. Until Athena. Until that cop. Now blood linked them, and blood was thicker than lead.

All those summers in the broiling sun, pretending to ignore his birthright. Watching that ungodly woman tarnish their family's name with that demon. He got through the day because he knew eventually the day would come when he could take up the mantle. When he could finally finally finally come out from the darkness and show the world that the throne was his now. It had merely been waiting for the new blood to carry it into the new century.

You'd think things would have changed in a hundred and thirty years, the Boy would say to the headstone. He would always say it out loud. He didn't care who heard him. If he didn't have the courage to take a few errant glances, he wouldn't be able to pull the trigger when the time came. You'd think they'd have changed, but they haven't. A hundred and thirty years and you'd be so sick of it you'd dust your guns off, brush all that dirt off your old, old bones and do what I'm doing.

His hands and legs ached. The rifle had a mean kick. The Boy hadn't gotten a chance to practice much with it, but the gun was every bit as true as he knew it would be. That gun had a reputation, and not the kind that came from some pussy who talked his own game up. This was the kind of rep that came through force, violence and blood.

He looked around the room. Grime covered the walls, and he could hear insects scurrying behind the plaster. Nothing bothered him. He tapped the rifle with his fingers and thought about the next kill.

He'd read the newspapers that morning. Read the ongoing coverage of Athena's murder. Only today it was sparring for coverage with the murder of Joe Mauser. He was surprised to see that he'd killed the cop rather than the mayor. But the more he read about this cop, the less guilty he felt. He read how the cop tracked down and nearly killed an innocent reporter named Henry Parker. The same Henry Parker whose words the Boy had written before killing Athena Paradis.

And as he knew, once your fate was revealed, you had to follow it.

The Boy read about how the death of officer Joe Mauser's brother-in-law had driven Mauser over the edge, how he relentlessly pursued Parker across the country before nearly dying at the hands of the real killer. And even though the Boy's bullet hadn't been meant for Mauser, fate was on his side. Joe Mauser was just as guilty as the rest of them.

The Boy looked out the window at the night sky, the beauty that was so close, and the beauty that he would help create. Then he

The Guilty

closed his eyes, dreamt of blood, blood that purified, blood that seeped back into an old, old grave. He dreamt that he was lying in the grave next to the man whose legacy he was carrying on, and the Boy slept in peace.

Chapter 10

I'd only met with a medical examiner once in my career as a reporter, and that was back in Oregon when I covered a b&e that turned ugly when the home owner confronted the burglar. The home owner was stabbed twice in the chest, the knife stolen from the his own bedroom. The ME confirmed the murder weapon was some fancy German blade, which the victim had bought on the black market. I ended up uncovering an unauthorized dealer ring in Portland, and was subsequently nominated for a Payne journalism award. The ME in Portland was a woman in her midforties, professional as hell, and willing to part with any and all information I needed for my story. From that encounter I assumed most MEs were similarly professional.

But when I met Leon Binks, New York County Medical Examiner, behind the rusty Dumpster on Thirty-first and First, let's just say it wasn't quite the professionalism I was hoping for.

Leon was wearing blue jeans and an unbuttoned work shirt, both dirty and disheveled. My guess was they were spare clothes for the times he had to run out and meet people behind Dumpsters. He was a fairly young man, mid to late thirties, with a wisp of a mustache and hair in desperate need of some Pert Plus.

He rubbed his hands together as he spoke, and I wondered what sort of compulsion that came from.

"So you know Jack," Binks said, more of a statement of fact than a question.

"I work with him at the Gazette," I replied.

Jack had called Binks and told him to meet me as soon as possible. Didn't ask Binks. Told him. I wondered what sort of coverage Jack had given—or shielded—to have the New York City medical examiner wrapped around his little finger.

"Good guy, O'Donnell," Binks said, his hands rubbing rhythmically.

"Yeah, he is." I waited for Binks to continue.

"Had a lot of good times with him," Binks said. "Well, not good

The Guilty

times, but good conversations. Like he's always been a good egg with me, a good egg. I figure any friend of Jack's has gotta be a friend of mine."

"That's right," I said. "So Leon, if I can call you that…"

"You can call me Binky," he said. "S'what my friends do, anyway."

"Right. So…Binky…you've done the initial on Joe Mauser?"

Binky nodded. "You'd be correct. Listen, Henry," Binky leaned in close. I could smell chemicals. Iodine and cheap aftershave. "Did Jack tell you about that…thing?"

"Uh…"

"I get it, you're playing dumb. It's okay, better you don't answer so neither of us have to lie. You know in case anyone comes asking."

No need to tell the Binkster that I wasn't playing dumb, since I had no idea what he was talking about.

"Just tell Jack I appreciate it, and so does my wife. I promise the bite marks will clear up and we'll be careful not to go out in public next time we want to role play."

"Yeah, anyway, let's talk about Mauser."

"Right," Binky said, winking. "Let's."

"Officer Mauser suffered from a single gunshot wound fired from a high velocity rifle."

"I knew it," I said.

"Knew what?"

"High-powered rifle," I said. "I know more about guns than I'd like to."

"Really? Well, would you like to tell me the rest of the autopsy? Please, go right ahead." Binky folded his arms across his chest petulantly. Finally he said, "May I continue?"

"Please, didn't mean to interrupt."

"No apology necessary. Anyway, the bullet entered Officer Mauser's chest and the left subclavian artery, causing a traumatic aortic rupture."

"Which means…"

"Which means Officer Mauser never had a chance."

I wiped my brow, took this in. Mauser wasn't the target of that bullet. This much was clear. Dozens of news crews had caught the whole speech and murder on tape, and a split second before the gun

49

went off, Mauser dove in front of Mayor Perez. Gave his life in the line of duty.

"The bullet then lodged in one of Officer Mauer's vertebrae, where I extracted it this morning. The bullet was turned over to ballistics for examination."

"Can you tell me anything about the bullet itself?"

"Hey Sherlock, I work at the coroner's office, not ballistics." Again I stayed silent. Hoping maybe Binky thought himself an amateur Man With No Name. "It was pretty big," Binky finally volunteered.

"Like how big?"

"Inch and a half, two inches long," he said. "Bullet was obviously distorted but I can't say for sure. Caused a whole lot of damage, whoever took that shot wasn't screwing around, wasn't looking to wing anyone. Even if the bullet had somehow miraculously missed the aorta, it shattered two surrounding vertebrae and severed Mauser's spinal cord. Guess we can be thankful the guy didn't suffer. I work a lot of GSWs, but I can't recall pulling a bullet this size from many victims."

"So we have some psychopath running around New York with a high-powered rifle and damn good aim," I said. Binky rubbed his hands together and nodded.

"Funny thing is," he said, his tone of voice anything but humorous. In fact, there seemed to be an edge of fear. "I've worked in the examiner's office nearly twelve years and I don't recall ever seeing a gunshot wound from that caliber weapon."

"Really," I said, that fear seeping into my veins too.

"Most GSW victims that end up the hospital or morgue are from .22 or .38 caliber bullet. Handguns, stuff you get on the street. But not this. This is a hard-core rifle, my friend. Kind you might hunt animals with. Kind of gun you only need one shot with, 'cause that shot counts."

"No shit," I said.

"None at all. Makes you wonder what kind of psycho this city's got loose."

"Yeah," I said. "Makes you wonder."

Chapter 11

I turned my key in the lock, unsure whether I hoped the apartment was empty or not. Before I could see the whole room I smelled perfume and knew Amanda was home.

She was sitting in an armchair reading a book. When she saw me her eyes picked up and the book clapped shut. She slowly rose from her chair, came over to me and wrapped me up in her arms. I laid my head on her shoulder and breathed in.

She looked me in the eyes and said, "If I had to guess, your day could have gone better."

I nodded. Took my jacket off and tossed it on a chair. Untied my shoes and kicked them off. Went over to Amanda and knelt down, put my head against her stomach. Soon I felt her fingers running through my hair, my scalp tingling as she pressed harder. I stood up, leaned in and kissed her. At first she seemed reluctant, then leaned in harder. Her hand was on the back of my head, pressing my lips against hers. I lost myself in it, felt her body lean towards me. Then I pulled away.

"What is it?" she said.

I looked at her, embarrassed. "Just hard to see these things happen. You know, and not be affected at all."

"That cop who was killed?" she said. "Mauser."

"Yeah. You know he was the one who last year...he almost killed me."

"I know," Amanda said softly. "He came to my house. Pointed a gun at you."

"Thing is, I never blamed him," I said. "If I'd been in that kind of situation, thought someone had murdered my family, I would have gone just as far as he did."

"Henry..."

"He was a good cop," I said, anger rising. "He didn't deserve to go down like some animal."

"What do you mean?"

"Whoever shot him, they're some sick bastard."

I took out my cell phone. Dialed Curt Sheffield's number.

"Sheffield," he said.

"Curt, it's Henry Parker."

"Hey man. Guess this doesn't mean you're hiding under a rock."

"I don't think I'd fit under a rock right now. Listen, we need to meet up. I talked to the medical examiner today, I think we can help each other."

"Name the time and place. But hey, Henry, be careful. Word's gotten around our friend Paulina Cole's been digging a little bit, asking questions about Mya Loverne, about your relationship. Don't know if she's going after you, but nothing she touches stays clean, know what I'm saying."

I cursed under my breath.

"Screw her," I said.

"I would if my lady wouldn't wear my balls for earrings. She's not a bad looking older woman. Wonders of Botox, I guess."

"Yeah, right. I need to know if you've heard anything about the ballistics analysis. Two deaths from what looks like sniper attacks, I'm willing to bet my bonus the same ammo and gun was used in both Mauser and Athena Paradis's murders."

"Don't be stupid, Henry, you know I can't just give out information Mayor Perez hasn't declared open for public consumption."

"Come on, Curt, you know the Dispatch is probably writing checks right now to cops and anyone else who can answer that question. Do you really want Paulina Cole and her BS responsible for the first impression of millions?"

"Watch your damn mouth," Curt said. "Those are my boys you're dissing."

"I'm sorry, man, but you know I wouldn't say it just to make conversation."

"No," he said reluctantly. "Listen, I got foot patrol duty tomorrow in Midtown. Carruthers wants my ass as public as possible. Guess they figure enough stuffy suits see me they might encourage their kids to sign up for the academy. Anyway, meet me on Fifty-second and Fifth tomorrow at five when my shift ends. Something else you should know."

"What's that?"

"They found another note. Same as before, taped to the roof where the sicko took his shot from."

"Jesus Christ, what'd it say?"

"Not over the phone man. I'll see you tomorrow."

"I'll be there. And Curt, I appreciate it. Really. We need to grab a drink soon. No business."

"Sure, Jimmy Breslin, no business my ass."

"I'm serious, none."

"In that case, I hear a bottle of Stoli Raspberry calling my name," he said. "And your corporate card, of course. You know, in case I get the munchies."

Sheffield hung up.

I looked over at Amanda. The book was on her lap. I knew she heard the whole conversation.

"He sounded good," she said.

"Always does."

"Are you worried about Paulina?"

I thought for a moment. Paulina had done her absolute best to ruin my reputation last year. I knew she had it out for me, but still wasn't sure if the vitriol was real or just a ploy to boost her career.

"The same way you worry about gum disease or cancer," I said. "You can brush your teeth and eat broccoli every day, but if it's going to fuck up your life it's going to fuck up your life."

"I don't want anyone to do that," she said.

"Hey," I said, wrapping my arms around her. She returned the gesture. "Whatever anyone does to me, you counteract it. You're my counterbalance, babe."

I kissed her, but knew her mind was elsewhere.

Chapter 12

Amanda tucked her hands into her peacoat as she walked down the street. Henry had ordered a half mushroom pie from the pizza place down the block (the one they probably kept in business). She'd told him she would pick up the pizza which she stepped out to grab some female products. Beautiful thing, those female products, as they could preempt any further questions.

The night was still cool, the remnants of spring still hanging on. Soon summer would come, and New York summers could be brutal. Damn Al Gore, guy was right all along. Maybe he really did create the Internet too.

She thought about Henry, their relationship. It was still a relatively new thing, still exciting, but neither of them really knew what lay around the corner. They'd been dating steady for nearly a year, though for the life of her she couldn't remember an official start date, other than the first day Henry introduced her as his girlfriend. It'd been a surprise but a pleasant one. After he was released from the hospital, everything just seemed to happen. Not that she had any problem with it—it felt good introducing him, holding his hand at night, saying the word boyfriend and knowing it meant more than some silly schoolgirl thing.

For years, Amanda didn't trust anybody. Not the nuns who ran the various orphanages she was shuttled between as a little girl, not the boys who claimed they liked her then split when the bra clasp remained fastened. Even Lawrence and Harriet Stein, the perfectly nice oatmeal couple who finally gave her a home, had a hard time earning any trust from their adopted daughter. And it still hadn't fully come.

She was amazed at the ease in which Henry settled into their relationship. She moved in with him just months after they met and he adapted like a dried fish being put back in water. He was romantic, honest, sincere. Even about the hard things. Mya. His father. He asked questions about her job, her family. He made her feel like she mattered. For Henry the process seemed purifying. For Amanda, the process was much more difficult.

She'd shared beds with boyfriends, made dinner for special guys and on some lucky nights had it made for her. But she'd never shared a laundry hamper. She'd never gone to work only to come home and see the same person she'd gone to sleep with.

It was a challenge, and some nights, all she wanted was space that their one-bedroom could not provide, all she wanted to do was scream, pull the notebooks from storage and wander the streets taking stock of everyone she came across.

But then she'd look at Henry. Sitting at his desk, reading a book or a newspaper. Writing on a notepad. She'd read his bylines in the Gazette and feel her heart swell with pride. And she would look at her man and smile, and he would smile back, and then Henry would come over and kiss her on the cheek and go right back to work.

Henry had been in a serious relationship. Mya. It was as serious as most college relationships went. It wasn't hard, Amanda figured, to move from one relationship to another. The person changes, but the habits carry over. He'd shared a bed. Shared a hamper. She supposed she could be thankful he wasn't awkward. But part of her wished they were both experiencing the doubts and fears for the first time, together.

Amanda's sense of trust seemed to come organically. Funny, since the very first thing Henry ever did was lie to her. He lied about his name to save his life, posed as someone else. But only on the surface. She could tell, from the moment they met, what kind of person he was. Maybe it was years of keeping journals, sizing up people in a quick glance. Because one thing Amanda always had a keen eye for was kindness. And in Henry she found that.

She knew the last year had eaten away at him. In between recovery from his wounds, the subsequent media frenzy, and then his attempt to settle back into a tenuous routine. Over the last few days, the sanctity of that routine had been threatened. Two horrible murders, one a man who, just twelve months ago, wanted nothing more than to kill him. She knew the guilt he still felt over John Fredrickson's death. Stroked his hair when he had nightmares. Even though Henry hadn't pulled the trigger, a family had been torn apart. That wasn't something you got over in a year.

When she saw that Athena Paradis's murderer had used a line written by Henry, again she feared that his work would endanger his life. Everything pointed to it being a terrible coincidence. Henry didn't want to dwell on it, and except for a brief conversation that night it had been dropped. She couldn't help but sit a little closer to him. Call him a few extra times a day. Just to make sure he was safe.

And now this witch, Paulina Cole, threatening to reenter his life. So she decided to do what any good girlfriend would do. Only she'd get more enjoyment out of it than most.

Amanda picked up a pay phone at the corner. She was twelve blocks away from their apartment. It would do.

She dialed the operator. Asked to be transferred to the main desk at One Police Plaza. When an operator picked up, she asked to be transferred to the press secretary. It rang twice, and was answered by a man with a high-pitched voice and wonderful enunciation.

"I'm calling in regards to the recent murders of Athena Paradis and Detective Joe Mauser. I'm a reporter, and I'd like to speak to Chief Louis Carruthers for a story I'm writing. It's of the utmost importance, so I'd appreciate if you connect me right this instant."

"Ma'am, all official statements regarding the murders of Ms. Paradis and Detective Mauser have been released, and are available on our website. If you need further information, you are invited to submit your queries and I will get the appropriate responses for you as soon as possible."

"Don't you ma'am me," Amanda said, affecting her best and bitchiest tone. Damn, this was fun. "You tell whoever your pansy-ass supervisers are, those pussy-eating faggots and butt pirates, and that spic mayor of yours who panders to all the kikes in city hall, you tell them that this is Paulina Cole of the New York Dispatch and I'll be damned if I let some queer tell me what I can and can't have access to. Now connect me to Carruthers or I'll send someone down there to snip your balls from your sack."

Amanda smiled at the click and dial tone. She checked her watch. The pizza would be ready in less than ten minutes.

Screw it. She still had time to call the mayor's office.

Chapter 13

The Boy looked at his rifle. Admired the straight grain walnut stock, well preserved and polished. This was a gun that had served well and been loved accordingly. Thank God he'd been able to free it from that glass prison, from all the idiot gawkers who never felt the power the gun accorded. With this gun, he was carrying on a legacy over a hundred years old, and every time he clicked the set trigger he felt the power of death over life.

So far the gun had been exactly what he'd hoped. Accurate and powerful. He hated how stupid most people were when it came to these guns, ignorant folk who assumed that the rifles of this kind that they saw in the movies were the real McCoy. Truth was, in the movies they usually used later models that were deemed more attractive. Only folks who could tell their ass from a cartridge chamber knew the truth. The Boy was being true to the legend, true to his heritage. And soon one more would fall.

And now he sat on the bed, gazing at the weapon that had won so many battles, claimed so many lives, knowing this gun was waging a battle that began over a century ago.

He heard a scuffling outside. He made two voices; male and female. The walls in the hotel were about as thick as linen, and he could hear every nearby squeak like it was right next to him.

The people seemed to be negotiating. The man's voice was eager. A little too eager. The woman was talking slowly. The Boy could feel his blood begin to rise, his fingers grinding against the wood stock of the rifle. Those two outside, they had no idea how close they were to death, that the person less than ten feet away could snuff them out faster than it would take to take exchange currency.

But he couldn't. He had to get the rage out, let it dissipate. He couldn't end the rampage before it had barely begun. He was strong, powerful, had that blood running through his veins. The only thing that could stop him was stupidity.

He heard her mention a dollar amount. The man said "Oh hell

yes" loud enough for the grimy bastard at the front desk to hear it.

"Told you I looked like her," he heard her say.

"No doubt, you got an ass like Athena Paradis," he responded. That made the Boy smile. "Just…just let me call you Athena. Please, baby."

She didn't say a word, but the moan of pleasure said it all.

They unlocked a door, slipped inside and closed it. Five minutes later, the Boy felt his bed beginning to shake. He closed his eyes. Took a deep breath. Fixing this nuisance would be relatively easy and painless, but nothing positive could be gained from it. There were more important homes for his lead. He took a deep breath, then turned his gaze from the rifle to the magazine splayed out in front of him.

He eyed the man whose photograph lay within its pages. He was portly, with graying hair that cascaded in waves past his ears, a gut reserved for men who'd lived their later years in a state of complacency rather than diligence. His half-cocked smile was one of condescension. His air was that of a royal walking amongst subjects who should consider themselves fortunate to lick the shit off his heels. He was one more battle for the Boy to win, boldly and violently.

He knew the man's schedule, when he arrived, when he left, when he ordered lunch, when his secretary came home with him, when he'd grown tired of her, and when his children were forced to visit. He knew the exact moment it would happen, knew where the security cameras were positioned, and knew he would be gone right as the fear sank in.

Athena Paradis was a masterstroke. He started the crusade by felling the biggest prize. The cop was a mistake, but looking into the man's background it was a mistake prompted by fate. The cop—Mauser—had shot Henry Parker last year, an innocent man. The same Henry Parker who wrote the quote the Boy had left up on that rooftop. He wondered how Parker felt, if, like the Boy, he was glad Mauser was dead.

The Boy looked at the gun one last time, could picture the bullet crashing through a helpless skull, and went to sleep.

Chapter 14

Paulina's telephone rang. She hesitated answering it, focusing instead on the morning edition of the Dispatch spread in front of her. Her hand gripped a red pencil. She was already worked up from having to explain to Bynes that a prank caller had impersonated her. That even though she thought Louis Carruthers was an idiot she wasn't stupid enough to spew a racist diatribe to a receptionist.

She was making small notes in the margins, passages that could have read better, accusations that could have been a little more salacious without bordering on libel. The article on Joe Mauser's murder had been written by some hack in Metro. Paulina's piece on Athena was on page three. Mauser got page seven. In the kingdom of selling newspapers, heroic cops were cow shit compared to rich heiresses. Way it went, and Paulina didn't think twice.

She looked at her caller ID, recognized the area code, figured if she didn't pick it up he'd just keep calling back. She picked it up.

"What?"

"Miss Cole, it's James."

"Hi…James."

"Hi?" Hi as a question. As if the word would offend her.

James Keach was a junior reporter at the Dispatch. About five foot ten, two hundred and ten cookie-dough pounds, with razor's-edge-parted hair that looked ready to recede the moment anyone said anything nasty about it. Just two years out of J-School, James never left the newsroom, followed reporters around like a beagle awaiting a biscuit, and was generally more of a nuisance than anyone you didn't either sleep with or work for had a right to be. The kid had pulled a solid C+ average, but his father was golfing buddies with Ted Allen and apparently promised to give Allen an unlimited supply of mulligans at Pebble Beach if his son was given a shot to learn the ropes. James didn't seem so much eager to learn the ropes as he did to simply climb halfway up and hang on for dear life.

Paulina had given James his very first assignment, which, she stressed, was every bit as important as any story she was working on that year. Seeing as how he'd spent every previous waking moment peeking around the water cooler in the hopes of overhearing gossip, she knew offering Keach a bone would make him salivate.

So last week, while laying out her eventual hatchet job on David Loverne, she decided to bring James into the fold. She wore her highest heels that day, a low-cut blouse, and a sweet new perfume called Sugar. James would have driven a lawn mower to Antarctica to report on penguin migration that day.

His assignment, she told him, was to shadow Henry Parker twenty four hours a day. Find out where he goes when he's not at home or at the office. Find out who he speaks with and what they speak about. Find out who his friends and enemies are, what he has for breakfast, whether he wears matching socks, everything. She wanted to tie Parker into the Loverne piece, show how a combination of her father's philandering and Parker's snubbing drove poor Mya Loverne over the edge.

For years, Mya had been the consummate politician's daughter. Bright, attractive, never a hair mussed or sentence misspoken. She got good grades, and never got into trouble. Her life and taken a turn for the worse when she was attacked by a man who broke her jaw during an attempted rape. Mya fought him off. But she had never been the same, Paulina attributed this to her disintegrating family and love life, her dreams vanishing in a puff of lies.

And so far James was everything she wanted in a bloodhound; loyal, dependent, and weak. If reporting didn't work out, he'd make a hell of a peeping Tom. Hell, just yesterday Paulina learned that Henry took his coffee with skim milk and three Splendas. Not exactly front page material, but Keach was getting close.

"So James, calling to shed light on more of Parker's dietary habits?"

"Oh, no Miss Cole, nothing like that." He paused. "So how are you this morning?"

She rolled her eyes. "I'm just fine, James. Skip the pleasantries."

"Right. No more pleasantries. Sorry about that, I…"

"James."

"Right. Anyway, I wanted to let you know that I followed Parker when he left his apartment this morning. He made one call, then

The Guilty

right after that another call came in. Then he went into the Gazette and I lost him. Maybe I'll see if I can get a temp ID, get into the building…"

"That's all right James, your daddy doesn't need you getting arrested. Who was the first call to?" Paulina chewed the swizzle stick from her coffee, wondering if snorting the Xanax would make it take faster.

"I didn't catch everything, but the guy's first name was Curtis. Parker said something about them meeting up later this afternoon. They sounded tight."

Lovers? Paulina wondered. That'd be a hell of a story.

"And who called him right after?"

"No last name, but at one point he called her Mya. And from the sound of it Parker didn't sound happy to hear from her. Cut her off pretty quick."

The straw fell from Paulina's mouth. A smile spread over her lips. Mya Loverne. Paulina knew that after his acquittal, Henry had broken up with Mya for a new airhead named Amanda Davies. Tossing aside his former love. Apparently, the goods weren't so happy to be tossed aside.

Paulina had despised Henry Parker the moment she met him. Given a cushy job by Wallace Langston despite the experience of a fetus. And to top it off, the court jester himself, Jack O'Donnell, took the kid under his wing. Paulina had sweat blood and tears over her ink for years, and Henry was being groomed as the heir apparent. The newsman of the twenty-first century whose balls had barely dropped.

And either directly or subversively, Paulina swore to be the wrecking ball that tore it all down. And if she happened to take down the Gazette with it, hell, that wouldn't be such a bad morning.

"James, you just made my coffee taste better."

"Oh, that's swell Miss Cole, and again I hope you know how much I appreciate your trusting me with this assignment. I'm…wait, Parker's moving. I'll call you back when I get anything new."

"You do that Jamesy, you do that."

"Hey Miss Cole?" James said apprehensively. "Do you think I can file expense reports for my breakfast? The bagels at this place are like three bucks each."

"Not a chance, Jamesey. Talk to you later." She hung up.

61

Chapter 15

I rounded the corner and saw him standing at a street vendor, paying for coffee and a muffin and waiting for change.

"Make that two coffees," I said.

"My friend here will take his with twelve sugars," Curt Sheffield said.

The vendor looked at me like I'd asked for a side of pork loin. "That's a lot of sugar, man."

"Three Splendas," I said. "I thought cops weren't allowed to lie."

"That's to suspects and witnesses. Not reporters. In fact, that's encouraged."

Curt took his change. I watched in awe as he inhaled the muffin in three bites.

"I think I've seen the same thing happen with boa constrictors. I bet if I look closely I can see a muffin-shaped protrusion in your uniform."

"Lay off, I haven't eaten since breakfast. You know at first I liked the idea of being the NYPD's poster boy, but you can't catch a break on the streets. Parents introducing their kids to me like I'm walking around in a Mickey Mouse costume or something."

"If Mickey carried a loaded Glock." He licked the crumbs from his fingers. "And aren't you guys supposed to eat donuts?"

Curtis sipped his coffee, wiped some crumbs from his mouth. He nodded, said, "Let's go," through a mouthful, and led me down the block. It was a cool afternoon, the streets lined with people preparing for the commute home.

"So tell me about the note," I said.

"What, no foreplay?"

"Not when two people have been killed."

"That's our job to deal with," Sheffield said. "You write about it, remember? That shit last year don't make you Dick Tracy."

The Guilty

"You're right, but you also know I'm one of the few guys in this town who'll give you a fair shake."

Curt sipped his coffee. "Word is Harvey Hillerman is hard up on Wallace to raise circulation. Says the Dispatch is growing and you're shrinking worse than my old man after joining the polar bear club."

Harvey Hillerman was the owner of the Gazette, and perpetually at war with the tabloid tactics of the other papers in town. But it was hard to keep the public's interest with payroll scandals when the Dispatch could just take a shot of Athena Paradis in a bikini, slap it on the front page and match your circulation rate.

"It's not my job to worry about Hillerman."

"It's your job to make sure you have a job, paisan."

"You know you're black, right?"

"What, paisan is reserved for Italians? Screw that."

We walked towards Sixth Avenue.

"So what have you got?" I asked.

"Well the ballistics report came back. I'll tell you, the pressure on Perez is unreal. Costas Paradis is watching every move he makes with a magnifying glass, and he's holding that glass up to the sun. Man's got eyes and ears from every lawmaker to every sewer grate in the city."

"His daughter was killed, what do you expect?"

"Carruthers has instituted mandatory overtime every day this week," Sheffield continued. "They have undercovers staking out every major nightclub, patrolmen inspecting every rooftop within line of sight. They have us watching any celebrity that goes anywhere after midnight. Problem is we don't know what we're looking for. Not to mention we're all watching our backs after Joe got killed."

I looked at the ground.

"Don't let it get to you. Guys in the department don't hold a grudge for the most part. And the guys that do hold grudges are all old school, the kind the department keeps on a tight leash because they might have had ties to Mike DiForio's crew. Carruthers knows Fredrickson was dirty, that he was taking money from that Tony Soprano wannabe. Until DiForio got barbecued, that is."

"When you say guys don't hold a grudge 'for the most part', what's that, like fifty percent? Ninety?"

Sheffield toed the cement. Then he looked at me. "Not gonna lie bro, there's definitely some bad blood. Fredrickson might have been dirty, but he went back a long way. The bad ones always have friends and there are always other people who covered their asses. Joe Mauser, though, he was a good cop. It's just a cumulative effect of what's happened to that family."

"What do you think?" I asked.

"Me? Shit. I wouldn't be here right now if I held a grudge. Fact is, city needs you on this story a whole lot more than it needs you digging up celebrity tampons to pad Hillerman's bottom line. Plus I like your stuff. Tired of reading news reports that read like they were written by fuckers who are stuck on typewriters and Geritol."

"I appreciate that."

"Appreciate it in private. I'm happy to give you dirt so it doesn't end up in Cole's witch cauldron. But after this, I gotta be a ghost, man."

I waited for him to continue.

"So ballistics confirmed the same caliber shot was used to kill Athena Paradis and Joe Mauser."

"No big shock there," I said.

"No, we figured it was the same sick son of a bitch. But they were surprised to find out the caliber bullet our man used."

"Unusual?"

"I'd say. 44-40 magnum rounds." Curt waited a moment. He expected my jaw to drop, but I must have slept through my NRA 101 course.

"Why's that surprise you?"

"Nobody uses .44-40 ammunition these days. Just an impractical caliber to use, on both sides of the good guy/bad guy coin."

"Why's that?"

"Magnum rounds are large, man. Heavy velocity, heavy impact. The recoil on those things will knock you on your ass. Forget everything Dirty Harry said, any cop who wants to be able to get off a second round in the same zip code would be an idiot to carry around a magnum. Only people who use it are idiot cons who think it looks pretty, but any perp who knows anything about weapons would prefer something lighter."

"Idiots don't kill women with a single shot from a hundred yards out," I said.

"No. That takes a different kind of mental defect."

"So what are magnum rounds used for?" I asked.

"Hunting, mostly," Sheffield said. "Got an uncle, lives out in Montana, goes big game hunting using magnum rounds. Got a black bear head on his mantle used to scare the shit out of me and my sister growing up. It's a good caliber for up to a hundred and fifty yards, after that the bullet is too heavy to maintain its accuracy."

"The killer shot both Athena and Joe Mauser from within two hundred yards."

"Right."

"Further reduces his idiocy quotient. Obviously the killer is smart enough to know his range."

"Question is," Sheffield said. "Why would anyone use magnum rounds for that kind of sniper shooting? Only an idiot would try to kill a person from far away using a magnum round. .22s are lighter, faster, and more accurate. Not to mention easier to get. I'm up there on the roof? I'm using .22s."

"Unless there's a reason for using magnum rounds," I said. "Whoever killed Mauser and Athena planned the murders out. They knew Athena was going to be at the Kitten Club, and they knew the setup outside city hall well enough to position themselves for a shot. You don't go through that kind of trouble and then randomly pick a gun and bullet that might separate your shoulder with the recoil."

"It is sexy ammo," Curt said, rather offhandedly. "Magnum."

We continued walking, both processing the information. Powerful, short range, heavy, high velocity. Sexy.

"Wait," I said. "What do you mean it's sexy?"

"Look, I'm not saying you'll find it at Victoria's Secret…"

"Come on. The killer chose this ammo for a reason. Why does someone choose magnum ammunition over something more practical? Especially when they have everything else planned to a T?"

"Well," Curtis said. "Dirty Harry made magnum ammo cool. Forget which one of the movies it was, but he used .44 caliber special loads, which are lighter and don't have the same recoil. Funny thing is they didn't actually use a magnum while shooting the movie, they used—"

"Come on," I said, impatiently. "What else?"

"Well, magnum ammo is probably the one ammunition that's actually known in pop culture. Ever see that movie, Winchester 73?" I shook my head. "Great flick. James Stewart and Shelley Winters. Anyway, the Winchester is commonly referred to as 'The Gun that Won the West'. Most popular rifle, probably ever, kind of a folk legend. The Winchester uses .44-40 magnum rounds."

"No shit," I said. "Winchester, huh?"

"Winchester."

"Think there's a chance our killer might have used a Winchester on Athena and Joe?"

"It's a possibility, man, but the Winchester plant shut down a few years ago. It's not even called Winchester these days, some conglomerate took it over. Probably called GunTex or something stupid. And trust me, nobody uses Winchester rifles any more. They went out with the dodo and bell-bottoms."

"Some people think bell-bottoms are hip," I said.

"Hey, what you and your girl do is between the two of y'all."

"Yeah, but maybe there's someone out there who thinks Winchesters are the new black. Or at least has a reason for using one."

"Well, I can't imagine there are a whole lot of working ones left, so you got yourself a lead there, Maureen Dowd."

"And the note," I said. "You told me another note was left at the scene again."

"No I didn't," Curt said.

"You did, asshole, give it."

Curt looked around, his eyes narrowing. "This is some creepy stuff man. Hard to get something like that out of your head."

"Do you have a copy of it I could take?" I asked.

"Nah. I didn't need one. You don't forget something like that."

"What did the note say?"

Curt stopped, seemed to think for a moment, then carefully spoke.

"It said, 'People thought me bad before, but if ever I should get free, I'll let them know what bad means.'"

"'I'll let them know what bad means,'" I repeated. "I didn't write that."

"He used a line from one of your articles after shooting Athena, right?"

"Yeah," I said. "Not exactly flattering. I was worried for a bit this guy had it out for me, but…guess he just liked my work."

"That make you feel better or worse?"

The Guilty

"Not sure," I said.

"Warm and fuzzy this guy is not."

I clapped Curt on the shoulder. "Listen Curt, I really appreciate it."

"Just do me a favor, wait until Carruthers makes his statement before you use that quote. Do all the research you want, just don't jump the gun." Curt warned.

"You scratch my back, I scratch yours. So now it's back to protecting and serving and all that good stuff," I said.

"You mean posing with tourists and keeping the kids away from my Glock. And you go back to being all fair and balanced and stuff," Curt replied.

"All the news that's fit to print," I said.

Suddenly I heard a crackling sound. Curtis looked at me. Both of our heads shot to his waistband where his walkie-talkie was attached. A voice came over the speaker. I only made out two words, and my blood froze.

"Shots fired..."

Curtis grabbed the walkie-talkie off his belt. The voice crackled again.

"10-10, shots fired, repeat, 10-10 shots fired at the Franklin-Rees building. All officers respond."

I looked at Curtis, saw a mixture of fear and determination in his eyes. "That's—"

"Four blocks from here."

Curtis turned and sprinted down the street, pedestrians parting, holding their children and backing against the wall.

I had no choice. I sprinted after him.

67

Chapter 16

I followed Curt Sheffield like a running back wisely trailing a bruising fullback. Oxygen burned in my lungs, and I felt my side tickle right below the scar where one year ago my perforated lung had to be inflated. Fear gripped me, my heart hammering. Shots fired. Why the hell was I running towards the shots? I heard sirens in the distance. Screams loud enough to be heard over them. Men and women were running past me. We were swimming against a terrified tide. And I saw one man run by, blood staining his shirt.

The Franklin-Rees company published many of the country's most popular magazines. A multibillion-dollar corporation, its head-quarters was a brilliant steel monstrosity with enough security mea-sures inside to stop a tank. But as I got closer, I could tell that all the security inside the building was useless to prevent the horror of what happened just outside.

I saw a dozen officers, guns drawn, massing around the en-trance to the Franklin-Rees building. Curt Sheffield was barking into a walkie-talkie. I heard sirens. Cop cars. An ambulance seemed to be drawing near. I stepped closer. And wondered why the ambulance was in such a rush.

A man lay on the sidewalk. A pool of blood was spreading around his head. Or at least what was left of it. When I saw the piece of brain sliding down the polished glass door, my stomach lurched and I felt dizzy.

Aside from the crowd of New York's finest, a small crowd of onlookers watched from across the street. Several officers were shoo-ing away ghouls with cameras. I could see a tuft of gray hair amidst the mass of blood and gore. Then the wind caught it, and took it away.

The dead man was wearing a tailored suit. From the liver spots on his hands, I guessed him to be in his late fifties or early sixties. A white handkerchief, once tucked neatly into the jacket pocket, now fluttered like a trapped dove.

The Guilty

When he put the walkie-talkie down, I approached Curt.

"What the hell happened?"

"Not now, Henry."

"Please, just one minute..."

"I said not now," Curt said, pushing me away.

Not now didn't compute. I had to know. And if Curt wasn't talking, none of the cops would. And enough people were milling about that somebody had to know something.

Pushing the nausea aside, I walked across the street, right into the mass of onlookers.

I took out my press pass and held it above my head.

"Did anybody see anything?" I shouted. "Please, we need witnesses."

Nobody said a word. They were either too frightened or too busy relaying the news to their entire address book. I scanned the crowd. Looked each person in the face, tried to understand their emotional state, if there was anything more to them being there.

One woman stood out. She had stringy brown hair, a cheap pantsuit, and a brooch that looked way out of her price range. There was a speck of red on her white blouse that I knew had to be blood. Her eyes were wide, her mouth open. She stared at me for a moment, then looked away.

Slowly I walked up to her. I extended my press pass, along with my hand. She stared at me, unsure of what to do. Her eyes were terrified, but something was shackling her to the scene. She had to be here. She was much closer to all this than she wanted to be.

"You were next to him, weren't you?" I asked softly. She nodded. "I'm Henry," I said, taking her hand in mine. Her whole body was shaking. I put my hand on her shoulder, tried to comfort her. I felt silly. I'd seen people die in front of me. And no hand in the world could comfort that.

"Betty Grable," she said. "I'm—was—oh God—I'm Mr. Lourdes's assistant."

My jaw dropped.

"That," I spat out. "That's Jeffrey Lourdes?"

She nodded again, then burst into tears.

Jeffrey Lourdes was the publisher of Moss magazine, and one of the most influential figures in popular culture for nearly thirty years.

He'd been credited for discovering dozens of headlining acts, some of the greatest reporting the country had ever seen, and now he was a mass of flesh torn apart by a piece of lead.

"I didn't know what was happening," Betty said. "I swear." Her hands were a trembling mess, tears cascading down her cheeks. "I was just telling him he had to be in early tomorrow for a photo shoot, then out of nowhere—"

She covered her mouth with her hand, choked sobs into it. I stayed silent. Had to let it come to her.

"Then he shot him!" she cried. "He shot him!"

"Who?" I asked.

"The young man," she said, her lip quivering. "He did it."

"Who was he? Young man? How old was he? What did he look like?"

"I don't know," Betty said. She looked at me as if having a revelation. "He looked about your age."

I stopped writing, looked at her.

"What happened?"

"We were standing there, Jeffrey was about to hail a taxi, and all of a sudden this man came out of nowhere. He was holding this giant—gun isn't even the right word—this giant thing. This fucking cannon. He just walked right up to Jeffrey and pulled the trigger, and then he ran. Oh God, Jeffrey!" She was staring at the body. One foot was visible through the sea of blue and white. I saw a police car pull up in front. An ambulance behind it. Two EMS workers popped out, ran to the body. I could tell from their body language they weren't going to work too hard on this one.

"What did he look like?" I said.

Betty shook her head. Not because she didn't know, but because she didn't want to.

"He was tall," she said. "Maybe an inch taller than you. Jeans. A jacket." She trailed off.

"What else?"

"I don't know!" she cried.

"Trust me, I know this is hard," I said. "But did he have any distinguishing features. Facial hair, tattoos, piercings…"

"The gun," she said.

"The gun?"

The Guilty

"The way he held it after he killed Jeffrey. I'll never forget that look in his eye. He stared at his gun for a second and then he ran. Looked at it the way somebody looks at a lover. This sick, sick boy. Oh my God..."

"The gun," I said. "What did it look like?"

She looked at me as if in shock that I could be asking such a trivial question.

"Please. It's important. Think."

"It...it looked like something out of a movie. Not a recent movie, something old. And the way he held it, like it was fragile."

"What about what the gun looked like?"

"The handle was brown..."

"Could it have been made from wood?" I asked. She nodded.

"There was this terrible explosion..." she stopped. "Please, I can't do this right now."

"Can you tell me anything else about it? Was it one barrel or two?"

"I don't know! I've never seen a real gun before in my life, now please leave me alone."

Just then a cop seemed to take notice and jogged over to us. He separated me, whispered, "Get the fuck out of here, scum." Then he said, "Miss, did you see the shooter?"

As I walked away, I looked over my shoulder long enough to see her nod and then collapse in his arms.

•

Ten feet from the carnage, a man clicked open his cell phone. Sweat was streaming down his face. He'd thankfully skipped lunch. Breathing heavy, he pressed Redial and waited for an answer.

"Hello?"

"Miss Cole?" He mopped at his brow with a shirtsleeve. "It's James Keach. You'll never believe what just happened."

Chapter 17

I arrived home tired to the bone. After spending hours writing my piece on the Jiffrey Lands march, my fingers ached, and my head throbbed. I'd had enough death for a lifetime, and I was growing tired of seeing it up close. I tossed my wallet and keys on the table, fell into the couch next to Amanda. She put her hand on mine. I squeezed it with whatever energy I had left.

We sat there. Tried to talk. Conversation came in bits and pieces. Amanda had ordered dinner for both of us. I wasn't hungry, just watched her poke at a salad. I stirred my pasta with a disinterested fork. All I could think about was Jeffrey Lourdes, and how ironic it was that the first time I ever saw him in person, his most recognizable feature had been reduced to blood and bone.

Betty Grable's words still rang in my ears. Between what Curt Sheffield told me about the ammunition used to kill both Athena Paradis and Joe Mauser, and her description of the weapon used to kill Jeffrey Lourdes, there was no doubt in my mind that the killer was using a rifle that took magnum bullets, and he was using that weapon for a reason. And somehow I had to find that reason, and use that to find the killer.

"How's work?" I asked Amanda. It was just a conversation starter, something to break the mood. Death was an inevitable part of reporting, but it had no place at the dinner table.

"The judge is still being a dick on the Mary Westin case," she said. "Three abuse complaints from the neighbors, two cigarette burns and Judge Jellyfish still doesn't realize it's in Mary's best interest to be taken the hell away from her sick-ass parents."

I nodded, picked at a piece of penne. On many nights I'd told Amanda how proud I was of her, both her work ethic and choice of profession. After graduation, Amanda had passed her bar exam and achieved high enough marks to warrant a position in the Juvenile Rights Division of the New York Legal Aid Society. The caseload for

The Guilty

lawyers working for the Legal Aid Society had increased nearly a hundred percent in the last few years, mainly due to some high-profile cases of child abuse and neglect that resulted in the horrific death of children who had slipped through the cracks. The Legal Aid Society had taken a beating in the press for their alleged inability to protect children whose parents were already the recipients of numerous abuse complaints. Because of this they were looking for fresh blood, cowboys and cowgirls who wouldn't stand for red tape.

Amanda worked long hours, alongside several other lawyers who were appointed "law guardians" by the court. It was incredibly enriching work for her, I knew. But spending all day every day around troubled and abused children took its toll. Sometimes she would come home, crawl into bed and appear on the verge of tears. She was too strong for that, though. She knew her tears were trivial compared to the reality of the situation. And her energy was better focused outward than in.

"You know I sit there sometimes," she continued, "and I want to scream. Not that I really hate the guys I work for, but in these cases you need to throw the book against the wall and just holler. Right and wrong doesn't stem from legal precedent."

I felt her staring at me, waiting for a response. I didn't want to talk about my day, but had to bite my tongue not to erupt. I hated making Amanda feel like my troubles were any more important than hers, but I couldn't focus on anything but this story.

"I have a lot of work for tomorrow," I said. "I'm pretty sure whoever's responsible for these murders is using an antique rifle or a replica, something that hasn't been used in a long time. There are thirty-two gun shops in the five boroughs alone, so I have my work cut out for me."

"You should talk to Agnes Trimble," Amanda said, sighing, wiping her mouth as a tomato spurted juice onto her plate. "She was my American History professor at NYU. Brilliant woman, but she scared the hell out of us during student conferences. She kept half a dozen model guns in her office, you know, like some people keep snow globes or toy fire trucks. Belongs to the NRA, all that good stuff. I can call her if you'd like, she should be in the city for the next few weeks and I'm sure she'd be happy to talk to you. Who knows, maybe she can help."

73

"Actually yeah. That'd be a huge help," I said. "Thanks."

"No problem."

We sat there in silence as I listened to Amanda chew.

"Did you see him die?" she asked me. There was a corner of lettuce sticking out of her mouth.

"No," I said. "I just saw what happened afterward."

Amanda chewed more.

"You don't want to know," I said.

"No," she replied. "Guess I don't."

As I got up and tossed the rest of my dinner into the garbage, the buzzer rang.

"Are you expecting anyone?" she asked. For a moment, my heart hammered. I could picture Mya waiting downstairs.

"No," I said. Amanda looked at me for a moment, surely knew what I was thinking. We walked to the window. Though we had no doorman to announce visitors, our apartment overlooked the building's entrance vestibule. Handier than an eye slot.

I grunted and heaved the window open, reminding myself to wipe down the grease and grime later, and poked my head outside. Looking down, I saw a man wearing a gray trenchcoat and hat. He looked up.

"Let me the hell up, will you?"

"Who is it?" Amanda asked.

"It's Jack," I said, with more than an ounce of relief. I closed the window and pressed the door release button.

"Doesn't he have his own home? What's he doing here at this hour?"

"I have no idea." I'd worked with Jack for over a year, and never once had we seen each other's apartments. I pictured his clean, full of polished wood and cracked books. Shelves lined with erudite literature and snifters of amber liquid, a fire roaring as he puffed a pipe and wrote great news of the day.

I looked around my apartment. Wondered if his vision of mine contained empty bottles of Pepsi and a subscription to Glamour.

"Quick," I said. "Hide stuff."

I picked up all the girly magazines, food wrappers, and rubber bands I could find and threw them in the trash. Which was already overflowing with girly magazines, food wrappers, and rubber bands.

The Guilty

"What are you doing?"

"Amanda, baby," I said, taking her hands in mine. "I idolized this man growing up. He's probably the only man I've ever dreamt about. And now he's coming up to my apartment." She eyed me like I'd just insulted her mother. "Okay, forget I said that. Just help."

For the next minute, we scrambled around the room tidying up as best we could. In those sixty seconds, our one-bedroom apartment went from resembling a tsunami-affected college dorm room to resembling an apartment lived in by two people who cleaned dishes after using them.

I heard a knock at the door. I looked around, panicked, then threw myself onto the worn polyurethane sofa and crossed my legs. Amanda glared at me.

"You expect me to open the door?"

"Would you mind?" She gave an exasperated sigh.

"Just so you know, you're sleeping on the couch tonight." She went to the door. Peered through the eyehole for dramatic effect. "Who is it?"

"Now it'd be some coincidence if it was someone other than the guy who was just downstairs," Jack said, his voice muffled by the door.

Amanda unlocked the door and opened it. Jack was breathing heavy, the trenchcoat seeming to weigh him down. He took off his hat, a few loose gray hairs sticking to it.

"You must be Miss Davies," he said.

"That's right."

"Charmed." He took her hand, kissed it as he looked into her eyes. She smiled demurely. "Henry here talks about you nonstop."

"Is that so? Well, at least one man here can call himself a gentleman." She led him into the apartment. "Can I get you a drink, Mr. O'Donnell?"

"Please call me Jack. And I'll take a Jack as well, if you have one, on ice." Amanda and I looked at each other. "It's been a long day."

Amanda disappeared into the kitchen. She came back with a glass full of brown liquid over ice. "Seagram's Seven. All we had."

"Do nicely," Jack replied. He moved over to the couch, let out a groan as he sat down. "How you holding up?"

"Me?" I said, incredulously.

"Heard you were at the Franklin-Rees building when…it happened."

"Nearby," I corrected. "I'm holding up fine. Jeffrey Lourdes is the one who was shot."

"Murder has a ripple effect, gets a lot of people wet," Jack said. "You better than anyone should know that."

Jack took a sip of his Seagram's. His cheeks were red, eyes tinged with veins. I wondered whether he was simply fatigued from taking the stairs, or if that Seagram's wasn't his first cocktail of the evening.

"I'm fine," I said. "Really."

"You know they haven't found a quote at the scene of Lourdes's murder," Jack said. "The first two were left in such prominent locations, either he dropped the whole thing, or…"

"Or he just didn't have time."

"You have to wonder, really, what kind of person walks up to a man in broad daylight and shoots him in the head."

"Same kind of person who shoots an unarmed woman and a cop from a distance," I said. "They're not dealing with your average run-of-the-mill lunatic. This guy has an agenda."

"You think so?" Jack said.

"Well, look at his targets. Athena Paradis, Mayor Perez and Jeffrey Lourdes. Remember, Joe Mauser was a mistake. All three of those people are celebrities, in some form or another. He's not killing random people, he's killing people whose deaths would pretty much dominate news coverage. I mean, just look at the metro papers the last few days. Athena, Mauser and tomorrow Jeffrey Lourdes will be everywhere."

"What do you make of the gun?" Jack asked, another nip of brown disappearing down his throat.

"I really don't know," I said. "Seems like he's using some sort of antique, something with a meaning. Don't quite know what yet, but Amanda has a contact from school who might be able to shed some light. I spoke to Lourdes's assistant at the scene. She got a quick glimpse of the killer and a partial of the murder weapon. Unfortunately she couldn't ID the actual shooter, and her police sketch is more vague than a Rorschach. Because of the chaos at the Franklin-Rees building, the guy was able to escape in the stampede."

The Guilty

"Mayor Perez, Athena Paradis and Jeffrey Lourdes," Jack said. "Not exactly three people you could imagine having brunch together on a Sunday morning."

"But someone sees them fitting in the same pattern."

"In this city," Jack said, "there's no shortage of people like those three. People who hog the front page. And though our great police force is locked up tighter than my grandma's cooter when it comes to terrorism, there's no defense for a sick fuck who wants to kill one person at a time."

"Lourdes," I said, "was surrounded by a hundred people when he died. His shooting caused a stampede. It couldn't have been any easier for the killer to disappear than if Scotty had beamed him aboard the Enterprise."

"Nobody disappears," Jack said, swallowing the last of the whiskey. "It's our job to find out what rug they're hiding under."

"I'm on it," I said. "You know the last quote he used. When he killed Joe Mauser. I'd told Jack about my tip."

"I'll let them know what bad means," Jack said.

"I looked it up," I said. "Guess quoting a junior reporter just wasn't scary enough, he had to upgrade to sicker game."

"Billy the Kid," Jack said. "Carruthers scowled during his statement, like he couldn't believe this thing could get any more macabre."

"He's moved on from quoting me to quoting mass murderers," I said. "Forgetting for a moment my disgust at being in that company, if the killer does see himself as some sort of avenger it probably means there's a longer list of people this guy doesn't like."

"Billy the Kid," Jack said. "You know the kid, or whatever the hell his real name was, pretty much started the trend of yellow journalism. His estate should get royalties from the National Enquirer and The Weekly World News. Reporters and hack novelists all over the country tripped over themselves to drool over this guy. Made him out to be some kind of hero. Some kind of Robin Hood. Idolizing celebrities practically began with the Kid."

"You think that's how this killer sees himself? Offing the rich and famous to help the poor?"

"Remember he also quoted your ass," Jack said. "Let's just hope all he's got is an affinity for scary words. In the meantime, we need to stay ahead on this story."

"Stay ahead? What do you mean?"

He took another sip and looked at me. And for the first time since I'd known him, Jack O'Donnell looked worried.

"Paulina," he said.

"What about her?"

"She's selling newspapers."

"Well that's her job," I said. "From what I hear she just didn't fit at the Gazette."

"Maybe not," Jack continued, "but if the Dispatch beats us to this story, they could see a double digit circulation growth by the end of the year." I stayed silent. "What that means, in lay terms, is we'd be fucked."

I considered this. "I know the Dispatch's circulation is up since she joined the paper, but I mean..."

"There's been a three percent swing this week alone, Henry. Whether it's our reporters getting beat to the punch or her articles attracting our readers, it's happening. These three murders are the biggest story of the year, everyone with a pen and a brain trying to get a piece. There's going to be a clear winner and loser here. We need to make sure we're not the ones holding the silver."

"They weren't beating us to the punch when I reported Athena's murder the morning she died," I said, my voice coming out angrier than I'd hoped.

"That was days ago, Henry," Jack said. He sighed, sank into the couch. "Since then it's neck and neck. Nobody is getting new scoops. So it comes down to juice, plain and simple. Paulina has it, we don't. People want salacious stories, headlines in bold, and photos of celebrities in bikinis. Only thing that can distract them from that is real, honest-to-God news. And until we get that, we're going to get creamed every day. If two people are tied during the race, everyone stares at the one wearing flashier clothing."

"I prefer jeans," I said.

"Don't be a smart-ass. And listen, Henry, you should be aware of it...Paulina knows you were at the crime scene today. Knew it before we did, actually."

"What—how is that possible?"

"I think she has some chumscrubber tailing you. But she's mentioning it in tomorrow's article on the Lourdes murder, claiming you always find yourself at the scenes of brutal crimes. Between Fredrickson, Mauser, your quote being found at Athena's crime scene and being seen talking to a witness today, she's got enough paint in her brush to paint some pretty brash accusations."

"That was a coincidence. I was talking to a friend. Any decent reporter would have done the same thing."

"A friend. You mean the cop."

"Yes, a cop friend, Curt Sheffield."

"I know Curt. Seen that recruiting poster everywhere but my refrigerator."

"Whatever," I said. "Bottom line is I have a lead on a hell of a story."

"You know, I thought you might."

"That gun, the one the killer is using, there's a reason he's using it. I'm going to find out what that is. Paulina doesn't have that. Combine that with this new quote, it's going to fit somewhere." I sat there silent. Watched Jack rattle his empty glass. Then he stood up, tipped his cap at Amanda, nodded at me.

"Find the story," Jack said. "Behind every murder is a motive. The cops don't care about that right now, they just want the man. Motive will come later, once they can be sure there aren't any more high-caliber bullets aimed at anyone's skull. So keep on keeping on."

"I will."

"Important work is silent until it needs to be heard. Keep that in mind. Other people want this story too." Then he left.

I turned to Amanda. "Your history professor," I said. "You think she's still awake?"

Chapter 18

The headline read, Head of Franklin-Rees, Now Without a Head.

Even I was shocked by the tactlessness and audacity of the Dispatch's front page. The lead story, naturally, was the murder of Jeffrey Lourdes, accompanied by a gruesome photo of the man's legs with blood pooling around them. In Technicolor.

The paper neglected to mention how Jeffrey Lourdes had revolutionized the magazine industry in the early seventies with several titles that captured the zeitgeist with aplomb and erudition, how he'd mentored many of the country's most talented writers and journalists from scruffy-haired hipsters to men and women who changed the face of American culture. Instead the Dispatch focused of rumors on money laundering, infidelity, drugs, and under-the-table deals. It noted how, over the last decade, Lourdes had been accused of letting his legacy go to seed, eschewing strong journalism for salacious stories and shoddy reportage that his younger self would have thrown in the fire. It also noted how, despite Lourdes's rumored twenty-million-a-year salary, circulation for Moss was way down, and the magazine had long ago ceded any cultural impact.

They would have had you believe Lourdes was as dirty as they come, a common rat working in an ivory tower.

Our article for the Gazette painted a more accurate, more even picture. Giving Lourdes credit where he deserved it. I expected the Dispatch to kick our asses at the newsstand.

If I didn't know any better, the Dispatch was suggesting that the magazine industry was better off with Jeffrey Lourdes dead.

At the same time, I knew I was on to something, that there was an even bigger story surrounding the deaths of Athena Paradis, Joe Mauser and Jeffrey Lourdes. I needed to find out why someone had murdered a famous socialite, tried to assassinate a government official and a publishing magnate mere days apart, and why the killer seemed to be using weaponry and ammunition completely impractical for someone who was smart enough to carry the murders to their grim conclusion.

I'd spent all night poring over the details given by Lourdes's assistant regarding the gun she saw, the man she saw wielding it, as well as the info Curt Sheffield gave me about the ammunition caliber. At eleven-thirty I'd left a message for Professor Agnes Trimble. I name-dropped Amanda, her former student, said I needed to talk to her about an important story. She called me back within fifteen minutes.

"I don't have much of a nightlife," she'd said. If what Amanda said was true, and she collected firearms, I wasn't totally surprised. But could a college professor help paint a clearer picture of a murder suspect?

I squinted as we walked towards the subway. Agnes was expecting us at eight thirty sharp. Not much of a nightlife, didn't care much about sleeping in. No wonder Amanda liked her so much.

"So you're sure Trimble isn't just someone who has a strange gun fetish," I said. "You really think she can help?"

"I went to a better school than you," Amanda offered. "I guess our history professors just take their jobs more seriously."

Guess it was that simple.

We took the 4 train down to West Fourth street and headed towards the NYU College of Arts and Sciences, located in downtown Manhattan by Washington Square South.

"You know, I did go to a pretty good college," I said.

"According to who, U.S. News and World Reports? Please. They know as much about academia as I know about horticulture. Most Ivy Leaguers are the kind of students who work twenty hours a day to make a three-point-eight, then get hit by a bus on your first day of work because you don't have enough common sense to know that red means 'stop.'"

"I've never been hit by a bus," I replied.

"Right. You just got shot."

She had me there.

Amanda had taken a class with Trimble, Professor of the Humanities, Professor of nineteenth-century American Cultural History, during her junior year. She claimed Trimble was brilliant, slightly loony, but if you wanted to know anything that took place between Maine and California between eighteen hundred and nineteen hundred, you could be sure it was rattling around in her brain.

Hopefully we could jar something loose, because aside from my employer losing ground to the print princess of darkness, three people had been killed and a murderer was still on the loose.

I'll let them know what bad means.

The killer had left that quote for us after killing Joe Mauser. Carruthers hadn't yet made public either that note or anything found at the scene with Jeffery Lourdes. Out of respect for Curt Sheffield I wanted to keep it to myself until it was made public. That didn't mean I couldn't conduct my own investigation, under the radar. Because if someone wanted the world to know what "bad" meant, and how bad they were, they didn't want for official statements. More lives were at stake. Hopefully Agnes had more than marbles rattling around up there.

It was early May, and Trimble had just finished up finals week. According to Amanda, she was spending her final days in the city packing up the office before heading off to Malibu for the summer. I wanted to ask more about this Malibu trip, but Amanda shushed me.

"Better you don't know," she said. "Let's just say her favorite movie is Point Break."

I hadn't been back to NYU since several people had wanted me for murder. That coincided with how I met Amanda. Needless to say, the school held some memories for me. Traded pain for pleasure, took a bullet in the leg in exchange for a lover at night. Fair deal, but if the bullet had been a few inches higher I wouldn't be thinking that.

The NYU College of Arts and Sciences had a storied history, and what was now known as the Brown Building was formerly known as the Asch Building. The Asch Building was the site of the infamous Triangle Shirtwaist Factory fire. The blaze, which occurred on March 25th, 1911, began on the eighth floor and quickly spread. Due to cramped working conditions and a lack of exits (including one that had been locked ostensibly to prevent workers from stealing), the fire killed a hundred and forty-six workers before it was put out.

It was purchased by real estate magnate Fredrick Brown, who donated it to the University where it became the Brown Building of Science. I didn't want to ask Amanda about it, but I don't how I would have felt taking classes in a building where nearly a hundred and fifty

The Guilty

people had died.

"Ah, home sweet home," Amanda sighed as we entered the CAS building. Despite the fact that summer was nearing and most sane students would have fled the campus weeks ago, there was a line twenty people deep waiting for an elevator than looked like it'd been erected by people who still wore shirtwaists. Amanda, though, seemed completely unsurprised.

"It's always like this," she said. "The elevator goes about a floor an hour. It's an excuse for students to be late to class. Professors can always tell who the serious students are because they're the ones who are panting and sweating when class starts. Come on, let's take the stairs."

Agnes Trimble's office was on the third floor. I was hardly panting when we arrived. I felt a small amount of pride at that. Then I felt ashamed for being proud of walking up two flights of stairs.

I followed Amanda down a whitewashed hall. Most of the doors were closed, the faculty having all adjourned for the summer, the corkboards adjacent to them holding naked staples and thumbtacks and occasional notices whose posters had neglected to take them down.

As we turned down one corridor, I heard loud noise coming from the end of the hall. As we got closer, I could hear the strains of the Grateful Dead's "Casey Jones" playing at full blast.

"That'd be her," Amanda said without an ounce of irony. "She's a huge deadhead."

We followed the music and came to an open doorway whose nameplate read Professor Agnes Trimble. And immediately my expectations were blown to hell.

Agnes Trimble was a small woman, sitting down I guessed about five foot three and a hundred ten pounds. She looked to be in her late fifties, with hair dyed so red I was surprised a horde of bulls weren't stampeding around the office. Her hair was done up in what I could best describe as a bird's nest, pretty much clumped together and held there with a brown scrunchy and a few terrorized bobby pins. On her ears rested a pair of horn-rimmed glasses, which I suppose helped her enjoy the two lava lamps in either corner. On her computer, a felt monkey dangled from a small American flag, its hands Velcro-ed to the top of the Stars and Stripes. Taped to one shelf looked to be an actual ticket stub from the original Woodstock, complete with authentic-looking mud stain. Her shelves were covered in books whose staid titles must have been hideously embarrassed by the rest of the décor. I debated relaying the information that the Partridge Family bus had left the parking lot a long time ago.

And resting among these hipster-drenched relics were dozens of toy guns. All makes and models. Rifles, cannons, small arms, and enough tanks to blow the hell out of the Indian in the Cupboard.

And somehow I was not surprised to see pictures of various male celebrities, many of them sans shirts or other commonly worn articles of clothing, taped to a corkboard behind her desk. I suppose reporting while staring at the nipples of Orlando Bloom and George Clooney had to happen sometime.

"Amanda, baby!" Agnes leapt up, leaned over the desk and wrapped her arms around Amanda, who leaned in awkwardly to reach the small woman. Agnes squeezed her eyes shut, sucked in a breath, and for a moment I worried she might be trying to inhale Amanda's soul.

When they separated, Amanda gestured to me and said, "Professor Trimble, this is who I was telling you about, Henry Parker. He's a reporter for the Gazette." I held out my hand to shake hers. She eyed me, squinted slightly.

"He your…boyfriend?" she asked, a sly smile on her lips.

"Uh…" I said.

"Actually, yes," Amanda said. "I didn't realize we were wearing name tags."

Agnes sat back down, reached into her desk and pulled out a candy cane. She unwrapped it and popped the whole thing in her mouth. Through a mouthful of peppermint, she said, "You didn't need name tags. Eighty-thirty in the morning, both of you dressed and showered, Henry wearing matching socks and the whole nine. Henry here is a reporter…no guy I've ever met under the age of thirty is dressed well and showered this early unless they're going to work, going to a funeral, or going somewhere with the person they sleep with. Do you have a funeral this afternoon?"

My cheeks grew warm, and Amanda's looked like they could catch fire at any moment. "Not that I know of," I said.

"Then you're boyfriend and girlfriend," Agnes said. "That's lovely. Please, sit. Candy cane?"

"No thanks," we echoed.

Agnes shrugged, as if she couldn't believe how anyone could say no to such a scrumptious treat at this time of day. In the meantime, Agnes seemed to have noticed me staring at the photos behind her desk. I'd also noticed that she wore a wedding ring.

"You never had pictures taped to your locker?" she asked.

"I did," I said, "back in high school." I glanced at her wedding ring. "How does your husband feel about them?"

"What are you, ten years old?" she asked. "He knows I'm not sleeping with Brad Pitt, and as long as that stays the case he could care less if I have pictures of him or Stephen Hawking on my wall. If you have a problem with them, you can leave any time."

There was a sharp pain in my side as Amanda elbowed me.

"Nope, no problem."

"So Amanda, how are you? It's been, what, three years?"

"Four," Amanda corrected. "Junior year, U.S. Nineteenth Century Intellectual and Cultural History."

"What'd I give you in that class?"

"A minus."

"That'll do. I refuse to put up with students post-graduation unless they've received at least a B plus. So what brings you to our humble university? Not soliciting donations, I hope."

I laughed. Amanda didn't. Clearly I'd missed a joke.

"So Mr. Parker," Agnes said. "Amanda tells me you're a reporter and you have some questions a women of my expertise might be able to assist you with. That correct?"

"Yes ma'am," I said. Agnes cringed.

"Don't call me ma'am, please. I'd rather die alone surrounded by cats than think I'm a ma'am. Call me Agnes."

"Right, Agnes. Anyway, you've heard about these murders, right? Athena Paradis, Officer Joe Mauser, Jeffrey Lourdes?"

She shook her head sadly. "Terrible, terrible things. How someone can murder people who've contributed so much to our society is just shameful and beyond me."

"The person who committed these crimes, I'm pretty sure they're using a weapon, specifically a rifle, that has some specific cause or reason behind its use. The killer is also using ammunition I've been told is quite out of the ordinary," I eyed her red hair, the lava lamps.

"Amanda said you were familiar with nineteenth-century weaponry…"

"Shoot," she said. Then she laughed. "Get it, shoot? Go on."

"Right. So my source in the NYPD told me that the bullet used to kill both Athena Paradis and Officer Mauser was a .44-40 caliber magnum round."

Agnes bit her lip, furrowed her brow.

"That's a powerful bullet," she said.

"So I've heard. Is it true that it's an uncommon round?"

"Depends," she said. "Hunters use them all the time. .44-40 bullets have massive stopping power, and just enough accuracy that if you're a decent shot, you'll only need one shot."

"I've scanned the police reports for every homicide in the five boroughs over the last five years," I said. "Three hundred and twelve murders. None of them with magnum rounds."

"Well, to be honest magnum rounds aren't the kind of ammunition you tend to see these days, at least not around here," she said.

"What do you mean?"

"Well, the area between the Hudson and East River isn't exactly known for their hunting grounds." She paused. "Unless this man is making them."

"I think he may be," I said.

"Listen, Mr. Parker…"

"Call me Henry."

"Right, Parker, I appreciate you coming down here, it flatters me to no end that a former student thinks so highly of me to believe I might be of some assistance on a murder case. But I'm a college professor. Nothing more, maybe a little less."

I looked around her office. "Mrs. Trimble, it's clear you have a passion for these weapons. Now regardless of what that says about you, I'd sure as hell trust someone who has a passion for something over someone who gets paid to do it. I think Amanda's right. But I'm not a cop, I'm not asking you to help catch a murderer. But I think there's more to this than simple killings. I think this guy has a motive, and I think his gun is a clue to that."

Agnes took the candy cane from her mouth, tossed it in the garbage. Looked me over. "You know my father took me to the range when I was a little girl. Had one set up in our backyard. Picket fence with empty paint cans on it. Only seven-year-old in my town who could shoot paint cans from twenty yards out with a nine-millimeter with eighty-seven-percent accuracy. I know guns. I don't like what they can do, but I'm in awe of them."

"I can see that," I said. "And that could be the difference here."

"Do they know what kind of gun it was fired from?"

"Not specifically," I said. "But there are clues. A witness to Jeffrey Lourdes's murder said she got a good look at the weapon. She said it looked old, like she'd seen it in a movie. It might have had a wood stock. That's as much as I know."

"Mr. Parker, hundreds of guns fit that description. If that's all you have…"

"Does the phrase 'gun that won the west' mean anything to you?"

Agnes's eyes opened wide. She brought a hand to her mouth, chewed on a fingernail. Suddenly she stood up, starting running her finger along the spines of various books on her shelf. She stopped at one. Took it out and laid it on her desk. She flipped it open. It was text heavy, filled with old photographs and illustrations. She turned to the index, flipped some more, scanned down, then stopped when she found what she was looking for.

"You say you think this rifle bears a significance to the case?" she asked. All the playfulness had left Agnes Trimble's voice. She was working now, the switch I assumed made her so good at her job now turned on.

"I don't know about the case, but it does to the man committing these crimes. I just need to prove it. I need to know why this gun is so special to him."

She turned the book around so it faced me.

"Could this be the gun?"

On the page was a photograph of a rifle. It had a wooden stock, like Lourdes's assistant said. Other than that, I didn't know.

"Look here," Agnes said. "Rather than a traditional trigger guard, it has a reloading mechanism with only one side attached to the frame. Makes for easy and fast reloading. These kind of rifles are as common as sequin jumpsuits. You asked about the gun that won the west? Well here it is."

The caption beneath the rifle read, Winchester 1873, First Model Rifle, S/N 27.

It was a beautiful piece of firepower. I examined it.

"At the time, this gun was given the highest production run of any rifle in history," she said. "As much as the Winchester won the West, it nearly drowned it in blood as well."

"Does the Winchester 1873 take .44-40 magnum rounds?"

Agnes nodded, her fingernail underlining a passage in the text.

The Winchester 1873 lever action rifle was originally chambered for the .44-40—a bottlenecked cartridge that has acquired legendary status and is often referred to as 'The cartridge that won the West.'

I read the line, wondered if this was the gun the killer was using. The rifle obviously had history, a literal one at that. But why would somebody use a nearly hundred-and-forty-year-old gun?

"The gun was accurate," I said to Agnes. "And fast. But it surely can't match some of the weapons around today. Hell…Uzis, semiautomatics, Saturday night specials."

"Yeah, I've seen movies too. And yes, there are many guns currently on the market that obliterate the necessity of this gun. But if this is the gun, and I'm assuming at this point that's a big if, this man is not using it for efficiency or posterity."

"So why use it?" Amanda said. She was into this, a little too much.

"The Winchester 1873," Agnes said, her voice taking on a reverential tone, "until the Uzi nine millimeter came along was the most famous and most recognizable gun in the world. Over half a million were produced and in circulation before the turn of the century. Between lawmen, outlaws, and other savory and unsavory types, just about anyone who needed to kill someone was doing it with a Winchester model 1873."

"What made it so popular?"

Agnes breathed out, whistled. "Oh, well, take your pick. The construction was far more rugged than the previous models. That beast could take a pounding. It had a lever-action mechanism, and what that does is allow the shooter to fire several cartridges without having to reload. The 1873 model was lighter and faster than its grandfather, the 1866. The 1873 had a steel frame, which allowed Winchester to use a centerfire instead of a rimfire for the first time."

The Guilty

Amanda said, "You know if I knew you knew all this, I might not have registered for your class."

"If I didn't know all this, I wouldn't have a dozen unregistered students every semester taking my class for no credit."

"So what's the difference between centerfire and rimfire?" Agnes seemed to get that I knew a little less about weaponry than your average twenty-five-year-old. She spoke with no condescension, and I could tell her interest was more than academic.

"The centerfire was one of the most important technological advancements in the history of advanced weaponery. See, with a centerfire, a gunman could use more than one cartridge at a time."

"Or gunwoman," Amanda added. "Hey, I know about Annie Oakley."

Agnes continued. "The older model Winchesters used a rimfire, which fired at a lower velocity and smaller caliber since the firing mechanism would often be damaged when using higher power ammunition. The steel frame made it the first rifle which could be used in just about any weather condition. It truly was an all-purpose killing machine."

I said. "Athena Paradis and Joe Mauser were killed by .44-40 magnum rounds. I'm willing to bet Jeffrey Lourdes was the same. My friend on the force told me the .44-40 rounds are pretty uncommon calibers to be used in an urban setting."

"They are, mainly because they're impractical as hell," Agnes said. "But in the 1880s, you didn't have Uzis. A good rifle, accurate, powerful and easily reloaded, could win a war, wreak havoc everywhere, or keep the law."

"So basically this was a bad-ass rifle of the first degree."

"I believe that's how pretty much any historian would put it."

I sat back and tried to digest all of this. According to all the facts we had so far, a young man could be running around New York with a rifle made famous in the nineteenth century. A rifle that would be described as a "killing machine." So far he had targeted three people who had seemingly no connection to each other aside from their propensity for front-page coverage. Popular gun, popular targets. I knew there was more to this story. That there was a very specific reason, if this was the right gun, that this monster was using it.

Agnes continued, confirming my thoughts. "Nobody would

be using this weapon today without a purpose."

"I know that," I said. "But we don't know what that purpose is."

"Where could someone find this gun?" I asked.

"Oh hell, I don't know. Someone who wants it bad, that's for sure."

"Look, Agnes," I said. "Three people are dead. Who knows how many more are targeted, or if the cops can catch this guy before he crosses anyone else off his list. Right now all I want to do is find out if this is the gun being used, and if so, why. I know in my heart if I can answer that question, we'll find out who this man is."

Agnes looked at me, looked at Amanda.

"You love her?" she asked.

Amanda's mouth opened. The question knocked me a bit, but I looked her in the eye and said, "Yes I do." I felt Amanda's hand on mine.

"Then promise this girl right here that if you feel yourself getting too close, you'll back off. The kind of man who would go out of his way to use a weapon with such a bloody history won't think twice about collateral damage. Reporters are no good dead."

"I know that," I said.

"Museums," she said. "Museums with old west exhibitions. Collectors, but antique and current. Start your search with everything below the Mason-Dixon line. Anyone who goes out of their way to possess a working Winchester 1873 knows its history well. And appreciates it."

"This killer surely does both," I said. "Hey, would you mind if I make a copy of this?"

"Not at all, Xerox machine is down the hall, second left, next to the Wet Paint sign."

I gently took the book, brought it to the machine, laid it flat and made three copies of the page featuring the Winchester. I put the copies in my backpack, then brought the book back to Agnes.

"Thanks," I said.

"Don't mention it. Now, what you do know," she said, "is that someone is looking to make a statement. The Winchester 1873 wasn't just any gun. This was the gun that won the west, back when our country was going through its bloodiest and most dangerous time."

"And now somebody's brought that gun back east," Agnes continued. "And you better pray to God they're not looking for this gun to do what it does best, and pick up where it left off. Because these dead people? They'll just be the beginning."

Chapter 19

She shivered in the morning air. She wore a tan polo shirt and skirt, the wind whipping through her uncombed hair. The weather report said today would be chilly and she could have easily worn a coat, but found herself caring less whether she was comfortable and more about getting out of the house.

Last night had been a disaster. She remembered dancing on tables. She remembered pouring alcohol down her throat seemingly by the gallon. She remembered going home alone, and her bloodshot eyes reminded her that she'd cried herself to sleep. She remembered making a phone call around three in the morning, but it went right to his voice mail. She woke up with mascara stains on her pillow, throwing it into the laundry in a fit of rage. It was then that she remembered her meeting this morning.

There were three messages on her cell phone. She didn't even remember it ringing. One was from her friend Shayla calling to make sure she got home all right. The second was from her friend Bobby, one of the bazillion gorgeous gay men of New York City who spent more money on clothing than the U.N. spent on military aid and seemed to have swept all the decent straight guys under some giant heterosexual carpet. Bobby had been positively shattered by Athena Paradis's murder. He owned an autographed copy of her book, had preordered her CD, and her image wallpapered his Mac. Bobby was also checking up on her. She'd gone to the bar with Bobby and her "friend" Victoria, though neither he nor Victoria seemed concerned enough to actually leave the bar to check on her. At least that's the sense she got, considering there was house music blaring in the background as they left the message.

The third was from her mother asking to meet up for dinner. Her mother sounded sad, even a little scared. She deleted the message and erased the call from her memory.

She wore dark sunglasses. Not that anybody would recognize her. Recently her jaw had been hurting. She'd seen a doctor a few weeks ago who said she might need another operation, that the first one might have damaged a nerve. She drank so much vodka to numb the pain that more than once she feared having to get her stomach pumped.

She was in no shape for this meeting, but when she remembered the woman's voice, the urgency, the *it's about your father, I just want your side of the story*, she knew she had to keep it.

The diner was just a few blocks from her apartment. She went there almost every morning, and it had been her suggestion to meet there. On weekdays she ordered a cappuccino to go, and the owner was always kind. On weekends she would treat herself to chocolate chip pancakes, then go straight to the gym to work off the calories.

They wouldn't miss her at the office today. She'd called in sick. They didn't much care whether she came in or not, as long as her last name was still Loverne.

Mya walked up to the diner and opened the door. She welcomed the smell of frying bacon, sugary syrup, and fresh eggs, felt like ordering all of them to get rid of the awful taste in her mouth. A bottomless cup of coffee would go a long way. She had a vague idea of who she was looking for. Then she saw a woman in the corner waving her hand. The woman mouthed *Mya?*

Mya nodded, walked over and slid into the booth. The woman extended a hand with perfectly manicured nails, and said, "Mya Loverne?"

Mya nodded.

"Paulina Cole. It's such a pleasure to meet you. Henry used to talk about you all the time back at the Gazette." Paulina looked her over. It made Mya uncomfortable.

Paulina Cole wore a tailored pantsuit. Her jewelry was fine but not ostentatious. She wore her hair tied back in a ponytail, a thin string of pearls around her neck. A tape recorder sat on the table next to two steaming cups of coffee. There was a smile on Paulina's face, like a friendly aunt pleased to see how well her niece is doing.

"You're much more elegant in person. I've only seen your picture in the society pages."

"The lighting always sucks," Mya said. "And the dresses make me feel like I can't breathe."

"Coming from a well-known family is as much a curse as it is a gift," Paulina said. "You know, it's a real shame that Henry is too stubborn to see what he's lost."

Mya didn't know whether to smile or throw a cup of coffee in Paulina's face.

"Please don't patronize me."

Paulina sat back, held up her hands. "I understand. But I can't apologize for saying it. Listen," she said, leaning forward again. "I'm embarrassed to say that we both know how stories in the news take on a life of their own. From what I gather, the last year has been hard for you."

"What do you know about it?"

"Well, after you were involved in Henry's altercation," Paulina said, as though they'd been in a fender-bender, "your career doesn't seem to have taken off the way you expected."

"What do you care about my career?"

"I shouldn't," Paulina said. "But the truth is we both know how hard it is for strong women to make it incorporate America. Add to that the pressure of being a Loverne. Whether it's law or journalism, it's still about who can claw the hardest and deepest. Cornell, then law school at Columbia, you have a pretty terrific pedigree. I imagine neither were easy to achieve."

"Easy is what you make of it. Some kids can study eight hours a night and still blow the bar. Some can soak it up while spending three years sucking down beers five nights a week."

"And which were you?" Paulina asked.

Mya shifted in her seat. "I don't really know. I think I used to be the former. Now...I don't know."

"Mya," Paulina said, her voice growing soft. "You know why I asked you here, right?"

"Not exactly," she said. "You said something about my father. What does he have to do with anything."

Paulina sighed. "I'm going to be straight with you. I'm writing an article on your father's campaign. Well, more specifically...his life. I think you can get where I'm going with this."

"No. Enlighten me."

"You're not blind," Paulina said, "and clearly not stupid. You must have heard the rumors. Or seen it with your own eyes."

The Guilty

"Seen what?" Mya said.

"The other women."

Mya nearly choked.

"You're writing an article about my father seeing other women? Are you fucking kidding me?"

Paulina offered her hands. "It's more than that," she said. "Your father is an important man. Important people need to gain the trust of their constituents. It's my job, it's what I'm paid for, to make sure people know the full story."

"Jesus," Mya whispered.

"It's going to be in the newspapers," Paulina said. "I have nothing against you or your father. I just want to know the truth. It doesn't need to be painful. If you just tell me what you know, the innuendos are kept out of it. The truth is all I want."

"I can't believe he's so stupid," Mya said, feeling her cheeks grow warm.

"Your father?" Mya nodded. "So you knew."

"Yes," Mya said, her voice barely a sound.

"Do you know who?" Mya shook her head. "Or how many?" Again.

"I don't know anything else, please, just leave it alone."

"Mya," Paulina said. "I honestly can't imagine how hard this is for you. Have you been able to talk to anyone else about it?" Mya stared into her coffee. "What about Henry?"

Mya looked at her, stared into Paulina's eyes. Then shook her head.

"We don't talk any more. At least he doesn't talk to me." Mya took a sip of her coffee, holding the mug in both hands. She let the warmth travel down her hands. She put it down, added some more sugar. "I'm not sure what else you want to know."

"Why doesn't Henry want to talk to you? Weren't you two close?"

"Were," Mya said.

"What happened?"

"It ended. Relationships do."

"You didn't want to stay friends?"

"I did," Mya said. Paulina leaned closer. Mya could smell her perfume. It smelled good, not too strong.

"The truth is, Mya, Henry is in an incredibly important position right now. I fear that the brain trust at the Gazette, that would be Harvey Hillerman and Wallace Langston, have placed too much pressure on Henry. Since the scandals last year, there haven't been many young reporters given access to the kind of stories he's had. Did you know he is covering Athena Paradis's murder?"

"I read his stories," Mya said.

"So much pressure though," she said, as though the weight of the world was on her shoulder. "If you're not up for it, in our profession there are catastrophic consequences."

Mya sipped her coffee, said nothing. Paulina offered a warm smile.

"My ex was addicted to coffee," she said. "If he didn't drink a minimum of six cups a day, he'd throw furniture around our apartment like he was shooting rubber bands. I think I spent as much money staying in hotels to get away from him as I did paying our mortgage."

"Really?"

"God yes. If you're ever in an abusive relationship, please take it from someone who's made too many mistakes in the love department, get your ass out of that place quick and don't ever look back."

They both laughed. Mya looked at Paulina. Her smile seemed so genuine, like she wasn't simply a reporter, but someone who truly cared. Mya thought about her friends, the ones who said they'd always be there for her. The ones who never called, never checked up, always assumed her tears came from happiness. Never stopping to think that she had nothing to be happy about. And hadn't for a long time.

"We were together almost three years," Mya said, sighing. "Then it ended."

"Just like that." Paulina spread some raspberry jam over a slice of toast. She bit into it, brushed some crumbs off her lip. "Was it one thing, or just a lot of one things?"

"Kind of both. You know how college relationships are. Eventually you either move in or get lost. I was a year older than Henry, and when I moved back to the city we just grew apart." Paulina kept chewing. "And then..."

Paulina stopped chewing. Waited. Mya stayed quiet.

"And then what?"

"You know, shit happens. Life. He was up there, I was down

96

here. Shit."

Paulina spoke faster now, like she'd sensed something. "No, I have a feeling it was something specific. Did Henry do something? Did you?"

Mya stayed silent. She didn't know if she could go on. Thought about her father. Thought about Henry. The two men in her life who'd promised to care for her, had in the end abandoned her. She stared at the tape recorder, cold gray, wheels turning. A memory that wouldn't be erased.

Paulina reached across the table. She placed her hand on top of Mya's. Kind. Mya felt her skin, smooth with just a hint of roughness around the fingertips. She looked at Paulina's lips, coated with a demure red gloss. Mya felt tears come to her eyes again. She wanted to excuse herself, to go to the bathroom and wail and pound the walls and let it all out, let all the shit ooze into the walls and cracks and disappear. Then she could come back and sit here silent, without feeling like a dam about to burst. But the woman's hand might as well have been a magnet holding her down. She couldn't get up. All she could do was talk. Afterwards wouldn't get lost in the cracks, but be recorded in those metal wheels. For some reason, she felt better knowing that.

"It was about a year and a half ago," Mya said. She felt the tears subside. Her jaw didn't hurt, but she could feel the scar. Her eyes dried up. It felt good to get it out. "Henry and I were in a fight."

Paulina listened to the whole story. She nodded, smiled, nearly looked to be in tears at the end. And while they spoke, the tape recorder sitting on the table disappeared from Mya's thoughts.

Chapter 20

"So if you were a hundred-and-thirty-year-old gun whose reputation was more notorious than Andy Dick on a bender, where would you be?"

"Do you really expect me to answer that?" Amanda said.

"It'd be helpful if you could," I replied. "But I won't be too disappointed if you don't.

Thankfully I had the deep resources of the Gazette archives at my disposal. Speed was key. With a thread this important, it was only a matter of time before other news outlets picked up on it. Once a story began percolating, you had to spill it before it grew cold. I had to find out if the killer was using a Winchester, and just what his motives were for killing three seemingly unconnected people.

"I'm gonna head back to the office, see what I can dig up," I said to Amanda. "Thanks for setting me up with Trimble, I knew there was a reason I keep you around." I gave her a playful nudge, then wrapped my arm around her. As she leaned in, I heard a beep come from my pocket. I always kept my cell phone on silent mode when talking to a source. Someone had called and left a message.

I checked my call log. One missed call. I recognized the number. I immediately shoved it back into my pocket. Amanda didn't need to see the number. She only had to look at my expression to know.

"It was her again, wasn't it?"

I nodded.

"You know I'm not a jealous girlfriend," Amanda said. "I don't need the password to your e-mail, I have a life outside of you, I don't sit around at night wondering when you'll be home, and I sure as hell don't care if you subscribe to Maxim. But raging jealousy and curiosity as to why your ex seems to think it's all right to call you every freaking day are two different things entirely."

"She's not calling me every day," I said, and immediately regretted it. That wasn't the point. Amanda was right. If the tables were turned and some other old boyfriend was calling her at freaky hours,

I'd be bugging the phone lines and setting up a tent outside the dude's house waiting for him to come home. The fact that she'd let Mya's intrusions go on for this long said a lot about her character and patience. And maybe mine too.

"Listen, Mya's had it rough the past few years. You remember what I told you about us, that night? When she was attacked?"

Amanda sighed, nodded. She knew about the attack. It was one of the first things I'd told her when we decided to be together. I thought it was important, to approach our relationship with all the cards on the table. It was a painful one to show.

A year and a half ago, Mya had been attacked. She was living in New York, while I was finishing my senior year. We were fighting constantly, and late one night she called me. Still boiling over an insult from before, I hung up on her. It turned out she pressed Redial in the middle of being attacked and nearly raped. She managed to fight him off, but he broke her jaw. I didn't know this until the next morning. It was as much consolation as knowing the surgery didn't leave much of a scar.

"I don't know why she keeps calling," I said. Amanda glared at me with one of those don't you dare patronize me looks. I had to remind myself that Amanda was much smarter than I was. "Okay, I know why she's calling. But she doesn't want me back. She's just hurting and needs someone to help."

"I don't have a problem with that," she said. "I know you're a great friend. But ignoring her, telling her to leave you alone, I feel like you're doing it for my sake rather than hers. If you want to do something, do it. But stop with the I don't know why she's calling crap."

"I don't want to do anything," I said. "I have you. That's where my attention deserves to be."

I wrapped my arm around Amanda, held her close, hoped she knew I was telling the truth.

"I turned my back on her once," I said. "I just don't want to be cruel. I know she's been having problems. I've heard she's been drinking too much, that she's alienated her friends. Being the daughter of a political animal is a full-time job, and Mya wanted to have her own life."

"Look," she said. "I'm not saying you should leave the girl to drown in a distillery, I'm just saying this isn't normal. Forget any girlfriend neuroses, it's just not healthy for someone to do what she's doing. If you don't clear things up, it's only going to get worse."

"You think so?" I asked.

"Come on, she's not the only girl who's ever wanted a guy she couldn't get." I stared at Amanda, cocked my head. "Oh, give it a rest. You think you're the first guy I've ever liked? Come off your high horse, Johnny, I had a life before we met."

"I know you had a life, I know there were probably other guys," I said. "I just don't want to know about them, hear about them, or think that they exist. I'd rather believe you wore a chastity belt your first twenty-five years, and the only guys you liked were flamingly gay men who wore big bushy mustaches and only called you 'girlfriend' in an ironic manner."

She laughed. "Now who's kidding who? Just think though, if you can react like that to me just insinuating I've liked other guys, imagine how I feel that a girl you actually had a relationship with is begging for your jock at 3:00 a.m.?"

"She's not…okay, you have a point."

"I usually do."

"Okay, I promise to talk to Mya. Now I have to get to work, time's wasting. I need to find out where this gun came from. First I need to talk to Jack."

I opened the phone, dialed O'Donnell's direct line. He picked up on the first ring.

"Hello?"

"Jack, it's Henry. You busy?"

"I was going to have my shoes shined, and hope a stray bullet didn't find my old ass."

"Listen, can you meet me at O'Grady's restaurant in twenty minutes?"

"You want me to leave the office to meet you somewhere. You'd better give me a reason, and it better not be that you're in the mood for an undercooked hamburger."

"No, but I might have a hell of a scoop on the Paradis murders, and I need some help."

"Are you stupid, kid? Half the Gazette goes to O'Grady's for lunch. Meet me at McPhee's pub in twenty, at least we can talk in private. Besides, it's the only bar in a ten-block radius that charges less than three bucks a beer. What's the occasion for this midday imbibing?"

"I need you to use the archives and run a search for me, then bring whatever you can find."

"A search for what?"

"Guns," I said. "I need to know what museums and collections carry authentic Winchester rifles, model 1873."

"The gun that won the west," Jack said, a sense of romance in his voice. "John Wayne would be proud. What does this have to do with the murders?"

"I'll tell you then," I said. "But I think this killer is more than just a fan of history—I think he's trying to recreate the bloodiest parts."

Chapter 21

I walked into McPhee's pub. And immediately decided that I never wanted to go back again. McPhee's was the kind of dive bar you were happy to get into in college despite your crummy fake ID, where the bouncer weighed upwards of six hundred pounds and was covered in tattoos that looked like they'd been painted on by an epileptic spider monkey. Where the bartender served beer whose advertisements settled for round men in green hats because they couldn't afford buxom women in bikinis. Where the decibel level never rose above "angry grumble."

Yep, this was Jack O'Donnell's kind of bar.

I walked past several booths that contained paper menus stuck under dirty glass. The walls were lined with flickering neon beer signs, the owners apparently making a statement (that statement being "we don't pay our electric bill").

I found Jack O'Donnell in the very back of the bar, sitting alone in a dimly-lit booth. He was sipping a brown liquid which, by the fill line, had been an inch higher before I arrived.

"Having a midday nip?" I asked.

"It's eleven in the morning. Either you don't get much sleep or you have no concept of what midday means."

"Actually I was just trying to make a bad joke."

"Bad jokes don't get funny just because you admit they're bad." Jack took another sip. A waitress came by, her hair done up in one of those fishing nets that all the classy ladies were wearing. She was also chewing gum. I could have sworn chewing gum while serving food had been outlawed alongside smoking and trans fat, but I stayed silent.

"Can I getcha?"

"Coors," I said.

"Bottle or draft?"

I looked at Jack's drink. Noticed an unidentifiable speck on the rim.

"Definitely a bottle." She smacked her gum and left.

"Probably the safe choice," Jack said.

"I've been known to make a few."

Jack took another long sip. His cheeks were red; I could even sense it under his beard. No doubt he'd had a nip or two before I got to the bar, but I wondered if Jack's drinking calendar had been more busy than usual.

"I have a few leads on the Paradis murders," I said.

Jack said, "I thought you asked me here on a date." I scowled at him. "So what have you come up with, boy wonder?"

The waitress came back with my beer. I felt relieved as she popped the bottle cap in front of me. Somehow I wouldn't put it past this place to refill empty bottles from the tap.

"It was confirmed that Athena Paradis and Joe Mauser were killed by the same caliber bullet. And it's only a matter of time before the cops release a statement confirming the same bullet and weapon was used to kill Jeffrey Lourdes."

Jack mimicked jerking off, yawning while he did so. Nobody ever said he wasn't a classy guy. "That's been running all morning, first or second lead in every major newspaper. It won't make Wallace bat an eye. What else you got, Nancy Drew?"

"You're an asshole, you know?"

"I know. So spill it."

"The actual bullet used was a magnum .44-40. Very uncommon usage due to its high recoil and over-the-top stopping power."

"That's true. Cops don't need to go around blowing suspects in half," Jack said.

"Exactly. So it seemed odd to me that a murderer who obviously went to great lengths to take down Athena and Mayor Perez, not to mention Jeffrey Lourdes, in such a public manner would use such an unusual bullet to do the job."

"You're thinking…"

"The killer chose the caliber of the bullets on purpose."

"Keep talking."

I smiled, took a gulp of my beer. Jack was interested. His shoulders were hunched forward. He hadn't touched his drink in several minutes.

"Figure if he's using a rifle, he's also gotta be carrying around something to transport it in," I said. "Suitcase, knapsack. And he's likely staying near transportation, a subway stop or bus terminal."

"You're not the only one who's thought of that. Rather than have cops sit in the subway and wait for guys in turbans carrying ticking packages to walk by, the NYPD has started searching of bags over a certain length and width that are brought into the subway. They're searching hotels within walking distance of the stops as well," Jack replied.

"That's a start, but we can't just follow the cops and report on Carruthers's statements. I want to go ahead and follow up on the gun. Amanda was able to hook me up with one of her old professors who's a hair away from certifiable. I gave her a description of the bullet and rifle, and we think the killer is using an 1873 Winchester. Like you said, the Winchester 1873 model is known as 'The Gun that Won the West.' It was by far the most popular model of that era, was used by every famous lawman and lawbreaker whose ass got sore from horseback riding."

"This sounds awful thin," Jack said. My heart sank. "But it also sounds awfully intriguing. And nobody's covered this angle yet?"

"Not that I know of. But take that gun and the quote from Billy the Kid, and I'd say this killer has a serious obsession with the old west. Somehow Athena Paradis, Mayor Perez and Jeffrey Lourdes are connected in this guy's mind. The other day you talked about Billy the Kid being some sort of Robin Hood." I stopped, looked at Jack. "What if this guy really thinks he was right in killing those people? You know Wallace won't let me run with the story as is."

"Not with your primary source being a college history professor, he won't. Even with the gun and ballistics it's too tenuous."

"Were you able to get those papers?" I asked.

Jack reached into his briefcase, pulled out a leather folder. From the folder he retrieved several pages of printouts.

"Every museum in the fifty that has a registered Winchester '73," he said.

"Oh man, this is beautiful. Thanks a ton."

"Don't sweat it."

"Can't imagine Wallace will green-light any expenses for this either."

"Doubtful. That assistant who witnessed Lourdes's murder," Jack said.

The Guilty

"Betty Grable."

"She had to be transferred to Bellevue. Seeing her boss killed like that, something snapped. Hate to say it, but it's a good thing you got a minute of her time."

"That's terrible," I said.

"Ripples, Henry. Not just the dead are affected by death."

"Guess not."

"That quote," Jack said. "Billy the Kid. You got something, but it's not nearly concrete enough for Wallace to let you print it."

"I'll find more," I said. "But I need time, resources."

Jack looked at me, seemed to be weighing something. Then he took a pen and pad from the briefcase. He opened the pad, scribbled something on it, then ripped off a piece of paper and handed it to me. It was a check for two thousand dollars.

"Jack, I can't possibly…"

"Take it," he said. "This will buy you some resources. And if it leads to anything, I expect to be reimbursed."

"And if it doesn't lead to anything?"

Jack smiled. "Then I expect one hell of a birthday present."

I had nothing to say, but, "Thank you."

"Don't mention it again," Jack said. He finished his drink, set it down. The waitress came over and he nodded for one more. He saw my eyes following his. "Trust me kid, once you get to my age you can't underestimate the importance of a good drink."

"I'll remember that, but I have a few years."

"Yeah, you do, but they go by quick. Wasn't long ago I was meeting my boss for drinks. Now," Jack said. "That girl you're with. Amanda's her name, right?"

"That's right." In the year and a half since I'd known Jack, we'd never discussed Amanda other than platitudes and pleasantries.

"And you two met during the Fredrickson fiasco."

"They say the best relationships are born out of extreme circumstances."

Jack's eyes had a flicker of recognition. "I think I heard that in a movie once."

"Probably."

"How are things going between you two?"

I shrugged my shoulders. "Good, I guess. We're living together. Soon, I know, after everything that happened, but it feels good."

"That's nice," Jack said wistfully. "Another thing you can never underestimate is companionship." Jack, I knew, had been married, and divorced, three times. "So I guess you'd say it's serious."

I laughed. "Yeah, I think so. Besides, if Amanda ever knew I said no to that question I'd wake up the next morning with no teeth."

"Feisty, is she?"

"She'd kick feisty's ass down the block."

"That's good," Jack said, smiling. "You know I look at you across this table, you look at me the same way I used to look at Petey Vincent."

"The name rings a bell," I said.

"Petey Vincent was my idol growing up. Those days, newsmen were the toast of the city. You reported the hot stories, had more groupies than ballplayers, went home to your Park Avenue homes and ate caviar. Nowadays the only way a reporter eats caviar is if an I-banker sends it to them at Christmas. It's a thankless job, so you gotta really love it."

"I do," I said.

"What I'm saying is," Jack continued, "If you want to be a great reporter, you need to keep Amanda this far from you." He held out his arm, as though holding up a wall.

"Why would I want to do that?"

"I'm not going to ask if you love her," Jack said. "Love is easier to find than you think. But nobody remembers great love. People remember great men and women for who they are, not who they love. At some point in every relationship, you have to make a choice as to what your priorities are. At some point this job will demand more of your time than your loved ones are willing to give up. And when that happens, you can either be prepared for it or you get overwhelmed. You'll end up a half-assed reporter and a half-assed husband. And then you'll have nothing."

The waitress came back with a refill of Jack's drink. She noticed that neither of us were speaking. "Getcha another?" she said, nodding at my half-finished beer.

"No thanks." She clicked her gum and walked away.

"I don't think I could ever give her up," I said. Jack sighed, looked down.

The Guilty

"Then you'll make a fine beat journalist. Live with exposed brick and take the subway because you can't afford taxis."

"That's not why I do this job."

"Of course it's not," Jack said. "But in any industry, the money level rises as the talent itself does. The better you are, the more you're needed. And when the money comes, so does love. It might not be the forever kind of love people with shitty mortgages have, it might not last until you die, but it's good enough to make you smile every once in a while. And that's what life is about, in the end. When you stare into the abyss, you want a smile to come back at you. Even if it's just sometimes."

"I have that," I said. I felt a pressure on my chest. I took a sip of beer and swallowed it down.

"You try to make everyone happy, you wind up making nobody happy. Anyway," Jack said, raising his glass. "Here's to the story. Let's find out more about this asshole, and hopefully put an end to it. Keep digging, Henry. Just don't stand too close to the hole."

Chapter 22

I needed to find out who might have gotten hold of an authentic 1873 Winchester, and how. Thankfully Jack had managed to pull together a file of many major gun collectors and museums. It was a haystack, to be sure, but one of these haystacks either sold their needle, or had it stolen. Jack had given me another thread, and now I needed to pull.

I went to the office, turned on my computer and ran a search for "Winchester 1873" and "stolen."

Only 149 hits came back. I searched through every entry, looking for anything that could be a piece of thread. Most of the articles were police and newspaper reports of replica Winchesters stolen from gun shows. No help there. I wasn't looking for a replica. Whoever was using that gun was using the real deal. None of the 149 hits went anywhere that looked promising.

I ran a new search, this time for "Winchester 1873" and "museum." Over four hundred responses came back. I refined my search by adding the words "authentic" and "working." Now we were down to thirty-two hits.

I sifted through each entry, arriving at the estimation of fifteen museums in the United States that listed authentic Winchester 1873 rifles among their collection, along with some sort of reference to the gun being in working condition.

My first call was to the Texas Ranger Hall of Fame and Museum, located in Waco. I got an automated system, press 0 for the operator. A nice woman with a wonderful Southern drawl picked up the phone.

"Ranger Museum, how may I help ya?"

"Hi, do you still have an exhibit featuring the Winchester 1873 rifle?"

"Gun that won the west, we surely do. It's open from nine ayem to six pee-yem. Day passes are a dollar fifty, year-round pass is twelve dollars. That's the better deal, y'ask me."

"How long have you had that rifle?"

"Oh heck, I've been here three years and it's been here long as I have, I'd have to ask for sure though."

"And you've had no other rifles come and go since then?"

"Why no...may I ask your interest?"

"That's okay, I appreciate the help." I hung up.

I called ten more museums. Each one could currently account for their Winchesters, and had seen none go missing in recent memory.

Then I dialed the twelfth number on my contact sheet, the Museum of Outlaws and Lawmen in Fort Sumner, New Mexico.

"MOL Museum, this is Rex speaking."

"Hi, Rex, I'm calling because I read somewhere that you have an authentic, working Winchester 1873 rifle in stock, is that true?"

"It ain't in stock," Rex said, "this is a museum, not a sidewalk sale, son."

"Sorry, but you do have one."

"Why yes sir, we do."

"Just one?"

There was a split second of silence before Rex answered, and I picked up on it.

"Why yes, one's just about all we need."

"Have any rifles come in or left the museum for any reason over the last year?"

"Listen, you care to tell me what all these questions are about?"

"I want just wondering..."

"Our gun is here, it's in great shape, and it looks a lot better in person than it does over the phone."

For a moment I assumed we'd been disconnected, but then I heard the dial tone and knew Rex had hung up on me. My heart began to beat faster. But I had to confirm it.

I dialed the number again. The same man picked up.

"Hi, I just called about your Winchester 1873 model rifle, and—"

"Hey, either come to the museum like all normal folks or stop calling."

Once again I was greeted by a dial tone. I stared at the phone for a moment. This museum clearly didn't like my line of questioning.

Then I recalled that the museum was in New Mexico. The heart of the old west.

I picked up the receiver and dialed again. This time a different number. It picked up on the first ring.

"Hey Henry," Amanda said. "Missed me much?"

"I have to go to New Mexico," I said. "And I need to leave tonight."

There was silence on the other end.

"Does that mean I shouldn't wait for you for dinner?"

"If you don't mind waiting until tomorrow to eat."

"As if I don't have enough trouble getting out of bed in the morning," she said. "So you found something out there? New Mexico?"

"Yeah, something to do with the murders, I know it."

"Something about the gun?"

"Yeah, I think I have a lead at a museum."

"Then go. Do whatever you can to find this guy," she said. "I'll be here when you get back. Dinner might be a bit cold, though. I'll just rename it Vichyssoise and call it a gourmet meal."

I laughed. "No way, when I get back you're getting the finest grilled cheese in North America."

"I'll keep a bowl of Kix nearby just in case."

"Thanks babe, I'll call you when I leave."

Then I hung up and booked my flight.

Chapter 23

I cashed Jack's check at a my local Chase branch, then took a cab home and threw a pile of clothes into a duffel bag, hoping I'd buck the odds and end up with a matching outfit or two. I took the Xeroxes from Agnes Trimble's book, packed them in a valise.

As I zipped up the duffel, I stared at the bed. Neither Amanda nor I had bothered to make it that morning. I could still make out the ruffled sheets where we'd lay the night before. I could recreate it; where Amanda's arm lain across my chest, where her legs curled around mine. My hand gently stroking her leg, the way she smiled and kissed my cheek.

I had to leave before I thought about it any more, because the more I did the more Jack's words resonated.

I made sure my phone was charged and I had a clean notebook and tape recorder. The bills made my wallet fat.

I thought about the last time I traveled across the country, several men wanting me dead and Amanda unaware of the lie I'd fed her. And she shared my bed. I still had to prove myself to her, and to do so I had to put her life before mine.

And yet for the first time since we started seeing each other, despite how much I loved her, I thought about my conversation with Jack and wondered if Amanda deserved better.

Another cab sped me to the Continental terminal at LaGuardia Airport. I ran to the reservations desk and made the seven-thirty nonstop flight to Albuquerque, New Mexico. I paid the five-hundred-and-sixty-dollar round-trip ticket with a handful of cash, drawing a slightly raised eyebrow from the woman at the ticket counter.

"How long is the flight?"

"Four hours and thirty five minutes," she replied, eyes down as she counted out the numerous crisp twenties.

"And what's the time difference in Albuquerque?"

"New Mexico is on Mountain Standard Time. Two hours earlier than New York."

"Is there an in-flight movie?"

"Let me check…that would be Shrek 2."

"Couldn't get Shrek 3?"

She did not find me funny.

My flight was scheduled to land at midnight, or ten New Mexico time. On arrival, I still had to rent a car and drive down to Fort Sumner, which was about a hundred and sixty miles southeast of Albuquerque. Barring any major driving mishaps or being kidnapped by a herd of mountain lions, I'd make the drive in two, two and a half hours, putting me in Fort Sumner at about twelve-thirty. The museum would be long closed, so I'd have to find a friendly bed-and-breakfast. All of this, of course, while having no clue about local customs or directions. You had to love seat-of-your-pants journalism.

I grabbed my boarding pass, bought copies of the Gazette and the Dispatch and headed towards the gate. There I sucked down a cup of coffee and a cheese danish, and waited. There were barely twenty people waiting for the flight, reading newspapers and paperbacks and counting the minutes until departure.

The plane boarded a mere twenty minutes late, and I was lucky enough to get a whole row to myself. I took the window seat, raised the armrests and spread my legs. I put the newspapers on the seat next to me and yawned, my head resting gently against the window, the fading light making my eyes heavy. The next thing I knew I woke up as the plane was landing.

I ambled drearily off the plane, then pissed off a dozen grumpy passengers when I had to double back and grab my carry-on bag. After a pit stop at a Coffee Beanery, I followed signs to the car rental area and filled out the paperwork for a beige 2001 Chevy Impala. I paid in cash, hemmed and hawed about insurance and finally caved in. With any luck Jack would get reimbursed. I took half a dozen maps of every conceivable location and asked the clerk to highlight the best routes for me to drive to Fort Sumner.

"Lot of history there," he said. "You going for business or pleasure?"

"Little of both."

"Well, don't spend so much time on business you don't enjoy

112

yourself. If you're an old west buff, you can't do any better than old Fort Sumner."

"That right?"

"Damn right. Buy me a few replicas down there every year, give 'em to the nephews to plays cowboys and Indians. Three littlest ones always fight to see who gets to be Jesse James. Funny, everyone always wants to be the bad guy."

"Guess being a good guy isn't as much fun."

"Guess not," he said.

"Is it hard to find a motel down there? Somewhere for a bite?"

"Shoot, not at all. Second most popular attraction Fort Sumner has after old guns is vacancy signs."

I thanked him and took the keys to my Impala. He told me to wait outside for a company shuttle, grabbed it for a silent seven minute ride to the lot.

I stepped outside, remembering to reset my watch. Then I took a deep breath. The Albuquerque airport resembled a mesa as designed by Frank Lloyd Wright—the façade a dark brown, with square geometric shapes and light blue cornering. The skies were clear, the air thick and humid, so I took off my jacket and wrapped it around my waist. Fashion be damned.

Unsurprisingly my Impala was one of several dozen available. I climbed in, put my coffee in the cupholder, adjusted my seat, and began the drive.

I took the I-25 North exit and headed towards downtown Santa Fe. Once I was reasonably sure I wasn't about to drive into a telephone pole or have a pack of wolves chase me, I took out my cell phone headset and called Amanda. Nobody picked up and it went right to voice mail.

"Hey it's me, just wanted to let you know I landed safe. I'm driving a seven-year-old Chevy Impala with thirty-seven thousand miles on it. There's barely anyone else on the road. Actually, I think I might be the only person driving in New Mexico right now. Anyway, I love you, call me when you get this."

The drive was much easier than I expected, the coffee keeping my blood percolating, but the breathtaking scenery was what really kept my eyes open. Despite the set sun, there was just enough light to make out the stunning mesas and even snow-capped peaks miles and miles away. It was a far cry from the city, where I'd become accustomed to metal towers and gridlock. I listened to the absolute silence, just stared into the black horizon and tried to take in a part of the country most people back east barely believed existed.

When I finally arrived in Fort Sumner, I stopped at a Super 8, parked the Impala and stepped inside.

The lobby was filled with framed documents that looked a hundred years old, and a kiosk held a handful of county maps and brochures for various tourist attractions. The night manager wore an actual cowboy hat, and booked my room with a sleepy smile. I studied the documents as I passed, and could immediately tell that not only did Fort Sumner house a great deal of history, it was damn proud of it. I grabbed a handful of brochures, including a pamphlet for the museum of Outlaws and Lawmen. It opened at 9:00 a.m. I wanted to be the first one there.

The rooms were like any typical hotel—brown drapes, floral comforters, paintings of old men fishing and settled lakes reflecting moonlight. My cell phone log had three missed calls; two from the Gazette, one from Amanda.

I set my alarm for 7:30 a.m., remembering the time difference. Figured that would give me enough time to shower and grab a quick bite.

My jeans felt like they were glued to my legs, so I peeled them off, tossed them on top of my shirt. I checked myself out in the mirror, patted my stomach. New York food had been good to me.

I did fifty pushups and thirty crunches and then fell into bed after my right tricep cramped up. I turned off the light and closed my eyes, and then my phone rang. It read Amanda Cell. I answered it.

"Hey."

"Hey yourself. How's the great outdoors?"

"I'm staying in a Super 8. And it does have a roof."

"Okay, how's the great Super 8?"

"Better than a Motel 6."

"Ooh, don't let Motel 6 hear that. So how was the flight?"

"Not too bad, actually left on time, which I don't think has ever happened to me before. I have to be up early tomorrow to get to the museum."

"Early bird gets the homicidal maniac's rifle, huh?"

The Guilty

"I think Socrates said that."

"So, you think there's a lead there?"

"Yeah, I do. You don't hang up on a question unless you've got something to hide."

"Guess they won't be able to hide much when you show up."

"That's the idea."

"Well, I'll let you get to sleep, Henry." I waited a moment to hear if she would say anything else. I wanted to ask it, but almost felt like by doing so I was ringing a bell that couldn't be silenced. But I had to.

"Amanda? Are we okay?"

"Yeah…" she said, hesitantly. "Why would you even ask that?" My stomach clenched.

"Just making sure. G'night babe."

"Sleep well. Go get 'em tomorrow."

"I will. Night babe."

She hung up. I placed the phone on the nightstand and closed my eyes. It was barely five minutes later when the phone beeped again. Just once. I had a text message.

I opened the phone, clicked Text Messages. The message was from Mya. It read: Im Sorry. ForGIve Me.

I stared at the phone for a moment, wondered what she meant by it. Then it hit me, and I smiled.

As my eyes closed, I was glad to know Mya was finally moving on with her life, offering the closure I'd needed for so long.

Chapter 24

I was dressed and ready to go by eight. Into my bag went a tape recorder, pen and notepad, and the copies of the Winchester 1873 Xerox from Agnes Trimble. I bought a muffin and slammed down a cup of coffee in the small motel dining room. My worry about standing out was assuaged, seems jeans and a T-shirt are common just about everywhere. The manager, a short, cherry-cheeked woman named Marjorie, inquired as to the purpose of my visit.

"I'm a history buff," I said.

"Ooh!" she squealed, nearly spilling the pot of coffee. "Then you've definitely come to the right place. Are you going to the Museum

of Outlaws and Lawmen?"

"That's actually my first stop."

"Oh goodness, if you love history, you won't be able to get enough of that place. My husband and I make a trip once a month, and as soon as the kids are old enough we're buying family passes. Jesse James, Annie Oakley, Pat Garrett, John Tunstall, Billy the Kid, gosh it's just enough to get a person excited." She gave me a mischievous grin and leaned closer. "Just don't be stealin' nothing."

I eyed her, confused. "What do you mean?"

"Oh, let's just say things have a way of disappearing around this town. Collectors and vagabonds are absolutely shameless. It's a real pity, how little respect some folks have. If you take a look at John Chisum's military sword in the museum," she said, leaning closer, "it ain't the real thing. Real sword was stolen ten ought years ago. They just tell people it's the real thing to keep up appearances, save money on insurance."

I took out the brochure, looked at the dozens of guns, swords and artifacts in the pictures. "Is that so," I said, not so much a question.

"Places like that keep this town going," she added. "Heck, there wouldn't be any need for this hotel without them. Anyway, enjoy your trip, don't worry 'bout what I said. There's enough real history in that place to send you home happier'n a pig in slop."

I thanked Marjorie, grabbed my recorder and notebook and headed out. The museum was on East Sumner Avenue, less than half a mile from the motel. It was just past eight thirty. All the houses and shops looked like they'd been pulled from old Western movies. Low-hanging awnings, typeface with old-style lettering, bright yellows and reds slapped on warped wooden signs. It was like the town was bending over backwards to retain its precious nostalgia.

The Museum of Outlaws and Lawmen was a one-story building that occupied most of one block. Sitting outside were two pitch-black cannons aimed at each other across the entryway, as though daring visitors to step past. Beside them stood a carriage-style wheel, painted bright yellow. The signage showed an image of a man leaning on a rifle. A rifle which, upon closer inspection, looked pretty darn like a Winchester 1873.

There were no lights on and the windows were barricaded. Not boarded, but barricaded as though the museum was defending itself from an impending attack. And if Marjorie was telling the truth, maybe it needed that line of defense.

I wiggled the front door, which was locked, but nothing that would have prevented anyone with amateur lock-picking skills and ten free minutes from circumventing. I stuck my hands in my pocket and waited.

At ten to nine, a thirty-something man with shoulder-length sandy blond hair, tattered jeans and cowboy boots, walked past the cannons. He nodded at me, took a ring of keys from his pocket and unlocked the front door.

He turned to me and said, "You here for the museum?"

"Yessir," I said.

"You a college boy?"

I smiled. "No sir, a few years out. Just came to visit." He nodded, as though that was a suitable answer.

"Just give me ten minutes to open up." He went inside and I waited.

Twelve minutes later he propped the front door open and waved me inside.

The museum was astonishing. It only consisted of four or five large rooms, but each room was packed to the gills with antique guns, bullets, cannons, actual carriages, bows and arrows, belts, rifles, and every and any other weapon that looked like it might have been used by, or against, John Wayne. The walls were covered with glassed-in documents that were remarkably well-preserved, along with photos of the writers and/or recipients of the correspondence. The air had a musty smell, the floor speckled with sawdust.

The manager took a seat behind a counter, put his feet up and opened a newspaper.

"You need anything," he said to me, "just holler."

Behind the counter hung several replica guns that were available for purchase. Several boxes of dead ammunition lined the shelves. A small sign read 10 shells for $5.

I paid the ten-dollar entrance fee. A few other visitors ambled in after me, also happy to pay and gaze at the history of violence.

I took a slow lap around, surveying the dozens of guns, even running my fingers along the cannons that guarded the entryway into each new room. One room was decorated to resemble an old west blacksmith's shop, complete with anvil and tools, bent metals and horseshoes. Along the walls were rifle parts in various stages of development, like a before-and-after of gun manufacturing.

After sating my curiosity, I made my way around the museum until I found the exhibit featuring the military cavalry sword of John Chisum which Marjorie claimed was a fake.

The sword was mounted in a glass case nearly four feet long. The blade was slightly curved. I examined the security glass, wondered if the sword had actually been stolen. And if so, why it had never been reported.

Behind the sword was a black-and-white photograph featuring a caravan of horses, and a portrait of a man who was presumably John Chisum. A black placard above the sword explained that Chisum was a cattle driver, and one of the first to send a herd into New Mexico. Chisum was a tangential part of the infamous Lincoln County Wars, a feud between businessmen Alexander McSween and John Tunstall and their rivals Lawrence Murphy and James Dolan. During these wars, Chisum had been accosted by a band of outlaws known as the Regulators. The Regulators were notorious cattle thieves, who pilfered from Chisum and other herders, but were deputized after Tunstall's murder. They hunted down the men who killed Tunstall, killing four including a corrupt sheriff named William Brady.

According to a placard on the wall, the Regulators consisted of men named Dick Brewer, Jim French, Frank McNab, John Middleton, Fred Waite, Henry Brown and Henry McCarty.

Next to the name of Henry McCarty, it read: aka William H. Bonney, aka Billy the Kid.

In the very last room of the museum I found what I'd come across the country for: an exhibit featuring the Winchester 1873.

Behind a crystal-clear glass case was mounted a pristine Winchester, along with various posters and propaganda leaflets. I took out the Winchester Xeroxes, compared them. The weapon in front of me looked identical to the one on the page.

Inside the case on a poster, written in big bold letters beneath two opposing firing pistols, were the words: Winchester 1873 edition: The Gun That Won the West.

There were several bullets mounted to the display below the weapon. A placard identified them as authentic .44-40 magnum ammunition, the very kind used by that edition Winchester.

I compared the gun and the Xerox until I was reasonably certain they were one and the same. Then I waited until the museum had quieted and the manager was free of troublesome tourists. He was reading a copy of the Albuquerque Journal, looked bored to death, but he set it on the counter when he saw me approach.

"Help you?" he said.

I pointed at the relics lining the walls..

"This is some pretty amazing stuff," I said, opening a window for him.

"Man, you don't have to tell me that. I get a buzz just sitting behind this desk." The Albuquerque Journal was still splayed open on the counter.

"No doubt," I said absently. I nodded at the display containing Chisum's military sword. "How'd you come upon that beauty?"

"John Chisum," he said without thinking. "One of the most influential cattle drivers in U.S. history. Blazed the Chisum trail from Paris, Texas all the way to the Pecos Valley. You know John Wayne himself played John Chisum in a movie?"

"No messing? Which one?"

"Was called Chisum."

"Guess that makes sense."

"Anyway, when Mr. Chisum passed on, died in Eureka Springs, his great granddaughter endowed this museum with the sword. D'you know Chisum's only children were born to him by a slave girl he owned?"

"I didn' know that."

"At's a true fact."

"Sword like that," I said, "probably worth, what, few grand?" I saw the man's eyes twitch, and he looked down for a split second.

"Try a few hundred grand. The country's swarming with collectors of old western antiques. Course most of em call it memorabilia, like a freaking baseball card. Most of em wouldn't know a Winchester from Worcestershire Sauce, and I never heard of a baseball card used in a gunfight."

"Speaking of antiques," I said. "Is that a real Winchester '73 on the wall?"

The man's chest puffed out with pride.

"You're darn right it is. Gun that won the west, gun that made this country what it is today. Winchester made over seven hundred thousand of those darlins back in the day. Nowadays, a '73 in working condition goes for upwards of six figures on the open market."

"Bet it goes for even more on the closed market," I said. The man winked at me, smirked.

"You'd probably be right there."

"Can't imagine the security you must have in place to keep valuables like that. I mean, there must be a few million dollars' worth of memorabilia here." The man bristled.

"We take the proper precautions," he said.

"Have you ever had a break-in? A robbery?"

The man took a split second too long to say, "Never."

"That Winchester," I said. "How long have you kept that particular Winchester in this museum?"

He took several seconds to say, "I reckon upwards of ten years."

"And you've never been robbed."

Finally he took a step back, eyed me suspiciously. "Mind if I ask what you're asking all these questions fer?"

"I'm sorry," I said. I reached into my bag, pulled out the tape recorder and notepad first, and then my press identification. "Henry Parker. Pleasure to meet you. I'm a reporter with the New York Gazette. And I don't think that Winchester in your case is authentic. In fact, I'm willing to bet the gun that's supposed to be in that case is the same one used in three recent murders in New York this past week."

The blood drained from the man's face, and his jaw dropped just a bit. "Murders, you're sayin? I read something in the papers, that pretty blond girl..."

"Athena Paradis," I said.

"She was killed by a..." he nodded his head towards the Winchester case, "Model '73?"

I said nothing, turned on the tape recorder. "That's a replica Winchester in your case, isn't it? Where's the original?"

"I'd like you to leave right now."

"If your Winchester was stolen, I need to know now. We need to alert the authorities in New York. More lives are in danger. Someone is using your gun and—"

"I don't know anything about that," he said, and picked up the phone. I had seconds before he called the cops and I was done. I looked at the nameplate. It read Rex Sheehan.

"Rex," I said. His eyes met mine. "Even if you call the cops, at the very least they'll want to run tests on the gun. If you tell me now, at least we can try to keep some people alive." Rex put down the phone. He bowed his head and crossed himself.

"I wanted to tell someone," he said solemnly. "But we don't have the money for security. We're not a government-funded museum like that fancy one down at New Mexico State. We get by on donations. And if you look around, I don't need to tell you we're not exactly the Met here."

"So somebody broke in and stole the gun," I said. "Did they steal anything else?"

He shook his head. His lip trembled. I felt sorry for him.

"Please don't tell anyone this," he said. "If people find out we're displaying a fake they'll just stop coming altogether. Besides, it doesn't really matter, does it? If people think it's real, who gets hurt?"

"There are three dead people in New York who can answer that better than me."

Rex bowed his head.

"But it still doesn't add up," I said. "1873 Winchesters are a rare model, but not extinct, right?"

"No, there's a few still out there. Collectors, mostly."

"So why come all the way out to Fort Sumner, New Mexico? Why would someone rob a museum when there had to be easier ways?"

Again Rex said nothing.

"Tell me about the gun," I said. "It's not just a model 1873, is it? There's something else." The man nodded.

"The gun that was stolen," he sobbed, "the one you're saying was used in those murders, well it belonged to William H. Bonney. Most people know him as Billy the Kid."

Chapter 25

Paulina Cole wrote long into the night.

She wrote until the other offices at the Dispatch were dark, until her colleagues had long ago gone home and surrendered to the comfort of a glass of wine and their inviting beds. She sewed together the interview like a trained surgeon, connecting arteries, nerves and capillaries together to create one body of work that would pump blood and live just the way she wanted it to. Read the way she wanted it to.

She could picture Mya Loverne's face, that poor, destroyed face, the shell of a girl whose life's flame had been snuffed out before its time. So many factors had driven Mya to the brink. Thanks to her father's chummy relationship with most gossip columnists, the majority of his philandering never made it to the printed page. That didn't mean it didn't ruin many a dinner conversation, estrange a daughter in the midst of the most difficult time of her life. Now it was time to collect on that debt. Mya had suffered terribly. But through pain she would regain her life. She was the victim. And the culprit was not only her lech of a father, but Henry Parker as well.

Henry had fractured Mya, literally and figuratively. All her troubles since the dissolution of their relationship had applied leverage to that emotional fracture, spreading it until she cracked open fully.

Paulina had dozens of pages scattered about her desk, three empty cups of coffee strewn about. She picked up the pages, plucked a sentence from different ones, felt her collar begin to burn when she read over all the stories about Henry she'd written last year. Henry who came to New York as Jack O'Donnell and Wallace Langston's golden boy. Who was accused of murder and embarrassed the profession she'd devoted her life to. If payback was a bitch, Paulina was its mother.

And just like Henry stuck the flint that burned Mya, this story was the spark that would burn down the New York Gazette. The kindling was there, David Loverne a juicy log, and she was going to blast that place apart.

Fuck Wallace.

The Guilty

Fuck Harvey Hillerman.

Fuck Jack O'Donnell.

Fuck Henry Parker and everything he was.

But for now, she had to keep working. Soon the paper would be printed. Soon enough, she would burn their whole house to the ground.

Just several blocks away, at a desk cracked and worn with age, an old man sat typing. The desk was covered in coffee stains and pencil markings, its owner never bothering to clean them, believing they added personality. The corkboard above his computer was adorned with pictures, awards, plaques, books with his name printed on the spine, and a life dedicated to his craft. It was here that Jack O'Donnell put the finishing touches on his story for the next day's Gazette.

When the story was done, after he'd saved it on his word processor, made sure he'd written enough inches, and combed through to minimize any errors that would drive his editors crazy, Jack O'Donnell sat back in his chair. He pulled a flask of Jack Daniel's from his leather briefcase and took a sip. It was a good story, one that dropped a potential bombshell on the Paradis investigation. No other paper had this. It was a Gazette exclusive.

After fifty years in news, his body still tingled at the thrill of a good story.

Before sending it off, Jack put the final touch on the article. Underneath the byline Jack added: With additional reporting by Henry Parker.

And come morning, the sparks would fly.

Chapter 26

I stared at the weak metal fence which contained three graves resting side-by-side, one of which belonged to the outlaw known as Billy the Kid. The fence was in the middle of a large patch of dirt, surrounded by piles of flowers, photographs, and even bullets. Never had I seen such gestures for such a shoddy excuse for a tomb.

A headstone sat behind the graves, three names engraved on it. The stone looked fairly well-maintained, as opposed to the rest of the mausoleum.

"The headstone's been stolen three times since 1940," Rex said. "At some point they figured it cost more to guard the darn thing than it did to throw up a new headstone. That's why you see here a gate my eight-year-old niece could pry apart."

"Kind of like the security system in your museum," I said, with more than a hint of sarcasm. Inside the cage were three burial mounds, side by side. At the far end of the enclosure was one large headstone engraved with three epitaphs.

"That's Tom O'Folliard and Charlie Bowdre, on the ends," Rex said. "Friends of the Kid. Billy, he's in the middle grave."

A marker sat in front of the graves. It was carved in bronze, about two feet tall, with a triangular top. It read:

THE KID
Born Nov. 23, 1860
Killed July 14, 1881
BANDIT KING
HE DIED AS HE HAD LIVED

Quarters were sprinkled atop the earth. "Tributes," Rex said. On the headstone was chiseled one word, Pals. Above the headstone was a garish yellow sign that read Replica.

And according to dozens of signs, brochures, and tourist bureaus, this was the grave site of Henry McCarty, also known as William

The Guilty

Antrim, also known as William H. Bonney, also known as Billy the Kid.

"This grave site's pretty much the only thing keeping old Fort Sumner alive," Rex said. "State legislature made us put that damn 'replica' sign up there, but once a year or so the cops come out here to arrest some hooligans looking to steal the damn thing. I swear, ain't nothin sacred anymore, they could buy their own sign for a buck ninety-five."

"But it wouldn't have been inside Billy the Kid's grave," I said. "There's a mystique to him. Just like to a murderer, there's a mystique to using his gun."

Rex scratched at his neck. I could tell he'd long ago given in to the lore and myth of this town. I didn't know a whole lot about Billy the Kid, only what movies or books passed down. I knew he was a celebrity in the southwest during the late 1800s, had allegedly killed over twenty people before his twenty-first birthday, and was eventually killed by Pat Garrett, a newly-appointed deputy who used to ride with the Kid. I remembered reading somewhere that other than Count Dracula, no other figure in popular culture had been immortalized so often on page or screen. He was a legend, plain and simple.

"If you used to have Billy the Kid's actual Winchester, the one he used to kill," I said, "why wouldn't you advertise the hell out of it? Why display it as a regular Winchester 1873 when it could be the highlight of your museum?"

"We did, for a while," Rex said. "Then it got stolen, and we didn't want to take the chance. Nobody knows who the hell John Chisum is, but everyone wants a piece of the Kid. Besides, people visit old Fort Sumner to see this grave site. They come to our museum for side trips, before they spend their money on souvenirs and lunch."

"And nobody cared that it suddenly was gone?"

"Anyone who asked, I told 'em some rich collector bought it."

I asked, "How long ago was it stolen?"

Rex stared at the ground.

"You know Billy built this town," Rex said, nodding at the grave site. "That man was a goddamn hero. Most don't look at it like that. But he fought for good."

"I bet the twenty-some-odd people he killed would disagree."

"Any war, man, you have to spill blood to do what's right."

"Said like a true patriot," I said, biting.

"You don't understand."

"Enlighten me."

"When he was young, Billy was hired by an Englishman named John Tunstall. Tunstall was a rancher, in a territorial feud with two men named Lawrence Murphy and James Dolan. John Tunstall aimed to take Billy under his wing, turn a troubled youth into a good man. John Tunstall was murdered by Dolan and Murphy, who'd paid Sheriff Brady to carry out the crime. After that, Billy and his boys united to form a band called the Regulators. The Regulators killed Brady, and because of that, the governor of New Mexico sicked the hounds of hell on Billy and his gang. But somewhere along the line, the Regulators traded places with the devil. The Regulators wanted to kill those who'd done wrong, folks who were contaminating everything that was good."

"There's a man in New York," I said, "using Billy's gun to kill people. There's no doubt in my mind he stole that gun from your museum. A witness said the killer looked young, in his early to midtwenties."

"Just like the Kid," Rex said. Then he cocked his head. "How old are you, Henry?" I looked at him. And didn't answer.

"Someone is looking to carry on Billy's legacy," I said. "You say Billy meant to create order. He wanted to kill those who'd done wrong."

"That's right." Rex thought for a moment. "You reckon this killer of yours is some screwed up kid, wants to play cowboys and Indians?"

"I doubt it. This is some kid who wasn't loved enough by his mommy and daddy," I said. "This guy has a motive. He thinks he's doing good."

We stood there in silence, staring at the grave site of one of the most legendary murderers in history. A man who died at the age of twenty-one, having ended one life for each of his years. And yet over the years the Kid had become a hero. A man worthy of legend. How could a murderer incite such passion? How could a man seemingly deputized by the devil himself be remembered as an angel?

A beeping sound broke the silence. I plucked my cell phone from my pocket, opened it. It was a text message from Jack. It was two sentences. When I read them, my blood ran cold.

There's been another murder. It's David Loverne.

I couldn't speak. Mya's father.

The last time I saw him was at his daughter's side at the hospital, where…

"I called you, Henry."

"I have to go," I said to Rex, shutting the phone. "I need to get home right away. I appreciate the help."

"You gonna be, you know, telling the police about this?"

"Yes I am."

"Figures. Anyway, you'll want to look at Brushy Bill. Dollars to dineros it's something to do with 'ol Brushy."

I nodded at Rex, then half-walked, half-sprinted back to the hotel. I threw everything in my duffel, jumped in the rental car, and headed towards Albuquerque.

The drive seemed to last for days. Visions in my mind reminded me of that night, seeing Mya's father there, holding her hand. Me not being able to apologize because words were useless. Knowing Mya had been hurt, and that I hadn't been there for her.

Athena Paradis, Joe Mauser, Jeffrey Lourdes, and now David Loverne. Somehow Mya's father fit in the killer's demented pattern. But how?

I'd heard rumblings about David Loverne's misdeeds. That his marriage wasn't as rock-solid as the façade he put on in public. Many felt that at some point scandal would hit, and hit hard. It was only a matter of time. I thought of Mya, how she was so damaged, how she'd been reaching out to me and I'd been slapping her hand away. If she ever needed a friend, someone who used to know her better than anyone, now was the time for me to be there for her.

I tried Mya's cell phone. It went right to voice mail. I couldn't leave a message. I had to see her. Then I remembered her text message.

I'm sorry. Forgive me.

I was numb when I arrived at the airport. They charged a hundred bucks to change my flight. I paid it in cash.

I called Amanda and left her a message. Then I called Jack and told him I would get to the office that night. He told me to read the Gazette and the Dispatch before I saw anybody in New York. His voice had both an urgency and sadness to it. My stomach turned over.

On my way to the terminal, I stopped by a news kiosk. I grabbed a bottle of orange juice and went to the newspaper rack. Thankfully they carried both the Dispatch and the Gazette. I paid for the drink and papers and took them to the gate. Sitting down, I took a long gulp of juice and then laid the papers out on my lap.

The Gazette's headline read:

Ballistics Sheds New Light on Murders
Killer Possibly Using "Gun that Won the West"
by Jack O'Donnell
with additional reporting by Henry Parker

Then I looked at the Dispatch. There were two stories competing for dominance. The first headline read:

Athena Paradis's Greek Boy Toy Speaks Out
Tells why murdered heiress was second to none in the bedroom

Then I read the second headline. I didn't hear the juice bottle hit the ground when I dropped it. Or the announcement that my plane was boarding. All I could see was that headline.

"He left me bleeding on the street"
Mya Loverne, David's daughter, comes clean about the relationship that nearly ended her life
by Paulina Cole

The Guilty

Chapter 27

Just months ago, voters looked at congressional candidate David Loverne as a man who held family above all else. A beautiful wife, Cindy. An ambitious daughter, Mya.

But all this is gone after a series of revelations that have shocked New Yorkers and destroyed a family that seemed indestructible.

David Loverne is being accused of perpetuating a long affair with a former aide, Esther Margolis. Ms. Margolis claims she is pregnant with Loverne's child, and that Mr. Loverne paid her sums totaling nearly ten thousand dollars in order to keep quiet and raise the child alone. Mr. Loverne refused comment for this article, but Ms. Margolis said, "I couldn't face looking at my son years from now and lying to him about who his father is."

I read the rest of the article, my heart hammering, hands shaking. Then I came to a line that nearly had me shouting in anger. It read Yet David and Cindy Loverne are not the only ones in that family whose worlds have been shattered.

Mya. Paulina was going to exploit Mya's fragility to sell newspapers. I read on, rage building inside me.

When you first look at Mya Loverne, you see a young woman brimming with possibility. Young, with strong green eyes and a confidence and solidarity that tells you she's taken on everything the world has thrown at her. At first glance you would think the world is this young woman's oyster.

But that isn't the case. In fact, far from it.

In the last eighteen months, Mya Loverne has been attacked. She's had her bones broken by an attempted rapist. And she's been abandoned by the one person who promised to be there for her.

For Mya Loverne, the wine has grown warm, the roses wilted. The one person to whom this misery can be pinned is young Gazette reporter Henry Parker, with whom Mya ended a three-year relationship last summer. The relationship ended in the most disgusting, careless way possible, when Henry dumped Ms. Loverne for another woman. This was prior to Mr. Parker being accused of murder, a charge that were not pursued, despite a nationwide manhunt that left several dead.

"We shared our bed and our lives for almost three years," Mya told me when we met yesterday at a coffee shop near her apartment. "Do you know what it's like to have someone know every intimate detail of your life and then not even return your phone calls?"

The original sin, however, was the night last year when Mya was attacked while on her way home from a party.

"A man pulled me into an alley," Mya told me, the pain from that night still evident in her eyes so many months later. "He wanted to rape me. He told me he was going to hurt me."

In an effort to call for help, Mya pressed the Redial button on her cellular phone. It dialed the last number she'd called. Her boyfriend, Henry Parker.

"I called him while this man was on top of me," Mya said. "And Henry hung up."

Thankfully Mya, ever resourceful, was able to get a shot of pepper spray off, deterring her attacker from committing the heinous crime of rape. It did not, however, prevent him from breaking Mya's jaw in retaliation. Henry Parker, though, did not see Mya until the next day, when after a frantic night of phone calls from Mya's parents they were unable to locate him. The reason they couldn't find Henry?

"He told me," said Mya, "that after he hung up he turned his cell phone off."

We all know how Henry Parker has destroyed the family of his former pursuer Officer Joseph Mauser, deceased, John Fredrickson, deceased, and Linda Fredrickson, widowed. We have seen the careless havoc he has wrought upon the lives of good and decent people like Mya Loverne. And yet he is allowed to cover the news for this city's "esteemed" newspaper, The Gazette.

Well, readers, if this is the kind of human being they have reporting the news, the kind of human being Harvey Hillerman and Wallace Langston claim is qualified to enter your lives every morning, I must say this is a dark day in the history of journalism, and for humanity itself.

The question is, fellow citizens, will you stand for men like Da-

The Guilty

vid Loverne and Henry Parker occupying prestigious roles in our society? If you're like me, the answer is obvious. Rise up, and demand more from our leaders. Demand they be held accountable for their actions. Demand that they not be allowed to harm one more innocent life.

I put the paper down. Noticed the newsprint smudged on my fingers. Didn't bother to wipe it off. My hand trembled as I laid the papers down. In an article about the infidelity of David Loverne, Paulina had stooped to a level lower than I imagined possible.

Mya.

The article had clearly been written and submitted before her father's murder.

I called you, Henry.

And I didn't answer. And now the whole world knows it. And the whole world sees me as a demon. But I'm not. And they won't believe me.

Oh God, Mya, how could you?

I stared out the window, alone in an airport in a strange city, thinking of the girl whose heart I'd broken, the girl whose destiny I had changed for the worse, the girl whose life would never be the same. I sat there and stared at the newspaper and thought of Mya, and thought of Amanda, and wondered if Paulina Cole was right.

Chapter 28

The flight touched down just before five o'clock. I turned on my cell phone while people were still prying their oversized luggage from the overhead bins. There were eleven messages waiting for me. And I didn't have that many friends.

I speed-walked through the terminal listening to the messages. The first was from Amanda. Wanting to know if I'd seen the Dispatch today. Wanting to know if I'd heard from Mya. Wanting to know if I was okay. Her voice was a combination of sorrow because I'd known David Loverne, and anger because of what Mya had done. Ordinarily I'd be thrilled to know a girl was willing to fight for me, but all I could think about was Mya. She didn't ask for this. And now her father was dead.

The second message was from Jack O'Donnell, telling me to expect hellfire and brimstone but not to say a goddamn word to the press until everyone at the Gazette had a chance to sort through the wreckage. He told me to call him as soon as I got the message.

The next two were from Wallace Langston. Asking me to call him as soon as I got his message. Telling me it was urgent beyond belief.

The third was from a reporter from the New York Times. The fourth was from a reporter for the Associated Press. The fifth through tenth messages were also from reporters asking for a quote on today's story in the Dispatch as well as my thoughts on the death of David Loverne. I knew nothing yet about the circumstances surrounding Loverne's death.

The last message was a hang up, but I heard a soft whisper say "Henry" before the line went dead. I didn't need to check the call log to know who it was from.

I checked the newsstand as I ran through the airport, hoping to see something about Loverne's murder, but there was nothing. It happened too late to make the papers. The only ink about the Lovernes at all, in fact, was Paulina's story.

The Guilty

As I waited in the taxi line, I couldn't help but think it was an awful coincidence that Mya's father was killed the day Paulina's story ran. That his dalliances seemed to have flown under the radar for so long, what were the chances of his being murdered on the very day they were made public, put under harsh light? The odds were too long to be a coincidence. Clearly Loverne was killed for a reason. I didn't have to ask anyone. I knew Loverne had been killed by the same sick son of a bitch who'd killed Athena Paradis, Joe Mauser and Jeffrey Lourdes. Another public figure. Another public execution.

I called Amanda first.

"Jesus, Henry," she said, picking up on the first ring. "Where are you?"

"I'm on my way back from the airport, I should be in the city in twenty minutes."

"Are you okay?"

How could I answer that?

"I'm fine," I said.

"You don't sound fine. Talk to me."

"I have to go right to the Gazette. They're going to want to know what the hell is going on."

"Babe, I want to see you, are you sure you're okay?"

"I'm fine," I said, this time my voice barely masking the irritation. "I don't know when I'll be home, but I'll talk to you then. I found a lot in New Mexico. I think I have a line on who the killer is. Or thinks he is."

"Well, I have to work late, but if you need anything please let me know. Hen, I'm so sorry about this. I know how close you were to that family."

It took a moment to gather myself.

"Henry, you there?"

"Yeah…listen, I'll call you when I know more. I might need one of those cyanide pills they give to soldiers in case they're captured."

"Don't say that."

"I'm kidding."

"Call me when you know more. Talk to Jack, I'm sure he can help. I'll see you at home. I love you."

I paused for a moment, letting those words sink in.

"I love you too."

As soon as I hung up I called Jack's private line. There was no answer. I cursed and left a brief message.

"Jack, it's Henry. Listen, I have something you need to hear. I know why the killer is using that gun. Call me as soon as you get this. I'll need your help before I go into the buzz saw."

As my cab veered towards the Grand Central Parkway, the sun began to dip below the clouds turning New York a beautiful dark blue. I could feel sweat dripping down my neck. Putting Loverne's murder aside, I had new information that would be vital to the reporting on this story. I just hoped it would be heard through all the noise.

The fare was thirty-five bucks. I tossed two twenties at the driver and raced into the Gazette office. There were two other days I'd felt this kind of queasy apprehension about going to work. My first day in the office, where I met Wallace and Paulina and nearly offered to polish Jack O'Donnell's shoes. My first day back on the job after running for my life from Joe Mauser and Shelton Barnes. And now today.

I entered the silent lobby, heard my shoes clacking on the marble floor. The security guard nodded hello and went back to reading his newspaper. From his polite demeanor, I guessed he hadn't read Paulina's article.

I swiped my pass and went to the metro floor. The doors opened, and standing right there was metro editor Evelyn Waterstone. Short, cold, mean—I couldn't tell if her reaction to my presence was based on general surliness or was simply her normal countenance.

"Parker," she said.

"Hey Evelyn," I replied.

"Nice reporting on the ballistics story with Jack."

"Thanks," I stammered, trying to remember the last time Evelyn had offered a pleasantry.

"Hope you're still around tomorrow," she added, before walking away.

As I threaded my way towards my desk, I noticed that every reporter, stringer and editor had stopped what they were doing to watch me. I couldn't look them in the eye.

Once again, I was the story.

I barely had time to sit down when Wallace was standing over my desk. His eyes were tinged with red and the red indents on his nose meant he'd stayed at the office overnight without removing his glasses. His hair was askew, tie loosened, like a school kid roughed up by the classroom bully. He pressed his lips together and said, "Come with me."

I felt eyes boring into my back as we walked to the elevator. I didn't have to ask where we were going. Wallace pressed the button, then shoved his hands back into his pockets. Then he looked at me.

"That was good work you did for Jack," he said.

"I think there's much more to these murders than the ballistic report," I said. "I've been in New Mexico, I—"

"Later," Wallace said. The doors opened. "Let's go."

My stomach surged upwards with the motion of the elevator. I wondered if the feeling in my gut was what prisoners felt like before their execution. We got off on the eighteenth floor. I'd heard about the eighteenth floor, but had never been there. Unless you were nominated for a Pulitzer or about to have the rug pulled out from your career, you never came up here. And I sure as hell wasn't up for a Pulitzer.

The digital counter stopped at 18. The doors opened.

Everything looked newer up here; the wood paneling looked dark and freshly polished, the newspapers in the waiting area were all folded, and even the receptionist looked like she spent a little more time at the gym than those on the metro floor. She guarded a narrow hallway with one set of double doors at the end. The office of Harvey Hillerman, Chairman and CEO of the New York Gazette.

Wallace nodded at the receptionist.

"You can go right in," she said.

"Thanks Gloria." Gloria went back to typing.

The doors swung open as we approached. Harvey Hillerman, chairman and CEO of the New York Gazette was standing in front of us, holding the door open, an unlit cigar in his mouth. The end was sopping wet and looked like a gangrenous limb that could detach at any moment.

His sleeves were a little too long for his wrists. His jacket seemed to billow out. On the wall was a framed portrait of Hillerman standing next to Bill Clinton, Hillerman's pants just a bit too baggy, as if the clothes he wore belonged to a larger man.

Harvey Hillerman's office was startlingly clear of any sort of clutter. Lining his walls were several dozen framed page ones from various Gazette editions. I scanned the headlines while Harvey and

Wallace exchanged awkward pleasantries.

April 4, 1996. Theodore Kaczynski, aka The Unabomber, is arrested at his remote cabin in Montana after his brother, David, notifies authorities.

February 5, 1997. O.J. Simpson is found liable in civil court for the wrongful deaths of Nicole Brown Simpson and Ronald Goldman and ordered to pay $33,500,000 in damages.

August 18, 1998. During Grand Jury testimony, President Bill Clinton admits to an "inappropriate" relationship with former White House intern Monica Lewinsky.

July 17, 1999. John F. Kennedy, Jr. and his wife are killed after the plane Kennedy was flying crashes into the Atlantic Ocean.

December 14th, 2000. Democratic Presidential nominee Al Gore concedes the presidential election to George W. Bush, over a month after election day.

September 12, 2001. The day after terrorists killed nearly three thousand Americans.

March 3, 2002. The launch of Operation Anaconda, the first large scale battle during the United States' war in Afghanistan since the Battle of Tora Bora in December, 2001.

March 13, 2003. Elizabeth Smart is found alive nine months after being kidnapped by two Morman fundamentalists.

December 14th, 2003. United States military forces capture Saddam Hussein.

December 27, 2004. An earthquake measuring between 9.1-9.3 on the Richter scale occurs in the Indian Ocean, triggering massive tsunamis over South and Southeast Asia killing over 180,000 people.

"Murder, calamity and scandal," Hillerman said. "They're usually the first things people look at." My eyes leapt from the frames to the chairman.

Harvey Hillerman was a tall man, gray neatly-coiffed hair, with round tortoiseshell eyeglasses and a Montblanc sticking out of his shirt pocket. His desk was covered with shiny things: trophies, awards, metallic pens and things encased in glass.

He motioned to the framed editions. "Each of those represents the best-selling newspaper of that calendar year." He gazed at them for a moment, reflective, then motioned to the oversize chairs positioned at forty-five degree angles in front of his desk. "Wally, Henry, please sit," he said. We both did so.

"Sir," I said, "before you say anything can I just say things didn't happen the way the Dispatch said they did. Paulina, she—"

"That's enough Parker," Hillerman said, depositing the unlit cigar into an empty silver ashtray. "Mind if I ask where you've been the last few days?"

"New Mexico, sir."

"New Mexico!" Hillerman exclaimed. "What in the bloody hell were you doing in New Mexico, vacationing?"

"No sir," I said. "I was following the lead Jack and I touched on in today's paper. The gun angle. It goes deeper—"

"Did you know about this trip to New Mexico?" Hillerman asked Wallace.

"O'Donnell made me aware of it last night," he said, looking at his shoes.

Hillerman squinted his eyes as he stared at me. I didn't know whether to stare back or let the visual beatdown continue.

"So Parker," Hillerman finally said. His voice wasn't reprimanding, it was…interested. "Tell us what you found in New Mexico."

I did a double take.

"Sir?"

"You went there for a reason, I'm hoping you didn't come up empty-handed."

"Well," I said, clearing my throat. "I was able to identify the murder weapon as a Winchester rifle, model 1873. That model is an extremely rare weapon, considering Winchester discontinued the gun a hundred years ago. There are barely a few dozen still in working condition."

Hillerman's eyes widened, but he kept chewing the cigar.

"I figured the gun had to have been stolen from either a private collection or a museum. Had a gun with that value been stolen from a collector, they would have filed the requisite insurance claims. There are less than twenty museums in North America with records of a Winchester 1873. Every museum still had the Winchester in their possession, except for one."

"Let me guess. It was in New Mexico," Hillerman said.

"That's right."

"And did you find this museum?"

"Yes sir, I did. The Museum of Outlaws and Lawmen in Fort Sumner."

"And?" Hillerman said.

"After getting railroaded at first by the manager, he eventually confessed that the model they were currently displaying was a replica, that the real one had been stolen several years back. They couldn't afford the insurance or security measures and couldn't risk losing tourist dollars by simply closing the exhibit."

"So the weapon this man has been using was stolen from a New Mexico museum and then brought to New York where it's killed four people," Hillerman said. "That's an awful long schlep, just to use a certain gun."

"Not for this killer. He stole that gun for a reason," I said.

"And why is that?"

"Because the gun he stole used to belong to Billy the Kid."

Hillerman sat back in his chair. The cigar was still hanging from his mouth, but Hillerman seemed to have forgotten about it.

"What you're saying it, this killer is using Billy the Kid's old gun—as in the Billy the Kid—shoot-em-up Billy the Kid—to kill people in New York City."

"Not just random people. He's got a motive, a pattern. The killer has some sort of connection to either the gun itself or the Kid."

Hillerman cocked his head and looked at Wallace. The editor-in-chief hadn't said a word in minutes. Wallace was between a rock and a hard place; attempting to keep control of his paper while having to account for his reporter being eviscerated in articles by their biggest competitor.

"Wallace," Hillerman said. "What do you think?"

Wallace seemed to come to life. "We've already gotten three calls from Louis Carruthers's office about Jack's ballistics article. Apparently they knew about the similarities and were hoping to withhold information until further notice."

"But you're saying Henry beat them to the punch."

"That's right."

"And this new information, the possible link between the killer and the Kid, what have you heard on that?"

"Complete silence from the NYPD," Wallace said. "And they haven't been silent about anything."

"Which likely means they weren't aware of it," Hillerman added.

"That's right."

Hillerman again leaned back in his chair, picked up the stogie and shoved it into his mouth. He gnawed on the end of it, then took it out and threw the soggy mess into a trash can.

"Here's what we do." His voice was angry, passionate. My heart was beating faster, my resolve growing stronger. "We report the living hell out of this story. Henry," he said, "I want you to chase this down like a goddamn shark smelling blood. I want you to get Lou Carruthers's office on the line and get the NYPD's cooperation. Since you seem to have scooped them on this, they'll give you a big wet one in return for the intel. I want copy for tomorrow's national edition about both the stolen Winchester and link to Billy the Kid. Just imply there might be a relationship, I don't want anyone jumping to conclusions, but we need your museum manager to go on the record. You got me?"

"Absolutely," I said.

"Right. Parker, get yourself home and clean up. You look like you just got mugged in the Gobi desert or something. Hell of a fucking job, Henry."

"What about Paulina Cole's story?" I asked.

"Fuck Cole," Hillerman said. "Good, honest, unbiased reporting beats out tabloid bullshit any day of the week. You give our readers something new about this case the Dispatch doesn't have, Paulina can pen hatchet jobs until her cooch defrosts, we'll sell more newspapers. Now get to work."

Wallace and I were out the door before he could fish out another cigar.

Chapter 29

I got out of the subway and walked towards my apartment. The last hour had been a whirlwind of debriefing, notes jotted down with the penmanship of someone born without opposable thumbs, and the sketches for what I knew would be a terrific and stunning article.

Jack filled me in on David Loverne's murder, which was nearly unbearable to listen to. I had to distance myself, look at the situation objectively, try not to think that the murdered man we were discussing had once hugged me, shook my hand, even told me he expected great things from me. Had things turned out differently, the man might have been my father-in-law.

I tried not to think about how it would leave Mya without a father.

I tried not to think about Paulina's article, written before Loverne's death. The two had to be related. I was still stunned by the audacity and hatred steaming from Paulina's article, but Wallace assured me that I would face no repercussions from Gazette management, and if need be they would defend me, publicly. I declined. They'd done enough of that already. After the debriefings, Wallace and I met with the Gazette's legal team to draft a response for any reporters looking for a quote.

The letter was brief. It said that Paulina's story was careless and inflammatory, and any more attempts by this allegedly balanced news organization to libel without facts would be met with legal reprimands from the Gazette, and moral reprimands from readers who wouldn't tolerate muckraking. That part was BS. Readers loved muckraking, and as much as it pained us we knew Paulina's article would sell newspapers.

The details of David Loverne's murder were gruesome in both their brutality and efficiency.

After Paulina's story ran in the Dispatch, in which she alleged that Loverne's history of infidelity would soon come to light, the press corps descended on the man's apartment building eager to take photographs of drawn curtains, berate cleaning ladies and doormen, and try to scrape up the scraps Paulina had left under the table. When a person was accused of wrongdoing, people didn't try very hard to photograph their good side.

Around five o'clock, Loverne left to attend a previously scheduled fund-raiser. He was swarmed by dozens of reporters. In what would be viewed as a colossal blunder, Loverne had no private security, and the elderly doorman was easily overmatched. As Loverne attempted to push his way through, a lone rifle shot shattered the commotion, blood splashed against the glass doors, and David Loverne died.

The photographers spent their entire rolls shooting Loverne's body, the blood pouring from his chest, as well as the rooftop where it seemed the shot had come from. Several photographers even tried to bully their way into that very building to either catch the culprit or take photographs of the crime scene before the police arrived. Thankfully that doorman was a former cop, realized what was going on, and locked the doors.

The shooter was long gone. But by the time the police arrived, hundreds of photos of Loverne's body were circulating among newsrooms, tabloids and the Internet.

I called Curt Sheffield to get the lowdown. He told me one of the investigating officers mentioned that another note had been left by the killer, but it was being kept quieter than a mouse fart. He didn't find it amusing when I asked him if he could hold a megaphone to the mouse's ass to hear it better.

"Doesn't matter if I tell you," Curt said. "Guy's as vague as my little sister when I ask her how a date went."

"He didn't leave a note with Jeffrey Lourdes. Now he changes his tune and leaves one with David Loverne. This is my ex's father, man, cough it up."

"Again," Curt said, "you use this before it's made public, I'll string you up to a lamppost. The note was just one line. It read, 'Because I had the power.' That's it."

"'Because I had the power'? That's pretty vague. What's it mean?"

"You're the reporter," Curt replied. "You ask me, this guy's been watching too much David Lynch."

As soon as I hung up with Curt, I did a search for that quote, only adding "William H. Bonney" to the search field.

What came back was most certainly not vague.

In 1878, corrupt sheriff William Brady arrested the Kid under the auspices of helping the Kid arrest John Tunstall's killers. When a reporter asked the lawman why he would arrest Bonney, a seemingly innocent man, Brady replied simply, "Because I had the power."

The connection was no longer a secret. This killer wanted us to know he had a foot in the past. The notes and public executions were garnering more media attention than anything I'd seen since coming to the city. Only not exactly in the way I expected.

The country was captivated by these murders, and the obsession had grown with every murder. Internet sites receiving millions of hits a day were all but praising the murderer. Paradis, many said, was single-handedly responsible for the downfall of popular culture, and, many said, morals and ethics as well. David Loverne had long claimed to uphold traditional family values, only in reality he'd bedded more sexual partners than most adult film stars. Mayor Perez—the intended target—another empty suit full of insincere promises. Jeffrey Lourdes, once a respected visionary, had been reduced to common gossip and smut peddler.

I couldn't believe these attitudes were so prevalent, that murder was being looked at by some as a reasonable means to an end. But they were. Somehow the man destroying lives was actually endearing himself to the public, by eliminating those deemed to be making our society ill. When I read those posts, shook my head at the stories, I knew what the link was. Why the man was killing who he did.

He was an avenger. A Regulator. Killing those who needed to be killed for the greater good.

Could there really be such a large portion of the population convinced that these murders were a good thing? Was it just cynical ghouls who would never know what it was like to lose a daughter, a father, a husband? That the person committing these crimes was not someone to erect a statue for, but rather a gallows?

I thought about Rex. Something was still troubling me about our conversation, but in my rush to return to New York I hadn't been able to follow up. Before I left, he mentioned a name. Brushy Bill. It sounded familiar for some reason, and I made a mental note to follow up with Rex later on. I had a full night ahead of me. I wondered when Amanda would be home. I missed talking to her, and hoped to God that everything Jack told me the other day could be chalked up to the ramblings of an old, lonely man. That just because he was going to die alone didn't mean I would. Amanda had saved my life; was my life. And I wouldn't give that up without one hell of a fight.

But then I rounded the corner to my apartment and saw the one thing I never expected to see. I stopped on a dime. Couldn't move. I didn't know what to do or what to say. Whether to go forward and confront it, or to turn and run. The anger inside me rose up, threatened to consume everything, but her tears, the misery etched on her face, they drowned it all out.

So when I saw Mya Loverne standing alone in front of my building, wearing an old sweatshirt, her eyes bleary and red from crying, I didn't know whether to scream at her, or to gather her in my arms and tell her everything would be all right. Like I should have done the night she got hurt. Like I hadn't done for her since.

"Henry," she sobbed, taking a tentative step towards me. I couldn't move. All I could do was stare at the woman who'd shared my bed so many nights, whose hand I'd held and caressed, who just the other day had thrown me under a bus driven by Paulina Cole. A girl who had just lost her father to a heartless monster. I didn't know what to say to this girl. But then I found myself taking a step forward.

"Henry," she said again, the sobs now wracking her small body. Mya looked like she'd lost at least twenty pounds since I'd last seen her, and she was a slim girl to begin with. She looked malnourished, pale, like she had given up on herself. "Henry I didn't mean to. I didn't mean to say all those things, they just happened. Henry I'm so sorry, please, my father, I don't know what to do."

My heart broke as I watched this, this shell of my former love. I took another step towards her, and she did the same. "My dad," she cried, her voice interrupted by staccato sobs, "my dad was killed. Oh God, Henry, please say something."

I took another step. I could feel her breath, caught the faint whiff of perfume sprayed on long ago and never washed off. Her hair was a ragged mess, her eyes streaked and bloodshot.

"Mya, I'm so sorry for your father…I…he was a good person."

"I know he was good," she shouted. "So why did he have to

die?" She came towards me, didn't hesitate, and suddenly Mya was leaning against my chest. Not in an embrace, but for support. There was no strength in her. If I moved she would collapse.

But I didn't move. I couldn't.

"Mya I'm going to find this guy. I promise. I'm sorry for everything I've done, everything I did."

She looked up at me. Her eyes blinked twice. She sniffed.

"You told me you would always be there for me," she said. My stomach burned as I drew in a breath. Then her eyes opened, I saw a fire in them, as she pounded her fists against my chest and screamed, "Where were you, Henry? Where were you when I lost everything? When my fucking father died? Where have you been?"

She brought her fists down on my chest, punching me with no force behind the blows. Then I took her arms and held them.

"I'm going to help you," I said. "I'm going to help you get your life back together. You've always been one of the strongest people I've ever known, Mya. And you can come back. You can do great things."

"I have nobody," Mya cried softly. "I lost you. I lost my father."

"You didn't lose me," I said gently. "You didn't want me. We weren't right together. You don't want me. You haven't for a long time. But I can help you. I will help you."

"I just want to be happy," Mya said. She wiped her eyes. A piece of lint from her sweatshirt caught on her eyelash. I plucked it free. She laughed through her sobs. "You used to make me happy, Henry."

I didn't know how to respond. Mya's arms had freed themselves, and I felt them wrap around my waist. Mya hadn't been this close to me in a long time. Yet there were no sparks. I held her like I would hold a small child. For comfort. For protection.

I wanted to hate her. I wanted to ask why she said those things to Paulina, why she took our private life and made it public, why she threatened to ruin us both. But I also wanted to squeeze all the pain from her body. Because she didn't deserve any of it.

Before I could think I felt Mya's breath on my face; harsh, sweet. She leaned in. I wanted to stop her but I couldn't. Couldn't say no to her right now. I felt her breath, didn't want it like this. But I couldn't break this girl's heart one more time. Her breath touched my lips, I wasn't going to stop her, and then they pressed against mine, hot and needy.

"You've got to be fucking kidding me."

My body went rigid. I pried myself from Mya's grip. Her hands slid off me. She'd heard the voice too. I was afraid to turn around, but I had to.

Amanda was standing on the corner. Watching us. A bag of groceries lay at her feet. Where she'd dropped them.

"No. No, no, no no no. You have got to be fucking joking," she said. She left the groceries and started towards us with a frightening urgency. I tried to open my mouth but nothing came out.

"Amanda," I said. It's not what it looks like. I can explain. Of course I would say those things. Isn't that what every guy said?

"You goddamn whore," Amanda spat. "You drag him through your filth and then you come to our house to spread it around? Get the fuck out of here, you disgusting tramp." Mya took a step towards Amanda, like she might do or say something, but then she turned and ran away. I turned back to Amanda.

"Wait," I said.

"So was she wearing perfume?" Amanda asked, her eyes wild, searching for some crazy answer. "Tell me she drugged you, that she had a gun, that she's the lunatic who's killing all those people and offered to sleep with you for the scoop. Tell me something other than you were just standing here playing tonsil hockey with the girl who dragged your name through the mud. Tell me there's more to it."

"Her father was killed," I said. "I didn't know what to do."

"No, you knew what to do. You decided to be hero Henry fucking Parker and swoop in for the rescue. Is that your M.O. now? You find these damaged girls and pretend to be their savior until the next basket case comes along? Is that what you did with me? You were tired of Mya so when I happened by you figured you'd take my broken ass for a spin?"

"It's not like that and you know it. I love you, Amanda."

"Then why were you kissing another fucking girl?" she shouted.

"I didn't...I...she held me," I said, realizing how lame it sounded as soon as the words came out of my mouth.

Amanda looked back at the groceries. "There's your dinner," she said. "Cook it yourself. Burn the apartment down. I'm going to stay at the office tonight." She turned and started to walk away.

"Amanda," I said, following her. My head was spinning, my heart felt like it was about to burst. This couldn't be happening.

"If you follow me I'll call the cops and tell them Mya's girl-friend-beating ex is coming after me." I stopped in my tracks, blinking rapidly. "Try me," she said, "I swear I'll do it."

Then her hand was in the air. A cab chugged up to the curb. I could feel the eyes of a dozen strangers watching the scene unfold. I watched as Amanda got into a cab, fleeing in a cloud of exhaust, leaving me alone on the street with a bag full of groceries.

Chapter 30

I stood on the street corner. My feet tapped involuntarily. My brain was running on about four gallons of caffeine, half of which probably hadn't even entered my bloodstream and would cause my eyes to pop out of their sockets any minute now.

I didn't sleep last night. I watched Amanda's cab drive off, picked up the discarded groceries, put them away neatly. I called Amanda. She told me not to call again. I didn't. Instead I took a cab to her office, saw the light on, and stood outside all night just to make sure she was safe. She didn't need to know I was there. But I did.

The next morning I decided to visit Agnes Trimble.

It was 8:45 a.m. I'd already plowed through the Gazette and the Dispatch. A reporter had written an article about the growing public sentiment that the killer might have done a public service by killing four people. Tomorrow more ghouls would come out of the woodwork and celebrate this murderer, and soon it would cross over from print to radio to television. Four lives were being trivialized, and a killer was being glorified. Undoubtedly reporters would eat each other to get the first scoop, pay loads of money to interview this beast. Pretend to be appalled by the killer's deeds while cashing the checks he helped rake in.

I waited outside the department building for Agnes. She got off the bus, then dropped her keys when she saw me. I guess if I saw a guy with messy hair, dark circles under his eyes and a heroin addict's jitters waiting in front of my office I'd be a little unnerved too.

"Professor Trimble," I said, trying to slow down my convulsions. "Do you have a minute?"

"Mr. Parker," she said, picking up her keys and smoothing out her clothes. "My taking your appointment with Amanda did not give you a free invitation to show up uninvited before I've had my morning scone."

"I understand that and I apologize for my abruptness and for interrupting your, uh, scone eating. But I need your help."

She sighed. "I should charge you a convenience fee." Then noticed I'd come alone. "Miss Davies isn't with you today?"

"No, just me," I said, eager to avoid any more discussions of Amanda. Agnes didn't need to know that the only way I could stop myself from thinking about Amanda was following this story.

Agnes entered the building, led me to her office. She unlocked the door and flipped the light switch, the lava lamp glowing a festive red and green and casting a Christmas-y glow over her replica firearms. "Did you have any luck with the information on the Winchester?" she asked.

"You have no idea," I said. I told her about New Mexico, about the stolen Winchester, and the connection to Billy the Kid. When I finished Agnes sat back and twiddled her lip with her thumbs.

"William H. Bonney," she said, "is one of the most misunderstood figures not only to come from the lawlessness of the Old West, but in all of history."

"How so?"

"For the most part, Billy the Kid had been portrayed as one of the most brutal men to ever raise a rifle. It's true Bonney killed over twenty men and almost single-handedly changed this country to the United States of Anarchy. But..." she trailed off.

"But what?"

"But as you may not know, Bonney wasn't always evil. He was a petty thief who actually wanted to do good."

"The Regulators," I said.

"That's right. See, Billy was the very first inspiration for tabloid journalism."

"Yellow journalism," I said, remembering my conversation with Jack.

"That's right. And let me tell you, some of the crock those papers put out would put the Weekly World News to shame. Every inch Billy took, they credited him with a yard. It's true that he was one of the most deadly men to ever hold a Winchester, but it wasn't until his killer, Pat Garrett, published a book about the whole ordeal that the legend took off. Fact is, Bonney was only confirmed to have killed nine men. The others were killed in larger gunfights. Most were likely killed by other members of the Regulators, but guess who got credit. Most of his closest friends thought the Kid was pretty easygoing, even funny, but dimestore novelists knew funny didn't sell a villain. Dangerous, cold-blooded and hair-triggered did."

"You look at the legend of Billy the Kid now," she continued, "almost a hundred and thirty years after his death, and the man has become a folk hero. Did you know that Count Dracula is the only figure in popular culture to have been immortalized in more books and films than Bill the Kid?"

I shook my head. "Does the name Brushy Bill mean anything to you?"

Agnes eyed me suspiciously. "Where did you hear that?"

"In Fort Sumner. A museum curator mentioned it."

"Never mind Brushy Bill Roberts. That's one myth grown from diseased roots."

"If it's all the same, Professor Trimble, I'd like the opportunity to check every tree and then decide if I'm barking up the wrong one."

She sighed. "It really is just a waste of time."

"Tell that to the four dead people."

Agnes sighed. "If you insist. Brushy Bill Roberts," she continued, "was a charlatan in the 1950s who claimed to be Billy the Kid."

"Wasn't the Kid shot and killed in 1881?"

"Yes," Agnes said. "But like Elvis, Tupac Shakur and the Loch Ness monster, some people simply love conspiracy theories and won't give them a rest despite all the evidence proving their insane delusions are complete bunk."

"I love bunk," I said. "Explain the bunk."

"In 1949, a probate officer investigated the claim of a man named Joe Hines. While interviewing him, the officer learned that Hines had been involved in the Lincoln County wars. Hines claimed to have known Billy the Kid. He said Pat Garrett never shot the Kid, and that Bonney was actually alive and well and living in Hamilton, Texas under the name of Ollie P. 'Brushy Bill' Roberts. Out of curiosity, the officer went down to Hamilton and found Roberts. After being confronted with the witness, Roberts confessed to being the Kid. Roberts then fought to reclaim his 'lost' identity, saying he wished to die with the pardon Texas Governor Lew Wallace had reneged upon over eighty years ago."

Agnes stopped.

"And?" I said.

"And Brushy Bill Roberts was quickly discredited and died the next year. End of story."

"Wow," I said. "That's a pretty abrupt ending."

"I don't deal in charlatans, Mr. Parker. They're not a legitimate part of history and aren't worth wasting my time or yours with. Brushy Bill is worth no more consideration than the boogeyman or Freddy Krueger. Now will there be anything else Mr. Parker? I haven't even touched my scone yet."

I leaned forward, put on my most soothing voice. Which, considering my girlfriend had just left me on the side of the street, was probably as soothing as sandpaper on dry skin.

"Let's just say," I said, "that I wanted to know more about Brushy Bill for entertainment's sake. You know, so I could win my next game of Trivial Pursuit."

She let out an audible sigh. Her eyes showed tremendous skepticism. Then they softened. She reached into her desk and pulled out a battered leather address book. She flipped through it, paused at a name, then scribbled something on a Post-it note which she then handed to me. Written on the note was the name Professor Largo Vance, retired. A phone number with a 212 area code was written next to it.

"Professor Vance lives in the city," Agnes said. "He was previously professor emeritus at Columbia, but was expelled due to scandal."

"What kind of scandal?" I asked.

"Of the grave-robbing kind."

"Oh. That kind of scandal."

"If you want to chase ghosts and waste time, do yourself a favor and speak to Vance, he's a master of both. And I hope for your sake you're not allergic to cats."

"Not that I know of," I said, standing up. I offered my hand. Agnes took it reluctantly. "Thanks for your help. Hopefully this will all lead to something."

"Piece of advice, Henry. If you go chasing false light, you'll end up in darkness. Don't bother."

I gave a courteous nod and left her office.

I wanted to stop at home and change, then call Professor Vance and meet with him as soon as possible. If there was any more to this story, I wanted to alert Wallace and Jack and hopefully make tomorrow's national edition.

I hailed a cab and headed home, plunging my head into the leather seat rest. I took a deep breath and could feel my body swimming away. The more I pulled on this thread the more spool there seemed to be. There had to be a core, some place where the full story was revealed. There was an emptiness. I was so used to calling Amanda, to actively ignore her was torture. I thought about what Jack said in the bar that day. For one terrifying moment, I wondered if what happened yesterday was fated to happen at some point. If people like Jack and I were meant to be alone. If loneliness would inevitably hunt us down.

I was still thinking about this when I paid the cab driver and trudged upstairs. I unlocked the door, flicked on the light switch, half hoping (and possibly expecting) to see Amanda waiting for me. I checked my phone again just in case. I hadn't missed anything. The emptiness was overwhelming.

I tossed my bag down and went into the kitchen. My stomach growled for food. I poured a drink of cranberry juice and seltzer, set the glass down on the counter, and reached into my pocket for Largo Vance's phone number. And that's when I felt a massive blow to the side of my head and everything went black.

Chapter 31

Amanda Davies sat in the high-back leather chair and stared out the window. She wanted to call Henry, desperately wanted to hear his voice if only for a moment. Several times over the last few hours she'd reached for the phone, felt the plastic beneath her fingers, only to retract like she'd touched a poisonous plant.

The office was empty, dark except for a desk lamp and her computer screen. The minutes seemed to stretch into hours. She watched the phone. He'd called once. She waited to see if he would call again. He didn't.

She'd told Henry she was coming here to sleep. She knew sleep wouldn't come easy. Not last night and not tonight. Not after what she saw.

Since joining the Legal Aid Society, Amanda had some witnessed horrible things. Mothers and fathers who beat their children within an inch of their life, starved them. Made seven-year-olds wear diapers for days and weeks on end. Boys and girls who were found caked in their own excrement while their parents were out drinking, stealing or fornicating. And no matter how hard they worked, how many children they rescued, it was like putting a Band-Aid on a busted dam. There wasn't enough manpower, not enough funding. As long as society remained this screwed up, as long as there were hedonistic parents who put themselves over their child, there would always be children without homes. Just like her. Until she met Henry.

She thought about Mya Loverne. Hated the fact that she felt even a whisper of sympathy for the girl. But she did. It was tearing her apart, because she could still see Mya's arms wrapped around Henry's waist, their lips touching, Henry seeming to give in.

He should have ended it months ago. He should have severed all ties with Mya Loverne. But he hadn't, and last night showed why. He wasn't ready to give her up. She'd lost the one person she could turn to, the one who showed her that there were relationships beyond her diaries.

The Guilty

She couldn't take it anymore. She grabbed the phone, nearly spilling a cup of water all over the desk, and dialed Henry's cell phone. She waited as it rang, hoping that any second he would pick up and she would hear his voice, hoping there was more to the story. Henry was not a bad guy, like so many of the douchebags and deadbeats desperate women seemed to flock to. Guys who smelled like skunk residue and wore enough hair gel to paste King Kong to the Empire State Building. Henry wasn't like them. She couldn't picture him cheating on her. Being with another woman. Pressing his lips

(stop it)

Henry's voice mail picked up.

"This is Henry. Leave a message and I'll get back to you as soon as possible."

She bit her lip, then spoke.

"Henry, it's me. We need to talk. Call me when you get this."

For a moment, fear gripped Amanda. What if he was with Mya? Couldn't be. He wasn't like that. He wasn't...

She hung up. Looked out the window again as the sun began to dip below the clouds, casting a golden hue over New York City. In a city of millions, Amanda had never felt so alone.

Jason Pinter

Chapter 32

Wake up, Parker.

I heard a voice in the distance, like a dream beginning to fade into the reality of morning. There was a beeping noise, like an alarm clock. Then just as abruptly it stopped. A gush of water hit me in the face, and the dream was shattered. I spit it out, coughed it out of my nose. My eyes opened. When I realized where I was, I wished I was still dreaming..

I was on the floor. Sitting up against the radiator. My hands were strapped behind my back. I couldn't see what was holding them together. My head throbbed and my neck felt sticky. My legs were numb, the tingling sensation of poor circulation. I had no idea how long I'd been here, but every muscle in my body felt some measure of pain.

The room was dark, a faint amber glow dying on the carpet. The sun was going down. How long had I been out? My heart beat fast, fear and adrenaline spreading quickly, my pulse racing as panic began to set in. Water dripped down my face. It got into my eyes and I tried to blink it away.

Then I heard a sucking sound, looked over and saw a man I'd never seen before sitting at the living room table, smoking a cigarette like he didn't have a care in the world. He was flicking ashes into a neat little pile on the floor. There was an empty glass in front of him, water beading down its sides. I recognized it as a piece Amanda bought from a mail order catalog a few months back. She'd said my glassware looked so worn it was ready to turn back into sand.

The stranger cocked his head and smiled at me, like he'd just noticed I was there.

"You're a heavy sleeper, Parker. I thought I'd have to bring a marching band in here to get those eyes open."

I blinked the spots from my eyes. The man in my living room was young. Mid twenties. His face had no lines from age, but looked slightly weather-beaten, like he'd grown up in the sun and hadn't yet

154

learned the dangers of UV rays. He was wearing jeans and a hooded sweatshirt. A blue bandanna was wrapped around his head. His eyebrows and sideburns were dirty blond, but the bandanna hid his hair's length and style. He wasn't from the city. Nobody got natural tans living here. Immediately I knew this man, like me, had come to New York from far away. He'd come for a reason. He'd killed four people without mercy or remorse. And now he was in my home.

The skin around his face was taut but smooth, like an older man squeezed into a younger man's body. His hands were veiny and strong, his expression one of both deep thought and intense malice, like he'd take a long hard thought before slitting your throat. This was the man who had ended four lives.

Mixed with fear, I felt a strange dose of excitement. The man sitting in my living room presented a fascinating story, one that I'd been dying to uncover. A spool that unraveled here—leaving me beaten and vulnerable, at a murderer's mercy.

He peered at me through a smoky haze as he took another drag and exhaled. I couldn't see any weapons on him, didn't know what he'd hit me with, only that it was heavy and knocked me out with one blow. I had a burning urge to write a very strongly worded letter to the landlord about the shitty security in this apartment building, but there were more pressing issues.

"How did you..." I said. My mouth felt like it was filled with cotton, my words slurred and slow.

"Please," he said. "Your building is easier to get into than my jeans. And it costs a whole lot less too."

He stood up. Moved closer until he was hovering over me. My heart was pounding. I tried futilely to struggle with my bonds. I could smell the stink of sweat. He was breathing hard, but not enough to keep a sick smile from spreading over his face.

"Part of me just wants to kill you right now," he said. "Lord knows you deserve it."

"Like Athena deserved it," I spat. "And Joe Mauser, and Jeffrey Lourdes, and David Loverne."

"Damn straight," he said. "Fact is, you belong right in with the whole lot of 'em. I could fucking kill you right now and nobody would know until some shitty two-line statement in your newspaper told 'em."

I had nothing to say. I tugged against my bonds, felt pain in my shoulder as I pulled and tugged. They were strapped. It was useless. My legs were asleep, and I had no leverage. The boy watched me with odd fascination, like watching a fly struggle to free itself from a web.

Finally I stopped struggling.

"If you wanted to kill me—" I started to say.

"I would have done it right after I knocked your ass out," he finished. "No, I don't aim to kill you just yet, Henry. You've been useful so far, I'm sure you were flattered I left one of your writings behind."

"You're demented."

He eyed me with disappointment. "Killing you is still a possibility, you don't get a lot smarter."

"Smarter?" I said, rather stupidly.

"I've read your paper," he said. "I've read all those stories about the guns and the bullets and the blah blah blah. Fact is your stories don't mean anything. What are you doing, son, other than just repeating shit that's already happened? You're a goddamn stenographer with a fancy business card, my friend, and just because you happened to look under a log nobody else wanted to get dirty enough to look under doesn't make you any less of a maggot than the dirt you find underneath."

"Like you," I said. "The maggot I found underneath."

"Maggot, whatever. All depends on your perspective," he said, dropping his cigarette onto the floor where he stubbed it out with the toe of his sneaker. "Funny thing about maggots is, people hate 'em, but the whole world would go to hell without 'em. Maggots strip dead flesh from bone, make sure the smell doesn't bother your pretty nostrils."

"Billy the Kid," I said, tasting my own blood. "What do you…"

"Shut the fuck up," the boy said. Without warning, he stomped on my leg hard with his boot. I let out a cry of pain. "You don't know anything. You know what you do, Henry Parker? You write about history. Me?" he said with a sharp laugh, "I am history. I decide what makes tomorrow's headlines. Without me you'd have nothing to write about Athena Paradis, her shitty singing, and David Loverne screwing some whore instead of his wife. Without me Jeffrey Lourdes would have nothing to write about except no talent hacks getting high and crashing their cars. Fact is, guys like you need a guy like me to survive in this world. You reap what I sow. Nothing you can do to change that."

The Guilty

"So why are you here?" I said, the words spilling out of my mouth. "You say I can't live without you, but I didn't break into your home and whack you over the head."

He laughed, one time, sharply.

"See my problem is, ungrateful asshole like you doesn't even know I'm doing you a favor. You might not be able to see it past your six-dollar coffee cup, but Athena Paradis, Lourdes, those people are ruining this place. You take the spotlight off of them you find what really matters. You talk about maggots? They're the vermin. Guys like you put a spotlight on the vermin, pretend you can't see how diseased they are. Then they infect you and everyone else. And what do you do? Blame people like me. And since you, Parker, are too chicken-shit to do it yourself, I'm going to do it for you. At some point there won't be no Athenas left. No more maggots to celebrate. And then you'll thank me."

"So why are you here, exactly? You have some grudge against the world? You didn't get laid until you were eighteen 'cause the girls didn't like some freak with a chip on his shoulder?"

He looked at me, as though confused and saddened by my ignorance. "You're even dimmer than I thought. Maybe I would be doing folks a favor 'n get rid of you."

"Then go ahead, get rid of me or get the fuck out of here."

"Trust me, I have something better in mind." His mouth curved into a vicious smile that made my skin crawl. "The real reason I'm here is because there's some history best stayed buried. I've seen you going to talk to all those people. I watched you leave that college professor's office this morning. And you know what I was thinking when you left? When I saw that broad's face watch you from her dirty window? I pictured what her head might look like with a rifle slug going through it at five hundred feet per second."

"A magnum slug," I said. "From your Winchester, you freak."

"That's right," the boy said. He took a step back. "I know about your woman. Amanda, right? Pretty hair, got that cute little birthmark under her neck. I know how she saved your life, Henry. Funny, she keeps your ass out of the ground and all you do is keep bringing 'maggots' like me into her world. What I'm wondering, Henry, is if her skin is that pretty on the inside. Rifles aren't the only things I know how to use pretty well. You don't get any smarter, we're going to find out what her skin looks like when we turn that girl inside out."

"Amanda," I breathed. "You go anywhere near her…"

"I could walk up to her on the street right now and stick a knife into her heart and you'd still be stuck here wriggling like a stupid fucking fish on a hook. If I go anywhere near her you can't do goddamn anything."

The boy's face seemed to unwind, the tautness leaving it. In other light it might have even looked kind.

"Amanda," he repeated. "Amanda Davies. Daughter of Harriet and Lawrence Stein of St. Louis. I got her name from someone at your office, that newspaper you work for that's going down the drain. People there are awful free with information. I know where she works, I know what train she takes to get to her office in the morning so she can save all the little children whose mommies and daddies didn't love them enough. Kind of like you and Amanda, right?"

"That's right, smart guy. So listen, Henry, you and me, we're on the same page, right? You can do all the storytelling you want, hell there must be a million stories out there in this big bad city. I'm asking nicely, stay away from this one. And as a token of my friendship, I'll make it a little easier on you."

The boy stepped around to where I was sitting. I saw something shiny, the glint of metal. He held a knife in his hands. I tried to crane my neck but I couldn't see him as he leaned down and reached towards where my hands were bound.

I started bucking like crazy, but between my head and the bonds my strength was gone. I felt a hand clamp down on my right wrist, holding it to the floor. I jerked my shoulder and tried to free it, gritted my teeth and attempted to pull away.

Suddenly I felt a searing pain on my right hand and a shout escaped my lips as the blade sliced through my skin. I cried out again as the blade kept cutting, tearing through me for what seemed like hours. I felt hot blood dripping through my fingers, I bit my lips to keep from screaming.

Finally the blade stopped. The boy stood back up over me. His hands and the blade were covered in my blood. I thought my heart was going to burst through my chest, the room fading away as blood leaked from my veins.

"Now I'm going to just use your bathroom, clean all this mess up and then I'll be on my way." He stepped away and I heard running water. The pain was unbearable, blood leaving my body with every heartbeat.

Then he came back. Squatted down. Pressed the tip of the knife against my chest, hard enough so I could feel the point digging in between two of my ribs. One small shove and he would pierce my heart.

"You have a lot to lose, Henry. Think about where you're going. Take one bad step," he said, before walking out the door, "and you'll know what bad means."

Chapter 33

I sat still as the nurse sewed my hand back together. After sinking the blade into my flesh, the man had traced every finger, carving a gruesome glove on my palm. He hadn't severed any tendons, and he'd missed or purposefully ignored the major blood vessels in my wrist. He wanted me hurt. Not dead.

Curt Sheffield sat on a stool next to me, watching as the black threads closed the wounds. He winced every time the needle pierced my skin, which was slightly disconcerting since between the novocaine numbing my hand and the extra strength aspirin for my head, I wouldn't have felt it if someone hit me with a two-by-four.

"Glad to know the boys in blue get squeamish at the sight of blood," I said to Curt.

"Blood? Uh-uh. I'm just wincing in sympathy 'cause you're gonna have one ugly-ass hand once those stitches come out." Curt looked at me, shaking his head as if he couldn't believe what he was seeing.

"Least I still have my looks."

"Yeah, right. I'd say you look like hell, but I don't want to hurt hell's feelings."

"Mmph," I replied, as another nurse placed an ice pack on my head and secured it with an Ace bandage.

"You're lucky Amanda came home when she did," Sheffield added. "Docs said if you lost any more blood they might have had to amputate the hand."

"They didn't really say that," I said. "Did they?"

"Nah, just jerking your chain."

"Please, just go away. I bet there are some strangers in the waiting room who'd find you just hilarious."

But Curt was right. Amanda had come home to try and make things right, only to find me passed out on the floor, my hand flayed open, blood everywhere. I couldn't bear to think what it must have felt like for her to see me like that. Because I knew how I would feel if the tables were turned.

"Where is Amanda?" I asked. "Curt, is she here? Excuse me, nurse? Are you sure you can't give me any more novocaine? I think it's wearing off." The look the nurse gave me confirmed that if she gave me any more novocaine I wouldn't feel anything for a long time. She kept on sewing.

"Amanda's waiting outside," Curt said. "Girl's all broken up, crying like she sprung a leak. Docs asked her to wait outside while they finished upholstering you."

"Christ," I muttered. There was a dull throbbing in my head, and my hand was stiff as a plank of wood. I watched as the stitches were sewn in, knowing they would undoubtedly leave one hell of an ugly scar.

"In the meantime," Curt said, "we have a security escort looking after Agnes Trimble. Our guy would have to be crazy or stupid to go after her now."

"He's definitely crazy," I said, "but not stupid. And he's not going to touch her. That was just a threat. He's killing people for a reason, and that doesn't involve spite."

"Nothing more dangerous in this world than a fool with a cause."

Prior to being loaded with painkiller, I'd managed to give a sketch artist the best description I could of my assailant. Of course due to my being knocked silly memory and his bandanna, it could have been any tan young white guy in New York City.

The nurse began laying strips of adhesive tape over the sutures. I watched with detached curiosity, like it was somebody else's hand being sewn up. From the corner of my eye I saw Curt playing with a spool of stitching. He was threading it between his hands and wrapping it around his fingers.

"Those are absorbable stitches," the nurse said to Sheffield.

"What's that mean?"

"They're made from specially prepared beef and sheep intestine."

Curt smiled and gently placed the spool back on the table.

Once the nurse finished taping me up, she said, "Keep it dry and clean for twenty-four hours. You can bathe again in forty eight hours, unless the wounds begin to bleed or you notice a discharge leaking through the adhesive. The tape should fall off on its own in about five days. You need to come back in ten days to have the sutures removed, unless you break a stitch during that time. But try not to. You also have a grade one concussion. You'll have a bad headache for a few days, but nothing that some extra strength Tylenol shouldn't help. If you still feel dizzy or disoriented after a week, or you find you can't remember certain things, come back immediately."

Sheffield looked concerned. "Gonna be awful hard to type with all that junk in your hand. Not to mention your brain floating around in your head." The nurse shot him a look.

"I think that was the idea," I said. "Make my job a little harder."

"I heard they've made some really good advances in voice recognition software," Curt added. "Or maybe you can hire a helper monkey or something."

"I think I'll manage." The nurse gave me a gentle pat on the arm to let me know she was finished. I stood up tentatively. My equilibrium was still off, and I had to lean on Curt for support. "You think this kind of thing ever happened to Woodward?"

"Not unless Bernstein got frisky with a tire iron. Besides, shadowy parking lots are much safer than the gutters you go digging in. But hey, Amanda's waiting for you outside," he said. "I swear, that girl gains Hulk-like strength when she needs it. They practically had to handcuff her to the bench to keep her in the waiting room."

"I don't know if I can see her," I said. "Not like this."

"Shut the hell up," Curt snapped. "You still have your hand 'cause of that girl. That shit happened to me I'd be writing parking tickets with a hook. Get your ass out there. Give her a hug. Let her know her big stupid boyfriend appreciates the fact that in a few weeks he'll be able to cop a feel with both hands."

"I got it, now give me a hand."

I wrapped an arm around Curt's shoulder as led me through the bright white corridors, navigating me around corners and blue-robed doctors until we reached the waiting room.

"I can stand," I said. Curt moved away, then opened the door.

Amanda was sitting in the waiting room, tucked into a beige chair, her feet tapping relentlessly. As soon as she saw me she leapt up, ran over and threw her arms around me. I winched as the blood flowed to my head, but I wrapped my good arm around her and squeezed as hard as I could.

"I'm tired of you being unconscious," she whispered into my ear. I could hear the pain and relief in her voice. I wanted to find the man who'd done this, who made Amanda feel this way.

"I'm okay," I said. "A little banged up. And I might need you to open my soda cans for a few weeks."

"Not a problem," she said. Amanda unwrapped herself and stepped back, wiping her face with her sleeve. Her eyes were red, a clump of tissues falling from her hand. "Let's go home."

I said goodbye to Curt and thanked him for his help. He told me he'd give me a call in a few hours to make sure my brain hadn't started leaking out of my ears. Nothing like a good friend to help cheer you up when you're in pain.

We hailed a cab outside the emergency room of New York/ Columbia Presbyterian hospital. Amanda helped me inside, as I made sure not to grip anything with my maimed appendage. When we pulled up to our apartment, Amanda again held the door and pulled me out of the cab. She paid and all but carried me upstairs.

I fell into the couch as Amanda took off her coat and hung it up. I took deep, slow breaths, closed my eyes, smelled something sweet. There was a mess of dried blood congealed by the radiator along with the twine Amanda had cut from my wrists. She saw what I was looking at and said, "I didn't have time to clean up. I called an ambulance as soon as I found you."

She was standing over me, her face a mess of confusion, fear and relief. "That's the second time you saved me," I said. "Or is it third?"

"I don't care," Amanda said, leaning down. Her hands rested on my thighs, sending waves of electricity up my body. "I'm sorry for leaving the other night. But when I saw you and Mya outside, I—"

"Stop," I said. "You don't have to explain anything." I wanted to stroke her hair with both hands, to hold her face with unscarred palms. "About Mya, it was nothing, it…"

"Stop. I don't want to talk about her. Not now, not ever." I nodded. She was still wearing her work clothes—a smart black skirt, a white blouse under a fitted black vest. I remembered the first time I met her—Amanda sitting in her car, wearing a simple tank top fit to her toned body, the floor of her Toyota strewn with empty fast food wrappers. There weren't many girls like her, who could look stunning both in elegant work clothes and pajamas. Who looked beautiful when they tried, and even more so when they didn't.

I mustered up some strength, leaned forward and gently kissed her on the lips. She was slightly surprised, but after a moment she pressed back hard. I could taste her strawberry lip gloss, felt her hand as it came up to cradle my face. The throbbing in my head and my hand quieted to a dull ache as Amanda straddled my legs, supported her body against my chest and kissed me harder and more passionately than she had in a long time.

Adrenaline began to kick in, and keeping my injured hand to the side I began to slide my good hand along her body. Up her side, across her chest, between her breasts. I felt her heart beating faster, her breath quickening. She ground against me, started to kiss my neck. I brought my right hand up, careful not to flex it too much, but Amanda took it and held it against the sofa.

"This stays here," she said between ragged breaths. She raised her arms and eased off her vest. I eased off her blouse with my good hand, pressed my palm against her bare skin, ran it up towards her bra, then underneath, cupping her warm breasts in my hand. Amanda sighed, reached behind and unhooked the clasp, letting the clothing fall free.

She stood up, giving me a moment to gaze at her body. A moment later our pants were undone and she managed to slip off my boxers. Amanda eased on top of me again until I was inside of her. We both groaned and began to move back and forth, up and down.

"I want to be so close to you," she sighed, her movements growing faster and faster. "I love you Henry."

"I love you too," I managed to gasp, as we rocked violently for another minute before collapsing onto the couch, Amanda's sweat-glistened body rising and falling against mine. Our lips found each other one more time, and then we fell asleep intertwined, as all the pain faded away.

Chapter 34

Jack O'Donnell sat at his keyboard, fingers flying as he typed away on the only story that currently mattered to him. When he told Wallace he was going to write it for the Gazette—they had to cover it, after all, as the crime was committed by a man who'd already killed four people—there was no argument, only a solemn nod and an assumption that the most accurate and unbiased story would be written. Wallace did point out that the Gazette would have an exclusive—the only paper in town to interview the victim, Henry Parker. All the other news organizations would simply have to credit Jack's piece when they copied from it.

Jack had arrived at the hospital less than ten minutes after the ambulance arrived with Henry. He'd watched them unload the stretcher. He saw Amanda leap out, doing her best to hold back tears. Jack offered a terse hello, then asked how Henry was doing. She said they didn't know, that he needed a CAT scan and that his hand was hurt something bad. Amanda looked at Jack in a way that made his stomach feel hollow, like somehow he'd been responsible for the attack.

He waited as they made sure there was no cranial bleeding, no fractures. When the tests confirmed a grade one concussion Jack sighed in relief, said goodbye to Amanda, and left. He went straight back to the office, locked himself in a conference room, pulled a flask of whiskey from his pocket and drank until his eyes were ruddy and the tears of frustration were sufficiently dammed up.

A year ago, when Henry had recovered after being shot, Jack had viewed him merely as a young reporter with potential. It was a professional relationship, nothing more, one that could be severed at any time for a multitude of reasons. Over the past twelve months, however, Henry had become more. For a man in his sixties who hadn't spoken to his own offspring in more than a decade, Henry Parker was the closest thing to a son Jack O'Donnell ever had.

Jack was a legend. He knew this, but did not brandish his legacy like some vulgar bayonet. Instead he cloaked himself in it, remembered it every time he began a story, every time he followed a lead.

Jack had torn through three marriages because he simply could not perform the duties most women expected of a husband. He would not come home when they pleased. He would not offer comfort or solace with any regularity. He stayed out late, drank often, was surly and emotionless depending on how a story was evolving. Every relationship was a bell curve. Passion and romance rose to a peak, then fell into a trough until they flatlined. And when that happened, it was time to move on.

But it made him a great reporter. He devoted himself to the craft, and in doing so became something more than just a reporter. Within Henry, Jack could see the same potential. He would have to make sacrifices. Sacrifices ordinary men could never make. Family, friends, even some happiness. But by doing so Henry would become what Jack believed he could be; someone who made a difference. Someone whose work lived on.

Amanda seemed like a nice enough girl, yet every loose thread a man had was one that could be pulled. One that could be leveraged. If a man had nothing, he risked nothing, and would stop at nothing. A woman could hold him back. Love could make him soft. Jack was unsure if he'd ever truly been in love, though if he had he would have retired years ago, spent his elder years in some pastel retirement community, flitting about in golf carts and wearing pants with shameful plaid designs. Eating lunch at "the club" with the other retirees before they went out and shot a hundred and fifty on the back nine. That was no life for him. That was no life at all.

He gulped down another hot sip of coffee, laced with just enough Baileys to give it a little kick, keep his blood pumping. He typed in his byline and got ready to send it off. It would be in tomorrow's national edition. He knew many people thought this killer was some sort of twisted hero, knocking off people whose deaths would somehow benefit the common good. They didn't think about the monster beneath, just what it took to pull a trigger and end someone's life. The families shattered. The soullessness of it all.

Jack was too old to go chasing villains. That was a job for a younger man, one ready to claim the mantle for his own. And Jack knew that if Henry kept his head on straight, snipped off any loose threads, the story would be fully told. And he could only hope it was told before the next victim fell.

Chapter 35

I tossed and turned the whole night, every position bringing a new bolt of pain. Whether it was my hand, my head, or Amanda accidentally kneeing me in the groin, I would have had a better night sleep covered in honey and stuck in an ant farm. Amanda didn't wake once. I tried to be jealous, but watching her sleep soundly, all I could do was smile.

After making love we fell asleep for an hour. When we woke, I threw on a pair of boxers, Amanda slipping into cotton underwear and one of my T-shirts that came down to her knees. We fell into bed and wrapped our bodies around each other, my head on two pillows and numbed by two aspirin, my hand stretched above my head to prevent undue pressure from ripping the stitches.

When the sun came up, I blinked the crust from my eyes and went to the bathroom. After peeing for what felt like an hour, I turned the water on for a shower.

"You're not supposed to shower for forty eight hours," Amanda mumbled from the bed.

"Crap, I forgot. Good thing I'm all sweaty from last night, I've always wanted to smell like a hobo at work." Though Amanda's face was mushed into a pillow, I saw the edge of a small smile.

I got dressed, and pulled out the note Agnes Trimble had written me yesterday. My stomach clenched as I wondered if the killer was watching me from the window. Watching Agnes. Watching Amanda.

I took out my cell phone and called Curt Sheffield.

"Hey Henry, how's the noggin feeling?"

"Feels like I went twelve rounds with Mike Tyson circa 1989."

"Damn, that's bad. Don't worry, give it a few years and you'll be biting off ears and threatening to eat people's children."

"Those are some nasty side effects."

"You're telling me."

"Listen Curt, I was wondering if you could get someone to watch Amanda. Just while I'm gone during the day."

"Bro," Curt said, laughing. "Look out your window."

Confused, I pulled open the window with my good hand and poked my head out. Below me I could see the sidewalk and the building's entrance. Parked right in front was a blue-and-white squad car. I could see two officers inside. And I swear I could make out the outline of a donut.

"They'll be on your ass every morning and night for the next week. You got a private escort to and from work, as does your lady-friend. You decide to shop for groceries, go to the Chinese laundry mat during the day, that's all you."

"Thanks Curt, I appreciate it."

"Don't thank me. Orders came down from Chief Carruthers's office. Guess there are people who want you to stay alive."

"I'll be sure to send Carruthers a fruit basket."

"No fruitcake, his in-laws send one every Christmas and he chucks it. Later Henry, give me a ring if you need anything." I hung up, then dialed the number Agnes Trimble had given me for Largo Vance. Hopefully Vance was an early riser. The phone picked up on the very first ring.

"Yes, who is this?" a high-pitched voice croaked out.

"Hello is this Professor Largo Vance?"

"If this is Jehovah's Witness, then no. If it's anyone else, depends who's calling."

"Mr. Vance, my name is Henry Parker. I'm a reporter with the New York Gazette and I was given your name by Professor Agnes Trimble—"

"Agnes! I haven't seen that minx in years." There was a moment of silence as I tried to think of what to say. "Oh come now Mr. Parker, don't be offended, I mean that with the highest compliments. Agnes is a randy little minx, she and I go way back."

"That's, um, wonderful. Anyway Mr. Vance, if you have a few moments today, I'd like to talk to you about Brushy Bill Roberts."

This time the silence came from Largo Vance's end. His response came sputtering out. "How fast can you be here?"

"Um, I don't know where you live, Mr. Vance…"

"3724 Bleecker. Be here in half an hour." He hung up.

"Who was that?" Amanda asked. She was sitting up in bed, clutching a pillow in her arms.

"A lead Professor Trimble gave me yesterday," I said. "An old professor. I think he has some more information on the Billy the Kid lead."

"Henry," she said, "please...be careful. Just yesterday you were in the emergency room and..."

"I know that." I went to the bed and sat down next to her. I took her hand in my good one, raised it to my lips and kissed her fingers. "I promise I'll be careful. There are policemen downstairs who are going to watch you, just to make sure this lunatic doesn't come after us again. If you go anywhere other than work, you know Curt's number. Call him."

"This lunatic killed four people," she said. "If he wants to kill, he's going to get them." I let that sink in, knew she was probably right.

"Call in sick today. Just this once. I have to go talk to this guy Vance. I have to."

"Then go," Amanda said. "The sooner you go the sooner you get back, the less time I have to spend worrying about you."

"Listen, that guy wouldn't have attacked me if he didn't have something to hide. He has an entire city police force looking to draw and quarter him, a newspaper reporter doesn't pose that much of a threat comparatively."

"If he was willing to break into our apartment and do what he did, it must be something awful he wants to keep a secret."

"That just means I'm going to find it," I said. "I'll call a locksmith, have him change the locks and get a security system installed."

"This apartment?" Amanda said. "That's like getting rims on a 1987 Yugo."

"Now that sounds like one crunked-up car. Don't worry about me," I said. I was having trouble pulling a shirt over my head, so Amanda came over to help. "I'm Mr. Incredible."

"Well, please ask Mr. Incredible why he needs help getting dressed. In the meantime Lois Lane would like it very much if he looks both ways before he crossed the street."

"Surely will. Besides, you'd make a sexy-ass Lois. My phone will be on if you need anything."

"Just remember not to open it with that claw of a hand."

"I won't."

"And Henry?" Amanda said. I turned to her, smiled, but the

smile quickly faded when I saw the look on her face. "Be careful. I can't say it enough."

"I will," I said. "Love you."

"Love you too."

I left on that sentiment. I nodded to the cops parked outside. They gave half nods back but otherwise did not acknowledge me. As I walked, I saw one plainclothes follow about ten yards behind me while the other followed in a squad car. When I entered the subway, plain-clothes followed, staying at the other end of the car, pretending to read a copy of one of those free newspapers that people toss onto the tracks and end up clogging the drainage systems.

I got off at Bleecker Street, picking up and swallowing a cup of lukewarm coffee and two more aspirin on the way. I buzzed an L. Vance at the given address, an elegant brown brick town house with a rusted front gate.

The buzzer granted my entrance, and I took a recently painted elevator to the third floor. When the elevator door opened, a man that had to be Largo Vance stood in the doorway. He'd been waiting for me.

"Henry Parker," he said. "Largo Vance. Get inside. Now."

Vance had a long gray beard, gray hair swept back in a less-than-neat ponytail. His overalls were covered with dried paint. What looked like a pound or two of cat hair had dried in the paint. I could smell fresh—and some not so fresh—kitty litter emanating from inside.

He ushered me inside, peeked around the hall (presumably to make sure no black helicopters had followed) and closed the door. A brown-and-gray striped cat snaked between my legs, rubbed itself against my jeans. Soon he was joined by another cat, and one more to complete the whole set.

"Don't mind them," Largo said. "That's Tabby, Yorba Linda and Grace. Say hello babies."

The cats did not say hello.

I followed Largo through a hallway to a small living room, where nearly every square inch was covered in either cat paraphernalia or large well-worn books, history and a few paperback novels whose spines had given out long ago. Largo sat in an overstuffed La-Z-Boy and beckoned me to a leather couch across from him.

I took a seat and minded the stench. Two more cats appeared. I couldn't tell if they were the same ones, new ones, or the first three had simply spawned in the last minute.

"So what brings you here about Billy Bonney?" Largo said. A cat leapt onto his lap and Largo began to scratch its chin absently.

"Not Billy Bonney," I said. "Brushy Bill Roberts."

"Same difference," Vance said. "Now go on."

"I uh…have you heard about the recent murders? Athena Paradis? Several others who were killed by a man using an old Winchester rifle?"

Largo shook his head. "I don't read the newspaper." This was going to be harder than I thought.

"Well, in the last week and a half, somebody has been—"

"I'm playing with you, kid. I may not know how to do the Google but I don't live under a rock."

"So you know that Billy the Kid's Winchester rifle was stolen from a museum in Fort Sumner."

Largo paused. "That, I did not know."

"But you know of Fort Sumner and the legacy of the Kid."

"I'm very well aware of the history of that town, and of Mr. Bonney. I've visited many times. I haven't set foot in that museum in years, though. But I do recall having a fine conversation with the proprietor—Rex is his name, I believe. Unfortunately the last time I visited was over ten years ago, and I left under less than pleasant circumstances."

At this point he must have stroked the cat too roughly, because it bared its teeth and jumped off his couch, leaving several red claw marks on Largo's hand. He rubbed it, then noticed the tape covering my hand.

"What happened to you there?"

I held up the hand for him to see. "The man I'm coming to talk to you about, he came to see me yesterday."

"I take it he also left under less than pleasant circumstances."

"You could say that."

"So Mr. Parker. It's been several years since a journalist has taken any interest in what I've had to say. And even then they didn't really take much interest in what I had to say."

"Wait," I said, "back up. What do you mean 'the last time'?"

"Back when I was trying to get something done about that

infernal and misplaced Bonney grave, and they dismissed me like some…loon. It's not quite so easy to secure federal funding when you threaten to reveal precious history as nothing more than bunk."

"I must have missed something," I said. "What exactly happened?"

Largo sat back, as a pair of cats circled his legs. He steepled his fingers and smiled. Despite the superficial idiosyncrasies of this man, I could sense tremendous intelligence. He looked like a man who still held himself with great honor and respect, but had turned his back on the very institution he sought to help.

"Ten years ago," Largo said, "I attempted to dig up the grave of William H. Bonney, also known as Billy the Kid. For years I fought to do this, and fought to have the story covered in the press. I wanted to inform the public of the travesty and secrets that had been kept hidden for over a century. But when you threaten the very sanctity of a legend—a legend that goes right to the heart of an entire culture—you're not going to find many friends."

I looked around, wondered if Tabby and Yorba Linda had replaced all those friends he'd lost.

"Who tried to stop you?"

"The name Bill Richardson ring a bell?"

"As in governor of New Mexico Bill Richardson?"

"As in presidential candidate Bill Richardson. You think he'd have a snowball's chance in Albuquerque without the support of his fellow southerners? You think anyone below the Mason Dixon line would be happy to have one of their biggest legends—not to mention juiciest cash cows—proven bogus?"

"I don't imagine that would make a whole lot of people down there happy. But why did you want to exhume the body of Billy the Kid? What would that have proved?"

Largo wet his upper lip with his tongue, slicked it back and forth, bristling the gray hairs. He looked at me as if debating whether to speak. "How much do you know about William H. Bonney? And by that I mean the methods in which he died."

"I know he was shot in the back by Pat Garrett, and that Garrett was a former riding mate of Bonney's. He was not a member of the Regulators."

"No, Garrett was not a Regulator," Largo said. "Garrett was a saloon keeper and small-time cattle rustler. To call him a former 'mate' of Bonney's is patently false, another story cooked up to give the legend bigger tits."

"I also know Garrett became a minor celebrity after killing the Kid, and published a book about the chase and capture," I said.

At this moment Largo let out a deep belly laugh. The cats circling his legs scattered. "A minor celebrity, you say? Certainly nowhere near as much of a celebrity as this Athena Paradis, or David Loverne. Actually Patrick Garrett was one of this country's very first victims of celebrity overexposure, as both his tawdry book and sketchy methods in which he dispatched Mr. Bonney left him disgraced and broke."

"What do you mean, sketchy?" I asked.

"By sketchy, I mean that only a fool would believe that Patrick Floyd Garrett killed William H. Bonney on July 14th, 1881. The real Billy the Kid lived for many years after his alleged death in Fort Sumner."

"Brushy Bill Roberts," I said.

Largo nodded. "The town of Fort Sumner would shrivel up and die without the legend of Billy the Kid to wet its whistle. As would most of the southwest, considering how much of its prosperity is built upon the house of cards that is the legend of its outlaws. Billy the Kid is perhaps the single most important card in that house. Pull it out, and the entire edifice crumbles."

"And you tried to pull it out."

"Yes, and you can imagine the good folks of New Mexico did not take kindly to having their stock in trade jeopardized. Yes I did try. And rightfully so. But those goddamn yellow bureaucrats in Washington and down south stopped me. Cowards are more afraid of the truth than they are of facing the fact that they've been lying for over a hundred and twenty-five years."

"You want to dig up the body of Billy the Kid," I said, "and do what with it?"

"Take a sample of the DNA contained in the so-called grave of Billy the Kid and compare it to DNA obtained from his birth mother, Catherine Antrim, who is buried in Silver City."

"And if you're able to prove that the DNA from that grave site doesn't match Catherine Antrim…"

"Then we'll know for sure that Billy the Kid was never buried in Fort Sumner, and Brushy Bill wasn't the charlatan folks would like to have you believe."

"So why didn't you go through with it?" I asked.

"Oh lord, where to begin," Largo said, kicking away a cat who'd begun scratching at the couch. "First off, Billy Bonney's alleged grave site has been robbed so many times that nobody knows for sure just who's buried under that tombstone. Plus the man who bought Catherine Antrim's cemetery plot in Silver City claims he moved the headstone years ago and isn't a hundred-percent sure just where Antrim's body is actually buried. He said he'd die and come back as Christ himself before we marched in there and accidentally dug up somebody's poor dead grandmother."

"It didn't matter, though," Vance continued. "The fact is if the government wanted to conduct the tests, they would have bent over backwards to do so. When it comes to proving a live man's guilt or innocence, there's no limit to what our government will do. But when it comes to proving the life and death of one of the biggest legends in human history, and in the process possibly destroying one of the most enduring American myths of all time, well, they'd rather discredit an honest old man, call him a loon, get his tenure revoked and make him live out his days miles from where he might crack their wall of lies.

"The truth is Pat Garrett did not kill Billy the Kid. William H. Bonney died under the assumed name of Oliver P. Roberts, in Hamilton, Texas."

"What makes you so sure?"

"Let me give you an example of the idiocy—or just plain ignorance—of those wishing to protect the legacy. As I was trying to have the bodies exhumed, both the mayor of Fort Sumner and the governor of Texas claimed that Brushy Bill and William H. Bonney could not be one and the same person, for the following reason. When Ollie Roberts died, it was a well-known fact that he was right handed. The most famous photo of Billy the Kid depicts him holding his beloved Winchester 1873 model in his right hand, with his single action Colt revolver in a holster by his left hip. By this photo you would deduce that Bonney was, in fact, left-handed."

"So they claimed that Bonney was left-handed but Brushy Bill was right-handed."

"That was their claim." Largo stood up and pulled a book off his shelf. He flipped to a page on which there were two photographs. Both depicted the famous photo of Billy the Kid, standing slightly awkwardly, holding his Winchester rifle, a mischievous grin on his face.

"If you look at this picture, the Colt is by his left hip."

"Okay," I said.

"But what the blue bloods in their marble castles failed to realize is that this photograph is actually a ferrotype. In other words, a mirror image of the actual subject."

"So in real life, Billy the Kid had the Colt by his right hip. Meaning he was right-handed."

"Just like our friend Brushy Bill."

"Would you be willing to go on record?" I asked.

Largo seemed taken aback. Another cat jumped onto his lap. He was too distracted to scratch it, so it simply nuzzled against his chest and closed its eyes.

"On record? You mean like in the newspaper? Would I be willing? Boy, I've been waiting for years for somebody to ask me that."

"Is that a yes?"

"Let me put it this way. If I'm not on the record enough, I'm coming down to that paper of yours and shoving a cat up your keester."

"That's fair," I said, pulling the tape recorder from my bag. "Now let's get started. Tell me everything you know about Brushy Bill Roberts, why you believe he was Billy the Kid, and leave nothing out."

Chapter 35

When I arrived at the Gazette, the newsroom was abuzz in a way I'd never seen it before in my brief tenure at the paper. The stringers seemed a little louder, the phone calls a little more urgent. A palpable electricity ran through the place. The whole organization seemed galvanized, charged, like a black cloud had been dragged away to let the sun back in.

It wasn't a minute after I stepped off the elevator when Wallace came jogging up to me. His hair was slightly askew and his right ear was slightly red as though he'd been pressing a phone to it the whole morning.

"Henry, glad you're here," he said, catching his breath. "Come with me. And don't say a word unless I tell you to." I opened my mouth to ask what was happening, but Wallace held up a finger and said, "not one word."

I followed Wallace, but quickly realized he wasn't leading me towards his office or my desk, but to the conference room at the end of the floor. The Kemper Room. In over a year at the paper I'd never set foot in it.

I desperately wanted to ask Wallace what was so important that he'd grant me access to such hallowed ground, but on the off chance he'd change his mind I stayed quiet.

The room was named after Peter Kemper, the Gazette's editor-in-chief from 1978 to 1984, but was more commonly known amongst the Gazette staff as the War Room. Every morning the editors from each department would gather in the War Room to go over the next day's stories. Each section editor would fight, scratch and claw for page one space, better coverage for their department. Each day every editor left the room either thrilled or disappointed. Then they would return the next day to keep up their good run, or dig their way out of the hole. Had they been shafted the day before they'd use pity points. If they'd been granted better placement, they'd claim sales were up due to them.

The Guilty

The War Room was where other bureaus such as Washington and Los Angeles would call in to battle for their share of the table scraps, often frustrated with their perceived lack of respect from the New York home office.

Jack would fill me in on War Room gossip from time to time. He took a little too much pleasure in recalling the greatest stories ever, like the time metro editor Jacquelyn Mills had a story negged and threw a glass of pomegranate juice in the editor-in-chief's face. The time Wallace himself told an editor that his stories showed as much life as Jimmy Hoffa, and smelled worse. Between New York and outside bureaus there was a natural conflict; reporters in Washington felt the ebb and flow of the political arena was the spark of the journalistic world, while the reporters in New York felt they were the center of the information universe. Los Angelinos felt their coverage of red-carpet shenanigans trumped all, that popular culture and celebrity scandal whet readers' appetites. They didn't win the battles very often.

As the War Room came into sight, I counted a dozen or so editors already seated, cups of coffee and bottles of water in various stages of being sipped or ignored. Far as I could tell, I would be the youngest person in the room by a good ten years.

When Wallace threw open the door, a dozen pairs of eyes focused on me. Not to mention the speakerphone in the middle of the conference table whose red "on" light meant another half dozen were listening in. And the guy in the corner with a pen and pad who was presumably there to take minutes. I coughed into my hand. Smiled meekly. The editors in attendance didn't seem to care much about meek smiles.

Wallace stated, "Henry, you know everyone here." I didn't, but remembered Wallace's "shut the hell up" rule. "Folks, this is Henry Parker. As you know Henry's been the lead on the Paradis murder story and the subsequent victims of this killer as well. He was attacked in his home yesterday, but as you can see he's alive and well."

"And glad to be here," I added. Wallace nodded his approval.

"Terrific scoops so far," said a man I believed to be the Arts editor. He had a neatly trimmed beard and thin glasses, a polite ink stain at the bottom of his shirt pocket. I'd only met him once, at the holiday party last year, the details of which ended up being reported on every gossip website between here and Mumbai. It well known that the arts editors always offered exclusive scoops to gossip rags in exchange for the rags making the Gazette seem like a hip place to work. If the definition of hip was Jack warbling Kenny Rogers while Wallace played acoustic guitar, both men having consumed their body weight in JD, then yes, I suppose you could call the Gazette a hip place to work.

I took an empty seat, trying hard not to meet any of the stares directed my way. I noticed several people staring at my bandaged hand, which I self-consciously tucked underneath the table. Wallace sat down at the head, and finally the eyes left me for more succulent meat.

"As I'm sure you're aware of this morning," Wallace said, "the reaction to Henry's story about the link between this killer and Billy the Kid has been off the charts. Based on our website traffic, it is the Gazette's most e-mailed article since we expanded our web capabilities three years ago. We've received dozens of phone calls, many supportive, many not so much, not to mention queries from at least three film scouts inquiring about film rights to the story. Needless to say we've struck a nerve with this article, and considering the demand I'd like each section to consider reporting on the phenomenon from a different societal perspective."

After a quick tug at his goatee, the arts editor piped in. "We can do an overview of the most famous movies, music, television shows and books to explore the legend of Billy the Kid. An IMBD search came back with at least two dozen films where the Kid was either a main or substantial supporting character. And you'd be surprised how often his name is dropped in contemporary music and literature."

Deborah Gotkowski, the business editor, said, "I have a call in to the tourism bureau at Fort Sumner. I'd like to know how much revenue they take in on a yearly basis from their various museums and tourism attraction, then analyze that data and compare it to the ten cities who receive the largest percentage of their revenue from one specific tourist attraction."

Jonas Levinson, the science editor, said, "We can do a comprehensive look at the DNA techniques Professor Vance was attempting to use, and determine whether they could actually tie Catherine Antrim to the alleged remains. That would have to have been some groundbreaking stuff."

I heard a loud grunt from the corner. It came from a large

man wearing a rumpled sports jacket and a white shirt with a moon-shaped mustard stain. Frank Rourke was the Gazette's sports editor, a man I'd never met, though I did enjoy his recent articles about steroid abuse in baseball. Unlike most city sportswriters, Frank wrote from a fan's perspective rather than writing as if he was the moral axis of the sports universe. He never chided athletes for their faults. That would have been the pot calling the kettle black, considering Frank had written two books—one about his marriage as a full-time sportswriter, the second about his divorce as a full-time sportswriter.

"I think the Knicks are looking to acquire a backup point guard for a playoff push. Maybe I can claim this Bonney guy is coming up in trade talks."

"You should do that," Jonas said. "I bet most of your readers would believe it too."

"My readers could beat your readers to death with one arm tied behind their back."

"I could throw your readers a tube steak and they'd forget all about it."

Frank leaned forward, half his body over the table. "Are you calling my readers stupid?"

Jonas shrugged. "If the GED fits."

"Fuck you, and fuck this kid Parker," Rourke spat. "I've been at this paper twelve years, I ain't never been so much as given a handkerchief by you assholes. Now we're sucking his dick about all this 'groundbreaking' reporting? Please. Once this twelve-year-old milk monitor earns his stripes he can come in here. Until then I'm not listening to this shit."

Rourke stood up and made a grand spectacle of tucking in his shirt, shooting his cuffs, and storming out. There was silence for a moment. Jonas's face showed a combination of pride and white-as-a-ghost fear, as though Rourke might be waiting for him at his desk with a pair of brass knuckles.

"Are we through?" Wallace said. " Because time is wasting and every other paper in town is looking for us to trip so they can pass us. I want a push on all fronts. Our early morning newsstand numbers are our highest in six months. Henry, I want you to stay on the murders. Jonas, I want you to look into the attempts made by Largo Vance and others to test the DNA contained in Billy the Kid's grave. Deborah, you look into the effects it could have on the present day economics of Fort Sumner and other towns such as Hamilton that are supported by this industry. I want all discoveries to be shared directly with the office of Chief Carruthers." Wallace paused a moment. "Most importantly, there's still a killer out there. If we can, in any way, aid the investigation and incarceration of this sick man, we owe it to the citizens of New York to do so. Err on the side of caution. If you think you have something that would be of use to investigating officers, run it by me and I'll make the final call. But get out there and report your asses off, and have your staff do the same. This is a story that reaches back over a century. And if you're like me, you all have that feeling, your pulses are racing a bit, you have that zing in your step because you know you're on the verge of a great discovery. Grab it. Let's make a great paper. Good luck."

And with that, Wallace dismissed us. I walked out with him. He put his arm around my shoulders, made it clear so the newsroom could see. This public display of affection was to let the newsroom know he was on my side.

"You're the lead dog on this," Wallace said, soft enough so only I could hear it. "But stay the hell out of the battle zone. The job of a journalist is to report the news, not become it. I've read too many briefs regarding your run-ins and injuries this past year."

"That's not my fault," I said, agitation in my voice, my blood pressure rising. "What happened last year was out of my hands. What happened yesterday won't happen again."

"You say that like a stupid kid playing in traffic just sure he won't get hit by a car. Until he does. You're a reporter, Henry, nothing more. It is your job to write and investigate the news. Neither Harvey Hillerman nor I want to see your name appear in the Gazette in any capacity except as a byline for the foreseeable future. If you can't comply with that, we can find a position here that will keep you safely behind a desk. Evelyn's assistant recently left to get her MBA, I'd be happy to put in a good word."

Being Evelyn's assistant held the same appeal to me as mopping up the public toilets at Shea Stadium. I knew where Wallace was coming from, but if a freak wanted to break into my house and Ginsu my hand, there was only so much I could do about it. Then again, if the Gazette had to keep defending me, readers would be smart enough to realize that the lady doth protest too much. It would only be a matter

The Guilty

of time before my byline overshadowed the story I was telling.

"I'll be careful," I told Wallace. "This is too important to me. I won't muck it up."

"You're damn right you won't. So report it right. Now get to work."

I went back to my desk, mentally rifling through all the work I had to do in order to get a fuller picture of Brushy Bill. As I walked past the other desks, I noticed most of my co-workers were gathered by the pantry. As I rounded the corner, they made an awkward attempt to stop giggling. I started towards them to see what was up, but then smelled something unmistakable in the air.

I looked over at my desk, noticed a paper bag sitting on my keyboard. As I got closer I noticed that a) my desk smelled absolutely rancid, and b) there was a small brown splotch at the bottom of the bag. I didn't need to get any closer to know somebody had put a bag full of shit on my desk.

I forced a smile, picked up the bag, walked it to the pantry. The other reporters parted as I approached. I dropped it in the trash, washed my hands, and said, "Looks like someone forgot their lunch."

I wasn't laughing as I returned to my desk. A killer was still out there. And despite what Wallace hoped, he wasn't planning to stop.

Chapter 37

"Last time we spoke," Paulina said, "you told me you were closer to Henry Parker than, let's see if I recall, 'white on rice.'"

James Keach loosened his tie and thanked God he was wearing a suit jacket because he was sure the pit stains on his blue Oxford were visible from across the street. "There's different kinds of rice," he stuttered. "There's brown rice, chicken fried rice. It's not all white."

"You said white. White on rice. So why the fuck is this Billy the Kid exclusive in the Gazette and we're sitting with another Britney crotch shot on page one?" Paulina's face was red, but he couldn't tell if it was from rage or more Xanax than usual. He hoped it was the latter, but doubted it.

"Parker was attacked in his apartment," Keach said, trying to regain his confidence. "The cops have assigned two protection details, one for Parker and another for this Amanda Davies girl. I tried waiting down the street from his apartment, outside a bagel shop, but one of the cops spotted me and started walking towards where I was standing. He was looking at me, Paulina! So I pretended I was buying a bagel and got the hell out of there. Better that than they knew who I was, right?"

Paulina closed her eyes, rubbed her forehead with her hand.

"And so Parker finds this crackpot Vance, and he snags the story while you're slurping cream cheese. James, do you know how close we are?"

"How close we are in what?"

Paulina rifled through some papers on her desk, pulled out a white sheet with a bunch of indecipherable numbers.

"These are the latest circulation figures for all five major New York newspapers, along with rates for the top twenty newspapers in the country. The latest numbers show the Gazette's circulation lead over the Dispatch at less than five percent. Five percent. That's less than yearly inflation these days. One major story can turn the tide, my rice-loving friend. So I don't care if you have to channel Houdini

The Guilty

himself, you shadow Henry Parker like your life depends on it. Because I can sure as hell make sure your job does. That is all."

Chapter 38

I could sense the men following me even though I couldn't see them. I knew they carried guns, had their eyes glued to my back, and sized up every person who came within five feet of me.

I told the cops the man had done his work, that their efforts would be better used fighting terrorism or searching for the killer himself. They disagreed. I told them the guy who cut up my hand wasn't stupid enough to go after me in broad daylight, that he had actual targets. He had a motive, a purpose, wasn't some fly-by-the-seat-of-his-pants, run of the mill murderer. He picked the Winchester for a reason. Stole it from that museum in Fort Sumner for a reason. Came to my apartment and tried to scare me off the case for a reason.

In the days since I wondered why he didn't just kill me. The man had already killed four others. He clearly wasn't averse to murder. There was a story he wanted to stay buried, and leaving me alive was just one more shovel that could keep digging. I guessed he just didn't know how brave—or stupid—I was.

To uncover more about the legacy of Brushy Bill Roberts, I had to start at the end. Roberts had lived in Hamilton, Texas and died in Hico. Roberts had since become the small town's only claim to fame, bringing in thousands of dollars in tourism every year. If Fort Sumner lived and breathed the legend of Billy the Kid, Hico lived on the whiff of conspiracy brought on by their most famous former resident.

I had to get out of the office and do research away from the madness that had become the Gazette newsroom. With the increasing battles between the Gazette and the Dispatch, I could tell Hillerman had come down hard on Wallace to make sure his reporters knocked this story out of the park. And if that was the case, I was his Babe Ruth, stepping to the plate and calling my shot, hoping for a moon rocket rather than a whiff.

The New York public library was quiet, had the same Internet resources as the Gazette, access to LexisNexis, and all the historical newspapers on microfiche I needed. I wanted to view the Roberts case from every media angle: not only Hico, but by the major metropolitan

The Guilty

papers in Texas, New York, Los Angeles and elsewhere. You could get a good grasp of how a story infected the national consciousness by how widely it was reported, and with what veracity the conspiracy was given.

It was a crisp summer day and the steps outside the library were teeming with people reading, hanging out, and even a few sleeping on the stone. The NYPL itself is a behemoth that takes up two full city blocks. The entrance was guarded by two stone lions named Leo Astor and Leo Lenox, after John Jacob Astor and James Lenox, both generous patrons. In the 1930s, they were renamed Patience and Fortitude by Mayor Fiorello La Guardia. Patience guards the south steps, Fortitude the north. As I passed them by, I hoped they'd grant me both. The three main doors are bracketed by six carved stone columns, which lead into the great reading room where I'd spent many hours wrenching my back while poring over old texts. The massive room is lit by grand chandeliers and surrounded by thousands of volumes. I was here to use CATNYP, the online system allowing subscribers access to the library's huge collection of journals, periodicals and newspapers.

I jogged up the steps and entered, making my way to a computer stall where I took a seat, cracked my knuckles, looked to see if the two cops had followed me inside. They hadn't.

I logged on to CATNYP and ran a search for Texas newspapers containing stories pertinent to the Brushy Bill case. I typed slowly with my index fingers, my right palm aching from the stitches. Guess I'd have to settle for old fashioned two-fingered typing for the time being.

The first article I came across was from the Austin Chronicle, and featured a story about one Judge Bob Hefner who, in 1986, published a booklet claiming Brushy Bill had in reality been the real Billy the Kid. The booklet gained notoriety when it was picked up by the Dallas Morning News. According to Hefner's story, "Brushy Bill had no children and was at the end of his life. Fame and fortune were not a consideration for the old man."

Hefner continued, saying that Roberts desired only to be granted the pardon promised by Governor Lewis Wallace years before. Hefner claimed that Pat Garrett had actually killed a friend of Billy the Kid's that night in 1881, solely for the purpose of collecting the five-hundred-dollar bounty on Bonney's head.

It seemed strange that Roberts would suddenly decide after years in hiding that he wanted to be pardoned for crimes committed in the 1880s. I noted that Hefner currently ran the Billy the Kid museum in Hico, making it two different states with two different museums claiming to be the final resting place for Billy the Kid. Of course he had financial motivation for keeping the theory alive. But that didn't make him a liar.

I then found an article published by the New York Times in 1950, concerning the spectacle surrounding a man who claimed to be the real-life Jesse James. James had been assumed murdered by two brothers named Bob and Charley Ford back in 1882, but in 1950 a man named J. Frank Dalton claimed to be the real James. After a media carnival descended upon the 102-year-old man during a hospital stay, Dalton died. Yet the rumors persisted. Finally in 1995, the body of Jesse James was exhumed from its grave in Missouri and the DNA was found to match 99.7 to that of James's family. Supporters of the Dalton theory did not give up hope, and in 2000 a court order was granted to exhume the body of J. Frank Dalton to end the speculation. Unfortunately the wrong body was exhumed, and attempts to discredit Dalton were halted. Dalton's body was never exhumed nor tested. I wondered if this botched exhumation was part of the reason Largo Vance was unable to do the same for William H. Bonney.

The article was accompanied by a photo of an elderly man with a long, scruffy beard lying in a hospital bed with two men standing by his side. When I saw the attribution given to the second of the two men, my heart nearly skipped a beat. He was wearing a leather jacket and bore a look of concern on his face. He was identified as one Brushy Bill Roberts, ninety years old, at the deathbed of J. Frank Dalton. The man thought to be the real Billy the Kid next to the man suspected of being the real Jesse James.

I ran another search, this time to determine whether Jesse James and William H. Bonney knew each other. According to news reports, Jesse James and Billy the Kid had met only once, at the Old Adobe Springs hotel near Las Vegas in July of 1879. The two were seen having dinner by an associate of Bonney's, though the witness's story was widely discredited. People simply couldn't believe history's two most famous outlaws had ever crossed paths, let alone met for a friendly dinner.

The Guilty

The Austin Chronicle, in a later story, said this "chance" meeting was even more unlikely considering James's daughter had been born merely ten days earlier.

I kept searching, and soon discovered another photograph, dated from 1942, again of Brushy Bill Roberts and J. Frank Dalton, this time of the two men standing side by side. The picture clearly identifies the two men by the names they went by at the time—Brushy Bill and Frank Dalton. According to records, it was not until after Dalton's 102nd birthday that he claimed to be Jesse James. Additionally, Roberts denied that he was Billy the Kid at first, only admitting to it after being confronted.

There were a slew of websites and conspiracy theory pamphlets printed and posted on the web, many claiming that Roberts and Dalton were two con artists looking to make a buck and gain notoriety. What made no sense is why the two men would wait until their deathbeds to claim this "notoriety." Both Roberts and Dalton died within a few years of their confessions, and neither made any sort of profit from their claims.

According to another report, a man named Homer Overton claimed that Pat Garrett's widow told him that the Kid's death was a sham, a ruse concocted by Garrett and the Kid to allow the outlaw safe passage into Mexico. Overton's testimony was entered into the record during an attempt to convince lawmakers to exhume the body of Catherine Antrim. Lincoln County sheriffs made a point of noting that Pat Garrett's likeness is featured on the logo of the Lincoln County Sheriff's department. If it were proven that Garrett did not, in fact, kill William H. Bonney, it would throw the entire county into upheaval.

I allowed this information to digest. For years Brushy Bill Roberts's story had been considered fraudulent. The ramblings of an old, broke man. Even an attempt to put the case to rest by comparing Billy the Kid's DNA to that of his mother never came to fruition. Likewise, J. Frank Dalton's DNA was never compared to that of Jesse James's family.

Two legends with cracks in their façade. Two legends protected either by governmental incompetence, or institutions with reasons to hide the truth. Without the prosperity of those legends to harvest from, several towns in the Southwest would shrivel up and die. And a large part of this country's history would be rent to pieces. If Oliver

P. Roberts truly was Billy the Kid, there were many people with clear motivations to keep that secret locked away.

I could see the connections between the legend of Billy the Kid and the man responsible for murdering Athena Paradis, Joe Mauser, Jeffrey Lourdes and David Loverne.

William H. Bonney was a Regulator, sworn to bring to justice those who had wronged him, wronged society and threatened to disrupt the very fabric of the land he was trying to protect. Using some twisted logic, the psychopath who went Mario Batali on my hand felt he was also bringing justice to the guilty.

I brought up the photo of J. Frank Dalton on his deathbed. Thought about the alleged report of Jesse James and William H. Bonney meeting near Las Vegas in 1879. Ten days after the birth of James's daughter.

Daughter. That word stuck in my throat. Mary Susan James. Born just three years before her father was allegedly killed.

On a whim, I checked to see if there were any records of Billy the Kid having children, a wife, any trace of a bloodline. According to the records, Bonney never married and it was unclear whether he had any children.

I looked up the family tree of Brushy Bill Roberts. Roberts had apparently married a woman named Melinda. Records showed that Roberts had one son, Jesse William Roberts, who was born in Hamilton, Texas, in 1897.

Jesse William Roberts. I looked at the photos featuring Brushy Bill and Frank Dalton together. Added that to the alleged meeting between the outlaws in 1879. It would be a mighty big coincidence—or a case of damn good foresight—for the man who'd later claim to be Billy the Kid to name his only son after Jesse James. Either that, or Jesse James and Billy the Kid were better acquaintances than people thought.

My fingers flew as I typed more searches into the machine, my mind ignoring the pain from my stitched-up hand. I couldn't stop. The spool was unraveling and I couldn't slow down. I knew I had stumbled upon something, a story that drove to the very heart of a century-old legend.

I looked for lineage records pertaining to Jesse William Roberts, son of Brushy Bill Roberts. Jesse had married a woman named

The Guilty

Lucy Barnett. Lucy gave birth to two of Jesse's children: James and Catherine.

Catherine Roberts. Brushy Bill's granddaughter. Who shared the same name as Billy the Kid's mother, Catherine Antrim.

Catherine Roberts died of tuberculosis in 1927 at just three years of age. James Roberts, Brushy's grandson, eventually moved to New Mexico, where he married Lucinda Walther. In 1957 she gave birth to a son named John Henry Roberts. John Henry Roberts married a woman named Meryl Higgins, and in 1987 Meryl gave birth to twins: Martha James Roberts, and William Henry Roberts.

William Henry Roberts.

The theories were true. William H. Bonney, known by millions as Billy the Kid, known by few as Brushy Bill Roberts, had fathered a son.

I knew why this killer was using the Winchester rifle. Why he had chosen the weapon and bullets he did. Why he had stolen that gun from the museum in Fort Sumner. Why he had waited twenty-one years to reclaim his heritage. To continue the destiny set forth by his ancestor.

The bloodline had survived. And one hundred and thirty years after his supposed murder, Billy the Kid's great-grandson, William Henry Roberts, had brought the lawlessness and bloodshed of the old west here to New York City.

Chapter 39

The vodka tasted cold and bitter as it slid down her throat, but the tonic dulled the taste and made it easy to swallow. She knocked the glass on the counter and signaled the bartender, a bohemian named Gregory who wore a ponytail pulled back so tight she feared it might tear his scalp off, and told him to refresh the drink.

"What, you going in for surgery and need a cheap anesthetic?" Gregory said with a laugh. He took a bottle from the well, gave her an inch and a half and topped the rest with tonic. "Hey Mya, you okay?"

Mya Loverne looked up at Gregory and managed a weak smile. She'd come to the Suave bar four times in the past week alone, drank herself into oblivion each time, and this was the first time Gregory had noticed her.

Drinking was all she could do since Henry abandoned her. Since Amanda had run her off. Since Mya had nothing left, nobody to lean on except the awkward embraces from sweaty drunks who weren't quite repulsive enough to turn down. The physical pleasure dulled the pain. Not for long, but long enough to gain a modicum of relief from the anguish inside her.

Mya took a small sip and saw Gregory watching her from the other end of the bar. As soon as he noticed her looking, he turned away, hiding a look of embarrassment, and pretended to clean a glass. She wondered what time he got off. If he had an apartment nearby.

Mya felt her cell phone vibrate through her purse. She took it out, saw it was her mother, and pressed Ignore. Mya had only spoken to her mother once since her father's murder. She made no effort to hide the fact that she believed her mother's ignorance led to his death. That if her mother wasn't such a goddamn passive bitch, wasn't such a pushover, had every now and then stood up for herself, her father would still be alive and not in a pine box in some cemetery surrounded by dimming memories of loved ones.

Mya could feel her blood warming as the alcohol swam through her veins. The door opened, and she felt a gust of cool air. Mya closed her eyes, knocked back the rest of the drink.

The Guilty

Then she heard a creaking sound, opened her eyes and saw a man pull out the stool next to her and sit down. He was young, early twenties, very tan with sandy blond hair and a sweet smile. His eyes flashed a striking blue, and Mya felt her cheeks grow warm. The guy raised his hand to order a drink. Mya noticed how cracked and calloused his palms were. He took off his coat, was wearing a blue T-shirt underneath. His forearms were tanned and toned. He looked like no other guy she'd seen at this bar. He was naturally lean, not possessing the kind of strength born in a gym, but born out of honest blue-collar work.

Gregory acknowledged him and came over. He placed a coaster in front of the stranger and said, "What'll it be?"

"Gin and tonic," the guy said. His voice sounded slightly older than Mya would have expected. "Light on the tonic."

Gregory held out his hand, palm up. "Lemme see some ID."

He looked moderately embarrassed, and offered Mya a sheepish smile before opening his wallet and handing the plastic over. Gregory looked the man over, looked at the picture, made sure the faces matched.

"William…Roberts?" Gregory said.

"That'd be me." Gregory, seemingly satisfied, handed the card back and poured the drink. He went heavy on the gin, surely in apology for the embarrassing age verification.

When Gregory left, the boy took a sip of his drink and said, "You think that'd never get old, but sometimes all you want is a drink." He said it softly without turning his head.

"I know what you mean. I still get carded half the places I go to."

The boy swiveled his stool towards her. He had a nice smile, dimples. "You're what, twenty-two, twenty-three?"

"Twenty-six," Mya said, failing to hide her pleasure in his guess.

"BS."

"You're right, I lie to pretend I'm older."

They shared a laugh. Mya took another sip of her drink, found she was sucking on ice. Her body felt warm. She was unsure if it was the alcohol or this stranger. Either way, she didn't want it to stop. "So let me guess. You walk into bars and try to flatter all the girls." Immediately she regretted uttering such a line, but what was the worst that could happen?

The boy laughed. "You're right," he said, a hint of sarcasm in his voice. "I have nothing better to do than wander around until I finally meet someone who needs flattery. Please. I talk to who I want, when I want. And right now I want to talk to you."

"I bet you say that to all the girls too," Mya said.

"Actually I do. You got me there."

"So here you are, I guess I should be flattered you're talking to me."

"Actually, I'm the one who should be flattered."

The boy smiled, his face a strange but alluring combination of youthfulness and maturity, like he'd seen more and done more than anyone his age had experienced. He wasn't in a hurry like most guys she met, hadn't overplayed his hand within the first ten seconds of their meeting. He looked confident enough that if she rebuffed any possible advances, he could pick up, move on, quickly find someone who wouldn't. Not that she wanted him to move on. But there was the deliciously dangerous possibility of it all.

"William Roberts," he said. "It's nice to meet you." He offered his hand.

"Mya Loverne." She took it, shook it. "So, William Roberts. Do you have a middle name?"

"You want to know my middle name? I don't know, that's a pretty big step. Once I've given that out, we're linked until one of us leaves this bar. Are you prepared for that kind of commitment?"

"Is it really that big a commitment?" Mya asked.

"Of course it is," he said. "See, a boy and a girl can sit in a bar talking for hours. They can share the most intimate secrets of their life, loves and hates, lovers and ex-lovers, pet peeves and fetishes, but there's always a layer of protection between them, this subtle, unspoken boundary where they both know the biggest intimacy has yet to be allowed." She felt the boy move closer, inching his stool towards hers. She pretended she hadn't noticed.

"See, once you cross that line, once you allow that intimacy, you can never go back. See, knowing my middle name isn't such a big deal on the surface, it's what it represents. So if I tell it to you, be sure there's no going back. Are you ready for that?"

The Guilty

"Mine's Helen," she blurted out. Everything seemed to stop for a moment, the boy seeming to soak it in. Now the night was open to all sorts of possibilities.

"Henry," he said. "William Henry Roberts. It's a pleasure to meet you, Mya."

Henry.

"It's a pleasure to meet you, William Henry."

William smiled. "Hey barkeep," he shouted. Gregory turned around. "Another round down here, if you please."

Chapter 40

William put down the copy of the Gazette. His fingertips had become black with ink. He licked his thumb, rubbed his fingers until the smudge had congealed, then wiped his hand on a napkin which he then tossed in the garbage by the bed.

The article was smartly written, insightful, and one hundred percent true. Parker had done a surprisingly good job. In a short amount of time, too. He wasn't quite sure how Henry had pulled all the facts together, and part of him was rather impressed. Still, William knew there were many unanswered questions to which Parker—and the rest of the city—would beg the answers. This was the beauty of the whole thing. William felt a great surge inside. Pride and ambition. Those four deaths were just the beginning. Athena Paradis, the other three martyrs, they were stepping stones to a greater good.

Two pages after Parker's story was an article about the turmoil at Franklin-Rees publications, as the empire ran around like a headless chicken hoping to find some stability. William knew, as soon everyone else would, that regardless of how many Frankenstein-esque heads they tried to bolt on, the animal itself was dying. Everything would crumble from the top down. And out of that rubble would come something beautiful.

Once the guilty had hanged, the innocent had nothing to fear. It was human nature to fear the executioner. Most never realized their job was to cleanse the earth of the guilty, the evil, those who poisoned society.

Despite the truths Henry Parker had unearthed, William felt no anger towards him. Being attacked and brutalized hadn't stopped Parker's pursuit of the truth.

Parker, of course, only knew what William wanted him to know. Because he was the Regulator. He was the last of the great bloodline. And even if the line died with him, it would have died claiming a destiny so abruptly halted many years ago.

Just as William had uncovered his history despite those who

The Guilty

had wished to keep it a secret, so would Henry Parker discover it as well. Two sides of a coin—one clean, one dirty—both needed to create the whole. The same way Billy the Kid had his chronicler in Pat Garrett, so would William in Henry Parker.

William heard a groan. She was waking up.

He nudged the prone body on the floor, gave her a little kick. She shifted, uttered a muffled cry through the rag soaked through with saliva.

William knelt down to her, gently shook her until those eyelids—crusty with eyeliner and mascara—fluttered open. The pupils took a moment to register, but as soon as they did fear came racing back to those pretty hazel eyes. The very eyes that had once gazed upon Henry Parker with an intense love that she still felt for him. Mya had made that clear in Paulina Cole's article. Surely Henry still felt something for her too. Perhaps he could still feel her pain. They'd find out soon enough.

The Boy smiled. He gently stroked Mya's cheek with the back of his hand. Her face trembled, lips quivering, blubbering.

"Don't be scared, Mya." William's fingers traced soothing circles over her forehead until her trembling lips began to calm. "You have no idea how important you are."

Chapter 41

Jack sat perched on the corner of my desk, swaying slightly, like a column debating whether or not to tip over. It was barely ten in the morning. After catching one whiff of his butane-flavored breath, it was clear that Jack was either coming off a night of wicked drinking, or that his wicked night of drinking hadn't yet ended.

"What you need to do now," Jack said, "to follow up on today's article, is start full court press into this Willian Henry Roberts's background. What did his parents do? Are any of his childhood friends willing to say he was 'the quiet type' or pulled the wings off of insects? You need to prove beyond a reasonable doubt that this psychopath is in fact the great-grandson of Billy the Kid. You planted the seeds, Henry, now you gotta water that sucker."

I leaned back in my chair, looked out across Rockefeller Plaza. Tried to let my mind wander, because when it did it usually ended up in the right place. The police had finally pulled their surveillance off of myself and Amanda, convinced my injury was just a warning and the officers would be better suited hunting than guarding a guy who sat at his desk typing while his eyesight got progressively worse.

And it was just as well. I needed to look into Roberts's birth certificate, family history, anything that could prove who he was and who he knew. He had parents—they would know if their son showed early signs of violence. Or if he had a preoccupation with family history. Perhaps a predilection towards antique weaponry. Or maybe he just spent a few too many hours with his Nintendo playing Duck Hunt.

I knew who William Henry Roberts was. Knew where he was from. When he had committed his atrocities in this city. What kind of monster he was.

"I need anything you can possibly help me with, Jack. I want to talk to anyone who's ever been in contact with William Henry Roberts. Schoolteachers, classmates—"

"Neighbors, pets, yada yada, I know the drill." For a moment Jack teetered on the edge of my desk before planting an unsteady hand on my keyboard to steady himself. He looked at me, a quick splash of embarrassment appearing and then vanishing. Like it never happened.

"Jack?" I said.

"Yeah kid?"

"Are you okay?"

Jack looked at me incredulously. "If by that statement you're asking whether I am in perfect health for a man of my age, with the virility of a tiger and countenance of a Viking—then yes, I am very much okay."

"No," I said, my voice pressing a little harder. "Are you really okay."

This time Jack didn't answer so quickly. The veined hand left my tabletop and mounted itself on my shoulder. Jack gave a warm smile as though flattered that I cared so much about his mental and physical state.

"I'm fine, Henry. People are full of bull. So don't believe everything you hear."

I blinked when he said this. Everything you hear?

My concern for Jack was based solely on what I could see right in front of me. His too-sweet breath. His slightly off-kilter equilibrium. His refusal to acknowledge any problems whatsoever. Nobody had said a word to me otherwise, and I had no clue if it was being discussed on the news floor. Obviously others were aware of the problem, as was Jack. Not that he cared one way or another.

We both stood up. Jack began to walk back to his desk.

"So," I said, "did you go out last night?"

Jack barked a laugh. "Go out? Kid, when you're my age going out means ordering in Chinese food and hoping they remembered the sesame chicken."

"So you stayed inside."

"Same as I do every night."

"Any company?"

Jack's eyes closed as he tried to understand what I was asking. "What's all this about?"

"I just want to know if anyone is there to, you know…just in case."

"Just in case what?"

"In case you need any help…anyone to talk to. If anything, you know, happened."

"Help?" Jack said. "What I hear, you need help more than I do. Don't think I didn't hear about Frank Rourke and his infamous crap-in-a-sack. You'd better work on your interpersonal relationships with the other reporters before you start asking if I'm okay. Otherwise that won't be the last bag you get. Help yourself, kid. There are only so many hours in the day."

As he left, I tried to think of something to say. Jack clearly had a problem, and if it were anyone else they would be confronted, put on leave, made to do something to right the ship. But Jack O'Donnell was a living institution. You didn't take the Michelangelo in for a cleaning until the marble was covered with so much grime you couldn't tell its ass from its elbow. Jack was still Jack, pumping out quality stories, but it was only a matter of time. And from the look of things, this wasn't an issue about to go away on its own.

I needed to focus. I still had a job to do, and there was still a killer out there. Maybe if I could uncover more information about William Henry Roberts, I could save more lives than just Jack's.

I logged into LexisNexis and performed a search for William's parents, John and Meryl Roberts. I found records of them owning two homes—one in Hico, Texas and another in Pecos Valley, New Mexico. Pecos Valley, if I remembered, was where John Chisum ended his famous cattle drive which began in Paris, Texas, and where Billy the Kid wreaked havoc during the Lincoln County Wars. Hico was where Brushy Bill Roberts had died.

I searched for all newspaper articles in the state of Texas containing references to either John or Meryl Roberts. Aside from previous known addresses, there were half a dozen other clippings. I sorted them chronologically from earliest to latest. Then I clicked on the first piece.

It was from the Pecos Valley News, a local paper from a town sleepy enough that high-school football was front page material. The article had run in the Church Briefs section of the paper, and was about the baptism of the Roberts's newborn son, William Henry. A photo accompanied the article, a robed priest holding an infant, nestled in between folds of cloth. I could just make out William Henry's eyes, which were peaceful, closed.

It was hard to imagine that this child, renouncing evil, would

The Guilty

eventually become a servant of the devil.

The second article was also from the Pecos Valley News, and it was written in 1979. The article was titled "Roberts Family Sells Home, Wish Them Luck in Texas!" An accompanying photo showed John and Meryl with their young children standing in front of a For Sale sign in their yard. The parents looked young, vibrant, like they were about to start a new chapter of their lives. An eight-year-old William stood to the side with an expression on his face that showed neither happiness nor sorrow. It was a blank slate, as though he was simply going along because there was nothing he could do to stop it.

I clicked on the third article. It was from the Hamilton Herald-News out of Hamilton County, Texas. It was dated August 23rd, 2004. The headline read Five Dead in Deadly Hico Blaze: Family of Four Trapped Inside Their Home, Die Along with Beloved Chaplain.

The accompanying photo showed the charred embers where a house once stood. There were police cars, ambulances and fire trucks spread out with abandon. Men and women in white jackets with filters over their mouths combed through the wreckage.

I could see at least one body draped with cloth and another, uncovered, lying amongst the timber.

My stomach clenched. I read further, my pulse quickening as I read the awful details.

Late last night John Roberts, his wife Meryl, their two children William and Martha, and beloved Pastor Mark C. Rheingold died in a four alarm fire at the Roberts ranch in Hico, Texas.

...bodies were burned beyond recognition...

...unknown how the fire began...

...Rheingold had just returned from a thirty-city tour for his latest book and was set to break ground on a new 15,000 seat church in Houston...

...the Roberts family had just moved to Hico three years ago...

...joined John Henry Robert's father, Oliver...

...William Henry and Martha James had recently graduated from Hamilton High...

...police have not ruled out arson...

I read the rest of the article, stunned. It was impossible. Either

199

I'd made a huge mistake, or something was terribly wrong. Because according to the newspapers, William Henry Roberts had died in Hico, Texas nearly four years ago.

The Guilty

Chapter 42

The next three articles were all follow-ups to the story of the tragic fire that had claimed the lives of four of Hico's newest residents, as well as the life of one of the state's most celebrated religious servants. The stories were competently written, relying on detail, but failing to get across the true horror of the blaze.

According to Sheriff Chip Youngblood, experts determined that the fire was electrical, and may have been exacerbated when one of the Roberts children foolishly attempted to extinguish it with water. According to the local energy supplier, there was a small spike in the Roberts family's electrical usage around the time the fire was believed to have started.

The county held a small, private ceremony for the burial of John Henry Roberts, his wife and their children. A photo ran of the burial. There were about twenty people in attendance, including several reporters from local papers.

The funeral service held for Pastor Mark Rheingold, however, was a very different story. The proceedings were held in Rheingold's old church in Houston, a ten-thousand seater that was filled to capacity for the ceremony. Ushers were needed to corral the crowds. At least four people were confirmed to have fainted. Another tried to drown himself in the hopes of meeting Mark Rheingold in heaven.

I came upon hundreds of photos of Mark Rheingold taken during his various pilgrimages in various newspapers, pamphlets and photo-ops. Rheingold was a thin man, not skinny but lean, with the lithe physique and stretched facial muscles of a jogger. His jet-black hair was always slicked back in a neat coif and his suits, like his wife's jewelry, were decent but not gaudy. Every photograph bore the pastor's thousand-watt smile. Though I did wonder why a man of God needed veneers.

Cards and flowers arrived from all fifty states and thirty foreign countries. Numerous politicians paid their condolences in person. Rheingold's closest friends and pastorial acquaintances read passages from his bestselling books. Rheingold's wife and young son remained stoic in the front row. The governor of Texas declared the day one of statewide mourning.

The following year, Rheingold's wife was given her own day-time talk show. His ten-year-old son published a book called Never Too Young to Follow the Lord, containing prayers and motivation for grade-schoolers.

There was very little reporting on the burial of the Roberts family. A grainy photo showed the four caskets being lowered. Two larger ones, for John and William. Two smaller ones for Meryl and Martha. John was noted as the grandson of Oliver P. "Brushy Bill" Roberts. Everything else was journalism-by-the-numbers.

One line from the article, though, threw me for a loop.

The Roberts family was buried in a closed-casket service presided over by Reverend Bert Brown. During his concluding remarks, Reverend Brown asked the heavenly father that the bodies of these four souls be looked after in heaven, and that any earthly remains not in these coffins find that everlasting peace.

Any earthly remains not in these coffins...

I immediately picked up the phone and dialed information for Hico, Texas. An automated voice answered.

"What listing?"

"I'd like the main number for the Hamilton County coroner's office."

"One moment please."

Muzak played in the background. I tuned out the newsroom chatter. Frank Rourke walked by the mail drop, turned and eyed me for what seemed like minutes, then kept walking.

"Hello, sir?"

"Yeah, sorry," I said. "Who is this?"

"Well my name is Helen, but I'm afraid there is no coroner's office in Texas."

"Do you mean Hamilton, Texas, or Texas as a whole?"

"I'm afraid that would be Texas as a whole."

"Then who's in charge of supervising wrongful death cases?"

"That would be the Justice of the Peace, sir."

"Then can I be connected to the office of the current Justice of the Peace?"

"Ab-so-lutely."

A minute passed as the line rang. Another woman picked up, her voice cheerful.

"Office of Justice Waverly's office, this is Brenda, how may I assist you?"

"Hi Brenda," I said, trying to make my voice sound as young as possible. Brenda sounded to be either in her late fifties or late teens. An aunt type. And aunts loved their young nephews. "My name is Henry Parker, and I'm with the New York Gazette. I'm a junior reporter."

"Oh, a junior reporter all the way up there in New York? That's wonderful. How can we help you, Henry?"

"If it's possible, I'd very much like to speak with Justice Waverly."

"Oh now, Justice Waverly is eating his breakfast and he doesn't like being disturbed during breakfast. Do you know that man can eat an entire stack of blueberry pancakes in one sitting? I swear I ain't seen nothing like it ever."

"That's fantastic, Brenda, really, but it's incredibly important I speak with him. We've had four homicides here in New York. And I think they might be related to an old case involving deaths in Hamilton County. Hico, to be exact."

There was silence over the phone as the word homicide seeped into Brenda's thoughts. As much as she wanted to protect Justice Waverly's breakfast routine, a good old gal like her couldn't bear to let such atrocities simmer.

"Now Henry, Justice Waverly will get mighty upset if I barge in there, make him get all messy and syrupy and this isn't an emergency of the important kind."

"Oh I promise Brenda, this is an emergency of the most important kind."

Brenda sighed as the good Samaritan in her kicked in. "Hold on just a sec."

Rather than put the line on hold, I heard a clang as she placed the phone down on her desk. I heard the sound of a door being opened, then the voice of a man none too happy about being interrupted. There was a brief spat, the sound of someone yelling with food in their mouth, and then more footsteps as Brenda returned to her desk.

"Hello Mr. Parker? Justice Waverly will be right with you."

"Thanks Brenda, you're a doll." Brenda giggled politely.

I heard a click as the line was picked up by another party.

"Hello?" a deep, male voice intoned.

"Is this Justice Waverly?" I said.

"Brenda I have it, hang up now." I heard a click as Brenda hung up her end. "Mr. Parker, Brenda tells me you're calling all the way from New York, that right?"

"Yes sir, Justice sir, I'm with the Gazette. I appreciate your taking my call."

"I didn't take no call, Brenda threatened to give me that terrible puppy dog look all day if I didn't. She tells me you said something about a homicide up there in the big city."

"That's right."

"Well if I'm not mistaken, you New Yorkers have quite a few homicides every year and you don't go calling me for all of those. So what makes you think my office can help with this one?"

"Well, sir, if I might answer a question with a question," I said, "were you the Justice of the Peace of Hamilton County in 2004?"

"I most certainly was," Waverly said. "I have been justice of this county for ought seventeen years."

"Then you probably recall notable criminal investigations during that time."

"I have a mind like an eagle, son. What are you getting at?"

"Well, Mr. Eagler, sir, then you'll remember the deaths of John Roberts, his family, and Pastor Mark Rheingold just a few years ago."

I heard a sharp intake of breath on the other end. And I knew I'd just pulled a big, dangling thread. I waited thirty seconds for a response. Waverly was still on the other end, but it was clear he wasn't dying to talk about the fire.

"Justice Waverly, are you still there?"

"Yes, Mr. Parker, I'm here."

"So you do remember those deaths?"

"I didn't say that."

"So you don't remember the alleged electrical fire that killed five people, including the most famous pastor in the state of Texas."

"I didn't say that either."

"Justice Waverly, I'm not the police," I said. "I'm a reporter trying to find out why four people have been murdered and how they might be connected to a fire that killed five people several years ago."

"I don't know how any of your murders are my concern, Mr. Parker. Now if you'll excuse me I have a meeting in just ten minutes and I still haven't had my coffee."

"Fine by me," I said. "Because my next call is to the FBI. I know Mike Sellers down at the Houston branch pretty well. And one thing he hates is red tape and bureaucratic doublespeak. So I hope you're not stringing any of that tape up for me."

I had spoken to Deputy Michael Sellers once, over e-mail. He had given me a terse no comment, though complimented me on a previous story about the treatment of prisoners at Rikers Island. I figured that brief correspondence was as good an opportunity as any to name-drop.

I heard a pounding sound, like something hitting wood. Sounded like Justice Waverly was getting frustrated and taking it out on his poor desk.

"No, now I wouldn't want that," Waverly said. "I'll answer any appropriate questions in order to help whatever story you're writing. But I won't go into tangential matters that are none of your business. So to answer your question, yes, I do remember the deaths of the Roberts family and the tragic passing of Pastor Rheingold. He was a pillar of this community."

"Would you say the Roberts family was a pillar of the community?"

"Shoot," he said. "John Roberts just moved his family down to Hico a few years back. He had some relatives down here got along pretty good, but I can't say they had as much influence as Pastor Mark."

"I read the news reports of the fire. You're sure it was electrical?"

"Goddamn right I am," Waverly said. "And I hope God's green ears don't hear you insinuating we didn't give that fire a thorough investigation."

"No, I'm saying the lady doth protest too much."

There was silence on the other end again. Then Waverly spoke.

"We turned that house inside out. There was nothing left. Not a doll, not a picture album, nothing. An entire family was destroyed in one night, I assure you it was a monumental tragedy. We didn't find any reason or need to pry more than we already had."

"So you're admitting the investigation wasn't handled as thoroughly as it could have been."

"I'm saying injury was bad enough without adding insult."

"Unless the insult and injury would have been to your town."

"I'm sorry Parker, you've lost me there."

"Let's see if you can follow: at the Roberts' funeral, the priest made a statement making it clear there were remains unaccounted for. That one or more of the coffins the Roberts family were buried were not full. Do you follow that?"

"I have nothing to say about such idiotic rumors. And if you don't mind me saying, I don't see how this has any relevance to your murders in New Yawk."

"I'll get to that," I said. "Now whose remains were never found?"

"This has nothing to do with you," said Waverly.

"Whose remains, Justice? I can be on the phone to Mike Sellers in thirty seconds and based on your lack of cooperation he can have those graves dug up in less time than it takes for you to stir your cream and sugar."

"You arrogant prick," Waverly spat. "Just who do you think you are? Do you have any idea who we are, what this town is? We have a thousand residents. You live in a city of millions, where nobody gives a shit about anybody else. Do you have any idea what something like this could do to our county?"

"Without the legend of Brushy Bill Roberts, your town dies," I said. "That's a fact. And by covering up a murder investigation, it will do the same thing."

"Who said anything about murder?" Waverly said. There was concern in his voice. It was trembling. He knew something.

"Whose remains were never found?"

"I don't have to talk to you?"

"Whose, Justice?"

"The son," he gushed. "William Henry. We found a piece of femur we believe was his, but…"

"But what?" I said.

"But we weren't sure. So we buried it."

"You buried an empty coffin?"

"It wasn't empty!" Waverly said. "There was a femur bone inside! Besides, the boy's body was nowhere. Either he died in that fire or he disappeared off the face of the earth. We figured his remains being too burnt up to find was a more likely scenario."

"Only those remains turned up alive in New York, pulling the trigger of a Winchester rifle four times, killing four people."

"Listen, Parker," Waverly said. "You don't know what it's like here. You don't know what this would mean to our township and its residents."

There had to be something else going on. Hico stood to prosper hugely if it was revealed Brushy Bill Roberts was, in fact, Billy the Kid. Waverly was hiding something else.

"What was Pastor Rheingold doing in that fire?" I asked. "Strange that he just happened to be at the Roberts home the night it goes up in flames."

"Enough!" Waverly said. "You got your damn story. Rheingold has nothing to do with it. Goodbye, Mr. Parker. I hope you sleep well tonight."

Waverly hung up. Sleep was the last thing I would find that night.

Chapter 43

Mya stirred. Not because her body awoke naturally. Not because sunlight from the outside had forced it, or because she had to pee, or any other number of reasons why nature might interrupt one's slumber.

No, Mya awoke because of the knife point she felt digging into her side.

"Wake up, Mya," he said. She opened her eyes, the lids dry and crusty. Her hands were still bound, her wrists hurt like hell. She hadn't been able to wipe the moisture or makeup away. The last thing she remembered was following this man back to his hotel room, having a drink, feeling his lips on hers, and then nothing. There was no other pain, and besides her bonds she was otherwise unharmed.

She was lying on the floor of some dingy hotel room. The bed was unmade. Ugly orange curtains dangled above her. The rusty air conditioner rattled, spewing a warm breeze. Under the bed she could see a small blue duffel bag, underwear and socks spilling out of it.

By the foot of the bed, Mya saw what appeared to be a gun. Not like the kind she saw in the movies. This one was long. The barrel seemed to have some kind of wood finish. The boy noticed her staring and said, agreeing, "She's a true thing of beauty."

Mya tried to squirm but it was no use. Her energy was gone. And a blade was ticking her ribs. If she bucked in the wrong direction, it could…

"How you feeling?" he asked. Mya blinked. What was his name? He'd told it to her at the bar. Where he'd been charming, funny, handsome and sweet. Of course all of this was before he kidnapped her. "Nod once for okay, nod twice for not okay."

Mya nodded twice, vigorously. She remembered his hands on her, her whole body tingling, feeling alive. She remembered his hands, strong and gentle, but then all of a sudden perfunctory, like they were only waiting to…

And here she was.

"You're not getting me, Miss Loverne. Nod once if you're okay,

The Guilty

as in not hurt. Nod twice if you are hurt. Forget about your hands. Can you walk?" Mya felt the blade dig in. She tried to cry out, but the tape prevented her from emitting anything but a pathetic whimper. She felt saliva coating the tape sealing her mouth.

She nodded once. That was all.

"You had me worried," the boy said with a grin.

William. His name was William.

"We have a busy night ahead of us," William said. "Are you up for it?"

Her first instinct was to try and scream. Or at least nod twice. But the knife made its horrible presence felt once again and she tilted her chin down once. A single tear streaked down Mya's cheek. The boy wiped it away.

Chapter 44

After leaving the office, I called Amanda. We hadn't spoken the whole day, mainly because I'd been swamped with Justice Waverly, then presenting the information to Wallace, Evelyn and Jack. Then I began to prep the outline of a blockbuster story that would both force the reopening of the fire in Hico, but present new information proving that Billy the Kid had lived long after his alleged murder. It was too soon to claim that Athena Paradis's killer was Billy's great-grandson, or that I thought he was. I knew it was true, but had to be able to convince others. Truth required proof, however, and since he was still at large the only proof were four silent corpses.

One thing was for certain, and Waverly had confirmed it, that William Henry Roberts was not among the victims who died in the fire.

So if William did not die in that fire, why was there no investigation into his whereabouts? Hamilton County police department came up empty, and they moved mighty quick to assume the body had simply "burnt up." Even I didn't think they would be that careless. At least not by accident.

Not a single newspaper report asked questions about the fire. They were too busy bemoaning the death of Mark Rheingold and four, less important, members of the Hico community. Everyone seemed more than happy to wash away any unpleasant memories and get on with their lives.

That brought up another question. What was Pastor Mark Rheingold, a statewide institution, a man who made millions of dollars a year and had thousands of rabid followers, doing at the Roberts house the night of the fire? I searched every archive available but couldn't find anything linking Rheingold to the Roberts family. It was a pretty big coincidence that Rheingold paid a house call the night a four-alarm blaze burned everything to the ground.

I dialed Amanda's line at work. It went right to voice mail.

"Hey babe it's me, I'm heading home now. You're probably still at work, just wanted to know if we should plan to have dinner together. Anyway, give me a call back. Love you."

Click.

I needed a night to relax, unwind. Everything this past week had come so suddenly. All those deaths—deaths of people I knew. The NYPD was beside themselves at this point, and the newspapers hadn't pulled punches in their criticism. And though New York had arguably the finest police department in the country, it was also a city in which it was all too easy to disappear. I knew that firsthand. Sooner or later the net would close in on Roberts. We could only hope it did before that Winchester fired again.

The Gazette's sales had gone through the roof the last few days. The city hadn't seen such juicy copy in a long time, and people were buying up papers in droves. Between Athena Paradis's murder, the turmoil at Franklin-Rees after Jeffrey Lourdes's death, the NYPD wanting blood for Joe Mauser, and the societal fallout from David Loverne's murder, it was a gold mine for newshounds.

Joe Mauser's death had been relegated to the back pages. A cop dying in the line of duty just didn't sell as many papers as a murdered pretty blond white girl. It was strange that this pissed me off so much, considering Joe Mauser's bullet had left a nasty scar on my leg. Just one year ago, Mauser wanted to kill me. Strangely enough, I held no ill will towards the man. If someone had done to my family what he thought I'd done to his, I would have wanted blood as well.

I got off the subway and began walking towards our apartment. The summer sun was dipping below the clouds, the shimmering towers of New York fading into night. The streets began to fill as people straggled home from work. Finally, after over a year I felt I was becoming a part of this city. It hadn't been easy, thanks to assholes like Frank Rourke. Since the dog crap prank, my desk had been left alone. I had gone along with it, laughed it up, threw it in the trash and left it at that. If you let guys like Frank know they'd drawn blood, they'd grow addicted to the taste. I could bleed on my own time.

I approached the apartment building and fished in my pocket for the key. I wondered if we should move, to a safer neighborhood, live in a building with a doorman. Now that Amanda was living with me I wasn't completely comfortable with her walking home alone, especially since most days she came home later than I did. I had to take care of the woman I loved. Put her needs before mine. I was determined to prove Jack wrong. I could balance work and relationships. I didn't have to give in just because he did. Jack was a legend, but an old school legend. I was strong. I could make it work.

As I turned the key in the lock, a voice broke the night and froze my blood. I recognized that voice, only now it was louder, angrier.

I heard it again, turned around. Saw several pedestrians staring up, up at the rooftops, their mouths open in masks of horror. A man dialed his cell phone frantically. A woman grabbed her son and ran.

Then I heard it again.

"Henry Parker!"

High above us, perched atop a four-story brownstone, illuminated by the descending moonlight, was William Henry Roberts. One hand was empty. The other held a knife. The knife was held to Mya Loverne's throat.

"Mya!" I shouted. Her eyes were frightened beyond rational thought. Some sort of towel or cloth was in her mouth. I ran forward, then stopped.

"Parker!" Roberts cried again.

"Leave her alone!" I shouted, unsure of what else to do. I wasn't close enough to get to them. No cops were in sight. Fucking Carruthers had pulled off my security detail, and now...

I called you, Henry.

Mya.

"This," Roberts said, his voice a mixture of pathos and breathless glee, like a man taking perverse excitement in reprimanding a dog. "This is what happens. I control information, not you, Parker. So consider this a present, Henry. From me to you."

And with that, before I could react, before my weak legs could respond or my mouth could cry out, William pushed Mya off the roof.

I shouted "No!" as her body plummeted out of view. The horde of onlookers gasped. Mya disappeared into the alley behind the building. I ran towards it, then heard the most horrible sound of my life. A terrible thump as something hit the ground.

Then I looked up, and Roberts was gone.

I ran as fast as I could, the world around me disappearing in

The Guilty

blur. I sprinted into the alley, then covered my mouth in shock.

Mya was lying on the ground. Her eyes were open, staring at the sky. I could see a small pool of blood below her.

I ran over and grabbed her hand.

"No," I whispered, frantically checking her wrists, her neck, anything. I thought I felt a pulse. Weak, but there. I could hear 911 calls being made somewhere behind me. "Mya, please, oh please God say something. Don't you dare die. Don't you dare. Please."

Then she blinked. Once, twice. Her mouth quivered. A noise came from her mouth, a small bubble of blood bursting over her lips.

"Somebody get an ambulance!" I shouted, wiping away the blood. "Please!"

"They're on the way," another voice yelled.

"Don't you go," I said to Mya. "Don't you go. You're going to be fine." My eyes darted, hoping to catch a glimpse of Roberts, but the murdering bastard was nowhere to be found. I took Mya's hand. It was growing cold.

I called you, Henry.

"I know you did, and I'm here. Please baby, please stay with me."

"Henry? Oh my God…"

I recognized that voice. I stood up, my footing unsure. Amanda was standing in the alley. Her face was white.

"Oh God Henry, what happened?"

"Amanda…"

I looked at Amanda. Her beautiful eyes. Those arms that had held me so close. The strong heart that had given itself to me. Trusted me.

Just like Mya had trusted me years ago. And now Mya was lying, broken.

No.

Amanda stepped forward. "Henry, oh God, is she alive? Please say something."

"I…"

I heard a gasp behind me. Mya's mouth was opening and closing. Another bubble of blood burst, coating her chin. I knelt back down and wiped it off. Not again. Not Mya. Not Amanda…

"Henry, please…"

213

"Get the fuck away from me!" I screamed, bolting up. My body felt ready to explode, and in my mind's eye I saw everything I touched, everything I loved, broken in pieces. I couldn't see Amanda. Not like this. Not like Mya. I'd already failed one woman. I couldn't do it again.

"Henry, please talk to me."

"Get the fuck out of here!" I yelled again, this time stepping towards Amanda, a fire in my eyes that I could see reflected via fear in hers. She stepped back. I stepped forward.

"Get out of here," I said, panting. "Don't ever come back. Leave now."

"No," Amanda said, tears flowing from her eyes. "Don't do this. I'm not Mya, I'm not..."

"Get away from me, and never come back." She didn't move. "I said get the fuck away from me!"

Amanda looked at me, crying, unable to say a word. Then she turned and ran into the night. And I turned back to Mya, took her hand. "Baby don't leave me...it's Henry...please don't leave me...I'm here..."

Chapter 45

Paulina Cole sat at her desk rifling through the transcription of an interview with a Republican senator she had just spoken to that afternoon. She didn't particularly like the man—primarily because she knew a great deal more about his predilection towards Guatemalan housemaids than did the voters—but he was a shoo-in for reelection and Ted Allen's instructions were to paint him in the most positive light. That Ted had contributed close to six figures towards his reelection campaign was not to be mentioned. Paulina had already picked out six good sound bites, thankfully all taken within some sort of context, and was in the midst of outlining tomorrow's front page story.

She was writing longhand when a sweaty, haggard James Keach appeared in her doorway. Keach staggered in, dropped into a seat across from her desk, his breathing hard, eyes frightened. It was the first time James had taken a seat without her express permission. Usually he stood by the doorway taking instructions. He didn't even think twice about plopping down, and it unnerved Paulina.

"Jesus, James, what happened to you?" she said, allowing a hint of concern to creep into her voice.

James looked up, as though startled to realize he was sitting in Paulina's office. He looked around, then locked eyes with her and leaned forward. James looked like he'd just witnessed something unspeakable, and would give anything to take it all back.

"I was trailing Henry Parker," James said. "And…oh God…"

"Spit it out."

James Keach's body began to convulse with sobs. She felt panic well up, but the flavor of excitement as well. Wherever there was fear was also a great story.

"Mya Loverne," James said. "I was following Henry and…"

For the next five minutes, James told her what he'd seen that night. The man atop the building. Mya's body hitting the ground. Henry Parker screaming, crying. The ambulances, the broken girl being sped away to the hospital.

The killer on the rooftop, grinning like the devil himself.

When James was finished, Paulina sat in silence. She recalled her conversation with Mya at the diner; the small, frail girl looking like she was one tap away from shattering. Mya Loverne. Was it possible…

Paulina cleared her throat, blew her nose into a handkerchief. She picked up the phone and dialed the metro desk.

"Fred, Paulina Cole here. Call Ted Allen. Tell him Senator Brisbane is being pushed back to page seven. We have a new page one story tomorrow."

She hung up. Looked at James.

"Did they say Mya is going to make it?" she asked. James shook his head.

"I couldn't get into the hospital, and nobody would speak on her condition. But it looked pretty bad."

Paulina closed her eyes, dismissed James with a wave of her hand. When he left, she sat back, folded her hands behind her head. Then with a snap she sat forward, pushing the sympathy from her mind. Then she turned on her computer, and began to type.

Chapter 46

There is no place whose atmosphere gives off such a potent mixture of calm and anxiety as a hospital room. The beeps come at such even intervals that if you forget their purpose for a moment, they could easily lull you to sleep. Then you remember what they represent and that knot swells up in your stomach, you look at the prone figure being monitored by machines, and you feel like you might never sleep again. Watching Mya breathe through a tube, that's how I felt.

Chairs in hospital rooms weren't any better. They were all metal and odd contours. As if the hospital didn't want you relaxing on the job.

I was alone in the room with Mya. Her mother, Cindy Loverne, was asked to leave by hospital staff. She arrived shortly after Mya and broke down immediately. Screaming. Crying. Asking how God could allow her husband and daughter to possibly be taken in the same week. She asked if God was testing her strength as a woman, as a person. It wasn't God who had done this to her family.

Cindy had hugged me. I hadn't seen her in almost a year and a half, the last time being in a different hospital room. Again, watching Mya breathe. It was hard not to apologize to Cindy Loverne; meeting me was the worst thing that ever happened to Mya.

The last time Mya was in the hospital she left with a barely visible scar. But I always knew it was there, might as well have been a bloodred tattoo.

If Mya survived this—the doctors had given her a thirty percent chance of doing so—she wouldn't be so lucky this time.

Mya had suffered multiple skull fractures and a shattered hip. It took three hours of surgery to reduce the swelling in her brain, to fuse her bones back together. And that was the good news. The doctors said thankfully she'd landed on her side. That might have saved her life. If she'd landed on her back or head, she would either be paralyzed or dead. At least now she had a fighting chance. And I knew Mya was a fighter. I knew it.

"Hey. Henry."

I turned around. Curt Sheffield was standing in the doorway. He was dressed in full uniform. The blue clashed against the white walls. I noticed the gun on his belt, holstered, safe. For a moment I thought about grabbing it, marching into the street and stalking around the city until that bastard Roberts showed his face. And then I would show him the same mercy he showed everyone else. None.

Curt gestured for me to join him outside. I nodded, stood up. Watched Mya's chest rise and fall.

I went into the hallway, followed Curt towards a small waiting area. We both took seats.

"How is she?" he asked.

"She's got a battle ahead of her."

"She looks like the kind of girl who's fought a lot of battles recently." I nodded, knew many of them were my fault.

"She's tough," I said. "Her hip will be fine. It's her head they're concerned about. They won't know how much damage there is until the swelling comes down."

"Jesus," Curt said, shaking his head. "Thing like this, kind of makes you want to become an atheist."

"Actually I've never prayed more in my life. But I'm pretty sure God is considering revoking my baptism right now."

"You know this isn't your fault, right?" Curt watched me, waited for a response. I didn't answer him. I couldn't. Because it wouldn't be the answer he was hoping for. "Henry, you know that, right?"

"Amanda," I said. "Have you…"

"She's staying with a co-worker tonight. You know she's worried sick about you man," Curt said. "Amanda's a hell of a catch. It hurt her to see Mya like that. She just doesn't want it to break you."

"It won't break me," I said. "But it might have broken us."

"Do you love her?" he asked. I said nothing. "I said do you love her?"

"Yes," I said. "I do."

"Then don't do this. You're a selfish prick you don't at least call. You think you're the only one hurting?"

"I can't see Amanda ending up like that," I said, pointing towards Mya's room. "That girl is in there because of me. Because of who I am and what I do. I can't control anything, man. I can't help myself from taking these punches, but I'll be damned if Amanda needs to feel them too."

"You don't think she's feeling it right now?"

"Not the same way Mya is. Emotional pain hurts, yeah. But physical pain can kill. I'd rather her be devastated than dead." I looked up at Curt. "Have you come any closer to catching this guy? Please tell me they've found the son of a bitch."

Curt took a deep breath. I saw a twitch as his hand went to his holster. I knew what he was wishing, because I felt the same way.

"No," he said. "NYPD is tripping over themselves to get at this guy, but the mayor's made everyone scared. Too many young guys in this city, too many potential suspects. One person gets an itchy trigger finger, Roberts is forgotten about and we have a crisis on our hands."

"So what then, we wait until he kills someone else, falls asleep at the scene?"

"First off," Curt said, "there's no 'we'. You're not a cop. You do your job, keep digging up leads, write shit people care about. We'll do ours and eventually we'll catch this guy."

"Bang-up job so far," I said.

"You know what, Henry? Go fuck yourself. You're not the only one hurting. Four people are dead and your ex is banged up bad. You want to vent? Go ahead. But don't crap on the only people left who give a damn about you."

"I don't need this," I said. "I have work to do. I have to find this guy."

"Yeah, right."

"You gonna stop me?"

"Stop you?" Curt said, laughing. "Why would I do that? Hell, I'll even walk you out. But listen man, Carruthers is going to make another statement tonight." He took a breath. "They found another quote. Where he pushed Mya."

"Jesus."

"Thought you'd be better off hearing it from me instead of the tube."

"Thanks for small favors. What did it say?"

"Was addressed to you," Curt said.

"To me?"

Curt nodded. "Said, 'Henry: Quien es?'"

Jason Pinter

"Quien es?"

"It's Spanish," Curt said.

"I figured that," I said. "What's it mean?"

"Means 'who is it?'"

"He asked me 'who is it?'"

"Guess he's not done with you yet. Be careful, my friend."

Cindy Loverne passed us in the hall. She grazed my shoulder with her hand, gave a weak smile.

"Gimme a minute to talk to Mya's mom," I said. "Then I'll head out."

"Take your time," Curt replied. "That family needs you more than I do."

I nodded, clapped Curt on the back, entered Mya's hospital room. Cindy was kneeling on the floor. She was holding Mya's hand, stroking it gently. I heard her whispering close to her daughter's face. I hadn't entered quietly. I watched Cindy speak to her daughter for several minutes before she stood up, walked to an empty chair and flung herself down.

"How are you, Mrs. Loverne?"

The woman's expression didn't change. She had a dreamy look in her eyes, slightly glazed. She was likely on some sort of sedative. If these things had happened to my husband and daughter I'd want to be knocked out too.

"I'm okay," she said, her voice slow and deliberate. "How've you been, Henry? It's been such a long time."

"I'm doing okay," I said.

"I see your name in the newspaper a lot. So proud that you're doing so well for yourself."

I said nothing. Felt proud of nothing. And receiving compliments made me feel worse.

"I'm so sorry about Mya," I said. "But she's going to make it and come out a hundred percent. She's going to recover and be a great lawyer. She's going to make you proud."

"That'd be nice," Cindy said. "David always said Mya had the brains in the family. I sure believed him. Did you know David used to watch 'Cops' every night? And those 'When Animals Attack' videos? I always said to him, 'David, how can such an educated man watch such tripe?' You know what he said?"

"No, what did he say?"

"He said every smart person needs some stupidity to take their minds off of life."

"Mya used to always make me watch videos of people getting tricked," I said. "Candid camera-type stuff."

"Oh!" Cindy said, clapping her hands together. "Like the one where someone drops a fake spider onto the shoppers at the mall."

"She almost burned out my DVD player at school, making me watch that."

Cindy's face was red, her smile long and genuine. She looked over at her daughter, her head swathed in bandages, and the smile quickly disappeared. "I hope you get to watch those with her again sometime," she said. "Henry?"

"Yes, Mrs. Loverne?"

"Would you like to watch those videos with me and Mya sometime? When she gets out of this place?"

"There's nothing I'd rather do more," I said. And I meant it.

"Henry, would you mind giving me some time alone with my daughter?"

"Of course not," I said. "You have my cell phone number in case you need anything, right?"

She held up her phone. "It's been programmed in here for a long time."

I smiled. "Please call me. For anything."

Cindy only nodded, and went back to staring at her daughter. I stood up, went over to Mya, kissed her lightly on the forehead. Cindy was beaming as I stood up.

"Take care, Mrs. Loverne."

"You, too, Henry. Such a handsome boy. I'm so glad my baby dated a boy with such ambition."

"Goodbye, Mrs. Loverne."

I left the hospital and met Curt outside. Then I caught a cab to Rockefeller Plaza.

Roberts had to have left a trail somewhere. Pastor Mark Rheingold. Something about him wasn't right. And where better to find a trail than to start with a man of God?

Chapter 47

"Do you want to talk about it?"

Amanda spun around. Darcy Lapore was standing by her desk, arms folded as though expecting an easy yes. Darcy was married, in her early thirties, made less than thirty grand a year, yet never came to work wearing an outfit that cost less than the net worth of the average Colombian drug czar. Her husband—a sweet man named Greg who just happened to work at a hedge fund—lavished expensive jewels and Caribbean vacations on her like the Gulf of Mexico might dry up at any moment. Despite this, Darcy still gave out her phone number to anyone who asked. Always off by one number, though, and thankfully men were pretty stupid.

Amanda had never been to the Bahamas. Or Mexico. She'd never been outside the continental United States. It wasn't that Lawrence and Harriet never tried to take her on family vacation, but they would always be that: Lawrence and Harriet. They would never be her parents—her family. She never had any desire to go away with them. It was like going away with a roommate you didn't particularly get along with. Children found themselves at odds with their parents all the time, but there was always an inherent love, a binding that surpassed most animosity. She never had that bond. So the animosity lingered.

It wasn't hate, they were good people after all, but there was never any desire to spend more time with them than she had to. Brief chats at the dinner table, superficial discussions about homework, friends, occasionally boys, and the future. Amanda loved to talk about the future.

Darcy was constantly stuck in the present. The "what now." Which is why Amanda liked her.

Today Darcy was wearing a stylish Versace pantsuit and a maroon tank top underneath. Her buoyant cleavage was visible above the lapels. Appropriate attire for a not-for-profit organization. A thin string of pearls danced around her neck, and the diamonds in her ears could have choked a horse.

"Baby, you want to talk?" she repeated.

"You know, I appreciate the gesture," Amanda said, "but I'm okay. Thanks anyway."

"You don't look okay, honey darling," Darcy said. That was another Darcy trademark—taking two NutraSweet words and sticking them together like syrup on top of fried sugar. "What's the matter?"

"Really," Amanda said, self-consciously pulling her v-neck sweater up a little higher. "It's okay."

Darcy rolled a chair over, nearly knocking over a potted plant in the process. "Is it boy trouble?" she asked with a mischievous smile, clearly hoping it would be. Though Darcy's idea of boy trouble likely consisted of "he doesn't pay attention to me" and not the "he just witnessed his ex-girlfriend being thrown off a roof" variety.

"Things could be better in that department," Amanda said. She began typing on her keyboard, nothing but gibberish, but hoping Darcy would get the hint.

"Oh, do tell! My Greg, any time he's not performing up to snuff I tell him. I say 'listen honeybabe, you know I love you, but we need to get a few things straight because my chi isn't being harnessed.'"

"Your chi?"

"Hell yes babycakes, my chi. If my chi isn't being harnessed I need to let my man know about it. It's like a tree root. It can go a few weeks without being watered, but unless you want it to dry up permanently you gotta feed it some water. Nourish that sucker."

"I think that's about all I need to know about your chi."

"Suit yourself. So what is it? Man trouble? Something else? Come on, babypie, tell me."

Amanda stopped typing. She didn't want to talk to Darcy but...

The truth was she had nobody else. For over twenty years, Amanda had grown up a stranger to everyone, even those supposed to take care of her. She was always introverted, never talking unless being talked to. It was great for developing sardonic comebacks, but meaningful conversations occurred as often as meaningful relationships. And that's where the notepads came in.

She hadn't written on them in months. Since she and Henry had gotten serious. Since she found someone who made her feel like she wasn't a stranger anymore. Someone who felt like he would be in her life longer than a leaf fluttering. Someone who felt like he would stay with her forever.

And yet here she was, sitting at work at seven o'clock at night, having finished up her daily tasks, biding the time until everyone left and she could fall asleep on her boss's couch.

Amanda had feared, early on, about what would happen if she and Henry split up, grew distant. After their first few months, she never imagined they could grow apart. She never feared tomorrow would bring an empty bed. Today, Amanda wondered if that tomorrow had finally arrived.

Amanda looked into Darcy's eyes. They were coated with makeup, brought out by jewels, but they were also honest. Darcy seemed genuinely interested, genuinely concerned. Whether it was a fleeting concern Amanda couldn't tell, but if she didn't let out some steam she would either explode or cry.

She smiled at Darcy. Opened up the web browser on her computer. Went to the home page of the New York Dispatch. Clicked on the headline banner, opening up their top story of the day.

The headline read: Murdered Politician's Daughter Critically Injured After Being Thrown from Rooftop.

"The same person who killed Athena Paradis," Amanda said, as Darcy scanned the article. "He threw Mya Loverne off a roof."

"That guy scares the shit out of me," Darcy said, seemingly oblivious. "I mean I'm not the biggest Athena Paradis fan, but I can't say the girl deserved to die. To think there's someone like that walking around out there…God, just gives me the creeps."

Then Darcy's eyes stopped scanning. She was reading a line three-quarters of the way down the page. She underlined a sentence with her fingernail.

"Is that…"

The line read: Loverne is also reported to have been romantically involved with Henry Parker, a junior reporter at the New York Gazette who himself was the focus of a murder investigation just last year.

Amanda felt a terrible lump rise in her throat.

"That…that's your boy trouble?"

Amanda laughed softly, didn't know why, then nodded, heard a patter as the first droplet hit her keyboard. Darcy's face was a mix of sympathy and confusion. That's your man??

Amanda leapt from her seat without turning the screen off, threw on her coat and fled the office, running into the New York night where the lonely streets awaited her.

Chapter 48

I walked to my desk without stopping for any hellos, any questions, queries or anything. I ignored everybody. I sat down at my desk knowing eyes were watching me, waiting to see what would happen, debating whether to offer support, taking mental wagers on who would be the first to break the seal and open conversation. I turned on my computer and immediately ran a search for the words Quien es and Billy the Kid.

I found several matches. And that vague Spanish line took on a whole new meaning.

When Pat Garrett allegedly killed Billy the Kid, the Kid's last words were Quien es. They were supposedly uttered in the dark, before Garrett put a bullet through Billy's heart. Words spoken from Billy to Pat Garrett, and now William Henry Roberts to me.

I was his Pat Garrett. The man who would make Roberts famous.

Quien es.

Who was this killer?

I opened up my files on William Henry Roberts.

From the corner of my eye I could see someone approaching. Turning, I expected to see Jack, but was surprised to see Frank Rourke standing in front of me.

"Hey," Frank said. He had a day's beard growth, red eyes. "I just wanted to say I'm sorry about your girl."

"Thanks," I said.

"And I'm sorry about the dog shit too. That was pretty low."

"Don't be. It was funny."

"Right," Frank said. "Funny. Listen, if you need anything—"

"Gotcha," I said, then turned away.

Frank took the hint, and left.

Mark Rheingold. The famous pastor. I didn't buy that he was at the Roberts ranch simply for evening tea.

As I scanned the articles, I looked at the framed picture at the right of my desk. Amanda and I had taken it last fall after a concert at Jones Beach. Her hair was wet; the skies had opened during the encore, rain and thunder making the music seem that much more powerful, one of those night you wished would never end. We were glistening wet, arms wrapped around each other, smiles big and bright. That night we went home and made love for hours. When the photo was developed Amanda pinched my butt, told me we needed more of those nights, especially if they all ended like that.

I turned the frame facedown. I couldn't have Amanda watching me. I couldn't think about her. I had to lose myself in the work. Finally, I had to listen to Jack. Which was apt, because Jack was heading towards my desk.

I stopped typing, turned around. Jack was wearing a suit that looked recently dry-cleaned, and breath that smelled recently minted. There was no red in his eyes or his cheeks, so the previous night was likely spent solely in the caffeinated company of his friend Juan Valdez.

He took up his familiar perch on the side of my desk. My face was blank. I didn't want him to be there; didn't want him to leave. I was ambivalent about his entire existence at that moment.

"How you holding up, kid?"

"How's what holding up?"

Jack's mouth twitched. "Come on Henry, you know what I mean. How's Mya?"

"She's in the hospital with a hole in her head and pins in her hip."

"Heaven help us," he whispered, running his hand over his beard. "Are you okay?"

"I'm just peachy."

"You don't sound peachy."

"Trust me, I'm peachy."

My face must have conveyed emotions that were definitely not peachy.

"Look Henry, about that talk we had a while back—about Amanda..."

"She's out of my life. You did your job. You were right."

"That's not my point, I know you kids had a good thing going..."

"I'm not your kid, Jack. I'm not your boy, sport, tiger, son or anything. I work with you. If you want to give me advice on how to do the job better, I'm all ears. If you want to tell me how to live my life, save it. I've heard it. It's done. Now unless you want to help me figure out what the hell Mark Rheingold was doing at the Roberts residence the night it burned to the ground, I have nothing to say to you."

"Mark Rheingold," Jack said. His eyes had strayed from me, rolled back into his head, combing his memory. I stopped talking. Jack knew something, heard something. Now I wanted him to stay. "Rheingold...Pastor, right? Had that big ass congregation down in Texas?"

"Houston," I said. "That's right."

"What house are you talking about? Is this Roberts related to William Henry?"

"A ranch belonging to his parents," I said, "caught fire about four years ago. The mother, father and sister were all killed, along with Mark Rheingold. The sheriff claims William Roberts also died, but I just spoke to the justice of the peace in Hamilton and after some prodding he admitted William's remains were never found. They buried a coffin with no body. So what I'm trying to figure out is why Rheingold was there in the first place."

"Rheingold," Jack said, "guy was making boatloads of cash, gave about ninety percent of it to the church and various charities. Wife was a hottie too, but that's beside the point. Big rumor was that Rheingold was taking kickbacks from his parishioners."

"Why would he take kickbacks if he was making so much money?"

"Henry," Jack said, shaking his head. "Kickbacks aren't always about money. Sometimes you can get back things that have no monetary value."

I thought for a moment. "You're saying he was sleeping with members of his congregation."

"I'm saying a lot of people thought he was, but there was never any proof to back it up. The woman would never tell because they were 'laying closer to God' or some bull, and their husbands kept their mouths shut because either a) they felt the same way, or b) what guy wants the world to know his wife is better satisfied by a man who's a servant of the Lord?"

"So you think Rheingold might have been doing the humpty Jesus dance with Meryl Roberts?"

The Guilty

"I don't keep a list in my pocket of all the church honeys Rheingold might have bedded, but you put two and two together chances are it's gonna add up to four."

"Unless one of those variables doesn't equal two."

"I was never very good at physics."

"That's math."

"I was an English major," Jack said.

"Me too."

Jack laughed. "No wonder you work here." His smile died with the conversation. "Give Mya's family my best. I hope she pulls through."

I nodded thanks, and Jack walked away.

As soon as he left, I pulled up a LexisNexis search for "Mark Rheingold" and "Meryl Roberts." It came back with four hits.

The first was an article in the Hico News about the second annual Texas Steak Cookoff, sponsored by the Hico High football team, featuring a special appearance by none other than Pastor Mark Rheingold. Meryl Roberts, whose daughter Martha was captain of the Hico girls' soccer team, was quoted as saying, "Hico is proud to welcome Pastor Rheingold. We know his presence will foster faith and support for our wonderful community, and lead these boys to the state championship."

The second and third articles celebrated the $7,000 raised by the event to help defray the cost of new football uniforms for the Hico Marauders. Leftover donations went towards purchasing new textbooks, as the school hadn't bought new ones in nearly a decade. The article ran next to a photo of Hico quarterback John Runyan. He wasn't holding a textbook, but his uniform looked spiffy.

The fourth article was about Pastor Rheingold's return to Hico after a six-month absence, in which he'd been touring around the country, speaking in auditoriums holding as many as ninety thousand worshippers. A church spokesman called it Rheingold's "God-appalooza" tour. He spoke at Madison Square Garden. The Staples Center. The freaking Rose Bowl.

The piece ran concurrent to a photograph of Rheingold being swarmed by a crowd of fans and supporters as he walked down main street in Hico.

In the photo, dozens of hands were reaching for him, but his eyes and embrace were focused on one woman in particular. Her hair was wavy and recently permed, her eyes sparkling, the cut of her dress just an inch or two lower than the other women. Pastor Rheingold was frozen in time, right about to wrap his suited arms around her. A big smile played on his face.

The caption read: An exhausted yet emboldened Pastor Mark Rheingold greets worshippers during his return to Texas.

The woman in the photo was Meryl Roberts.

That look in her eyes was not of an adoring fan, or heaven-obsessed parishioner. It was the same look I saw at the airport, when husbands returned to their wives. When lovers reunited. When dormant embers were rekindled.

John Roberts was standing next to his wife in the photo. A smile was on his face. A smile that knew more than he was willing to tell.

And in the background, over both of their shoulders, was the face of the man who had killed four people, cut up my hand and thrown my former lover off a rooftop. It was the face of William Henry Roberts.

He was staring at Mark Rheingold. I recognized the burning in his eyes as the same expression he had right before pushing Mya off a building. That he'd enjoy the violence about to take place.

Chapter 49

William Henry Roberts lay in bed, naked excerpt for a pair of loose-fitting shorts. The window was open, his skin dry from the cool summer air. He could hear sirens like crazed bees flying down the New York streets, looking to quench fires that could only be put out briefly before igniting again. They were looking for the source of these flames, and so far they'd come up empty.

William read the papers. He knew they were looking for a ghost. He could be anybody. Someone's friend. Someone's brother. Someone's son.

In one life he had been all of these.

He could sense the panic in the streets as men and women tried to figure out who might be next. They promised to keep their children locked up, to come home early from work. That made him laugh. He wasn't targeting normals moms and pops. All of his victims shared the same bond, and once he'd taken out as many as possible, in the end they would all thank him.

Some called him heartless.

Cold.

Evil.

A demon.

The devil himself.

Others called him a warrior.

A prophet.

An apostle.

One said that God worked in mysterious ways.

One referred to his beloved Winchester as the weapon with which God was raining brimstone down upon the city of sin. That only through darkness and devastation could light eventually emerge.

William Henry Roberts read all of these, and knew that with the right fire the whole city could burn. Just like the fire that had lit up the Texas sky years ago.

It took a fire to clean William and awaken him. It would take a fire for this city to see the light.

Just like his great-grandfather had done all those years ago, riding with fearless men who tried to right the wrongs of so many evils only to find backs turned, his very motives questioned, an army amassing against his fellow Regulators.

He was forced into hiding to save his life. He had to live a lie, denying his heritage until he was nearly on his deathbed.

Bonney was a great name. Billy the Kid was the mythological name bestowed upon him. William's parents had tried to hide that legacy from him. Better for them to die than to bury the legend, stem the blood.

The heiress and the mogul were all targeted from the beginning. The cop was a mistake, but a fortunate one. David Loverne was a split-second decision. After reading Mya's interview in the Dispatch, it was an easy choice.

Mya, though, was another story.

She had to go because of Henry.

William Roberts was a Regulator. Some thought him a villain, others a savior. Whichever side of the coin he was on, Henry Parker was on the other, the one chosen by fate to chronicle William's myth. Parker was young man, just a few years older than Roberts's twenty-one. Henry himself had been hunted, narrowly escaping death.

We're the same.

Even if Henry didn't understand what William was trying to accomplish, he would be the one to spread the gospel. Patrick Floyd Garrett didn't agree with Billy the Kid, but it was his sensational storytelling that cemented Billy's legend. And for Henry to be able to tell the story with the passion necessary, he needed to feel anger. He needed to feel hate. He needed to feel loss. Only then would his words have the desired effect. Once Henry Parker saw the world the way William did, that thin line separating life and death, innocent and guilty, their two sides would amount to a perfect whole.

William remembered back to the night he learned the truth about his family. The first was the truth about his legacy. Though his parents had fought their hardest to distance themselves from it, William knew his grandfather Oliver well. And when he learned the full extent of his legacy, there was no way he could let that mantle simply fall to the floor. He had to pick it up, shepherd it into a new millennium. And New York, more than New Mexico or Texas, needed it.

The Guilty

The second truth was about his mother and that smiling bastard. His parents told him they loved him, would never lie to him, that they would always put William and his sister above everything.

They forgot to leave out the "almost" before the everything.

William's mission had been clear. When a patient's limbs become gangrenous, you had cut them off before they killed the whole. Sometimes you had to lose limbs vital to who you were. Limbs you never believed you could live without.

But he did.

William picked up the Winchester, ran his fingers along the cold steel, tried to envision all the lives shattered, worlds changed by this weapon. He squeezed it tight, believed he felt his ancestor, the great Billy the Kid, transferring his strength.

William felt it, felt ready. He knew where he had to go. He knew who had to die next. Mya Loverne was a stopgap, a bonus, but to get to Henry he had to strike closer. Because for Henry Parker to truly be the other side of William, he would have to learn to deal with the death of his loved ones as well.

Chapter 50

When I first moved to New York, I would often find myself wandering the streets at night. Walking for blocks and blocks for no real reason other than to soak in the city, bask in the dimming sun and reflections off the towers. I dreamed of being part of this town, and like a lover I wanted to caress and explore every inch of it.

I would walk down to the South Street Seaport, breath in the salty air, stroll along the historic district with ports that looked like a relic from a Melville novel, made you forget it was a city with 3.2 coffee shops per square block.

I would walk all the way west to the Hudson, then down to Chelsea Piers, watching young teenagers skateboarding and couples bowling while a mammoth cruise ship took young lovers around the Hudson, down past where the World Trade Center once stood, around the East River where they could see the majestic arches of the Brooklyn Bridge, the grace of the Statue of Liberty.

Most of these sojourns took place while my relationship with Mya was deteriorating. In prior months we would have spent every moment of every evening together, cuddled up on a couch, watching a movie. Mya would wear one of my sweatshirts, purposefully drop popcorn all over my lap. Eventually we'd fool around and pass out, start the next day fresh.

Then our relationship dimmed, and we began to avoid each other at all costs. Then after I met Amanda, after I nearly died, Mya and I lost touch completely.

I didn't mind. I loved Amanda. It may have been cruel to leave Mya hurting, but it would have been worse to lead her on.

Ordinarily walking the streets alone at night wouldn't have been such a big deal. I wouldn't have thought twice about it. But tonight I was walking alone, knowing Amanda was somewhere else. Not because my relationship with her was similar to my relationship with Mya—a Band-Aid slowly being peeled off—but because it had been painfully ripped away.

Suddenly I looked up and I was standing at the apartment building of Linda Fredrickson. I hadn't planned it, at least not consciously.

Linda Fredrickson was Joe Mauser's sister. Her husband, John, had died from a gunshot wound after I confronted him. If John had never met me, Linda would still have a husband.

After it was revealed that John Fredrickson was a dirty cop and I was exonerated of the murder charges, I attempted to contact Linda. At that point I wasn't really thinking about whether or not she would forgive me. It just seemed like the right thing to do.

A year ago I had come to this very apartment building, gone upstairs and knocked on her door. She opened it and stared at me with a befuddled look, the kind you might give a Jehovah's Witness who simply won't stop soliciting you. I told her I was sorry. She slapped me hard across the face. She slammed the door and I left.

For uncertain reasons, tonight I felt I had to speak to Linda. If anyone could understand what was happening, she could. Mya was in the hospital. I had to cut Amanda from my life before she got hurt. I had nobody to turn to.

But this wasn't about me. Linda had her own life. She was still grieving over the loss of her brother. I never knew Joe Mauser beyond the frantic cross-country chase last year when he tried to kill me in revenge for his brother-in-law's death. Funny thing is, I never held a grudge. Mauser was doing his job, avenging the death of a family member. If anything I respected him more for that.

I stood in front of the awning, debating whether to call on Linda Fredrickson. The doorman sighed and walked over to me. He knew I didn't live there. His eyes were raised as if to say either come in, or get the hell out of here.

"May I ask who you're here to visit?" He wore a red uniform and a square hat with gold tassels. I could see several newspapers littering his tiny counter; the flicker on the glass told me he kept a small television set to pass the time.

"Nobody," I said. "Just walking around the neighborhood."

"All right then," he said, with a suspicious tone. He left me and went back inside, immediately picking up the newspaper. He raised the cover and for a moment I had a terrible sense of déjà vu. On the cover was a police sketch of William Henry Roberts. It looked both exactly like him and nothing like him. He was a young man. Like thousands of others in this city. Like me.

I wondered if the doorman had been paranoid, thought I could be the killer.

I hurried away.

The entire city was being combed for William Henry Roberts. Yet as the noose tightened, the picture was becoming clearer. I knew Roberts thought he was the great grandson of Billy the Kid. I knew he'd killed his entire family. The problem was I had no proof. The proof had been reduced to ashes four years ago.

I begged Wallace to let me run the story, knowing full well my claims couldn't be fully supported by facts. They were unsubstantiated, and I offered to provide full disclaimers and editorialize much more than usual. In the end Wallace nixed it. And rightly so. But that didn't mean I couldn't try to print it elsewhere. Or let someone else print it.

I pulled out my cell phone and dialed the one number I swore I would never call again.

The phone rang and the operator picked up.

"This is the New York Dispatch, how may I direct your call?"

"I'd like Paulina Cole's desk."

"One moment."

I held my breath, waited for the call to go through. Paulina screened her calls. One of the benefits of having worked beside her for a few months. Unsurprisingly it went to voice mail.

"This is Cole. Leave a message."

"Paulina, this is Henry Parker. Meet me at Ollie's diner in an hour. I have a story for you. No tricks, just business."

I hung up and began walking towards the diner.

Chapter 51

I was in the middle of chewing a ham-and-cheese sandwich when Paulina burst through the door. I'd been inside just ten minutes, but decided to order without waiting. This wasn't a date.

Paulina's hair was disheveled, her makeup ready to cascade down her face at any moment, and her purse clung to her shoulder by one overworked strap. She perused the diner until she saw me. Then she took an enormous deep breath and came over. I leaned across the table and pushed the seat out for her. I was nothing if not a gentleman.

"Henry," she said, placing her bag on the floor, then thinking better of it and hanging it over the chair back. "It's been a long time, we need to do this more often."

"We need to do this once and only once," I said. She cocked her head like I was speaking ancient Sumerian.

"That's not how I feel," she said. A waiter came by and handed her a menu. He began to walk away, but she snapped her fingers and he turned around. "I'll have a bagel and cream cheese, with the bagel scooped out and light cream cheese. I also want capers, but not too many. And a glass of pineapple juice." The waiter nodded and left.

"So how's the Dispatch treating you?" I asked, taking a swig of coffee.

"Oh, you know. Always busy, always hustling." She made a running motion with her hands to denote that she did, literally, hustle. "Listen Henry," she said, leaning forward slightly. She was wearing a tight black sweater with a V-neck that exposed the top of her remarkably perky breasts. I wondered if she had them done. Then I decided I'd done enough thinking about her breasts for the rest of my life. "I know things haven't been great between us. But I'd like to make amends."

"I'm sure you lose tons of sleep over it," I replied, "but everything I say today is off the record."

"You can't be serious." I pulled a tape recorder out of my bag, held it up for her to see. "Let me guess. You got that 'off the record' bit on tape."

"Just making sure my off the record is on the record."

Paulina laughed. The waiter arrived with a glass of pineapple juice, pulpy and thick. Paulina took a small sip, then pointed a long fingernail at me.

"You know, I always thought Wallace was smart to bring you onboard at the Gazette. That place is an old man's club. And old men don't get younger—they die. And if nobody is there to take over when they finally kick the bucket, the paper will die too. It was smart of him to inject some new blood."

"You've spilled enough ink calling for my blood this year, I didn't think you cared so much."

She dismissed it with a wave of her hand. "This is business honey. You sell newspapers. Cute, young guy like you. Remember that actor from The Sopranos, supposedly killed a cop? Every day his mug was on the front page we couldn't print enough papers. Half the people that buy our rags don't read them, sweetie, they look at the headlines and the pictures and move on to pictures of Paris Hilton in a bikini. The least we can do is give them something to hold their interest."

"Like Mya and David Loverne."

Paulina shrank back. I could tell I'd struck a nerve. It felt good, but I couldn't dig too deep. I was here for a reason.

"You know I never wanted to see either of them hurt." She meant it. "Mya is a lost soul. People like reading about lost souls, and they like to have someone to blame for it. You and Get-Around-Town Loverne were easy marks. But you're not so innocent yourself. I checked the hospital records. She was admitted with those facial wounds. You really did hang up on her when she called you. Your own girlfriend, lying beaten on the street, and you turn the ringer off. Brave man."

"Keep punching, if it makes you feel better. I've lived with it for a year and a half and I'll never forgive myself. But I wasn't the one who hit her. And I've learned to live with the rest of it."

"You say potato, I say poh-tahto. So here's the deal," Paulina said, ignoring the waiter as he brought over her bagel. "You don't like me. That's fine. I have a man who makes me come twice a night so I don't need more friends. But you called me, Mr. Parker. So why am I here?"

"Because I've got a story for you," I said.

Paulina eyed me while she smeared cream cheese into the crater where the bagel had been dug out. "You've got a story for me? I hope it doesn't end with you squeezing sour grapes, because that's a boring story and you're the only schmuck who wants to read it."

"It's not sour grapes," I said. "Those are there, don't get me wrong, but that's not why I called you. I have another story. A better story. A story that will help you beat the Gazette tomorrow if you have time to make it into the national edition."

"I'm sorry, did Ted Allen put you on the payroll without telling me?" Paulina asked. She took a bite of her bagel, washed it down with pineapple juice. That combination couldn't taste good.

"I have a once-in-a-lifetime lead. But Wallace won't let me run with it. He said it'd stir up a ton of controversy and he doesn't need more of that from me right now. He wants me to lay low."

Paulina's eyes lit up at the word controversy.

"So why come to me?" she said. "Why not take it to a magazine?"

"It needs to run as soon as possible. There's a maniac out there and I think this could smoke him out. And if Wallace is too scared to run it, it's my duty to make sure it runs somewhere. I'm a journalist. My duty is to the truth first, my paycheck second."

"It has to do with this Billy the Kid angle," Paulina said.

"That's right."

"Do tell."

"Does the name Mark Rheingold ring a bell?"

She thought for a moment, tapping her nails against the tabletop. "Religious guy, right? Had some big church down south."

"Close enough. Do a little digging and you'll find out just how big this guy was."

"So what's your point?"

I told Paulina what I'd discovered. Every word of it. I told her how the Roberts family had died in that fire, along with Pastor Rheingold. I told her how William Henry Roberts's body was never found, and the county covered it up. How Roberts had been presumed dead for four years, and was continuing the bloody legacy of his ancestor, Billy the Kid.

Paulina listened transfixed. Yet there was fear in her eyes. She knew I'd done enough digging so that this wasn't some half-baked concoction. She could tell from my eyes that the closest thing to a real demon this city had ever seen was currently walking the streets, had killed David Loverne and three others and tried to kill Mya. I told her all of it.

"I still don't understand," she said, her voice much softer, the confidence gone. "Mark Rheingold, why was he at that house? If William Roberts really did…" she paused before she said it "…kill his whole family, why kill Rheingold too?"

I told her about the rumors of Rheingold's affairs with his congregants. I told her about the photo I'd unearthed.

"I think Rheingold was having an affair with Meryl Roberts, William's mother. I think William's father knew about it. That's why he killed Rheingold. He was killing the man who brought disgrace to his family, Billy's family. Cutting off an infected bloodline."

"Jesus," Paulina said. She looked like she'd aged ten years in the last ten minutes. "And you want me to print this?"

I reached under the table and unzipped my knapsack. I handed her dozens of pages of documents. Copies of all the research I'd done, the photos I'd unearthed. Everything proving Brushy Bill Roberts was Billy the Kid, and that William considers himself heir to the throne.

"Between William and Billy they've killed almost thirty people." I looked at Paulina, her face grave. "You got into this business for the same reason I did. At least at first. You wanted to tell the truth. You wanted to find the stories that matter. Well, here's one that will rewrite history, and with any luck save some lives. I don't want a byline or any credit. You can take that. But it needs to run tomorrow. And if anything I said gets on the record in my voice, I swear to God I will make you pay for the rest of your life. I've lost my girlfriend. I've lost Mya. There's nothing more dangerous than someone with nothing to lose. Right now all I have is my integrity. You take that, I will make your life a living hell. I will sue you and Ted Allen and the Dispatch for printing that shit about Mya and me. I will lie through my teeth and tell people I fucked you and then dumped your ass and that's why you're so spiteful."

"What happened to the truth?" Paulina said sarcastically.

"Just this once, I'll not only stoop to your level, I'll wave hello from six levels deeper."

"I'll run it," she said, knowing I was serious. She tucked the file into her purse. It barely fit. I knew she'd take good care of it. "But if it's going to run I need to leave. I have a story to write."

I gave her a military salute.

"I'll pick up the check."

"Next time it's on me," Paulina said. She stood up, threw on her coat and purse.

I laughed, shook my head. "If I ever have a meal with you again, expect a healthy dose of arsenic in your pineapple juice. So you'd better hope there's no check to get."

"I like this side of you, Henry," she said. "You act all nice, like you're the cub reporter who can do no wrong, but you've got some ice in those veins. Keep 'em cold, tiger."

And she left.

I sat there sipping my coffee, having made either a brilliant calculation or a horrible mistake. I was pretty sure it was the former. I'd find out tomorrow.

Chapter 52

Nobody really noticed him as he walked by. His suit was tailored and his shirt was neatly tucked in. His bright red tie practically screamed POWER! from the rooftops. His shoes were shined, hair combed back and soaked with gel. He looked like any one of a million investment bankers or traders on their way to becoming the twenty-first century master of the universe. He was one in a million.

A few did glance at the guitar strapped over his back, assumed after leaving the office he would play a gig at some dank bar with his other gel compadres, where drunken patrons would worship him for exactly forty five minutes before going home to either puke or screw some desperate groupie.

The truth was, the guitar case was made out of a lightweight carbon, the whole thing weighing less than five pounds. The Winchester rifle housed inside made the whole contraption weight just over ten. It was easy to run with, narrow enough to fit through subway doors and turnstiles, scamper down fire escapes and disappear into the city crowds. And since he always dressed as either a young, rich broker or some near-homeless schlub looking for that one gig that would get him discovered, as far as New York was concerned he was faceless. Voiceless. Like a million more of his generation looked upon by their elders as those who sucked the life from the system and gave nothing back.

Unlike those faceless assholes, he would be remembered. Like his grandfather was. Twenty-one when Billy allegedly died, yet that was enough time to carve a legacy that would live for generations.

William's legacy would be a new chapter. The Winchester was more than an heirloom, it was an artery through which their bloodline flowed.

When he woke up this morning, though, William knew there was a chance he might never use his beloved gun again. It had served him better than any weapon he could imagine, but the gun was old, not meant to be fired so many times in such a short span. At least in a museum it wasn't exposed to the elements. But legends weren't meant to be kept on display.

One more shot. One more kill.

William was sure that Amanda Davies' death would deal Henry Parker that one grievous blow that would finally push him over the edge.

William had paid his last night at the hotel, and the nearly blind old man who ran the place said he was sorry to see him go. William couldn't help but laugh, wondered if he should correct the man. Sorry to hear you go.

Yesterday's newspapers had been the most heartening yet. One editorial admitted that William had become some sort of folk hero, that each of his victims had some penance to pay and the devil had come to collect. Just like his grandfather had.

And just like Billy would have done, William had his escape route planned out. The building across the street had a foot-high ledge from which he could rest the gun yet remain hidden. The fire escape was a mere twenty feet away. Just a few days ago the police had been watching both Henry and Amanda, so he had to play it safe. There was a good chance he'd have to run. Which meant leaving the Winchester behind.

He could live with it.

The gun was a means to an end. And once Henry Parker felt what he felt, experienced the same loss he had, knew what it was like to cut the disease away, the fuse would be lit. Henry would mythologize William Roberts, and the legend would be made. Billy the Kid wasn't made a legend until Pat Garrett created the myth. Like Garrett, Henry Parker had the power of the written word. The power to create a legend.

It was fate that William chose to use Henry's quote when he killed Athena. And so a hundred and thirty years after his great-grandfather changed this country, so would William.

Yet as he walked down the street, William felt a cold stir in the pit of his stomach. Every so often, another stranger would glance his way. Eyes scanning his face, like they had recognized him from somewhere. Like they knew him somehow.

A twinge of panic began to rise in William's gut. He walked faster. Began to sweat. He didn't like this. Didn't like people looking at him. So far he had survived by blending in, looking like every other young punk in this city that people were happy to dismiss. But now there was recognition, and from random people on the goddamn street.

William passed a small bodega. He thought about stopping for a pack of gum, just to calm his nerves. He went over. Debated getting a pack of cigarettes too. People avoided smokers. He tried to remember how much money was in his wallet. Then he looked at the newspapers.

They were neatly arranged under triangular metal paperweights. The headline of the New York Gazette read The Face of Sorrow. It ran beside a picture of Cindy Loverne crying at her husband's funeral. A picture alongside it showed Mya Loverne, taken the day before he'd thrown her from the roof. She was smiling in the pic. The caption read Injured Daughter Hanging On.

William smiled. Looked like the girl could make it. Wasn't that from Rocky?

If she lives, she lives. If she dies…

Then the smile faded. The pit in his stomach opened up, and he felt a wave of nausea overcome him. Then the nausea turned to anger, the anger turned to hate, and he ripped the paper from the kiosk.

It was the New York Dispatch. The page one headline read: The Face of Evil?

There was a photo on the front page. He recognized it. He hadn't seen the photo in years, but knew exactly when it was taken. Clearly visible in the photo were three men and a woman.

One of the men was his father.

The other man was Pastor Mark Rheingold.

The woman was his mother, Meryl, and she was reaching for the pastor, preparing for a deep embrace. William's father looked on in joyous approval.

And in the background William recognized himself, just four years ago, staring at his mother and her lover as they mocked their family name.

William H. Bonney would never have stood for that.

And so neither would William Henry Roberts.

Despite the newsprint, the tiny pixels, William saw the fire in his eyes. He remembered setting fire to the house, the fire that claimed the lives of his father, sister, mother, and his mother's God-fearing lover.

They were the same eyes he was showing to the world right now.

Millions seeing his face in black and white.

Millions recognizing him on the street.

His heart beating faster than it had since the night he sent a bullet through Athena Paradis's head, William Henry Roberts turned and sprinted down the street.

He couldn't waste any more time. He had to find her.

It was only a matter of time before somebody recognized him and called the cops. Tried to end his crusade before he was ready.

Amanda Davies had to die before that happened.

Chapter 53

Louie Grasso picked up the phone. He gently placed the receiver to his ear and wondered if there was anywhere near this godforsaken building he could grab a shot of whiskey to throw in his coffee. If the rest of the day went the way his first half an hour did, he'd quit his job by noon. He'd been working the lines at the Dispatch for nearly seven years and had weathered complaints and grievances from all walks of life. Never, though, had he heard such anger due to a story. Goddamn Paulina Cole, at some point she was going to get them all killed.

Louie took a breath, said, "New York Dispatch, how may I direct your call?"

"You have two choices," said the man with the southern twang on the other end. "You can either put this shithead Ted Allen on the phone or that sassy bitch Paulina Cole. Your choice, either one will do, but I'm not hanging up until one of those worthless dungheaps is on the line."

Louie recited what his boss had told him to after the first barrage of calls came in.

"Any complaints you have regarding Ms. Cole's article in today's edition should be addressed in the form of a typewritten letter or e-mail directed to the New York Gazette public relations department. Your concerns are duly noted. They will be responded to either individually or as a whole."

"Listen, I got my whole extended family just waiting to call in as soon as I hang up, and my grandma Doris is ready to hop on the plane and whack Allen upside the head. So I'll fill out your stupid forms, but I hope you're ready to repeat those directions another few thousand times this morning. So 'duly note' my ass."

Louie sighed as the line went dead. He drained his coffee and picked up another one of the dozen lines that hadn't stopped flashing in hours.

"New York Dispatch, how may I direct your call?"

The Guilty

Paulina had just hung up the phone when James Keach appeared in the doorway. Sweat was streaking down his face, and his work shirt looked several different shades of blue.

"This is not the time, James."

"I need to know what to do. People are calling me asking for a statement. Some guy from the Associated Press, another one from the Times. I don't know how they got my number."

"Our company directory isn't a secret. What are you telling the people who call?"

"I've been hanging up on them."

"Good," she said. "You say one word to anyone who doesn't work inside this building I'll roast your nads in my Foreman Grill. Now get."

Keach disappeared.

Paulina turned back to her computer. Her inbox had three hundred new messages, and another ten were appearing every minute. They all bore colorful subject headings like You're wrong and eat shite and die and does your mother know you lie for a living?

Never in her career had Paulina witnessed such an onslaught of offended readers, and that was counting the time they ran a still photo from Pamela Anderson's sex tape with her nipples blocked out. Hundreds of angry readers were calling in, demanding her head, and every new message was directed at the story she'd written for today's Dispatch. The story Henry Parker had dropped on her lap. That sneaky shit knew it would provoke this response. He wanted that story to run, but didn't want the Gazette to go through exactly what the Dispatch was right now. She'd have to remember to send him a cyanide fruitcake for Christmas.

Once the brushstrokes are painted, the picture becomes clear as a Midwestern day. One hundred and twenty-seven years ago, a lie was told, and that lie has been perpetuated for generations by deluded, small-minded townfolk whose entire lives and economies live and die on the wings of a myth. Once you know the truth of Brushy Bill Roberts's identity as Billy the Kid, once you know how William Henry Roberts burned his family's house with his family inside, once you know that William's mother had an affair with a millionaire man of God (with his father's blessing, no less), you know that a hundred years too late, the truth has come to collect its revenge.

Soon the facts will prove that William H. Bonney did not die in 1881 in Fort Sumner, New Mexico. He and his bloodline lived on. This country has been living in denial for years. And it is because of this veil of ignorance that nine people are dead, with another young woman fighting for her life.

If there is any justice in the world, if the truth is regulated at all, then the entire citizenry of New Mexico, Texas and all those who convinced themselves that the nightmare was over will wake up to the violent reality and confront a demon who manifested himself right here, today.

Never had Paulina seen such an outraged reaction from a "concerned" group of citizens. But to her surprise, many of the protesters were from far outside the delusions of Texas and New Mexico, and the sandblasted states who perpetrated the myth. She'd only received about twenty messages from Fort Sumner, ten or so from Hico and Lincoln County, but the vast majority were from New Yorkers, Californians. She had even received harsh rebukes from several members of Congress, writing to say that at best her article was in poor taste, and at worst a selfish attempt to discredit one of the most enduring legends in history.

She didn't bother to respond to the irony of calling a mass murderer an "enduring legend," but therein, she supposed, was the point.

William H. Bonney, despite his violent history, was now considered a hero, a vigilante, a romantic icon. And having read the dozens of articles about William Henry Roberts's deadly spree, she knew that more than a fair share of "concerned citizens" considered him the same way. Roberts was a bandit, an outlaw. And like Bonney's Regulators years ago, he was purging the landscape of those who poisoned the well.

Yet unlike other articles she'd written that had stirred up controversy, there was no joy at the Dispatch at the prospect of increased circulation. There were no high fives in the hall or talk about holiday bonuses. Nobody from senior management had stopped by Paulina's office to congratulate her on a terrific story. In fact, nobody had come by at all. And if there was one thing that frightened Paulina more than anything, it was silence.

Ordinarily she might respond to one or more complainant, just for kicks. But today she merely forwarded all the messages to their PR department. They'd be earning their paychecks this week. Then one e-mail popped up in her inbox that made her forget all the others.

The sender was Ted Allen. The subject heading read We need to talk.

She took a deep breath before opening the message.

...hurts the credibility of our newspaper...

...true or not the Dispatch had been placed under a magnifying glass...

...witch hunt...

...my mother grew up in Texas...this is akin to pissing on the Pope's grave...

He requested her presence in his office in fifteen minutes. The Dispatch's legal team and PR department would be on hand. She had no doubt her job would be safe, but this fire had to be handled with extreme caution.

Henry had gotten away clean. She couldn't mention his name. If the public found out she'd received information from a reporter at a rival paper, the Dispatch would lose its credibility faster than Jack O'Donnell downed a shot of whiskey. Take credit for your successes, take credit for your mistakes, hope the former outweighed the latter.

Paulina picked up her phone, dialed James Keach's extension.

"Ms. Cole?"

"Where is Henry Parker right now?"

"I...I don't know. Work, I assume?"

"Find him. Then call me. You have half an hour."

She hung up, stood up, smoothed out her skirt, and headed for Ted Allen's office.

Chapter 54

There was no stopping it; the juggernaut had begun lurching forward. Reports stated that the Dispatch was receiving more complaints and hate mail than at any point in the last ten years. The most since they ran a story about a presidential candidate paying off a cocktail waitress with whom he'd had an affair. The complaints weren't about the story, of course, but of a photo on page one in which readers claimed they could see more than fifty-one percent of her left butt cheek.

Nobody ever said people didn't have their priorities straight.

The gossip websites and blogs claimed that Ted Allen was considering canning Paulina Cole. They paid her to piss people off, under the maxim that controversy created cash, but now it looked like she'd pissed off too many people who spent the cash. Challenging an American legend, as well as asserting that a beloved (and deceased) clergyman had an extramarital affair, was too much to handle.

The story on William Henry Roberts was out. It was public. And despite the protests and pitchfork-waving townsfolk, there would be inquiries. There would be investigations. This kind of scandal could not be covered up.

When I got to my desk my voice-mail light was blinking. I checked it; it was from Largo Vance.

"Hey Henry, I don't know how she got it or why, but I have a feeling I have you to thank for Paulina's story, you little devil you. With any luck those pussies in D.C. will have no choice but to exhume the proper body this time. If they screw this one up they'll have more important people than yours truly to answer to. Anyway, the wool's been pulled down long enough. Now catch that Roberts prick and then give me a call. I have an unopened bottle of Johnnie Walker Blue with your name on it."

Before I could hang up the phone I saw a shadow hovering over my desk.

"Hey Jack," I said.

"Hey yourself. So, read any good stories today?"

The Guilty

"I just got in a minute ago. Why, is something breaking?"

"Something already broke," Jack said. He opened up a leather valise and pulled out a copy of today's Dispatch. I'd passed it on the way to work but didn't bother to buy a copy. I knew what would be on the front page, and ignoring some basic sentence structure I was pretty sure I knew exactly how the article would read. Jack opened it, spread the paper across my desk.

Looking back at me in a salacious full two page spread were the glistening veneers of Mark Rheingold, a faded family portrait of John Henry and Meryl Roberts with their two young children, and a photo of Ollie P. "Brushy Bill" Roberts at the deathbed of the man claiming to be Jesse James.

The headline read: Sex, Murder, and the Gun that Won the West.

Not Paulina's finest hour as far as headlines went, but she more than made up for it with the story. I scanned it quickly while Jack stood there. She covered all the important bases: Mark Rheingold's affair with Meryl Roberts, the fact that John Henry likely knew about it and approved. And their son William's disgust at the shaming of Billy the Kid's legacy.

"You have any idea where Paulina got these leads?" Jack asked. "Seemed to me you were on top of this story a week ago, and all of a sudden Jackie Collins is scooping you."

I held up my hand, still sutured together. "In case you forgot, I had a bit of an altercation a few days ago. Oh yeah, my ex is in intensive care. Oh yeah, and I broke it off with Amanda. So pardon me if I've been off my game for a few days."

"Come on, kid, I don't buy that for a second. Don't get me wrong, I'm not saying you haven't had, you know, stuff on your mind, but the day you get scooped on your own story is the day I start drinking wine coolers and dating British women."

"What do you want me to say?"

Jack looked me in the eyes. I held his gaze, unsure how to respond. Then he stepped back.

"You don't need to say anything. I know what you did."

"Really? What's that?"

"Doesn't matter. I understand why you did it. But if you ever fucking do it again, I don't care if you're Bob Woodward the second or

251

spawn of Jimmy Breslin and Ann Coulter, I'll stuff your body down the trash compactor and make sure you never work at this newspaper again. Understand me?"

"I don't know what you're talking about."

"Of course not. Glad to see you understand. If Wallace asks—which he will—tell him exactly what you told me."

"I will."

"And Henry," Jack said, his eyes growing soft. I'd never seen the man show a tender side, and it unnerved me. "I want you to know I'm sorry about Amanda and Mya. I know I said some things a while back, I don't know how much you actually listened to and how much you passed off as the loony ramblings of an old idiot, but everyone lives their life differently. I never found the same kind of happiness a lot of others have, but that doesn't mean what I did is the right way to live."

"Right or wrong, you made a career to be proud of."

A small choking sound came from Jack's chest.

He said, "You know what I consider the best story I ever wrote, Henry?"

"It wasn't Michael DiForio?"

Jack laughed. "No offense to the guy who tried to rub you out, but not even close. No, it was February third, nineteen-eighty-seven. Not just because that's the day Liberace died—not a lot of people paying attention to human interest stories that day—but I wrote a piece about a woman in Nebraska who'd lost her husband to cancer and her son to a carjacking. Childless and widowed at forty-one. She'd never worked a day in her life, and suddenly decided to join the police force, and became a cadet on her forty-second birthday. Her name was Patti Ramona, and I remember she told me that if she saved just one life doing her job, if she prevented one family from going through what she went through, then their deaths wouldn't sting so much."

Jack coughed into his hand.

"A week after the article came out, I got a letter from a man in Idaho, Robert something, his name escapes me. Robert had lost his wife and daughter and had been dying of loneliness for a decade. Robert told me the moment he finished reading my story he went out and became a volunteer firefighter. He said thanks to Patti he knew his life could still have a purpose. You see what I'm saying, Henry? You don't need a whole city to remember you. If you make your mark on just one person, change one life for the better, that's the noblest thing you can ever do. It's easy to be a celebrity. It's harder to actually mean something."

He clapped me on the shoulder and left without saying another word. I watched him turn the corner and disappear. And then I was alone.

Sitting at my desk, my mind was blank. I didn't know what to write about. I stared down at the paper Jack had left on my desk. My phone was silent. E-mail inbox empty. I had a sudden and terrible feeling of déjà vu, remembering walking the streets of Manhattan after Mya had been attacked a year ago. Getting drunk and hoping the needle in a haystack would cross my path. I remembered the anger and sadness, a dangerously potent mixture. I felt that way now.

It was easier when there was a story. Something to focus on, something to prevent my mind from wandering. But right now all I could focus on was that emptiness. And hope it didn't consume me.

And suddenly everything changed.

I saw Wallace running from his office down the hall. Evelyn followed from Metro, her short legs having trouble keeping up. Then two more got up and ran after them. Frank Rourke ran past my desk. I grabbed his shirtsleeve.

"What's going on? Where's everybody running to?"

"Anonymous tip just came in, there's a hostage situation going down. Some maniac took a girl."

"Where?" I asked.

"Downtown," he said. "199 Water Street." Then he ran off.

I couldn't breathe. 199 Water Street. That building housed the New York Legal Aid Society. Where Amanda worked.

But the stringers…there was no police activity. Yet everyone at the newsdesk knew about it. What the hell was happening?

My heart racing, I picked up the phone and dialed Curt Sheffield's cell phone. He picked up, said, "This is Sheffield."

"Curt, it's Henry. Have you heard anything about a hostage situation down on Water street?"

"That's a negative, nothing's come over the radio, and I'm downtown right now so I would've heard something. Why, what's going on?"

"I don't know," I said. "Somebody called in an anonymous tip about a hostage in the building where Amanda works. But if it hasn't been reported to the cops yet…I'll call you back."

I hung up, dialed Amanda's number at the office. We hadn't spoken in days. I didn't know how she'd sound, what to expect, but I needed to know what was happening, that she was all right.

I regained my breath when the line picked up and I heard Amanda's voice say, "New York Legal Aid Society, this is Amanda."

"Amanda, it's me."

"Henry…hi…"

"Listen, is everything okay over there?"

"Of course it is, what do you mean?"

"Are you in trouble? Have you seen or heard anything strange?"

"Other than your calling me just now, I was having a pretty uneventful day."

"Thank God."

"Thank God I was having an uneventful day?"

"No, not that at all, I…well, yeah…I'm just glad you're safe."

"Safe? Why wouldn't I be? If there's something I should know—"

And that's when I heard a woman scream over the phone, followed by a gunshot so loud it rattled my teeth. I recognized that sound. I'd heard it this week. It was the sound of a Winchester rifle. William Henry Roberts was in Amanda's office.

"Amanda? Amanda! What's happening?"

"Oh God, Henry, there's someone here—help us!"

The line went dead.

I leapt up, heart hammering. I had to get down there. Everyone was piling out the door, going to the scene of the crime.

And then it hit me, just what he'd done.

He called us. William Roberts.

You write about history. I am history.

Chapter 55

At first Amanda thought that the sound of shattering glass came from outside. A construction crew had been tearing up the building across the street for what seemed like a decade, and anything more than a dropped pen in their office was cause for excitement. But then she recognized Darcy's high-pitched voice as she screamed for help, and Amanda knew that whatever was happening was happening terrifyingly close.

Then she heard the gunshot, a blast so loud it seemed to shatter the air, and for a moment she heard nothing but ringing in her ears. When her hearing returned, Amanda heard Henry on the line.

"Amanda? Amanda, what's happening?"

She didn't know what she said next, or if she said anything at all, but suddenly Amanda was scrambling away from her desk, trying to bide her time while figuring out what the hell was going on.

She crouched down, surveyed the office.

Their suite housed three shared offices and one large conference room, as well as a smaller waiting room by the elevator. The waiting room door was made of glass. The others were metal. She immediately knew that the breaking glass was the sound of somebody crashing through the waiting room door.

She wondered how he'd gotten past the security guard downstairs, waited until he'd gone on break. Or something more horrible.

Oh God...

She heard another scream, someone yelled, "Get away from me!" and then Amanda heard a loud thud like something heavy had hit the floor.

She saw Phil the intern run past her muttering "Sweet Jesus, sweet Jesus" over and over again. Amanda still couldn't see what was happening, but if praying to Jesus or any other deity meant she'd make it out of the building alive she'd happily renew her faith in the Lord.

Crawling on all fours, Amanda moved past her desk until she

Jason Pinter

was next to the door to the conference room. She peered up, looked through the small window pane. She gasped when she saw what was happening inside.

Violet Lawrence was lying on the floor, facedown. Amanda recognized the purple sports jacket she'd complimented her on just that morning. She couldn't see anything else, couldn't see Violet's face. But she heard a small moan, and that meant at least she was alive.

Nobody else was running. The office had grown deathly silent. The water cooler gurgled. Then she saw the man walk into the room, and Amanda froze.

He was tall, maybe six one or two, lean with short blond hair. He was wearing a suit, the sleeves rolled up, sweat beading through the fabric. His face was tan, eyes wild yet focused.

He was holding a gun. No, not a gun, a cannon. And immediately she remembered their meeting with Agnes Trimble, the image her professor showed them. The one Henry was captivated by.

The Winchester rifle.

That's what he was holding. The man in their office had killed four people. Killed his family, all in cold blood. What the hell was he doing here?

Another woman ran past, screaming. The boy—William, the papers had called him—grabbed her by the ponytail. She let out a shriek. He spun her towards him. Amanda could see the veins and muscles in his forearms. The woman was crying, blubbering, tears streaking her mascara. Then he suddenly let her go, pushed her towards the doorway. She disappeared and Amanda heard the familiar chime of the elevator call button.

He let her go.

The man was standing in the middle of the room. He was holding the rifle by his side. She could see no other movement. William scanned the room, quickly crouched down to see if anyone was hiding under a desk, then stood back up.

"Amanda?" he said. Her blood ran cold. "Amanda Davies?"

It wasn't phrased as a question. He said her name the same way Henry did when he got home from work. Said like he knew she was there and couldn't wait to see her.

"Amanda," he said, holding his arms out wide, the rifle barrel pointing at the ceiling. "I've been wanting to meet you for a long time.

The Guilty

Don't keep a friend waiting."

She knelt, silent, hoped he would search the other offices, turn his back so she could make a run for it. Her heart felt like it was ready to burst through her blouse, she could feel sweat dripping down her sides.

"Henry and me, we bonded the other day." She heard footsteps, looked up, saw he was moving through the office. "Like brothers from different mothers, we might have been. Every yin needs a yang, every bad penny needs a good one to even things out. He's my bad penny."

The footsteps grew closer and Amanda dropped back to the ground. She scuttled behind her desk, crawled underneath and curled her knees to her chest. She bit her lip to keep it from trembling. She was too scared to cry.

Roberts moved closer. She heard a squeak as the doorknob turned. Suddenly she heard a bump come from the other office, and the knob stopped turning. The footsteps grew fainter.

Amanda crawled back to the door, looked up just in time to see Roberts disappear into the conference room.

"Where's Amanda?" she heard him say. There came a wheezy response from a male voice—she recognized Phil, the intern. Poor Phil had only been here a week. She hoped he was making a killer stipend.

Amanda brought her hand up to the doorknob, slowly it turned until it stopped. Looking up, she saw that the adjacent office was empty. Slowly she eased the door open just enough to fit her slim body through. She eased the door shut. The stairwell was less than twenty feet away. She could make it. There were still noises coming from the other room. Now or never.

She crawled along the wall, keeping her eyes on the other office where Roberts had entered. Saw William's black shoes pointing away from the door. She took it a step at a time, taking deep, slow breaths to slow her heart rate. Twenty feet. Eighteen. Fifteen. She was past the door, closer to the exit than Roberts. She slowly stood up. Took one more step. Peeked around, braced herself, planted her feet to sprint away.

Just as she took her first step, she felt a sharp pain as a hand gripped her hair and spun her around.

Her breath caught in her throat as Amanda looked into the

grinning face and wild eyes of William Roberts.

She couldn't fight back. His hand was on her neck. The Winchester was slung over his neck. And in his other hand was a knife nearly half a foot long, a streak of glistening red blood on the blade.

"Miss Davies," he said, his voice metallic and calm. "If you'll please join me."

"Wh…what do you mean? Where?"

"Somewhere a little, oh, scenic. The last girl, Mya, sad to say she's probably going to make it." He smiled at her. Then he said, "Problem is, I didn't drop her from nearly high enough. That's a mistake won't happen again."

Chapter 56

I shared a cab with Jack. My legs were jittery as I kept redialing Amanda's number on my cell phone. It went right to voice mail every time. I called 911. Tried to figure out what the hell was going on. I got the feeling from the exasperated woman on the other end that I wasn't nearly the first to call it in. I hung up without learning anything.

I called Curt Sheffield, praying there was some sort of mistake. His voice instantly told me the situation was worse than I imagined.

"Dude, 911 got about a hundred calls in a three-minute span," he said, his voice breathless and uneven. "All from newspapers and television stations. The NYPD has a freaking battalion on our way down there, but man they're going to be a few minutes, the choppers say there's already a few dozen reporters at the scene. Somehow you guys at the news desks got wind of this before the cops did. Listen, Carruthers is on the rampage. I'll call you soon as I know anything."

Curt hung up.

"What'd he say?" Jack asked. His voice was scared, his breath slightly sour.

"Nothing we don't know," I said. "But it seems like the news crews got tipped off somehow before the NYPD. There might be a few reporters down there already."

The cab rounded the corner, arrived the building at 199 Water Street. Or at least got as close as it could. Because when we saw the crowd in front of the building, both of our jaws dropped.

Jack said, "I have a small quibble with your definition of the word 'few.'"

Surrounding the building's entrance were at least a hundred reporters and a dozen news vans. They lined the street like a cattle drive stuck in neutral.

"What the..." Jack said.

"Hell..." I finished.

Dozens of sports-jacketed journos were in the middle of writing copy while news correspondents were already being primped for their on-camera reporting. Cameramen were pushing and shoving, jockeying for the best lighting to both hide their stars' blemishes and capture the best angle of the building behind them. It was an unmitigated madhouse.

And there wasn't a cop in sight.

"This has to be a mistake," Jack said. "I've never seen anything like this."

"No way," I said. "This is no mistake."

Looking at the building, I could see several confused people staring out their office windows down at the gathering outside, oblivious to what was going on just a few floors above or below them. And in the time I took to assess the situation, three more news vans pulled up, five more nattily dressed reporters piled out, followed by several burly not-as-nattily dressed cameramen. They all joined the horde and began applying makeup.

There were no cops anywhere to be seen.

Roberts.

He couldn't have taken the office more than twenty minutes ago. That's when I spoke to Amanda. That's the last I heard from her.

"Crazy son of a bitch," I said. "Roberts tipped off the press before hitting Water Street. Only a sick fuck would call the press prior to a crime he intended to commit. He called the press so they'd show up before the cops. He wanted it like this."

"This isn't just one newspaper," Jack said. "I think everyone who's ever held a press badge is here. Informing a thousand reporters about a hostage situation in New York is like throwing a slab of rancid meat into an ant farm."

Roberts wanted the press to have the kind of unimpeded access cops would normally prevent. Right now, the news crews were free to roam. There was no yellow tape, nobody holding the crowd back, no gruff detectives or crisis management teams giving inconvenient "no comments."

This was the very definition of a free press.

A reporter wearing a two-thousand-dollar suit and fiberglass hair walked up to the main entrance, cupped his hands and peered inside. He cocked his head, turned back and shouted, "Jesus, I think I see someone lying down behind the security desk. I think I see blood, I think the security guard is dead." He turned to the cameraman. "You think we should go inside?"

His cameraman, six four with a body that looked like was fueled at the local Krispy Kreme, carried the camera over to him. He glared inside.

"Why not? Let me get a light reading, make sure this thing will transmit."

Suddenly I was sprinting over to the entrance. I shoved fiberglass hair against the side of the building and pressed my forearm into his chest.

He struggled, tried to pry my arm away, yelped, "Get the hell off me!"

"Goddamn it, you don't know who's watching. If you so much as touch those door handles I'm going to break them off and strangle you with them."

He could see in my eyes I wasn't kidding. He relaxed. So did I. He smoothed out his jacket, told the cameraman, "We're good out here." Then he turned to me. "I had a great spot out front. If someone steals it I'll have your ass."

"You'll have to try it with broken arms. Look, there's a nice spot, go set up. Get away from here."

He walked away. Then I turned back to the building. That's when I heard the first siren. I could see the reflection in the doorway as half a dozen squad cars pulled up and a phalanx of uniformed officers filed out. Radios came out as the first cops to arrive called in reports. They circled the building's entrance.

One cop came closer. I heard him say, "We don't know what floor they're on."

"Ninth floor," I said.

"And who are you?"

"Henry Parker, I'm with the Gazette. My girlfriend is up there, she works here. Amanda Davies."

The guy waved his arms and another cop came over. This cop was tall, thin, with a handlebar mustache.

"Captain James O'Hurley."

"Henry Parker."

"You have knowledge of this situation?"

"I just know I was on the phone with my girlfriend, she's an employee who works on the ninth floor, when I heard a gunshot. Then the line went dead."

"Who's your girlfriend?"

"Her name is Amanda. Davies."

"Can you think of any reason why Miss Davies or her co-workers would be in danger?"

I took a breath. "William Henry Roberts. He's up there."

O'Hurley's face darkened. I saw a flash of anger in his eyes. The other cop looked at him.

"That's the guy killed Joe." O'Hurley nodded. "Roberts is supposed to be the grandson of Billy the Kid or something, right? Hey kid," he said, clearly meaning me, "you work at the Gazette, didn't you write some stuff about this guy?"

"Yeah," I said. "I did."

"How much do you know about him?" O'Hurley asked.

I held up my hand, the stitches still embedded in my skin. The cop whistled.

"Manners aren't his strong suit. Let's say I know Roberts a lot better than I'd like."

"He did that to you," O'Hurley said, "and that's your girlfriend up there, then…" he paused, realized what was going on. "Maybe you shouldn't be here."

"You try and drag me away," I said. "And it won't be pretty."

"Fine," O'Hurley said. "But stay out of the way. If we need your help we'll ask for it."

"No problem, but Roberts is in there and I know he's going to hurt Amanda. I know it. That's why he came here. That's why he called the press first. He wants people to see every second of this. You don't do that kind of thing if you're looking to steal a few grand and disappear to the Caribbean." I noticed the rest of the cops were hanging back. "Are you going in?"

"Not yet," O'Hurley said. "We need to assess the situation, take his demands if there are any, and then figure out a strategy. Rushing in there might cause panic, stress, and force Roberts's hand."

"This sick bastard killed one of our own," the other cop added. "He's either spending the rest of his life getting reamed up the ass in the shower or he's getting a one way ticket to the juice chair."

"But what about Amanda?" I asked.

O'Hurley said, "We have no reason to believe she's in immediate danger. If she is the intended target, we have the hostage negotiation team en route."

"Your might be negotiating for a body, captain."

"Listen, Parker, I can imagine what you're going through. Trust me, this freak will get what's coming to him. But we need to minimize collateral damage."

"By collateral damage you mean my girlfriend."

"That's right."

"You think he called the press just so he could try out his new stand up routine? He's going to do something terrible, and if you guys don't do something soon it'll be too late."

"That's enough, Parker." O'Hurley pointed to where several cops were putting up blue sawhorses, stringing up yellow tape. "Wait behind the line with the rest of the press."

I watched as the cops herded several reporters behind the barricade. They put up a fight. They always did. But in the end they always moved back, docile.

Docile wasn't going to cut it today. Roberts was pure evil. He wasn't going to wait for the cops to "strategize."

I waited until O'Hurley's back was turned, then I pushed the other cop aside and bolted towards the building.

I heard someone yell, "Stop that guy!" but it was too late.

I shoved the glass doors open, saw that the elevator was stuck on nine and not moving. Without hesitating I sprinted towards the end of the hallway, banged through the stairwell door and began my climb to the ninth floor.

When I got to five, my breath beginning to leave me, I looked down. Nobody was following me.

Four flights above was a man who was preparing do something unspeakable to Amanda. Clenching my right fist, feeling the stitches threaten to pop, I began to climb.

Chapter 57

When I reached the ninth floor I stopped to catch my breath. If we lived through this, I promised to use the StairMaster on a more frequent basis..

Guys like Roberts always looked like they would be a pushover in a fight. Not too big, not too heavy, but their muscles were trained. They were sleeping attack dogs waiting to be prodded. First fight I ever won was against Bruce Baumgarten in the sixth grade. Bruce was a hundred and ninety pounds, a Mack truck in seventh-grade weight. But I literally ran around him until he could barely see straight, then one punch to the stomach took away the last of his wind. He went down like I'd stepped on an empty bag of potato chips.

The first fight I ever lost was against Kevin MacGruder in the eleventh grade. I outweighed Kevin by twenty pounds. He was president of the Math club. He had freckles and acne and a rail-thin girlfriend we called Olive Oil, and we mocked him mercilessly. What I didn't know is that to burn off the rage from our taunts Kevin hit the free weights five times a week. He dislocated my shoulder, and I pissed blood for two days after he kicked me in the stomach. I never messed with Kevin again.

In a strange way I was glad I knew this. William Roberts would tear me to pieces. Even if I was able to separate him from the Winchester—which seemed as doable as separating Linus from his blanket—I had to deal with the fact that he could pound me into sirloin expending less energy than it took me to climb the stairs.

I was prepared to fight dirty.

But that didn't mean I wasn't scared shitless.

Adrenaline was pumping through me. It was working, my rage concentrating.

I'd only visited Amanda at her office once. Actually I'd meant to come more, but I could never get away from the Gazette during working hours. Or more accurately, I didn't want to get away from the

The Guilty

Gazette.

I tried to recall the office layout, seemed to remember there being a conference room with a long, mahogany table, several long-backed chairs, and a speakerphone. I remembered Amanda's desk. There was a picture of us in a silver frame. I'd had it engraved for her. Only Happiness Lies Ahead.

I stood in the stairwell, moved closer to the door and pressed my ear up against it. The stairwell was painted gray, dirt coated the steps, and the metal was rusted. I glanced around, couldn't see any security camera, so I was fairly confident Roberts wasn't aware of my presence. I couldn't hear anything inside the office, but the metal was likely muffling all sounds. But it couldn't muffle a gunshot. And I didn't hear any cops storming the stairs. Roberts hadn't killed anybody. Yet.

I gripped the doorknob, turned it ever so gently just to see if it was locked. For a moment panic gripped me. If it was locked from the inside, I wouldn't be able to get in unless our friendly neighborhood rifleman decided to let me join the party. And I knew the cops wouldn't greet me with open arms if I slunk back downstairs. But the knob turned. I stopped for a moment.

The last time I barged through a closed door unannounced and unwanted, a cop ended up dead and I ended up on the run for my life.

I took three short, quick breaths, then three long deep ones, and gripped the knob. It turned easily, and I eased it all the way to the left until it wouldn't go any further. Then I listened.

Nothing.

I pushed the door slightly to make sure it moved inward.

It did.

I pushed it just enough to create a small crack between the door and the jamb. I peeked inside.

I could see an elevator. An unmanned receptionist desk with a tall, white orchid. Nothing else.

I pushed the door further in, enough so that I could slip inside. There were no sounds, nobody in view.

I stuck my head in, did a quick sweep, then crept inside and tiptoed over and ducked behind the receptionist's desk. I poked my head out the side. There was a door which I recalled as leading to the conference room. I couldn't see anything. No Roberts. No Amanda.

Nothing except for a quarter-sized circle of blood on the middle of the carpet. My heart raced. I couldn't see any bodies. Nobody was screaming or crying. But there he was here. Somewhere.

And when I felt the muzzle of the Winchester rifle press against the back of my neck, I knew for sure.

Chapter 58

"You were watching the whole time," I said as I stood up. The gun followed me, the muzzle pressed against my flesh. If my heart beat any faster, all I had to do was turn around and it would burst through my chest, killing Roberts. Might be worth a try.

"Yessir I was," he said. "Everything's more exciting when you're being watched."

"Sure it is. That's why you called the press before the cops could come," I said. "You wanted us on the scene to 'make things more exciting.'"

"Yessir," he said.

"If we got here first, the cops wouldn't be prepared. You knew I'd try to contact Amanda. You knew I'd try to get inside."

"Yessir," he said.

"Then you also know that this building is surrounded by more ammunition than every Schwarzenegger movie combined. And cops whose trigger fingers will get epilepsy the second they get you in their crosshairs."

"Yessir I do," he said. Roberts didn't seem the least bit upset by this. His face was calm, serene even, like everything was playing out perfectly.

This was the first time I'd had a chance to study him from close up. No bandanna, no bonds holding me down. He was younger than I remembered. His short blond hair made him look like a young twenty-one. It must have been easy for him to pass through the city. Easy to get lost. He looked like anyone's brother. Son. His eyes didn't contain the hate or evil I thought they would. They contained as much levity as mine. What lay behind those eyes might have been pure evil, but the prism it shone through disguised it, altered it. He could have been anyone.

"Same time, you can plan all you want but never really be sure what's gonna happen." Roberts clicked his tongue. And if my eyes weren't deceiving me, even nodded his head in an appreciative way. "Glad you're here, Parker. Glad you could make it."

Jason Pinter

"Where's Amanda?"

"Safe," he said. "One thing I'll say, that's a strong female there. Didn't cry one bit. Didn't beg for help. She did say your name once, kinda like she expected you to come. Guess you two have some sort of telepathic link. That right? Can you read each others' minds?"

I shook my head. "No," I said softly.

"Come on," Roberts said, his voice like a goading friend. "You can tell me. You and Davies, you hear each others' thoughts. Complete each others' sentences. Do all those goopy things lovers do. I bet you even talk to her after you're done fucking. Don't just snooze off like most guys. Bet you talk to her about your feelings and shit."

"What the hell are you talking about, you sick asshole?" I said. Clearly that was the wrong thing to say, because the muzzle bit into my skin harder than before. I winced. Roberts sensed this. Dug in harder.

"I care because I want to know just how close you and Davies are. I need to know, man. I need to hear you say it."

"Why?" I asked.

He walked around the side of the gun, eyed me, then lightning-quick, smashed me in the stomach. I doubled over, pain shooting through my abdomen. I coughed, felt a speck of blood hit my hand. Wiped it off. Stood back up.

Robert smiled. "Come with me."

He grabbed me by my jacket collar and pulled me into the main office. Aside from the smashed window, blood on the floor and an overturned chair, everything looked like business as usual. Except for the sprinkles of plaster on the floor. I looked up, saw the hole in the ceiling where Roberts must have fired the Winchester.

"I see you asserted your authority," I said. "Guess you needed to scare all these vicious not-for-profit workers."

"I'm not a fan of violence," Roberts said. He looked at me. "You seem surprised."

"Considering you've killed about ten people, yeah, I'm surprised."

"Only killed those people because they needed to go. Same way you'd burn a tick, step on a spider. Doesn't mean you like to kill. Means you don't want vermin spreading disease."

"So that's what Athena was doing," I said. "Spreading disease?"

"I'm not a killer," Roberts said. "I'm a liberator. You can't see it

268

now. They couldn't see it with my great-grandfather either."

"Billy the Kid was no liberator," I said. "He was a butcher who killed twenty-one people. He should have died in the womb."

Roberts laughed. "You're fucking clueless, man. The country exists because of my great grandfather. America, man. Cowboys and Indians. Outlaws and lawmen. The old west gave birth to the new world because of men like my grandfather. He killed the people who impeded progress. The people who lied and cheated and stole."

"Like Joe Mauser?" I said. "Like Mya Loverne? Like your family?"

"You don't get it," Roberts said. "You and everyone, ignorance is the new intelligence. Athena Paradis and David Loverne don't exist. They're shells, Parker. Husks. As soon as their public life overtook their private life, as soon as who they were became more important than what they were, they ceased to exist. People like you, you're happy to stare at the shell and as long as it's pretty, you don't care what putrid shit is underneath. My great-grandfather understood this. He was the only one who had the balls to make things right. He brought together the Regulators to kill the disease that everyone else ignored. Jeffrey Lourdes? Athena Paradis? All I did was kill what needed to be killed. You should be thankful. And you will be. See, to realize my destiny, I had to cut off everything that weighed me down. Soon I'll do the same for you. Then you can report my story with a clearer head. You're gonna make me famous, Parker."

He pushed me towards another closed door. Looked at me. Then pushed the door open.

Amanda was tied to a chair, her hands bound behind her back. A handkerchief wrapped around her mouth. Her eyes widened when she saw me. Pleading. Helpless.

"Amanda!" I shouted. Lunged for her. Felt the butt of the gun come down on the back of my neck, driving me to the ground. Amanda shrieked as loud as she could. Which wasn't much.

Roberts knelt down next to me. I could feel his breath on my face. He smelled like tobacco and sweat. He grabbed my shirt in his hand, pulled me closer. He was breathing heavy, and the calm in his eyes had been replaced by a manic anger. I was sure the eyes I was seeing right now were the same eyes that killed Athena. Joe. Jeffrey. David. And nearly Mya.

"See, Henry, you're a shell. You're one of them. I know about you. I know what happened to you last year. I know about all those reporters who love you, think you're a hero, and the ones that hate you, think you go against everything that's noble about your profession. Who you are has become more important than what you are. I can fix that."

"You can kill me," I said. "But leave Amanda out of this. Let her go."

"Not on your life," Roberts said. "If you hadn't noticed, I already let all the other useless ones go. I need Amanda for this. You can do a whole lot more good than she ever can. You have a voice. I need that voice to reach people, so they understand what I've done. But you also have a shell. You have a protective skin. All I'm going to do is remove that skin. I don't plan to leave this building alive. But neither will Amanda. And then you'll be free, Henry."

Amanda was listening to every word he said. Listened to the ravings of a murderer as he discussed why he was going to kill her, her eyes growing wider. The fear in her eyes made me want to forget the gun pointed at my head, run over and throw my arms around her. But I knew I couldn't. I was the reason Amanda was here right now. I mouthed I'm sorry. Amanda didn't react.

"So here's what's going to happen," Roberts said. "Davies, you're going to come with me. Parker, you're going to sit and watch like a gentleman."

"What makes you think I'm going to do a damn thing?" I spat. Roberts took a step back, then drove the butt of the gun into my stomach. I doubled over, gasping for air, bile surging upwards.

While I was on the ground, he went over to Amanda, grabbed her by her bound hands and lifted her up out of her chair. She tried to struggle, but Roberts was strong.

He pushed her in front of him, the rifle pointed at her head. He marched Amanda into the conference room. The windows faced the street. It was a beautiful day. Ordinarily I could sit at my desk and watch the sun reflect off the towers in Rockefeller Center. Now I had to watch dozens of cops and reporters crowd the sidewalk. Cameras recording every second, waiting for something to headline their newscast or make their page one.

I crawled into the room, my legs still too weak to carry me.

The Guilty

Roberts walked up to the window, then he took the rifle and swung it at the glass, shattering it. Dozens of shards tumbled outward and I heard them sprinkle against the pavement.

Suddenly he shoved Amanda's face towards the window. I could hear her gasps, her sobs, still trying to get free. I struggled to find my footing. I knew that all those cameras were focused on the face of William Henry Roberts as he held my girlfriend, Amanda, hostage. And I knew, in that instant, he was going to kill her for the cameras. He was going to give them their page one.

"You sick fuck," I breathed, holding a table for balance. "This isn't about her or me. It's about you. You and your sick fucking family."

Roberts turned slightly, looked at me. "I wouldn't expect you to understand, Henry. But after Amanda dies, you will."

I heard a click, knew that the Winchester was loaded and ready to fire. Amanda struggled, but his other arm was clamped around her neck, nearly cutting off her air supply.

"Billy the Kid was a fraud," I said. "He was as much a hero as a donkey's ass. He was a scrawny little prick who happened to have good aim. His legacy is worth squat, just like yours. Nobody will remember you tomorrow. You'll be dead, and people will move on like you never existed." The anger seethed through my voice, my veins felt like they were on fire. I took another step closer, saw Roberts's finger tighten on the trigger.

I heard a fluttering sound from outside, a fwap fwap fwap that could only have been a helicopter, homing in on us from an unseen direction. Staring at the building across the street, I could see windows opened, marksmen waiting for a clean shot to take out Roberts. They couldn't do it with Amanda in the way. They needed a clean shot. They needed separation.

Roberts was ignoring me, speaking to Amanda. "Miss Davies, like so many others before you, you will accomplish much more in death than in life. Henry, I trust you'll know what to make of all this. I know you'll know how to properly record my history."

I stepped forward again, spoke louder.

"Tell me," I said. "How did it feel to see your mother getting fucked by that priest?"

Roberts's finger slipped off the trigger. I saw the gun waver slightly. He didn't turn. Didn't look at me.

"Your mom, Meryl, I guess your father couldn't show her God so she had to try someone a little closer to the almighty. Bet Dad was proud, too. Bet he watched them. Bet you listened in, you freak, watched Mark Rheingold leave your house late at night, early in the morning. Bet your mom left him something nice on the collection plate."

"Shut your fucking mouth," Roberts said.

"You claim all this is about bringing down Sodom and Gommorah, I say this is about some poor little kid who saw his mommy getting drilled by the guy who passes around communion wafers. You were pissed, so you killed him and your whole family. How's that for the legacy of Billy the Kid. His descendants were so messed up they couldn't satisfy their wives. Think I'll take another trip down to Fort Sumner, fix up that tombstone of his. Right now it says 'Pals'. I'm thinking it should say Billy the Kid: Always Shooting Blanks."

For a split second, Roberts's face turned away from Amanda and his eyes met mine. They burned in a way I hadn't seen before. They were unfocused, angry, like he'd begun to lose a bit of control. Though he was in fact a cold-blooded murderer, in William's mind he was a savior.

"See," I said. "The way you're looking at me right now, those aren't the eyes of a Regulator. They're the eyes of a guy who kills for his own sick pleasure."

He swept his gaze back to Amanda, the rifle muzzle still digging into the nape of her neck. Sobs were wracking her body. I had to separate them, get some distance. Just a little more…

"This whole show for the cameras? Might get page twelve in tomorrow's paper, somewhere after the ninth episode of Lost. You'll be forgotten before restaurants get their morning sushi deliveries. And all that'll be left is your dead granddaddy. You saw today's Dispatch, right? You know nobody believes the truth. Nobody thinks Brushy Bill actually was Billy the Kid. You're a fucking failure, Will. Just like your whole family."

Suddenly Roberts swung the rifle my way, that muzzle aiming to blast my heart out. I knew it was coming. Once I saw the look in his eyes, I knew he would kill me if I pressed further. So I was ready.

I managed to grab the rifle's barrel before it measured my chest, swatted it upwards as a gunshot shattered the air, white plaster

The Guilty

raining down like ash. I only had seconds. One thing I'd learned about Winchesters, they were quick to reload.

"Amanda, run!" I shouted. She tried to move, but Roberts's hand snaked out and grabbed her by the hair. He tried to hold the Winchester with his other hand, but the long, heavy rifle seemed to be too much. He struggled to bring it around and get off another shot. Instead he whipped the barrel around and caught me in the face.

I went down, my legs giving way. Blood began to trickle into my eyes. I wiped it away, got back to my feet, saw that horrible black muzzle lining up with my forehead. Roberts had a sick grin on his face.

Then another shot rang out, and the grin disappeared.

A swell of blood blossomed just over Roberts's left shoulder. I heard another sharp crack, saw a spark of light come from the building across the street. The cops had set up snipers. And they finally got their separation.

The second shot blew out a portion of Robert's jacket by his midsection, a gout of blood splashing onto the floor. His eyes began to roll back in his head. He tried to bring the Winchester back up, but I grabbed it from his trembling hands.

Then everything just seemed to happen. Roberts began to topple backwards, and in a moment of horror I saw his body was destined for the open window he'd shattered. His left hand was still clutching Amanda's hair. Her hands bound, her mouth gagged, she didn't have the balance to resist.

"No!" I shouted, as Roberts stumbled backward, hitting the back of his legs on the windowsill. He teetered for a moment, grinning at me, his face and chest a mass of dark blood.

Through bloodstained teeth I heard him say, "Let's go, angel," before he fell backwards, taking Amanda with him.

I rushed forward, still holding the gun, and thrust the upper half of my body out the window. Amanda was teetering over the ledge, holding on with her legs as Roberts clung desperately to her outstretched arms. His hands were slipping. Below them I could see dozens of people scattering about as they looked above, saw the three of us perched nine stories high.

And then he fell. Roberts's hand slipped off of Amanda's wrists, and then he tumbled down, faster than I could have imagined, that sick smile embedded in my eyes like it would never leave, his body falling faster and faster until it thudded on the pavement below.

And that's when Amanda's knees gave way, and she fell over backward. Without thinking, I thrust the Winchester into the loop between the bonds on her hands.

It held.

And there we were, hanging a hundred feet from the ground, Amanda's bound hands caught on the barrel of a rifle that had been used to kill four people.

Her mouth was still gagged. Her eyes fluttered, more gasps escaping as she tried not to die.

"Amanda, baby, reach up with your hands and grab the barrel," I said. Her hands managed to close around the rifle, but the weight was too much for me to hold. I braced my legs against the wall, tried to leverage the rifle upwards and give Amanda a place to find her footing.

Then I heard the sounds of bending metal. The rifle was old, wasn't meant to carry any load, let alone a grown person. Amanda was slipping.

"Hold on!" I yelled. I braced my feet ever harder, felt the stitches in my hand pop as I yanked as hard as I could, feeling the rifle barrel moving upwards as I carried Amanda. Then the load lightened, and I saw Amanda had found her footing, just barely, on an outside ledge.

"Amanda, baby, count to three and then lean forward. Please, I promise you'll be fine." Tears streaked down her cheeks but she nodded.

"One," I said, my voice leaving me. "Two."

I looked at my love, knew in this next second she would either live or die.

"Three."

At once I dropped the Winchester and Amanda leaned forward. I leapt forward, clasped my arms around her waist, pulled her as hard as I could, and suddenly she came toppling over the windowsill, landing on the ground next to me.

We both lay there for a minute, breathing heavy, until I saw that Amanda was still bound. I grabbed the knife Roberts had dropped and cut the ropes from her hands. Then I gently pulled the cloth tape from her mouth and kissed her hard. Her salty tears found their way into my mouth as I held Amanda, knowing I could never hold her like this again.

Chapter 59

You never know how much damage is done until you pull back. Survey the scene from a distance. And even then it needs a few days to metastasize.

What Largo Vance had started, Costas Paradis was about to finish. The man had donated nearly half a million dollars to perform an exhumation of Brushy Bill Roberts and compare his DNA to William Henry. His alleged grandson, and the sole surviving heir to Billy the Kid. And this time they were going to do it right. Costas would make sure of that. Or at least his money would.

In the meantime, as expected, residents of New Mexico and Texas were apoplectic over the Dispatch's revelations. They were planning to fight the exhumation tooth and nail. My old friend Justice Waverly was quoted in the Dallas Morning News saying, "They can come with shovels and backhoes, but if they try to destroy the legacy of the old west we'll meet them with rifles and cannons."

In New York that kind of talk could get a politician impeached. In Texas it guaranteed Justice Waverly would be reelected every term until he finally keeled over in his morning pastry.

I spoke to Curt Sheffield the day after Roberts died. The cops had found a receipt in his bag for several nights at a seedy forty-dollar-a-night hotel room. I didn't even know they ran that cheap in New York. The manager didn't remember seeing Roberts, mainly because the man was half blind.

The cops found blood stains on the floor that they were running against Mya's type, to confirm Roberts had stayed there. They also found a note on the nightstand next to the bed where Roberts slept. It gave no further explanation for the murders. It contained two brief sentences.

Up in heaven I'll see my friends.
Bury me next to my blood.

If the DNA tests confirmed what I assumed they would, there

was a question of whether William Henry Roberts would be buried in Fort Sumner, New Mexico next to the alleged grave site of Billy the Kid. Even though it wasn't where the true Kid was buried, it was where his legacy lived. And that legacy, that myth, I'd learned, was far more important than the truth.

Most argued a murderer didn't deserve such a burial. Those in power argued what was good enough for one killer was good enough for another, that evil should be contained.

After running the hostage crisis on page one the next day, the next day Dispatch relegated the Roberts story to page seven, where it was given quarter page treatment in deference to a color picture of a senator's wife who had an allergic reaction to her Botox injection. After that, William Henry Roberts wasn't mentioned again.

Paulina Cole was suspended for three weeks. But I knew that her suspension was merely window dressing. Ted Allen was forcing her to fly under the radar until everything quieted down. Besides, with Costas Paradis looking to dig up Brushy Bill Roberts, the Kid's defenders had bigger fish to fry than a newspaper reporter.

On page three of the Dispatch was a small item about the custody fight for the Winchester rifle Roberts had used on his rampage. Rex Sheehan claimed it was still legal property of the museum in Fort Sumner. Costas Paradis wanted to buy the gun to smelt the metal and burn the wood. Despite my desire for Costas to get some sort of closure and to see the rifle destroyed, part of me felt the gun was part of American history and should be treated as such. Provided, this time, Rex got a security system worth a damn.

When I finished reading the day's papers, I put them in a neat pile underneath the chair. It was only then when I noticed the steady beeping, the humming. It came from Mya's bedside.

Staring at her small, frail body, a far cry from the strong, vibrant girl I once knew, something inside me had burst. I couldn't leave. Didn't want to. I told Wallace and Jack I needed a few days off, that the trauma from the week's events combined with the new sutures in my hand made it difficult to write, difficult to work. This was all bullshit, but it sounded better than the truth. A lot of things were sounding better than the truth.

Mya came and went. Her eyes fluttering open and shut. The doctors said she would make it. She would recover. Physically. Mentally, it would take time. It would be hard. And I would be there for her. Like I hadn't been before.

I called you, Henry.

And I wasn't there.

No more.

Cindy Loverne entered, holding a cup of coffee. She sat down, blew some steam off the top and crossed her legs.

"How are you, Henry?"

I felt guilty even answering such a question.

"Feeling a bit better," I said.

"That's good. Listen, I want to thank you for being so good to Mya. I don't know what she's done to deserve such a good friend, but—"

"Please," I said. "Don't finish that sentence. She deserves much better than anything I've given her. And I want you to know, I know she can't hear me right now, but I'll be there for her and your family. It's the least I can do after everything."

Cindy smiled warmly. Then her eyes moved to the bed. She looked back at me.

"I think somebody can hear you."

I looked over. Mya's eyes were open. They were filmy, groggy, squinting to regain focus.

I nearly leapt off the chair, went over and knelt down by her bedside.

"Hey you," I said.

"Henry," Mya said, her voice still weak.

"I'm here," I said. I took her hand in mine, gently stroked her dry skin. "I'm here."

I waited outside the hospital. The sun had dipped below the buildings, the sky turning a harsh gray. The air felt cold and I cinched up my jacket. I'd asked Amanda to meet me here, unsure why I chose this particular location, but in the back of my mind I knew the reason full well.

I watched her as she walked towards me. Her eyes were streaked with red, and I didn't have to ask why. She came up to me. Her hands were in her pockets. She moved her toe back and forth across the pavement, afraid or unwilling to make eye contact.

"Hey Amanda," I said.

"Hey," came the flat reply.

"Were you able to find—"

"Yes," she said, cutting me off. "A friend said I could sublet her studio for a few months. Rent's not too bad. Commute is kind of a killer. Guess you take what you can get."

"Yeah," I said. "Guess so."

She looked at me, the pain and hurt and confusion in her eyes nearly tearing me apart, letting loose everything I wanted to say but knew I couldn't.

"So what happens now?" she asked.

"I don't know," I replied. "I do want to see you again."

Amanda shook her head, and it was just then that I saw she'd begun to cry.

"Nope," she said. "If we end this…I want to end it. I don't want to have to think about this every time I see you. I just want to pull it off. Like you said."

"Amanda." I never wondered, in all my life, what it would feel like to tell the girl I loved, who loved me back, that I couldn't be with her. Part of being in love, part of being a man was putting your loved ones above yourself.

I didn't love Mya anymore. Not like that. But she'd paid a price for my failures. I had a debt to pay her back.

To keep Amanda safe, to keep her alive, I had to leave. I knew pulling away from her would tear open a wound that would probably never heal. But at least at some point the bleeding would stop; it would scar over.

I noticed her hand had left its pocket and was fidding with her jeans absently.

"What's that?" I asked. She seemed surprised.

"Nothing," she said. "Just, you know…guess old habits die hard."

"Show me," I said, but had a feeling in the pit of my stomach that I knew what it was. She stared at me as she brought it out. A small spiral notebook. Just like the kind she wrote in back when we met. Back when she had nobody, and every person she met was catalogued in one of those notebooks. For a girl who'd grown up with no real family, no real identity, those notebooks helped her hold on.

The Guilty

I hadn't seen her write in them in the year we'd been a couple. And now that we were coming apart, she needed them again.

It's for the best, I told myself. She's smart. She's beautiful. She has the world waiting to open itself for her. If you stay with her, you selfish bastard, you could steal all from her.

And so I knew I had to end it.

"If you ever need anything," I said. "Someone to talk to…"

"I won't," she said. "But I appreciate the gesture."

"Right," I repeated blindly. "Gesture."

She wiped her nose, sniffed once.

"Well then, goodbye Henry." She turned to leave.

"Amanda," I said. She turned back. The tears were flowing from her eyes, and all I wanted to do was gather her in my arms, kiss her and tell her everything would be all right. But to do that would allow events like the other day to happen. Jack was right. He'd been right all along. And Amanda nearly paid for my ignorance with her life.

"If you want to say something, Henry, say it." My mouth opened but nothing came out. So she said, "Goodbye, Henry."

Amanda walked away without saying another word. I watched as her hand went to her pocket again, then wiped at her eyes, and before I knew it she'd turned the corner and disappeared.

I stared at the empty street for several minutes, half hoping something would happen, the rest of me praying it wouldn't.

And when I was sure it wouldn't, I turned around and went back inside.

About the Author

Jason Pinter is the bestselling author of five novels in his Henry Parker thriller series, which have over one million copies in print worldwide and have been published in over a dozen countries, as well as the Middle Grade adventure novel Zeke Bartholomew: SuperSpy. He has been nominated for the Thriller Award, Strand Critics Award, Barry Award, RT Reviewers Choice Award, Shamus Award and CrimeSpree Award. Two of his books—The Fury and The Darkness—were chosen as Indie Next selections, and The Mark, The Stolen and The Fury were named to The Strand's Best Books of the Year list. The Mark and The Stolen both appeared on the 'Heatseekers' bestseller list in The Bookseller (UK). The Mark was optioned to be a feature film.

He is the Founder and Publisher of Polis Books, an independent publishing company he launched in 2013. He was named one of Publisher Weekly's inaugural Star Watch honorees, which "recognizes young publishing professionals who have distinguished themselves as future leaders of the industry." He has written for The New Republic, Entrepreneur, The Daily Beast, Medium and The Huffington Post, and been featured in Library Journal, Publishers Weekly, Mystery Scene and more.

He was named one of the top writers on Twitter (@JasonPinter) by Mashable and the Huffington Post, and his articles and essays have been covered in the New York Times, Los Angeles Times, CNN, The Atlantic, Boston Globe, New York Observer, Baltimore Sun, Salon and as far as Australia's Sydney Morning Herald. He was born in New York City and currently lives in New Jersey with his wife, their daughter, and their dog, Wilson.

Visit him online at
www.JasonPinter.com
and on Twitter at @JasonPinter

CPSIA information can be obtained
at www.ICGtesting.com
Printed in the USA
LVHW021603040421
683400LV00013B/194

9 781947 993198